Finding
Sky

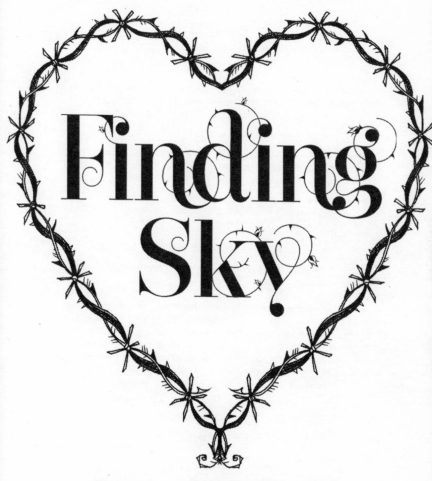

Finding Sky

Joss Stirling

OXFORD
UNIVERSITY PRESS

OXFORD
UNIVERSITY PRESS

Great Clarendon Street, Oxford OX2 6DP
Oxford University Press is a department of the University of Oxford.
It furthers the University's objective of excellence in research, scholarship,
and education by publishing worldwide in

Oxford   New York

Auckland   Cape Town   Dar es Salaam   Hong Kong   Karachi
Kuala Lumpur   Madrid   Melbourne   Mexico City   Nairobi
New Delhi   Shanghai   Taipei   Toronto

With offices in

Argentina   Austria   Brazil   Chile   Czech Republic   France   Greece
Guatemala   Hungary   Italy   Japan   Poland   Portugal   Singapore
South Korea   Switzerland   Thailand   Turkey   Ukraine   Vietnam

Oxford is a registered trade mark of Oxford University Press
in the UK and in certain other countries

British Library Cataloguing in Publication Data
Data available

ISBN: 978-0-19-273213-2

1 3 5 7 9 10 8 6 4 2

Printed in Great Britain

Paper used in the production of this book is a natural,
recyclable product made from wood grown in sustainable forests.
The manufacturing process conforms to the environmental
regulations of the country of origin.

For Lucy and Emily

Acknowledgements

With thanks to Leah, Jasmine and the wranglers at the Tumbling River Ranch, Colorado. Also my family, for taking the trip across the US with me, and risking the white-water rafting expedition in the Rockies.

Chapter 1

The car drew away, leaving the little girl on the verge. Shaking with cold in her thin cotton T-shirt and shorts, she sat down, arms locked around her knees, her light blonde hair blowing messily in the wind, pale as a dandelion seed head.

Be quiet, freak, or we'll come back and get you, they'd said.

She didn't want them to come back for her. She knew that for a fact, even if she couldn't remember her name or where she lived.

A family walked by on their way to their vehicle, the mum in a headscarf, carrying a baby, the dad holding the hand of a toddler. The girl stared at the worn grass, counting the daisies. *What's that like,* she wondered, *being carried?* It was so long since anyone had cuddled her, she found it hard to watch. She could see the glimmer of gold that shone round the family— the colour of love. She didn't trust that colour; it led to hurt.

Then the woman spotted her. The girl hugged her knees tightly, trying to make herself so small no one would notice. But it was no use. The woman said something to her husband, handed over the baby, and came closer until she could crouch beside the girl. 'Are you lost, sweetie?'

Be quiet or we'll come back and get you.

The girl shook her head.

'Mummy and Daddy gone inside?' The woman frowned, her colours tinged an angry red.

The girl didn't know if she should nod. Mummy and Daddy had gone away but that was a long time ago. They'd never come for her in the hospital but stayed in the fire with each other. She decided to say nothing. The woman's colours flared a deeper crimson. The girl cringed: she'd upset her. So the ones who had just driven away had told her the truth. She was bad. Always making everyone unhappy. The girl put her head on her knees. Perhaps if she pretended she wasn't there, the woman would feel happy again and go away. That sometimes worked.

'Poor little thing,' the woman sighed, standing up. 'Jamal, will you go back inside and tell the manager there's a lost child out here? I'll stay with her.'

The girl heard the man murmur reassurances to the toddler and then footsteps as they went back towards the restaurant.

'You mustn't worry: I'm sure your family will be looking for you.' The woman sat beside her, crushing daisies five and six.

The girl started trembling violently and shaking her head. She didn't want them looking—not now, not ever.

'It's OK. Really. I know you must be frightened but you'll be back with them in a minute.'

She whimpered, then clapped a hand over her mouth. *I mustn't make a sound, I mustn't make a fuss. I'm bad. Bad.*

But it wasn't her making all the noise. Not her fault. Now there were lots of people around her. Police wearing yellow jackets like the ones that had surrounded her house that day. Voices talking at her. Asking her name.

But it was a secret—and she'd forgotten the answer long ago.

Chapter 2

I woke up from the old nightmare as the car drew to a halt and the engine fell silent. My head pressed against a cushion, sleep dragging on me like an anchor, it took me a while to remember where I was. Not in that motorway service station, but in Colorado with my parents. Moving on. Moving in.

'What do you think?' Simon, as my dad preferred to be called, got out of the dodgy old Ford he'd bought in Denver and threw his arm dramatically towards the house. His long grey-streaked brown hair was getting loose from its tie in his enthusiasm to show off our new home. Pointy roof, clapboard walls, and grimy windows—it did not look promising. I half expected the Addams family to lurch out of the front door. I sat up and rubbed my eyes, trying to drive off the gritty fear that remained after one of my dreams.

'Oh, darling, it's wonderful.' Sally, my mum, refused to be daunted—the terrier of happiness, as Simon jokingly called her, seizing it in her teeth and refusing to shake free. She got out of the car. I followed, not sure if it was jetlag I was feeling or dreamlag. The words I had in my head were 'gloomy', 'wreck', and 'rotten'; Sally came up with some others.

'I think it's going to be brilliant. Look at those shutters—they must be original. And the porch! I've always fancied myself a porch kind of person, sitting in my rocker and watching the sun go down.' Her brown eyes sparkled with anticipation, her curly hair bouncing as she jumped up the steps.

Having lived with them since I was ten, I'd long ago accepted that both my parents were probably *off* their rockers. They lived in a little fantasy world of their own, where derelict houses were 'quaint' and mould 'atmospheric'. Unlike Sally, I always fancied myself as the ultra-modern kind of person, sitting in a chair that wasn't a haven for woodworm and a bedroom that didn't have icicles on the *inside* of the windows in winter.

But forget the house: the mountains behind were stunning, soaring impossibly high into the clear autumn sky, a dusting of white on their peaks. They rolled along the horizon like a tidal wave frozen in time, caught just as it was about to curl down upon us. Their rocky slopes were tinged with pink in the late afternoon light, but, where shadows fell across the snowfields, they turned a cold slate blue. The woods climbing their sides were already shot through with gold; stands of aspens burned against the dark Douglas firs. I could see a cable car and the clearings that marked the ski runs, all of which looked almost vertical.

These had to be the High Rockies I'd read about when my parents broke the news that we were moving from Richmond-on-Thames to Colorado. They'd been offered a year as artists-in-residence in a new Arts Centre in a little town called Wrickenridge. A local multi-millionaire and admirer of their work had got it into his head that the ski resort west of Denver needed an injection of culture—and my parents, Sally and Simon, were to be it.

When they presented me with the 'good' news, I checked

the town website and found that Wrickenridge was known for its three hundred inches of snow each year and not much else. There would be skiing—but I'd never been able to afford the school trip to the Alps so that would put me about a million years behind my contemporaries. I was already picturing my humiliation at the first snowy weekend when I stumbled on the nursery slopes and the other teenagers zipped down the black runs.

But my parents loved the idea of painting among the Rockies and I didn't have the heart to spoil their big adventure. I pretended to be OK with missing out on sixth form college in Richmond with all my friends and instead enrolling in Wrickenridge High. I'd made a place for myself in south-west London in the six years since they'd adopted me; I'd struggled out of terror and silence, overcoming shyness to have my own circle in which I felt popular. I'd shut off the stranger parts of my character—like that colour thing I'd dreamt about. I no longer looked for people's auras as I had done as a child, ignored it when my control slipped. I'd made myself normal—well, mostly. Now I was being launched into the unknown. I'd seen plenty of films about American schools and was feeling more than a little insecure about my new place of education. Surely normal American teenagers got spots and wore crappy clothes sometimes? I'd never fit in if the movies turned out to be true.

'OK.' Simon rubbed his hands on the thighs of his faded jeans, a habit that left every item of clothing he owned smeared with oils. He was dressed in his usual Bohemian scruff while Sally looked quite smart in new trousers and jacket she'd bought for travelling. I fell somewhere between the two: moderately rumpled in my Levis. 'Let's go and see inside. Mr Rodenheim said he'd sent the decorators in for us. He promised they'd do the outside as soon as they could get to it.'

So that was why it looked a dump.

Simon opened the front door. It squeaked but didn't fall off its hinges, which I took as a little victory for us. The decorators had clearly just left—gifting us with their dust sheets, ladders, and pots of paint, walls half done. I poked my nose in the rooms upstairs, finding a turquoise one with a queen bed and a view of the peaks. Had to be mine. Maybe this wouldn't be so terrible.

I used my fingernail to scratch paint splashes off the old mirror over the chest of drawers. The pale, solemn girl in the reflection did the same, staring at me with her dark blue eyes. She looked ghostly in the half light, her long blonde hair curling in unruly tendrils around her oval face. She looked fragile. Alone. Prisoner in the room through the mirror; an Alice who never made it back through the looking-glass.

I shivered. The dream was still haunting me, tugging me back to the past. I had to stop thinking like this. People—teachers, friends, you name it—had told me I was prone to drifting off in melancholy daydreams. But they didn't understand that I felt . . . I don't know . . . somehow lacking. I was a mystery to myself—a bundle of fragmented memories and unexplored dark places. My head was full of secrets but I'd lost the map showing me where to find them.

Dropping my hand from the cool glass, I turned away from the mirror and went downstairs. My parents were standing in the kitchen, wrapped up in each other as usual. They had the kind of relationship that was so complete I often wondered how they found space for me.

Sally circled Simon's waist and laid her head on his shoulder. 'Not bad. Do you remember our first digs off Earls Court, darling?'

'Yes. The walls were grey and everything rattled when the tube passed under the house.' He kissed her froth of short brown hair. 'This is a palace.'

Sally held her hand out to include me in the moment. I'd trained myself over the last few years not to mistrust their affectionate gestures, so took it. Sally squeezed my knuckles, silently acknowledging what it cost me not to shy away from them. 'I'm really excited. It's like Christmas morning.'

She was always a sucker for the stocking thing.

I smiled. 'I never would have guessed.'

'Anyone home?' There was a rap on the porch door and an elderly woman marched in. She had white-flecked black hair, dark brown skin, and triangle earrings that dangled almost to the collar of her gold padded jacket. Loaded down by a casserole dish, she efficiently kicked the door closed with her heel. 'There you are. I saw you arrive. Welcome to Wrickenridge.'

Sally and Simon exchanged an amused look as the lady made herself at home, putting the dish on the hall table.

'I'm May Hoffman, your neighbour from across the street. And you are the Brights from England.'

It seemed Mrs Hoffman did not require anyone else to participate in her conversations. Her energy was scary; I caught myself wishing for a tortoise-like ability to creep back into my shell to take cover.

'Your daughter doesn't look much like either of you, does she?' Mrs Hoffman moved a pot of paint aside. 'I saw you pull up. Did you know your car's leaking oil? You'll want to get that fixed. Kingsley at the garage will see to it for you if you say I recommended him. He'll give you a fair price, but mind he doesn't charge you for a valet service—that should be complimentary.'

Sally grimaced apologetically at me. 'That's very kind of you, Mrs Hoffman.'

She waved it away. 'We make a point of being good neighbours here. Have to be—wait until you experience one of our winters and you'll understand.' She directed her attention in

7

my direction, her eyes shrewd. 'Enrolled as an eleventh grader at the high school?'

'Yes . . . er . . . Mrs Hoffman,' I mumbled.

'Semester started two days ago, but I expect you know that. My grandson's in junior year too. I'll tell him to look after you.'

I had a nightmare vision of a male version of Mrs Hoffman shepherding me around the school. 'I'm sure that won't be—'

She cut across me, gesturing to the dish. 'Thought you might appreciate some home cooking to start you off right in your new kitchen.' She sniffed. 'I see Mr Rodenheim finally got round to doing the place up. About time. I told him this house was a disgrace to the neighbourhood. Now, you get some rest, you hear, and I'll see you when you've settled in.'

She was gone before we had a chance to thank her.

'Well,' said Simon. 'That was interesting.'

'*Please* fix the oil leak tomorrow,' Sally mock-begged, holding up her clasped hands to her chest. 'I couldn't bear to be here if she finds out you've not taken her advice—and she'll be back.'

'Like the common cold,' he agreed.

'She's not . . . um . . . very British, is she?' I ventured.

We all laughed—the best christening the house could have had.

That night I unpacked my suitcase into the old chest of drawers Sally had helped me line with wallpaper; it still smelt musty and the drawers stuck, but I liked the faded white paint-job. Distressed, Sally called it. I know how it felt, having spent many years at that end of the emotional spectrum.

I found myself wondering about Mrs Hoffman and this strange town we had come to. It felt so different—alien. Even the air at this altitude wasn't quite enough and I had the faint buzz of a headache lurking. Beyond my window, framed by the branches of an apple tree growing close to the house, the mountains were dark shapes against the charcoal grey sky of a cloudy night. The peaks sat in judgement over the town, reminding us humans just how insignificant and temporary we were.

I spent a long time choosing what I'd wear on my first day at school, settling on a pair of jeans and a Gap T-shirt, anonymous enough so that I wouldn't stand out with the other students. Thinking again, I pulled out a snug-fit jumper with a Union Jack worked in gold on the front. Might as well accept what I was.

That was something Simon and Sally had taught me. They knew about the difficulty I had recalling my past and never pushed, saying I would remember if and when I was ready. It was enough for them that I was who I was now; I did not have to apologize for being incomplete. Still, it did not stop me being plain scared of the unknown that was tomorrow.

Feeling a bit of a coward, I accepted Sally's offer to accompany me to the school office to enrol. Wrickenridge High was about a mile down the hill from our neighbourhood, near the I-70, the main road that connected the town to the other ski resorts in the area. It was a building that had pride in its purpose: the name carved in stone over the double height doors, the grounds well maintained. The hallway was crammed with noticeboards advertising the wide range of activities open to— or maybe expected of—the students. I thought of the sixth form college I could have been attending in England. Tucked away behind the shopping centre in a mixture of Sixties buildings and portakabins, it had been anonymous, not a place you belonged to but passed through. I got the sense that *belonging* was a big part of the Wrickenridge experience. I wasn't sure what I felt about that. I supposed it would be OK if I did manage to fit, but bad if I flunked the test of blending in to a new school.

Sally knew I was anxious but chose to act as if I was going to be the most successful student ever known.

'Look, they've got an art club,' she said brightly. 'You could try pottery.'

'I'm useless at that stuff.'

She sucked her teeth, knowing that was the truth. 'Music then. I see there's an orchestra. Oh look, and cheerleading! That might be fun.'

'Yeah, right.'

'You'd look sweet in one of those outfits.'

'I'm about a foot too short,' I said, eyeing the giraffe-legged girls that made up the cheerleading team on the team poster.

'A pocket-sized Venus, that's what you are. I wish I had your figure.'

'Sally, will you stop being so embarrassing?' Why was I even bothering to argue with her? I had no intention of becoming a cheerleader even if height wasn't an issue.

'Basketball,' continued Sally.

I rolled my eyes.

'Dance.'

It was a joke now.

'Maths club.'

'You'd need to club me over the head to get me in that,' I muttered, making her laugh.

She squeezed my hand briefly. 'You'll find your place. Remember, you are special.'

We pushed open the door to the office. The receptionist stood behind the counter, glasses attached to a chain around his neck; they bounced on his pink sweater as he stacked the mail in the teachers' pigeonholes. He managed this at the same time as drinking from a takeaway coffee cup.

'Ah, you must be the new girl from England! Come in, come in.' He beckoned us closer and shook Sally's hand. 'Mrs Bright, Joe Delaney. If you wouldn't mind signing a few forms for me. Sky, isn't it?'

I nodded.

'I'm Mr Joe to the students. I've a welcome pack for you here.' He handed it over. I saw that I already had a school swipe card with my photo. It was the one taken for my passport where I looked like a rabbit caught in headlights. Great. I slung the chain around my head and tucked the card out of sight.

He leant forward confidentially, giving me a whiff of his flowery aftershave. 'I take it you are not familiar with how we do things here?'

'No, I'm not,' I admitted.

Mr Joe spent the next ten minutes patiently explaining what courses I could attend and what grades I needed to graduate.

'We've made a timetable here based on the choices you made when you filled out your application but, remember, nothing is set in stone. If you want to change, just let me know.' He checked his watch. 'You've missed registration, so I'll take you straight to your first class.'

Sally gave me a kiss and wished me luck. From here, I was on my own.

Mr Joe frowned at a crowd of loiterers by the late book, scattering them like a collie herding recalcitrant sheep, before leading me towards the history corridor. 'Sky, that's a pretty name.'

I didn't want to tell him that we chose it together only six years ago when I was adopted. I'd not been able to tell anyone my birth name when I was found and hadn't spoken for years afterwards, so the Social Services had called me Janet—'Just Janet', as one foster brother had joked. This had made me hate it more than ever. A new name was meant to help make a new start with the Brights; Janet had been relegated to my middle name.

'My parents liked it.' And I hadn't been old enough to foresee how embarrassing it could be on occasion with my surname.

'It's cute, imaginative.'

'Um, yeah.' My heart was thumping, palms damp. I was not going to mess up. I was so not going to mess up.

Mr Joe opened the door.

'Mr Ozawa, here's the new girl.'

The Japanese-American teacher looked up from his laptop where he'd been running through some notes on the interactive white board. Twenty heads swung in my direction.

Mr Ozawa looked over the top of his little half-moon glasses at me, straight black hair flopping over one lens. He was good-looking in an older guy kind of way. 'Sky Bright?'

A snigger ran through the class but it wasn't my fault my parents had not warned me when we picked my name. As usual their heads had been full of fanciful images rather than my future torment at school.

'Yes, sir.'

'I'll take it from here, Mr Joe.'

The receptionist gave me an encouraging nudge over the threshold and walked away. 'Keep smiling, Sky.'

That was so going to happen when I felt like diving for cover under the nearest desk.

Mr Ozawa clicked to the next slide entitled 'The American civil war'. 'Take a seat anywhere you like.'

There was only one free that I could see, next to a girl with caramel-toned skin and nails painted red, white, and blue. Her hair was amazing—a mane of gingery brown dreadlocks falling past her shoulders. I gave her a neutral smile as I slid in next to her. She nodded and tapped her talons on the desk while Mr Ozawa passed round a handout. When he turned away, she offered her palm for a brief brush rather than a shake.

'Tina Monterey.'

'Sky Bright.'

'Yeah, I got that.'

Mr Ozawa clapped his hands to gain our attention. 'OK, guys, you're the lucky ones who've chosen to study nineteenth century American history. However, after ten years of teaching juniors I have no illusions and I expect the vacation has driven all knowledge from your brains. So, let's start with an easy one. Who can tell me when the Civil War started? And yes, I want the right month.' His eyes scanned a class of expert head-duckers and came to rest on me.

Bummer.

'Miss Bright?'

Any American history I had ever known vanished like the Invisible Man taking off his suit, piece by piece, leaving me a blank. 'Um . . . you had a civil war?'

The class groaned.

I guess that meant I really should've known that.

At recess, I was grateful that Tina didn't abandon this clue-less Brit despite my dismal performance in class. She offered to show me around the school. Many things I came out with made her laugh—not because I was being funny, but because I was being too English, she said.

'Your accent's neat. You sound like that actress—you know, the one in the pirate films.'

Did I really sound so posh? I wondered. I'd always thought I was too London for that.

'You related to the Queen or something?' Tina teased.

'Yes, she's like my second cousin twice removed,' I said seriously.

Tina's eyes widened. 'You're kidding!'

'Actually, I am—kidding I mean.'

She laughed and flapped her face with her file. 'You had me for a moment there; I was getting worried I'd have to curtsey.'

'Go ahead.'

We helped ourselves to lunch from the canteen and took our trays into the dining hall. One wall was composed entirely of windows, giving a view of the muddy playing fields and woods beyond. The sun was out, silver-plating the peaks a glistening white, so some students were eating outside, gathered in groups arranged roughly by style of clothing. There were four years in this high school, ages ranged from fourteen to eighteen. I was in the eleventh grade, the so-called 'junior' year below the senior class of those graduating.

I waved my can of fizzy spring water towards them. 'So, Tina, who's who?'

'The groups?' She laughed. 'You know, Sky, I sometimes think we are all victims of our own stereotypes, 'cause we do conform even though I hate to admit it. When you try to be different, you just end up in a group of rebels all doing the same. That's high school for you.'

A group sounded good: somewhere to take cover. 'I suppose it was the same back where I came from. Let me guess, those lot are the jocks?' These had featured in every film I'd seen from *Grease* to *High School Musical* and were easy to spot thanks to the team strip for lunchtime practice.

'Yeah—the sports mad ones. They're mostly OK—not many fit guys with six-packs, sad to say, just sweaty teenagers. It's mainly baseball, basketball, hockey, girls' soccer and football here.'

4

'American football—that's like rugby, isn't it, except they wear loads of padding?'

'Is it?' She shrugged. I guessed then that she was not sporty herself. 'What do you play?'

'I can run a bit and have been known to knock a tennis ball about, but that's it.'

'I can handle that. Jocks can be so boring, you know? One track minds—and it's not girls they're thinking about.'

Three students walked by, discussing gigabytes with serious expressions worthy of Middle East peace negotiators. One twirled a memory stick on a keyring.

'They're the geeks—they're the clever ones who make sure everyone knows it. Almost the same as nerds but with more technology.'

I laughed.

'To be fair, there are also other bright ones—they're clever but wear it well. They tend not to hang together in packs like the geeks and the nerds.'

'Uh huh. Not sure I'll fit in any of those groups.'

'Me neither: I'm not dumb, but I'm not Ivy League material. Then there's the arts type—the musicians and drama people. I kinda fit in there as I like fine art and design.'

'You should meet my parents then.'

She clicked her nails on her can in a little drum roll of excitement. 'You mean you're *that* family—the ones coming to Mr Rodenheim's Arts Centre?'

'Yeah.'

'Cool. I'd love to meet them.'

A group shuffled past, boys with trousers hanging off their butts like mountain climbers clinging to an overhang with no safety rope.

'That's a few of the skater dudes,' snorted Tina. 'Enough said. I mustn't forget the bad boys—you won't see them hanging round here with us losers—they're way too cool for us. Probably out in the parking lot right now with their groupies comparing, I dunno what, carburettors or something. That's if they haven't been suspended. Who have I left out? We have some misfits.' She pointed to a little group by the serving hatch. 'And then we have our very own skiing fraternity, special to the Rockies. In my opinion, that's the best game in town.' She must have seen my worried expression because she hastened to reassure me. 'You can be in more than one—ski as well as be a jock, do the play and get the best grades. No one has to be just one kind of thing.'

'Except the misfits.' I glanced over at the group she had indicated. They weren't really a group, more a collection of oddballs who had no one else to sit beside. One girl was muttering to herself—at least, I saw no evidence of a hands-free headset for her phone. I felt a sudden panic that I would be among them when Tina got tired of me. I'd always felt something of an oddity; it wouldn't take much to knock me over into the group of the seriously weird.

'Yeah, don't mind them. Every school has them.' She opened her yoghurt. 'No one makes a big deal about it. So what was your last school like? Hogwarts? Posh kids wearing black gowns?'

'Um . . . no.' I choked on a laugh. If Tina could've seen us at lunch in my comprehensive, she would not be reminded of Hogwarts but a zoo as two thousand of us tried to fight our way through to the cramped dining hall in forty-five minutes. 'We were more like this.'

'Great. Then you'll soon feel at home.'

Being new is something I'd had a lot of experience of in my life before Sally and Simon adopted me. In those days I had been shuffled from home to home like a chain letter no one wanted to keep. And now I was back to being a stranger. I felt horribly conspicuous wandering the hallways, map in hand, completely at sea as to how the school functioned, though I guess my obviousness was all in my mind; the other students probably didn't even notice me. Classrooms and teachers became landmarks to orientate by; Tina a kind of rock I could cling to when I washed up in her area from time to time, but I tried to hide this as I didn't want to put her off developing friendliness into friendship from fear that I would crowd her. I went hours without talking to anyone and had to force myself to ignore my shyness and make conversation with my classmates. Still, I had the impression I'd arrived too late; the students of Wrickenridge High had had years to form groups and get to know each other. I was on the outside, looking in.

As the school day drew to a close, I wondered if I was always going to be doomed to this feeling that life was a shade out of focus for me, like a poor quality pirated film. Dissatisfied, and a little bit depressed, I made my way out of the main doors to head home. Threading through the crowds pouring out of the building, I got a glimpse of the bad boys Tina had mentioned at lunchtime. Caught in a shaft of sunlight in the car park, there was nothing fuzzy about these guys, though they certainly looked illegal. There were five of them, lounging against their motorbikes: two African-American boys, two white guys, and a dark-haired Hispanic. At any time, any place, you would have identified them immediately as trouble. Their expressions matched—a sneer at the world of education as represented by all us good students dutifully filing out on time. Most pupils gave them a wide berth, like ships avoiding a dangerous stretch of coast; the remainder shot them envious looks, hearing the siren call and tempted to stray too close.

Part of me wished I could do that—stand there, sure of myself, flipping off the rest of the planet for being so uncool. If only I had legs from here to eternity, quick cutting wit, looks to stop people in their tracks. Oh yeah, and being male helped: I could never carry off that hipshot look, thumbs linked in belt loops, kicking the dirt with my toe caps. Was it natural to them, or did they calculate the effect, practising in front of the mirror? I dismissed the thought quickly—that was something losers like me would do; they surely had such inbred coolness they were their own little ice age. The Hispanic fascinated me in particular—his eyes were hidden by shades as he leaned, arms folded, against the saddle of his bike, a king in his court of knights. He didn't have to struggle with the conviction that he was lacking in any way.

As I watched, he mounted his bike, revving it like a warrior prodding a monstrous steed awake. With brief goodbyes to his companions, he shot out of the car park, other students scattering. I'd give a lot to be on the back of that bike, dismissing the school day as my knight whisked me home. Better yet, be the one driving, the lone superhero, fighting injustice in her skin-tight leather outfit, men swooning in her wake.

A gust of self-mocking laughter stopped my random thoughts. *Just listen to yourself!* I chided my overheated imagination. Warriors and monsters; superheroes? I'd been reading too much Manga. These boys were a different breed from me. I was not even a blip on their radar. I should be thankful that no one could see inside my head to know just how fanciful I was. My grasp on reality could seem a bit shaky at times as I let my daydreams colour my perceptions. I was plain old Sky; they were gods: that was the way of the world.

chapter 3

I drifted through school for the next few days, gradually filling in the blanks on my map and learning the way things were done. Once I'd caught up with the work, I found I could cope with my classes, even if some of the style of teaching was unfamiliar. It was way more formal than in England—no first names for the students, all of us seated in individual rows rather than in pairs—but I thought I had adjusted OK. So, lulled into a false sense of security, I was unprepared for the rude shock of my first gym lesson.

Mrs Green, our evil sports teacher, sprang a surprise on the girls early Wednesday morning. There should be a law against teachers doing that so we at least had time to get a sick note.

'Ladies, as you know, we've lost six of our best cheerleaders to college so I'm hunting for new recruits.'

I was not the only one to look crestfallen.

'Come now, that's no way to react! Our teams need your support. We can't have Aspen High out-dancing, out-chanting us, can we?'

Yes we can, I chanted under my breath in Obama-Bob-the-Builder fashion.

She tapped a remote control and Taylor Swift's 'You belong with me' started to blare over the loudspeakers.

'Sheena, you know what to do. Show the other girls the steps for the first sequence.'

A lanky girl with honey-blonde hair loped with antelope grace to the front and began what looked to me a fiendishly difficult routine.

'See, it's simple,' declared Mrs Green. 'Fall into line, the rest of you.' I shuffled to the back. 'You there—new girl. I can't see you.' Precisely: that had been the idea. 'Come forward. And from the top—one and two and three, kick.'

OK, I'm not completely hopeless. Even, I managed to do an approximation of Sheena's moves. The minute hand on the clock crawled towards the end of the period.

'Now we're going to step it up,' announced Mrs Green. At least someone was enjoying herself. 'Get out the pompoms!'

No way. I was not going to shake those ridiculous things. Glancing over Mrs Green's shoulder, I could see some of the boys from my class, already back from their run, were spying on us through the window in the sports hall canteen. Sniggering. Great.

Alerted by the attention of the front row to what was going on behind her, Mrs Green twigged that we had an audience. As smooth as a Ninja, she swooped on the boys before they knew what had hit them and dragged them in.

'We believe in equal opportunities in Wrickenridge High.' Gleefully, she thrust pompoms in their hands. 'Line up, boys.'

Now it was our chance to laugh as the red-faced males were forced to join in. Mrs Green stood at the front assessing our skill—or lack of it. 'Hmm, not enough, not enough. I think we need to practise a few tosses—Neil,' she picked out a broad-shouldered boy with a shaved head, 'you were in the squad last year, weren't you? You know what to do.'

Tossing sounded OK. Chucking pompoms was better than shaking them.

Mrs Green tapped three more recruits on the shoulder. 'Gentlemen, I'd like four of you up front. Make a cradle of your arms—yes, that's it. Now, we need the smallest girl for this.'

No, absolutely not. I sidled behind Tina, who loyally tried to look twice her normal girth, pompoms on hips.

'Where's she gone—that little English girl? She was here a moment ago.'

Sheena spoilt my plan to hide. 'She's behind Tina, ma'am.'

'Come here, dear. Now, it's quite simple. Sit on their crossed hands and they'll throw you into the air and catch you. Tina and Sheena, bring a crash mat over here, just in case.' My eyes must have been like saucers, for Mrs Green patted my cheek. 'Don't worry, you don't have to do anything but point your hands and feet and try to look as if you are enjoying yourself.'

I eyed the boys with distrust; they were looking at me closely, possibly for the first time, estimating just how much weight I was carrying. Then Neil shrugged, making his mind up. 'Yeah, we can do this.'

'On the count of three!' bellowed the teacher.

They grabbed me and up I went. My shriek probably could've been heard in England. It certainly brought the basketball coach and the rest of the boys running in the belief that someone was being brutally murdered.

I don't think Mrs Green will be picking me for the squad.

Still in shock, I sat at lunch with Tina, barely eating a thing. My stomach had yet to return to earth.

'They got a fair bit of height on that toss, didn't they?' Tina flicked my arm to interrupt my blank stare.

'Oh. My. God.'

'You make a lot of noise for such a small person.'

'So would you if a sadistic teacher decided to torture you.'

Tina shook her mane. 'Not going to be a problem for me—I'm too big.' She thought it funny, the traitor. 'So, Sky, what're you going to do with the rest of your recess?'

Spurred out of my stupor, I dug out a leaflet from my welcome pack and put it between us. 'I thought I'd go along to the music practice. Want to come too?'

She pushed it away with a wry laugh. 'Sorry, you're on your own. Me, they don't let me near the music room. Glass shatters when it sees me coming with my mouth open. What do you play?'

'A couple of instruments,' I admitted.

'Details, sister, details.' She beckoned with her fingers, drawing the words out of me.

'Piano, guitar, and saxophone.'

'Mr Keneally is going to die of excitement when he hears. A one-girl band! Do you sing?'

I shook my head.

'Phew! I thought I was going to have to hate you for being sickeningly talented.' She dumped her tray. 'Music's this way. I'll show you.'

I'd seen pictures on the school website but the music suite was much better equipped than even I had hoped. The main classroom had a glossy black grand that I was already itching to get my hands on. Students were milling around when I entered, some strumming on their guitars, a couple of girls practising scales on flutes. A tall, dark-haired boy with John Lennon glasses was changing the reed on his clarinet, his expression serious. I looked for somewhere inconspicuous to sit, preferably with a good view of the piano. There was a space next to a girl on the far side. I made towards it but her friend sat down before I could.

'Sorry, but this seat's taken,' the girl said, seeing I was still hovering at her shoulder.

'Right. OK.'

I perched alone on the edge of a desk and waited, avoiding meeting anyone's eye.

'Hey, you're Sky, right?' A boy with a shaved head and complexion of rich roast coffee took my hand, giving it a complicated shake. He moved with the easy grace of the long-limbed. Put into one of my comic book dreams, he'd be called something like Elasto-man.

Stop it, Sky, concentrate.

'Um . . . hi. You know me?'

'Yeah. I'm Nelson. You met my grandma. She told me to watch out for you. Everyone treating you well?'

OK—so he wasn't like Mrs Hoffman after all, way too cool. 'Yes, everyone's been very friendly.'

He grinned at my accent and dropped down beside me, putting his feet up on the chair in front. 'Awesome. I think you'll have no problem fitting right in.'

I needed to hear that because just then I was having doubts. I decided I liked Nelson.

The door banged open. Enter Mr Keneally, a hefty man with the ginger hair of a Celt. Doodling on my pad, I immediately had him tabbed: Music Master, Harbinger of Doom to all disharmony. Definitely not a candidate for spandex.

'Ladies and gentlemen,' he began without breaking step. 'Christmas is coming with its usual alarming swiftness, and we've a big programme of concerts scheduled. So you can all expect to let those little lights shine.' I could hear his signature tune now: lots of drum and building tension, a kind of revved-up version of the '1812' overture. 'Orchestra starts on Wednesday. Jazz band Friday. All you budding rock stars, if you want to book the music rooms for your own band practice,

23

see me first. But why do I bother—you know the drill.' He dumped the papers down. 'Except perhaps you.' Music Master had brought his X-ray vision to bear on me.

I hate being new.

'I'm catching up fast, sir.'

'Good for you. Name?'

Hating my parents' whimsical choice more and more, I told him, receiving the usual giggles from those who'd not met me before.

Mr Keneally frowned at them. 'What do you play, Miss Bright?'

'A bit of piano. Oh, and guitar and tenor sax.'

Mr Keneally rocked on the balls of his feet, reminding me of a diver about to take the plunge. 'Is "a bit" some English code for "really good"?'

'Um . . .'

'Jazz, classical, or rock?'

'Er . . . jazz, I suppose.' I was happy with anything as long as it came on a stave.

'Jazz, you suppose? You don't sound very certain, Miss Bright. Music is not take it or leave it; music is life or death!'

His little speech was interrupted by the arrival of a late-comer. The Hispanic biker sauntered into the room, hands thrust in pockets, his mile-long legs eating up the floor as he strode to the windowsill to perch next to the clarinettist. It took me a moment to get over the surprise that the biker actually participated in any school activities; I'd imagined him above all that. Or maybe he'd come just to make fun of us? He leaned against the window as he had his saddle, ankles crossed negligently, an expression of amusement on his face as if he'd heard it all before and no longer cared.

All I could think was that they don't make them like that in Richmond. It wasn't so much that he had the poster boy looks, it was more to do with the raw energy that rippled under the skin, pent-up rage like a tiger pacing a cage. I couldn't tear my eyes away. I was by no means the only one affected. The atmosphere changed in the room. The girls sat up that little bit straighter, the boys were put on edge—all because this godlike creature had deigned to come among us mere mortals. Or was it the wolf among the sheep?

'Mr Benedict, so kind of you to join us,' Mr Keneally said in a voice dripping with sarcasm, his previous good humour chilled. A little scene flashed through my head: Music Master facing up to the Wicked Wolfman, weapons a bullet spray of notes. 'All of us are thrilled you've torn yourself away from your no doubt far more important schedule to make music with us, even if your arrival is somewhat tardy.'

The boy quirked an eyebrow, evidently unrepentant. He picked up a pair of drumsticks and rolled them in his fingers. 'I'm late?' His voice was deep as I had imagined it, a shrug of bass tones. The clarinettist bravely elbowed him in the ribs, a reminder to behave.

Mr Keneally's buttons were definitely being pushed. 'Yes, you are late. I believe it is a custom in this school to apologize to the teacher if you arrive after they do.'

Drumsticks stilled, the boy stared at him for a moment, his expression arrogant like some young lord contemplating a peasant who dared correct him. Finally, he said, 'Sorry.'

I had the impression that the rest of the room gave a subtle sigh of relief that conflict had been averted.

'You're not—but that'll have to do. Watch your step, Mr Benedict: you may be talented but I'm not interested in prima donnas who don't know how to treat their fellow musicians. You, Miss Bright, are you a team player?' Mr Keneally turned back to me, dashing my hopes that I'd been forgotten. 'Or are you afflicted with the same attitude as our Mr Zed Benedict?'

A very unfair question. This was a battle of superheroes and I was not even a sidekick. I'd not yet spoken to the Wolfman and I was being asked to criticize him. He had the kind of looks that made even the most confident girl a little in awe of him and, as my self-esteem was way down at rock bottom to start with, what I felt was closer to terror.

'I . . . I don't know. But I've been late too.'

The boy's gaze flicked to me, then dismissed me as no more than a fleck of mud on his Wolfman superboots.

'Let's find out what you can do. Jazz band fall in.' Mr Keneally shot music out like Frisbees. 'Mr Hoffman, you take the sax; Yves Benedict, clarinet part. Maybe you can prevail upon your brother to delight us all on the drums?'

'Of course, Mr Keneally,' John Lennon specs replied, shooting the biker a dark look. 'Zed, get over here.'

His brother? Wow, how did *that* happen? They might look a little like each other but in attitude they were on different planets.

'Miss Bright can have my place at the piano.' Mr Keneally caressed the grand fondly.

I really *really* didn't want to perform in front of everyone.

'Um . . . Mr Keneally, I'd prefer—'

'Sit.'

I sat, adjusting the height of the stool. At least the music was familiar.

'Don't mind the prof,' Nelson muttered, giving my shoulder a squeeze. 'He does this to everyone—tests your nerves, he says.'

Feeling mine were wrecked already, I waited for the others to settle.

'OK, take it away,' said Mr Keneally, sitting in the audience to watch.

With the first touch, I knew the grand was a honey—full

toned, powerful, capable of a great range. It relaxed me as nothing else could, providing a barrier between me and the rest of the room. Getting lost in the score chased off my jitters and I began to enjoy myself. I lived for music in the same way my parents did for their art. It wasn't about performance— I preferred to play to an empty room; for me, it was about being part of the composition, taking the notes and working the magic to weave the spell. When playing with others, I was aware of my fellow performers not as people but as the sounds: Nelson, smooth and loose; Yves, the clarinet player, lyrical, intelligent, sometimes funny; Zed—well, Zed was the heart-beat, powering the music along. I sensed he understood the music as I did, his anticipation of shifts in mood and tempo faultless.

'Very good, nay, excellent!' Mr Keneally pronounced when we had finished. 'I fear I've just been bumped from the jazz band.' He gave me a wink.

'You aced,' said Nelson in a low voice as he passed my back.

Mr Keneally went on to other matters, organizing the choir and orchestra rehearsals, but no one else was asked forward to play. Unwilling to give up my barrier, I stayed where I was, gazing at the reflection of my hands in the raised lid, fingers tapping the keys without pressing down. I felt a light touch on my shoulder. The students were leaving but Nelson and the clarinet player stood behind me, Zed further off still looking as if he'd rather not be there.

Nelson gestured to the clarinettist. 'Sky, meet Yves.'

'Hi. You're good.' Yves smiled, pushing his glasses further up the bridge of his nose.

'Thanks.'

'That idiot's my brother, Zed.' He waved a hand towards the scowling biker.

'Come on, Yves,' Zed growled.

Yves ignored him. 'Don't mind him. He's like this with everyone.'

Nelson laughed and left us to it.

'You twins?' They had the same colouring and golden-brown skin, but Yves was round-faced with sleek black hair, a young Clark Kent. Zed had well-defined features, strong nose, large eyes with long lashes, and a head of thick curls, more likely to be one of the colourful bad guys than be found among the boring good. A fallen hero, one of those tragic types who turn to the dark side like Anakin Skywalker . . .

Keep with the programme, Sky.

Yves shook his head. 'No way. I've a year on him. I'm a senior. He's the baby of the family.'

Never had I seen anyone less like a baby. My respect for Yves soared as it was clear he wasn't intimidated by his brother.

'Gee, thanks, bro, I'm sure she wanted to know that.' Zed folded his arms, foot tapping.

'See you at band practice.' Yves tugged Zed away.

'Yeah, sure,' I murmured, watching the brothers. 'I bet you can't wait.' I hummed an ironic little exit tune, imagining them both leaping into the skies as they departed from the sight of us mere mortals.

chapter 4

That same afternoon, Tina ran me home in her car, saying she wanted to see where I lived. I think she was really angling for an invitation to meet the parents. Her vehicle only had two seats, the boot devoted to tool space for her brother's plumbing business. You could still make out the words *Monterey Repairs* on the side.

'He gave it to me when he upgraded to a truck,' she explained cheerfully, honking the horn to move a cluster of teenagers out of the way. 'He's officially my favourite brother for at least another month.'

'How many brothers do you have?'

'Two. More than enough. You?'

'It's just me.'

She chatted away as we wound through town. Her family sounded wonderful—a bit chaotic but close. No wonder she had bags of confidence with that behind her.

She gunned the accelerator and we shot up the hill.

'I met Zed and Yves Benedict at music practice,' I said casually, trying to ignore the fact that I was being thrown back in the seat like an astronaut on take-off.

'Isn't Zed gorgeous!' She smacked her lips enthusiastically, swerving round a cat that dared to cross the road in front of her.

'Yeah, I suppose.'

'There's no suppose about it. That face, that body—what more could a girl want?'

Someone who noticed her? I thought.

'But he's got a big attitude—drives the teachers mad. Two of his brothers were similar but they say he's the worst. Almost got kicked out of school last year for disrespect to a staff member. Mind you, none of us liked Mr Lomas. Turned out he liked some of us too much, if you know what I mean. Got fired at the end of term.'

'Yuck.'

'Yeah, anyway. Seven sons in the family. Three still at home in the house at the top of town next door to the cable car station and the older ones in Denver.'

'Cable car?'

'Yeah, their dad runs it during the season; their mom's a ski instructor. We all think the Benedict boys are the kings of the slopes.'

'There are seven of them?'

She hooted at a pedestrian and waved. 'The Benedicts kept to a pattern: Trace, Uriel, Victor, Will, Xavier, Yves, and Zed. Helped them remember, I guess.'

'Odd names.'

'Odd family, but they're cool.'

Sally and Simon were unpacking art supplies when we arrived back. I could tell they were delighted that I had brought home a friend so soon. They worried about my shyness even more than I did.

'Sorry we've nothing to offer you but shop-bought biscuits,' my mother said, rustling up some refreshments from the grocery box on the kitchen counter. As if she were the kind of mother who would be baking her own!

'And here was I hoping for a full English tea,' said Tina with a twinkle in her eye. 'You know, iddy-biddy cucumber sandwiches and those cake things with jelly and cream.'

'You mean scones and jam,' said Simon.

'Sc-*own*-es,' Sally and I corrected him automatically.

'Sorry, did I miss something?' Tina asked when we laughed.

'Old joke—not funny,' Simon said briefly. 'Cut it out, girls. Sky told us you were into art, Tina. What have you heard about the new centre?'

'I've seen the building—totally awesome. Mr Rodenheim had big ambitions for the place.' She sneaked a peek at a sketchbook Sally had just unpacked. She looked impressed, taking time to study each one. 'This is great. Charcoal?'

Sally stood up and tossed her scarf over her shoulder. 'Yes, I like that medium for sketching.'

'Are you going to hold classes?'

'That's part of the deal,' Sally confirmed, shooting Simon a delighted look.

'I'd like to come, Mrs Bright, if I may.'

'Of course, Tina. And please, call me Sally.'

'Sally and Simon,' added my dad.

'OK.' Tina put down the sketch pad and shoved her hands in her pockets. 'So did Sky here pick up artistic genes from you then?'

'Er . . . no.' Sally smiled at me, a little embarrassed. It was always like this when people asked. We'd agreed we'd never pretend to be other than what we were.

'I'm adopted, Tina,' I explained. 'My life was a little complicated before they took me in.'

Read 'seriously messed up'. I'd been dumped at a motorway service station when I was six; no one had been able to

31

trace my birth parents. I'd been traumatized, not even able to remember my name. The only way I had communicated in the next four years was via music. Not a time I liked to remember. It had left me with the haunting feeling that maybe one day someone would turn up and claim me like a suitcase lost by an airline. I knew I didn't want to be traced.

'Oh, sorry—I didn't mean to put my foot in it. But your parents are awesome.'

'It's OK.'

She picked up her bag. 'Cool. Gotta go. See you tomorrow.' With a cheery wave, she was gone.

'I like your Tina,' Sally announced, hugging me.

'And she thinks you're awesome.'

Simon shook his head. 'Americans think shoes are *awesome*, someone offering them a lift is *awesome*: what are they going to do when they meet something really awe-inspiring? They'll have run out of road with that word.'

'Simon, stop being an old fuddy-duddy.' Sally slapped him in the ribs. 'How was your day, Sky?'

'Fine. No, better than fine. Awesome.' I grinned at Sally. 'I think I'm going to be all right here.' As long as I steered clear of Mrs Green's cheerleaders.

Jazz band practice fell at the end of the week. During the intervening time, I didn't come across the two Benedicts in the hallways as our timetables appeared not to overlap. I did see Yves in the distance once when he was playing volleyball, but Zed's schedule did not coincide with mine.

Tina saw him.

Nelson shot a few hoops with him. Brave man.

But not me. Not that I spent all my time looking out for him, of course.

I heard a lot more about him. He and his family were one of the favourite topics for gossip. Three of the Benedict Boys—Trace, Victor, and now the youngest, Zed—were notorious for roaring through Wrickenridge on their motorbikes, getting involved in fights in the local bars, leaving a trail of broken hearts among the female population—mostly from their failure to date the local girls. The oldest two, Trace and Victor, had settled down a little now they had jobs out of town, ironically both in law enforcement, but that didn't stop their past exploits being related with great relish and some fondness. 'Bad but not mean' seemed to be the verdict.

Tina's summary was the most succinct: 'like Belgian chocolate—absolutely sinful and completely irresistible'.

Guilty in the knowledge that I was far too interested in someone I'd met just the once, I tried to shake the habit of looking for him. This wasn't my normal behaviour—in England, I'd rarely taken an interest in boys, and if I'd chosen a candidate to flip the switch, so to speak, it wouldn't have been Zed. What was there even to like about him? Nothing but a sneer. That made me shallow for taking such an interest. He might have become the anti-hero of my ongoing graphic novel plotting, but that didn't make him a good candidate for my attention in real life. Maybe the fact that he was so far out of my league made him strangely 'safe' to fancy; it would go no further because the moon would fall from the sky before he noticed me.

Our paths did cross once, but that was out of school—and definitely not to my advantage. I'd dropped by the grocery store on my way home to pick up some milk and got cornered by Mrs Hoffman. In between grilling me as to how I was getting on in every single one of my subjects, she also enrolled me in fetching goods for her.

'Sky, honey, I'd like a jar of dill sauce,' she said, gesturing to a small green bottle on the very top shelf.

'OK.' I put my hands on my hips and looked up. It was out of reach for both of us.

'Why do they make these pesky shelves so tall?' huffed Mrs Hoffman. 'I've a mind to call the manager.'

'No, no.' I didn't want to be there for that particular episode. 'I can get it.' I glanced down the aisle, wondering if there was a handy ladder available and caught sight of Zed at the far end.

Mrs Hoffman spotted him too. 'Well, look there, it's that Benedict boy—Xav—no, Zed. Foolish names if you ask me.'

I didn't ask because I had no doubt she'd also have something to say on the subject of mine.

'Shall we call him over?' she asked.

That would be great: 'Excuse me, Mr Tall-and-Good-looking Wolfman, but can you help the English midget reach the sauce?' I think not.

'It's OK; I can get it.' I climbed on the lowest shelf, pulling myself up by the middle one, reaching up on tiptoes. My fingers curled around the topmost jar—almost . . .

Then my foot slipped and I landed on my backside, the jar flying from my hand and smashing on the tiles. The row of dill sauces rocked precariously, looked sure to fall, but miraculously stayed on the shelf.

'Bummer!'

'Sky Bright, I won't stand for such unladylike language!' said Mrs Hoffman.

The assistant arrived, towing a mop and bucket on wheels behind her like a tubby dog.

'I'm not paying for that, Leanne,' Mrs Hoffman announced immediately, pointing to the mess I'd made with the jar.

I struggled to my feet, feeling a bruise already forming at the base of my spine, but I resisted the temptation to rub the offended part. 'It was my fault.' I dug in my pocket and pulled out a five dollar bill. There went my chocolate treat.

'Put your money away, honey,' said the shop assistant. 'It was an accident. We all saw that.'

Without a word, Zed sauntered over and plucked another jar of dill sauce from the shelf with no difficulty whatsoever and tucked it in Mrs Hoffman's basket.

Mrs Hoffman beamed at him, perhaps not realizing she was smiling at the school's bad boy. 'Thank you, Zed. It is Zed, isn't it?'

He nodded curtly, his eyes flicking over me with something like derision.

Zap—he paralyses his enemy with a flick of an eyelash.

'How are your parents, Zed dear?'

Wonderful! Mrs Hoffman had found another victim to interrogate.

'They're OK,' he said, adding as an afterthought, 'ma'am.'

Wow, was America weird! Even the town bad boy had a polite streak drummed into him—not like his British equivalent who wouldn't have dreamt of calling anyone 'ma'am'.

'And your older brothers, what are they doing these days?'

I slipped away with a soft 'bye'. I wouldn't swear to it, but I thought I heard Zed mutter 'traitor' as I abandoned him, which made me feel a lot better about doing a prat-fall before his very eyes.

I'd not got far before I heard a motorbike behind me. I looked over my shoulder to see Zed manoeuvring a black Honda up the street, weaving expertly between the streams of traffic returning home for the night. He was obviously better at cutting short a conversation with Mrs Hoffman than I was. He slowed down when he spotted me but didn't pull over.

I carried on walking, trying not to worry that it was getting dark and he was still on my tail. He followed until I reached my gate, then zoomed off, doing a wheelie that made a neighbour's little poodle yap as if she'd been electrocuted.

What had that been about? Intimidation? Curiosity? I thought the first was most likely. I would die of embarrassment if he ever knew how much time I had spent wondering about him that week. It had to stop.

Friday morning and the local news carried non-stop coverage of a gang shooting in the nearest city, Denver. Family members had got caught in the crossfire—all now in the morgue. It seemed a long way from the concerns of our mountain community so I was surprised to find everyone was talking about it. Violence of the 'ka-pow!' sort was OK in the imagination, but the real thing was sickening. I didn't want to dwell on it but my classmates were unstoppable.

'They say it was a drug deal that went down real bad,' Zoe, a friend of Tina's, told us over lunch. She had an irreverent attitude to life and I particularly liked her because she was only a shade taller than me, thanks to her petite Chinese mother. 'But five members of the same family were killed including a baby. How sick can you get?'

'I heard the gunmen have gone on the run. An APB is out over the whole state,' added Tina knowledgeably. Her older brother worked in the sheriff's office. 'Brad's signed up for extra duty.'

'Tell your brother not to worry: Mrs Hoffman will spot them if they come here.' Zoe snapped her celery and dipped it in salt, deftly slicking her long black hair over her shoulder with her spare hand. 'I can just see her taking them out.'

'Yeah, she'll have them begging for mercy,' agreed Tina.

Mrs Hoffman—Judge Merciless, dealing out justice with her wooden spoon of doom, I mused.

'Do you think the gunmen will come here?'

The two girls stared at me.

'What? Something exciting happen in Wrickenridge? Get real,' laughed Zoe.

'No, Sky,' said Tina. 'Not a chance. We're at the end of a road going nowhere. Why would anyone come here unless they've skis strapped to their feet?'

It was a good question. I realized too late that I'd been stupid not to guess that they were joking about Wrickenridge getting involved in the big story, but Zoe and Tina were more amused than scornful of my intelligence. Being foreign cut me a little extra slack.

Making my excuses to get away from all this talk of murder, I arrived outside the practice room five minutes early. I had the place to myself and indulged my wandering fingers on the grand, dipping in and out of a Chopin nocturne. It helped cleanse me of the shivery feeling I got when thinking of the Denver shooting. Violence always made me feel panicked, as if it was about to release a tiger from a cage of memories inside me—something I couldn't fight or survive. Not going there.

We didn't yet have a piano at home and I was having serious withdrawal symptoms. As I weaved my way through the notes, I distracted myself by wondering what reception Zed would give me today. Chopin melted into something more funky, with the *Mission Impossible* theme tune interlaced.

The door banged and I spun round in anticipation, pulse leaping, but it was only Nelson.

'Hey, Sky. Yves and Zed aren't in school.' Elasto-man bounded in and got his instrument out of its case.

I felt a huge wave of disappointment which I told myself to put down to being denied the chance to play, not because I was missing out on seeing the object of my secret obsession.

'Do you want to try out a few things together anyway?'

31

I ran my fingers over the keys.

Nelson's mouth twitched. 'What kind of things you have in mind, sweet thing?'

'Um . . . I'm sure there are a few songs here we could take for a test drive.' I got up and leafed through the stack of music on the table.

He laughed. 'Aw, shucks: you're brushing me off!'

'Am I? I am?' I could feel my blush getting to the top of the embarrassing scale. 'How about this?' I shoved a random piece of music towards him.

He looked down. 'Show tunes? I mean, *Oklahoma* has some good ones but—'

'Oh.' I snatched it back, getting more flustered by the knowledge that I was amusing him.

'Take it easy, Sky. Better idea: why not let me pick?'

Relieved, I abandoned the scores and retreated to my piano stool where I felt more in control of things.

'I make you nervous?' Nelson asked seriously, shooting me a curious look. 'You shouldn't mind me—I was just fooling around.'

I tugged my long plait over my shoulder and wrapped it around my fist. It had to be kept plaited or it got out of control. 'Not you.'

'Just guys?'

I thumped my head lightly on the piano lid. 'Am I that obvious?'

Nelson shook his head. 'No. I'm such a sensitive soul for recognizing it.' He grinned.

'I've got a few issues.' I wrinkled my nose in disgust at myself. My problems were many, all rooted in my deep sense of insecurity according to the child psychologist I'd been going to since I was six. Well, gee, as if I couldn't have worked that one out for myself, seeing that I was abandoned and all.

'I'm a bit out of my comfort zone.'

'But I've got your back, remember.' Nelson pulled out his choice and showed it to me for my approval. 'You can breathe easy round me. I ain't got no nefarious designs towards you.'

'What's nefarious?'

'I don't know, but my grandma accuses me of having them when she thinks I done something bad and it sounds good.'

I laughed, relaxing a little. 'That's right—I can rat you out to her if you step out of line.'

He gave a mock shudder. 'Even you can't be so cruel, Brit Chick. Now, are we going to sit shooting the breeze all day or play some music?' Nelson grabbed his sax and tested the tuning.

'Music.' I propped the score open on the stand and jumped right in.

chapter 5

I had no plans for the weekend.

Doesn't that sound pathetic? Tina and Zoe had Saturday jobs in the local stores and Nelson was out of town to see his dad so there was no one to hang out with. Simon had mentioned something about hunting for second-hand pianos but that idea got shot down by the manager of the Arts Centre asking my parents to come in and sort out their studio space. I knew better than to get in the way. It would be like standing between two chocoholics and their candy supply. That left me circling Planet Wrickenridge, a lone comet in my own orbit.

'Come and find us for lunch,' Sally said, handing me a twenty dollar note. 'Go and see what's what in town.'

That didn't take long. Wrickenridge was American-quaint; even Starbucks masqueraded as a Swiss-style chalet. There was a small selection of upmarket shops, some only open during the skiing season, a couple of hotels with posh looking restaurants waiting for winter, a diner, a community centre, and a gym. I stood outside that for a while wondering if it was worth a closer look but in the end felt too shy to try it. Same went for the adjoining spa and nail parlour. I wondered if *Neat Nails* was where Tina got hers done. I'd pretty much bitten mine to the quick.

Wandering further on, I headed up Main Street towards the park, enjoying the municipal flowerbeds spilling over with bright autumn blooms. Passing the duck pond that doubled as an ice rink in winter, I walked until garden planting faded into an arboretum of mountain trees and shrubs. A few people strolling in the sunshine greeted me as we passed, but I was mostly left to myself. I wished I had a dog to make my presence less conspicuous. Perhaps I should suggest it to Sally and Simon. A rescue pup that needed a home because someone had abandoned it—I'd like that. Problem was we were only certain on staying a year—not long enough to be fair on a pet.

I followed a track up, hoping to reach a viewpoint I'd seen marked on the map at the park entrance with the intriguing label of 'ghost town'. My leg muscles were burning by the time the path led me out on to a rocky outcrop that had a great vista of Wrickenridge and the rest of the valley. The label hadn't lied: the ledge was home to a street of abandoned wooden buildings; it reminded me of a movie set when filming had finished. I read a plaque hammered into the ground.

Gold Rush township, built 1873 when the first nugget was discovered in the Eyrie River. Abandoned 1877. Seven miners died when the Eagle shaft collapsed in Spring 1876.

Only four years and the miners had thrown up a whole little community of lodging houses, saloons, stores, and stables. Most of the dark wood buildings had lost their roofs, but some were still thatched in tin which creaked ominously in the breeze. Rusting chains dangled over the edge of the escarpment, swaying over the golden wild flowers that clung to the ledges, mocking the lost dreams of the pioneers. It would make a great backdrop to a really spooky story—'Revenge of the Miners', or something. I could hear the spine-chilling themes already, incorporating the lonely clank of the chain and the hollow notes of the wind blowing through the abandoned buildings.

But it was a sad place. I didn't like to think of the miners buried somewhere in the mountainside, crushed under tons of rock. After poking around in the buildings, I sat down, crossed my legs on a bench, wishing I'd thought to buy a Coke and a chocolate bar before climbing all the way up here. Colorado was just so big—everything on a scale unfamiliar to a British person. Mist drifted off the mountain slopes, cutting the sunlit summits off from the dark green base like an eraser rubbing out a picture. I followed the progress of a yellow van winding its way along the main road, heading east. Cloud shadows moved across the fields, rippling over barns and roofs, dimming a pond then moving it on to leave it a bright eye gazing up at the heavens again. The sky arched over the peaks, a soft blue on this hazy morning. I tried to imagine the people living up here, faces turned to the rock rather than the sky, watching for the glint of gold. Had any of them stayed on and moved down to Wrickenridge? Did I go to school with descendants of people who arrived in the madness of the Gold Rush?

A twig snapped behind me. Heart thumping, head full of ghosts, I twisted round to see Zed Benedict hovering at the point where the track left the trees. He looked tired, shadows under his eyes that hadn't been there last week. His hair was mussed, as if he'd been running his fingers through it repeatedly.

'Perfect, just what I need,' he said with cutting sarcasm, backing away.

Words not calculated to make a girl feel good about herself.

I got up. 'I'm going.'

'Forget it. I'll come back later.'

'I was just heading home in any case.'

He stood his ground and just looked at me. I had the strangest sensation that he was drawing something out of me, as if there was a thread between us and he was winding it in.

I shivered and closed my eyes, holding up a hand, palm towards him. I felt dizzy. 'Please—don't do that.'

'Don't do what?'

'Look at me like that.' I blushed a furious red. He would now think I was completely mad. I'd imagined the thread after all. I turned on my heel and strode off into the nearest building, leaving him the bench, but he followed.

'Look at you like what?' he repeated, kicking aside a fallen plank of wood in his pursuit. The whole place groaned; one puff of a strong wind and I was sure it would collapse on our heads.

'I don't want to talk about it.' I marched ahead, making for the empty-framed window overlooking the valley. 'Forget it.'

'Hey, I'm talking to you.' He caught my arm, but seemed to reconsider. 'Look . . . er . . . Sky, isn't it?' He cast his eyes upwards as if seeking guidance, not quite believing what he was about to do. 'I've got to tell you something.'

The breeze got under the eaves, making the tin roof creak. I suddenly realized just how far we were from other people. He released my arm. I rubbed at the places where his fingers had dug into my skin.

He frowned, reluctant even to speak to me, but made himself do so. 'There's something you need to know.'

'What?'

'Be careful at night. Don't go out alone.'

'What do you mean?'

'The other night I saw . . . Look, just be careful, OK?'

No, not OK. He was one scary guy.

'You've got that right.'

What? I hadn't said that aloud, had I?

He swore and kicked the broken mining gear in frustration.

The chain clanked to and fro, reminding me of a body swinging on a hangman's scaffold. I hugged my arms to my chest, trying to make myself a smaller target. This was my fault. I'd done something—I don't know what—something to set him off.

'No, you haven't!' He said the words sharply. 'None of it is your fault, you hear?' He dropped his voice. 'And I'm just scaring the hell out of you, aren't I?'

I froze.

'Fine. I'll leave.' He strode off abruptly, disappearing between the empty buildings, swearing at himself under his breath.

So, that went well.

chapter 6

Three weeks into the semester and high school had proved to be mostly fun apart from the weird feeling left over from Zed's warning. What was that boy on? And what did he think he had seen? How could it possibly have anything to do with me not going out after dark? The last thing I needed was some bad boy to take an unhealthy interest in me.

I tried to shrug it off. Too much else was going on. I had a few bad moments with some of the students teasing me about my accent and ignorance of things American, but on the whole they were OK. A couple of the girls in my social studies class, including the cheerleading Sheena—ones I'd privately tagged as Vampire Brides due to their preference for blood-red nail varnish—stole my ID off me for a joke when they'd heard me moaning to Tina about how bad my picture was. Unfortunately, the Draculettes agreed with me and dubbed me the 'blonde bunny' when they saw my photo, which I found more than annoying. Tina advised me to let it pass, arguing it was more likely to stick if I made a fuss about it. So I bit my tongue and kept my school swipe card hidden at all times.

'Activities day next week—Juniors can choose to go rafting,'

Nelson told me one Friday afternoon as he walked me home. He was on his way to fix his grandmother's lawnmower for her. 'Wanna come?'

I wrinkled my nose, imagining Robinson Crusoe lashing together tree trunks. 'Rafting—you have to build one or something?'

He laughed. 'This isn't the Boy Scouts of America, Sky. No, I'm talking white-water, white-knuckle, high octane excitement on the Eyrie River. Imagine an inflatable boat with room for six or seven. You've got the main man on the rudder at the back, the rest of us with the paddles sitting on the sides, just barely holding on as we plunge through the rapids. You've gotta give it a try if you want to count yourself a Coloradan.'

Whoa, high school wasn't like sixth form college after all—this was immense. I could see the images flashing before my mind now as I expertly navigated my way down a foaming river, saving the child/dog/injured man, music swelling to unbelievable heights, heavy on the strings, tight with tension . . .

Yeah, right.

'They've got a beginner's level?'

'Nope, gonna send you down the trickiest run with no life jacket and no guide.' Nelson laughed at my expression. 'Course they have, you muppet. You'll love it.'

I could do this: start small, graduate to hero status once I'd got the hang of it. 'OK. Do I need any special kit?'

He shook his head. 'No, just wear some old clothes. Sky, I don't suppose you'd ask Tina if she'd like to come in our group?'

My suspicions were instantly alerted. 'Why don't you ask her yourself?'

'She'll think I'm coming on to her.'

I smiled. 'Aren't you?'

He rubbed the back of his neck in an embarrassed gesture.

46

'Yeah, but I just don't want her to know it yet.'

The day of the rafting trip and the weather looked a little cloudy, the mountains a sullen grey and breeze stiff. There was a definite chill in the air, even a few spots of rain. I'd put on a thicker hoodie, my favourite one with 'Richmond Rowing Club' on the front which I thought was funny considering this was absolutely no Thames. The minibus bumped down the dirt track that led to the rafting school. The first gold leaves were drifting off the aspens and falling into the river to meet a violent end in the rapids. I hoped it wasn't a sign of things to come.

When we arrived, the rafting school receptionist doled out helmets, waterproof shoes, and life jackets. We then gathered on the bank to listen to a briefing given by a stern-faced man with long dark hair. He had the dramatic profile of a Native American, broad forehead and eyes that seemed eons older than his years. It was a face made to be drawn or, better yet, sculpted. If I'd written a melody for him, it would have been haunting, plaintive like the South American panpipes, music for wild places.

'Great—we've got Mr Benedict—Zed and Yves's father. He's the best,' whispered Tina. 'He totally rocks on the water.'

I couldn't pay attention, my eagerness to launch myself out on to the rapids dwindling now I actually faced the turbulent river.

Hearing our murmured discussion, Mr Benedict gave us both a keen look and I had a sudden glimpse of colours surrounding him—silvery like the sun on the snowy peaks.

Not again, I thought, feeling that strange sense of dizziness. I refused to see colours—I wasn't letting them back in. I closed my eyes and swallowed, snapping the contact.

'Ladies,' Mr Benedict said in a soft voice that still managed to carry over the noise of the water, 'if you would listen, please. I'm running through vital safety protocols.'

'You OK?' Tina whispered. 'You've gone a little green.'

'It's just . . . nerves.'

'You'll be fine—there's nothing to worry about.'

I hung on to every word Mr Benedict said after that but few of them lodged in my brain.

He finished his little lecture, stressing the need to obey orders at all times. 'Some of you said you were interested in kayaking. Is that right?'

Neil from cheerleading raised his hand.

'My sons are out on the course right now. I'll let them know you want a lesson.'

Mr Benedict was gesturing towards the upper reaches of the river where I could just make out a series of striped poles suspended over the channel. Three red kayaks were racing down the rapids. It was impossible to tell who was in each boat but they were evidently all skilled, playing the river in a series of almost balletic movements, pirouettes and turns that brought my heart into my mouth. One shot through to the front of the trio. He seemed to have an edge over the others, able to anticipate the next churn of the water, the next flip of current, a fraction ahead of time. He passed under the red and white finish post and punched the air with his paddle, laughing at his brothers lagging behind.

It was Zed. Of course.

Mesmerized, we all watched the other boats cross the finish. Zed was already at the bank getting out of the kayak when his brothers reached him. After some rowdy arguments in which the word 'unfair' was shouted several times, the tallest one picked Zed up and threw him in. He went under—but it was a calm backwater so he merely bobbed up to the surface. He grabbed his brother and pulled him over. From the easy way the boy fell, I guessed that this was not unexpected. That left Yves on the bank but he was getting royally splashed before lending a hand to haul his brothers out. They collapsed on the bank, laughing, until they got their breath back. It was odd to see Zed happy; I'd come to expect nothing but dark looks from him.

'My younger sons,' said Mr Benedict with a shrug.

As if hearing a whistle out of the hearing of the rest of us, the Benedict boys looked up.

'Get the raft launched, Dad, and I'll be right with you when I get changed,' shouted the tallest one. 'Zed'll take the kay-aker.'

'That's Xav,' said Tina. 'He only left school this year.'

'Is he like Zed or Yves?'

'How do you mean?'

We tagged along after the rafting party as it headed to the landing stage.

'Hostile or friendly. I think Zed's got it in for me.'

Tina frowned. 'Zed's got it in for a lot of people, but not usually girls. What's he done?'

'He . . . it's kinda hard to explain. When he notices me— which isn't often—he seems really irritated. Look, Tina, is it me? Have I done something wrong? Is it because I don't understand how things are done here?'

'Well, there are these vicious rumours that you prefer drinking tea to coffee.'

'Tina, I'm being serious!'

She put her hand on my forearm. 'No, Sky, you're doing fine. If he's got a problem with you, that's what it is exactly: his problem, not yours. I wouldn't worry. Zed's been acting kinda strange for a few weeks now—more of everything, more angry, more arrogant—everyone's noticed.'

Our discussion ended as we had to pay attention to Mr Benedict's instructions as to where we were going to sit. 'River's running high since the rain over the weekend. We need the smallest and lightest in the centre of this seat so you don't get flipped out.'

'That'd be you, Sky baby,' said Nelson, nudging me forward.

'One of my sons will take the paddle at the front, and you,' he pointed to Nelson, 'take the other side. That leaves you two girls to sit behind them near me.' He beckoned Tina and another girl from high school forward. They both were issued with paddles; I was the only one without as I had to be in the middle.

Zed approached, having dumped his wetsuit and put on shorts and a life jacket.

'Xav and Yves are taking the kayaker,' Zed announced.

His father frowned. 'I thought that was your job.'

'Yeah, well, I saw that he was going to be a jerk. Yves's better at handling that.'

I decided there and then that Wolfman had missed out on the devilish charm-school part in his anti-hero training.

Mr Benedict looked as if he wanted to say something—a lot of somethings—but was prevented by us listening in.

We took our places in the inflatable raft. This arrangement had the unfortunate consequence that I was next to Zed with Nelson on the other side. Zed appeared to be studiously avoiding looking at me—I'd become Miss Invisible Sky.

'Girl in the middle at the front—Sky, isn't it?'

I turned round to see Mr Benedict was speaking to me.

'Yes, sir?'

'If it gets rough, link arms with your neighbours. Girls up my end, make sure your feet stay in the toeholds on the bottom of the raft when it starts to buck. They'll keep you from falling in.'

Nelson grunted with disgust. 'Not worried about the boys then, is he?'

Zed overheard him. 'He thinks men should be able to look after themselves. Got a problem with that?'

Nelson shook his head, feeling the dig. 'Nope.'

Sally would just love this, I thought. As a card-carrying feminist, she would think Mr Benedict a complete dinosaur. She wouldn't be too impressed by Zed either.

Mr Benedict pushed the raft off from the moorings. With a few strong pulls from Zed and Nelson, we were out in the current. From here on, paddles were mainly about steering as there was only one direction on this stretch of the river—downstream very fast. Mr Benedict shouted instructions, plying the rudder-paddle at the rear. I hung on to the seat, biting back my shrieks as the raft spun round a rock jutting out into the water. When we passed it, I saw what lay ahead.

'Oh my God. We're never going to survive that!'

The water looked as if there was a giant whisk churning away on the fastest setting under the water. Froth flew in the air; rocks pierced the surface at irregular intervals, making navigation round them impossible as far as I could see. I'd watched what happened to eggs in a food mixer—that was going to be us in two seconds.

With a great kick, the boat surged forward. I screamed. Nelson roared with laughter and shouted 'Yee-ha!', swinging his paddle to help stave off the rocks. On my other side, Zed calmly did the same, showing no sign that he felt the exhilaration, the danger or even noticed that I was having a minor panic attack.

'Devil's Cauldron's looking a bit frisky,' shouted Mr Benedict over his shoulder. 'Keep us central, boys.'

The stretch he referred to looked more than frisky. 'Frisky' is what you call boisterous foals on a spring morning, gambolling in the sunshine; this was an autumnal savaging bear in a killing frenzy, wanting to stock up for winter with extra body fat. A raft-load of humans seemed to me the perfect menu.

The strains of the *Jaws* theme tune thumped in my mind.

The raft plunged in. The nose momentarily dipped under the surface, dowsing us in icy water. Tina shrieked but she was laughing as the water sloshed away. We were buffeted on all sides. I was thrown against Nelson, then into Zed. I slipped my arm through Nelson's elbow, but didn't dare do the same on the other side, Zed looked so forbidding. Nelson gave my arm an encouraging squeeze.

'Having fun?' he bellowed, water dripping down his face.

'In an awful "I'm-gonna-die-any-moment" way, yes!' I shouted back.

Just then, the nose of the raft got wedged between two rocks, pressure of water pushing us sideways. Waves slopped over the side.

'I'm going to push us off!' Mr Benedict shouted. 'All to the right.'

He'd taught us this drill on shore—it involved piling over to one side of the raft to make it lift half out of the river. I ended up sandwiched between Nelson and Zed, the stem of Nelson's paddle clipping my chin.

'Left!'

On the order, we lurched to the other side. The raft began to slide free.

'Back to your places!'

As I scrambled to obey the order, Zed suddenly threw his arms around me, tackling me to the floor, face down in the water that sloshed ankle-deep. 'Keep hold or you'll fall in,' he yelled in my ear.

Water going up my nose, I panicked and struggled free, just as the raft leapt down another rapid. Floundering on the floor,

I was propelled towards the side. I had no grip so I parted company with the boat and tumbled backwards into the water.

Cold—rushing water—screams—whistles. I thrashed to the surface. The boat was already ten metres behind as I was swept like an aspen leaf through the Cauldron.

Float! The order punched its way into my brain—a voice in my head that sounded like Zed.

I had no choice but to let the current take me where it would, trying to lie as flat as possible to stop my legs hitting submerged rocks. Something scraped my calf; my helmet collided briefly with a boulder. Finally I was spat out into the slack water of an eddy. I clung to a boulder, fingers frozen white spiders spread on the stone.

'Oh my God, Sky! Are you OK?' shrieked Tina.

Mr Benedict steered the boat to my side so Zed and Nelson could heave me out of the river. I lay gasping on my back at the bottom of the boat.

Zed briskly checked for injuries. 'She's fine. A bit scraped up but fine.'

We completed the rest of the course in a subdued mood, the fun having been swept away when I had. I felt cold, numb, and angry.

If Zed hadn't pounced on me, I would've been all right.

Mr Benedict steered us to the landing area where a jeep and trailer waited to take the raft back up the river. I refused to look at Zed as I got out on to the bank.

On dry land, Tina gave me a hug. 'Sky, you really OK?'

I forced a smile. 'Fine. Whose brilliant idea was this anyway? What is this—kill-a-foreigner week?'

'I thought we'd lost you.'

'You know something, Tina: I'm not cut out for this great outdoors stuff you Coloradans do.'

'Sure you are. You were just unlucky.'

Mr Benedict and Zed finished loading the raft, then came over to us.

'You all right, Sky?' Mr Benedict asked.

I nodded, not trusting myself to speak.

'What happened?' The question was directed to Zed.

I got my side in first. 'He flattened me—made me lose my grip!'

'I realized what was going to happen—I tried to warn her,' countered Zed.

I scowled. 'You *made* it happen.'

'I tried to stop it—shoulda just left you to it.' He scowled at me, eyes chilled as the river.

'Yeah, perhaps you should—and then I wouldn't be freezing to death here!'

'Enough!' Mr Benedict separated us. 'Sky, get in the jeep before you get any colder. Zed, a word.'

Swathed in towels, I watched father and son continue the argument until Zed stormed off, heading on foot into the woods.

Mr Benedict climbed into the driving seat. 'I'm sorry about that, Sky.'

'It's OK, Mr Benedict. I don't know why but your son seems to have a problem with me.' I shot a glance at Tina to say 'I told you so'. 'I don't need an apology. Perhaps he could just keep his distance or something. I don't like people laying in to me without cause.'

'If it's any comfort, he's got a lot on his mind at the moment.' Mr Benedict's sombre eyes followed his son. 'I've asked too much of him. Give him a chance to work things out.'

'See what I mean?' I whispered to Tina.

'Yeah, I do. What was that about?'

'I dunno—I really don't.' I needed her advice so badly; she was rapidly becoming the Obi Wan to my clueless apprentice.

I hoped she understood boys, or at least Zed, better than I did.

'That was weird.'

The windscreen wipers swished to and fro as the rain began to fall in earnest: he hates me, he hates me not, he hates me . . .

'You've not been pestering him, have you?' Tina asked after a pause.

'No, of course not.' I kept quiet about the number of times I had looked out for him at school. She didn't need to know the details of my pitiful obsession with the guy. Today had cured me of that.

'You wouldn't be the first. Lots of girls throw themselves at him, hoping to be the one.'

'Then they're seriously stupid.'

'After what he said, I'd have to agree with you. There's a lot of anger in that boy and I wouldn't want to be around when it gets out.'

I spent the evening and much of the night pondering Tina's warning, transposing it in my mind to fit her new role in my internal storyboarding: *the force is strong in this one but the boy has much anger.* Good advice, Obi Tina. Zed was too much for me to handle. Leave the Wolfman to chew on his own resentments. I was making light of it, but part of me instinctively cringed away from violent emotions like his, knowing that they could hurt. I had an uneasy sense I'd once lived too close to someone who flew into rages—someone from the time before I was found. I knew that harsh words became fists and bruises. Added to this, I was furious with myself. I had to be the prize idiot for obsessing about hearing Zed's voice when I was in danger. I needed to get a grip and leave the whole Zed thing well alone.

My good intentions were still intact as I crossed the school car park with Tina the following morning, that was until I saw the look I got from Zed. He was standing with the other boys by the motorbikes, arms folded, scanning the crowds entering the building. When he saw me arrive, he took one long examination and then, as if deciding I didn't measure up, dismissed me.

'Ignore him,' murmured Tina, seeing the exchange.

How could I? I wanted to go over and slap him, but, let's be honest here, I'm not the kind to have the guts to make a scene like that. I was sure I'd get halfway and bottle out. I'd promised myself I'd leave it alone.

Go on, do it, my anger told me. Girl or mouse?

Mouse every time.

Every time but this. There was just something about Zed Benedict that was like a match to my fuse and I was fizzing up to the point of explosion.

'Excuse me a moment, Tina.'

Before I knew it, I had changed direction and started towards him. I was having an Aretha Franklin moment—'Sisters are doin' it for themselves' blasted through my head, giving me the foolhardy courage to close the gap. The intent behind my furious charge must have transmitted itself to the other students because I could see heads swivelling towards me.

'Just what is your problem?' Whoa, had I really said that?

'What?' Zed dug in his pocket and pulled out his shades, putting them on so I was now looking at myself in double in the reflection. The four other boys were smirking at me, waiting for Zed to slap me down.

'I almost get drowned yesterday thanks to you and you made it sound like it was my fault.'

He stared at me silently, an intimidating tactic that *almost* worked.

'You were more to blame than I was for what happened in the raft.' Aretha was leaving me, her voice dying to a whisper.

'*I was to blame?*' His tone was marvelling that someone dare address him like this to his face.

'I knew zilch about rafting—you were the expert—go figure who was most in the wrong.'

'Who's the angry chick, Zed?' asked one of his friends.

He shrugged. 'No one.'

I felt the punch—and it hurt. 'I am not "no one". At least I'm not an arrogant pain-in-the-backside with a permanent sneer.' *Shut up, Sky, shut up.* I must have developed a death wish.

His friends howled at that.

'Zed, she's got you nailed,' said the one with slicked-back red hair, looking at me with new interest.

'Yeah, she's something else.' Zed shrugged and nodded his head into the building. 'Run along, BoPeep.'

Mustering all the dignity I could, I clutched my books to my chest and strode into school, Tina at my side.

'What was that?' she marvelled, touching my forehead to see if I was running a temperature.

I puffed out the breath I'd not been aware I was holding. 'That was me being angry. Was I convincing?'

'Er . . . some.'

'That bad?'

'No, you were great!' She didn't sound very certain. 'Zed had it coming. Just you'd better get good at hiding when you see him coming; he's not going to be pleased you ripped into him in front of his mates.'

I hid my face in my hands. 'I did, didn't I?'

'Yeah, you did. He isn't used to girls criticizing him—they're usually too much in awe. You know he's the hottest date in Wrickenridge, right?'

'Yeah, well, I wouldn't date him if he were the last breath of air on the planet.'

'Ouch, that's harsh!'

'No, it's fair.'

Tina patted my arm consolingly. 'I wouldn't worry. He'd never look at you in a million years.'

After that conversation, I watched the hallways like a commando in enemy territory so I could take cover if I saw Zed coming. At least I now had a group of friends to hide amongst should he decide to retaliate with some choice sneers for my outburst. First was Obi Tina, of course, but Zoe, who would fit the role of a slightly wicked Catwoman with her sense of humour, along with the original Elasto-man Nelson were also now part of my gang. They stood up for me against the Vampire Brides, Sheena and Co., who continued to pick on me, partly I think because they sensed I was vulnerable. VBs have this thing for drawing blood. Word must have gone round about the scene in the car park, with people coming to the understandable conclusion that I had a streak of insanity. Tina, Zoe, and Nelson were all that stood between me and a fringe life with the misfits. I could picture them in my head, my three defenders, arms folded, standing as a shield between me and all harm, cloaks rippling in the breeze, cue swelling heroic music . . . and cut.

I really had to get out more. These daydreams were invading every part of my life.

On the last Friday in September, I received some unwelcome news from Tina on our way to school in her car.

'We *all* have to show up to play soccer, boys and girls?' I asked her, horrified by the notion.

'Yeah, it's a junior year tradition before first snowfall so that means first Monday in October. It's supposed to build team spirit or something.' Tina blew a bubble with her gum and let it pop. 'As well as show up any hidden talent to the coach. I personally think Mr Joe is behind it—you must realize by now he's the power behind the throne in the school. He likes the chance to pretend he's a coach.'

She didn't seem too bothered by the prospect, not like I was.

'This is worse than dental surgery.' I hugged my arms defensively across my chest.

'Why? I thought you Brits loved soccer. We're all expecting great things from you.'

'I suck at sports.'

Tina laughed. 'Too bad.'

After pleading with my dad for him to explain the offside rule, I realized that I was heading for another disaster. But there was no escape. The whole year group—all one hundred of us—were told to report to the coaches out on the bleachers on Monday. The computer had selected a random collection of names to make up the teams. Mr Joe, in a misguided attempt at making the English girl feel at home in her national sport, crowned me captain of team B, which meant we were the first to play against A. And guess who was their captain?

'OK, Zed, you win the toss.' Mr Joe tucked the coin away and blew his whistle. He had really entered into the spirit of the game, even having one of those little notebook-thingies in his top pocket. 'It's fifteen minutes each way. Good luck!' He patted me on the shoulder in passing. 'Now's your chance to shine, Sky. Do England proud!'

I was sure this place was going to crop up in my nightmares from here on: rows upon rows of people watching from the bleachers and me without a clue what to do. It was like those dreams where you go out naked.

Major humiliation. Duffy started begging for mercy on my internal soundtrack.

'OK, captain.' Nelson grinned at me. 'Where do you want us?'

The only position I knew well were centre forward and goalie. I put Nelson up front and myself in goal.

'Are you sure,' asked Sheena. 'Aren't you, like, a bit short for a defender?'

'No, it's fine. I'm best back here.' Out of harm's way, I meant. 'The rest of you . . . um . . . share out the other positions—do what you do best.'

After kick off, I found that I had seriously miscalculated. I'd forgotten that when the opposition are captained by a player who makes minced meat of your defensive line—half of whom had as shaky a grasp of the game as I—then the goalie suddenly has a very busy time indeed.

We were 5–0 down after ten minutes. My team began making mutinous noises. If the strikers on Zed's team had left me alone for a moment, I would have dug a hole in the goal and hidden in it.

At half time we were a mammoth nine goals behind. I'd let in ten, but Nelson had achieved a miracle and scored once. My team gathered round me, the spirit of the lynch mob in the air.

'Tactics?' sneered Sheena.

Invite a meteor to fall on the pitch, obliterating my goal? Drop dead from plague? Stop it, Sky: this wasn't helping.

'Um . . . well—well done, Nelson, great goal. Let's have more of those, please.'

'That's it? Your tactics? *More goals, please?*' Sheena inspected her nails. 'Sheesh, look, I broke one. Do you think they'd let me retire injured?'

'I don't play football—I mean soccer—back home. I didn't want to be captain. Sorry.' I gave a pathetic shrug.

'This is so humiliating,' grumbled Neil, who until then had always been quite nice to me. 'Mr Joe promised you'd be great.'

I was beginning to feel a lot like crying. 'Then he was wrong, wasn't he? Expecting me to be good at football is like expecting all Welsh people to be able to sing.' My team looked blank. OK, so they hadn't heard of Wales. 'Just stop letting so many of them past you with the ball and then I wouldn't have to save so many.'

'Save!' Sheena shrieked with derision. 'You've not saved a single one. And if you do, I'll eat my sneakers.'

The whistle blew for the second half. I trekked up field to

my goal, only to be stopped by Zed. 'What now?' I snapped. 'Gonna rub it in some more that I'm rubbish? No need, my team's done that already.'

He looked over my head. 'No, Sky, I was going to tell you that you're down that end this half.'

Sheesh, I *was* going to cry. I scrubbed my wrist over my eyes and pivoted on the spot to set off for the other end of the pitch. I had to run the gauntlet of mocking faces.

I blinked. Zed's team were all surrounded by the raspberry pink glow of amusement. Mine had a charcoal grey aura shot through with red. Was I really seeing this—or imagining it? Stop it!

Sometimes I'm such a nutcase.

The massacre—sorry, game—continued until it was embarrassing for everyone, even the spectators. I'd not managed to save a thing. Then Sheena brought Zed down in the box and I was facing a penalty. The jeers and laughter from the stands grew louder as all realized that a classic high school moment was in the making: Zed, the best player in the year, was facing the talent-challenged foreigner.

'Go on, Sky, you can do it!' yelled Tina from the bleachers.

No, I couldn't, but there spoke a true friend.

I stood in the centre of my wretched goal and faced Zed. To my astonishment, he wasn't gloating; if anything, he looked a bit sorry for me—that's how pathetic I was. He placed the ball carefully on the spot and glanced up at me.

Dive to your left.

His voice in my head again. I was certifiable. I rubbed my eyes, trying to clear my brain.

Zed held my gaze. *Dive to your left.*

What the hell: I was now so far gone I was hallucinating. I had no hope of stopping the ball, so I could at least make a flamboyant, if hopelessly unnecessary, dive. Maybe I'd knock myself out on the post—let's think on the bright side.

Zed ran up, kicked, and I spreadeagled myself sideways to the left.

Ooof! The ball struck me square in the stomach. I curled round it in agony.

An enormous cheer went up—even from Zed's team mates.

'I can't believe it—she saved it!' yelped Tina, doing a celebratory dance with Zoe.

A hand appeared in front of my eyes.

'Are you OK?'

Zed.

'I saved it.'

'Yeah, we saw.' He cracked a smile and pulled me up.

'Did you help me?'

'Now why would I do that?' He turned his back, reverting to the rude Zed of our first acquaintance. Great.

Thank you very much, O mighty one.

Spurred on by irritation, I'd acted on instinct and sent the thought the same way I'd heard his voice. It was as if I'd taken a plank of wood to his head. Zed spun round, reeling, to stare at me—I couldn't tell if he was horrified or amazed. I froze, momentarily stunned, as if I'd just brushed against a live electric fence. I clamped down on the shriek of emotion shooting through me. He hadn't heard my sarcasm, had he? That was just . . . just impossible.

Mr Joe jogged between us, blowing his little whistle. 'Well done, Sky. I knew you had it in you. Only one minute to go—get the ball back in play.'

We still lost. 25–1.

In the girls' changing room, I played with my shoelaces thoughtfully, not really having the desire to get started on the shower with so many people around. Quite a few girls came over to say something about my performance on the pitch, most finding my fluke save off Zed Benedict a cause of great hilarity. That one act seemed to wipe out my tragic performance in goal. Sheena's friends were ribbing her that she'd have to eat barbecued sneaker for dinner.

Tina pounced on me from behind and slapped me on the back. 'You showed Zed, girl! He'll never live down you saving that kick.'

'Maybe.'

But what had that all been about—his voice in my head? I really felt as if he was speaking to me—telepathy, wasn't it called? I didn't believe in that freaky stuff. Like the colours. I was—what was the word my psychiatrist had used—projecting. Yeah, projecting.

'So, you think they'll pick me for the team?' I joked, trying not to let Tina see my distraction.

'Yeah, you're a sure thing—when Hell freezes over. But maybe the athletics coach might come knocking. You move like lightning when you want. I've never seen anyone run *off* the pitch so fast.' She crammed her track gear in her sports bag. 'Something going on between you and Zed I should know about? More than that hate-at-first-sight stuff?'

'No.' I slipped off my trainers.

'He didn't seem pissed that you saved the penalty. He was staring at you all through the other matches.'

'Was he? I didn't notice.' I am such a liar.

'Maybe he likes you now.'

'Does not.'

'Does too. What are we: in first grade?'

'I don't know—I never was.'

'That explains it. You've got a lot of infantile behaviour to catch up on.' She shoved me towards the showers. 'Hurry up. I want to get home before I'm due to graduate.'

Chapter 8

The next few days at school I suffered under the minor celebrity status my lucky save earned me. Nelson thought it hilarious and never lost an opportunity to make the most of my notoriety.

'Make way, citizens of Wrickenridge, for the hottest new property in women's soccer!' He jogged backwards in front of me as Tina, Zoe, and I headed for Science.

'Nelson, please,' I mumbled, aware of the laughter around us.

Tina did better: she dug him in the ribs with one of her talons. 'Give it a rest, Nelson.'

'You her agent, Tin girl?'

'Yeah, and she ain't giving you an interview.'

'You're a hard woman.'

'You've got that right. Now back off.'

'I'm already gone.' Nelson turned and ran to his class.

'That boy is a major league pain in the butt,' pronounced Tina.

'He thinks he's funny,' I offered.

'He is—about half the time,' said Zoe, curling a lock of her dead straight hair round a finger thoughtfully. 'I always figured he gets at Tina because he likes her so much.'

'Repeat that and die,' warned Tina.

'He's had a thing for you since fourth grade and you know it.'

'I don't want to hear this. Not listening.' Tina flapped Zoe away.

Zoe considered she'd won that exchange so dropped the subject. 'So, Sky, you gonna come and watch the school baseball team today? We're playing Aspen.'

'If I do, will one of you explain what's going on?'

Zoe groaned. 'Don't tell me—you don't know the rules of baseball. Where you been living all your life? Under a rock?'

I laughed. 'Nope. Richmond.'

Tina elbowed Zoe to get her to lay off. 'Sure, we'll fill you in, Sky. Baseball's fun.'

Zoe gave Tina an arch look. 'Zed's on the team, you know.'

I pretended interest in a leaflet pinned to the notice board outside the lab. 'I could've guessed.'

'An extra reason for coming along.'

'Is it?' I replied airily.

'That's what they're saying.'

'I would've thought it a reason for giving it a miss.'

Zoe giggled. 'I'm more of an Yves girl myself—those cute little glasses and studious air gets me every time. He's like a hot Harry Potter.'

I laughed as Zoe expected, but my mind was working overtime. Was everyone speculating about Zed and me? Why? We were the least likely pairing in the school. Just because he helped me up in front of the year and stared at me for the rest of the afternoon . . .

'Look who it is!' crowed Tina, elbowing me in the ribs.

Enemy at twelve o'clock: Zed was just leaving the lab, in

conversation with another boy. I tried my commando camou-
flage technique, hiding behind Tina.

'Hi, Zed,' said Zoe in a falsely girly voice.

I withered with embarrassment. It made us sound like a
bunch of groupies.

'Oh, hi.' Zed's gaze skimmed us, then scooted back to me,
just visible between Tina and the wall. Letting his friend go
on ahead, he stopped in front of us. 'I didn't get a chance to
congratulate you, Sky. You made an awesome save.'

Damn him—he was laughing at me.

'Yeah, I thought it pretty unbelievable,' I said ironically.

'I'm telling everyone you got lucky.' Zed tweaked the strap
of my bag back on to my shoulder.

My stomach did a flip. The gesture felt almost territorial.
And what was this? Zed Benedict being *nice* to me.

'And I say I had a little help.' I gave him my hardest stare.
What was his game? Had he really told me what to do? It was
driving me mad not knowing what was real and what I had
imagined.

'You're rumbled, Zed: we all know you didn't bend the ball
like you usually do.' Tina gave me a worried smile. She hadn't
missed the casual way he'd touched my bag strap.

Zed held up his hands in surrender. 'I was just lulling Sky
into a false sense of security. Next time I won't be so easy on
her.'

Zoe hooted, enjoying the flirtatious undercurrents to the
conversation even if Tina and I weren't. 'No way. Zed Benedict,
you built up this image of the meanest guy in the year and now
we know you're a sucker for little blondes looking all dewy-
eyed and defenceless.'

'Zoe!' I protested, her remark too close to the bunny stuff
for comfort. 'Don't make me out to be dumb.'

'Miss Congeniality shows her temper! I knew you had

to have one somewhere,' said Zoe, fascinated by my prickly response.

'You'd be like that if you had to live with looking like I do. No one takes me seriously.'

My temper only rose a notch when all three of them snorted with laughter. 'So I'm a joke, am I?'

'Sorry, Sky.' Tina held up a hand to prevent me storming off. 'It's just that you looked so fierce when you said that . . . '

'Yeah, really scary,' agreed Zoe, struggling not to laugh. 'Like Bambi with an Uzi.'

'And, just so you're clear, none of us think you're dumb,' said Tina. 'Do we?'

'Definitely not,' Zoe chipped in.

'But I have to agree with Zoe,' Zed said, suppressing a grin. 'You don't do mean as well as me. Maybe I should give you lessons. Be careful, won't you?' He brushed his hand lightly down my arm and walked off, leaving my insides doing a little tap dance.

'Man, that's one cute butt,' sighed Zoe, enjoying the rear view.

'Don't talk about his butt,' I said crossly. That set them off again. 'And stop laughing at me!' Had he been warning me again?

'We'll try, but it's hard when you say things like that.' Tina nudged me. 'Tell us it's your butt to protect, then we'll stop looking, won't we, Zoe?'

'Well, I might look but I'll stop saying stuff.' Zoe grinned, ignoring the rest of the class filing into the lab. Teasing me was far more enjoyable than anything the Biology teacher could offer.

'It's not my butt,' I ground out.

'But I think it could be yours. He's definitely circling you.' Zoe shouldered her bag.

Tina stood back to let Zoe go in, then dropped her voice. 'We were just joking, Sky, but, seriously, I get the impression Zed's up to something. I've never seen him act so, well, so nice around a girl.'

I glanced down the corridor to check he'd really gone. 'You noticed?'

'Hard to miss. Last time you were both together, you almost drew blood.'

'Yeah, but he's still Mr Arrogant.'

'And then some.' She tugged my bag strap to make her point. 'He's always kept his distance before. I wish he would now. He's not your type.'

I frowned. 'So what is my type?'

'Another Bambi, I guess.' She smiled at my groan. 'I mean someone who will be gentle. I can see you going for romance, long walks, roses—that kinda thing.'

'And Zed's not that?'

'You don't need me to tell you that. For a girl with a tough shell, that'd be OK, but you're more a marshmallow, aren't you?'

Was I? 'Maybe. I don't know what I'm like really.'

'You'll be careful?'

That's what Zed had said. 'I don't know what to think. He can't expect me to fall for him after the way he's treated me.'

'Just you remember that.'

'I don't know he's after me.'

Tina glanced at her watch and tugged me into class. 'Don't you?'

I was fast learning that Wrickenridge High School was obsessed by sport. I'm not even thinking of the absurdity of cheerleading; it went much deeper than a weird desire to wear short

69

skirts and shake pompoms. For one, we were all expected to turn out to support our team even if we didn't play. It was so unlike England—I didn't know if my sixth form college even *had* a team.

'OK, so baseball is about how fast you can get a team out and then how many runs you can score when you're in?' I repeated, helping myself to a generous handful of popcorn. Zoe's father, manning the refreshment stand run by the PTA, had given us an extra large serving and treated us to drinks. 'You swap over once three men are out.'

Tina settled her shades over her eyes and stretched out her legs. It was cool at this altitude but the sun was really powerful. 'That's it.'

'And they choose to wear these peculiar uniforms because . . . ?' I thought even Zed struggled to make the baseball strip of long white shorts look cool. They resembled teens gathered for a bizarre kind of pyjama party.

'Tradition, I guess.'

'Protection,' countered Zoe—she turned out to be a bit of a baseball fanatic. Had her own catcher's glove and everything. 'Need to cover the skin if you slide for home.'

The teams were milling about. Aspen had just annihilated our batsman and were now up for their inning.

'And Zed's our best player?'

'He could be. He's a bit erratic. Drives Coach mad.' Zoe popped her soda. 'All his brothers, apart from my lovely Yves, were in the team when they were at Wrickenridge, but none of them went on for a sports scholarship. Coach Carter is trying to persuade Zed—his last chance at a Benedict—but he can't get Zed to commit.'

'Hmm.' I watched Zed run his fingers over the ball. His face was stern with concentration but somehow distant as if he was hearing a strain of music no one else could. His first pitch beat the batsman by miles. The spectators screamed their approval.

'He's on form,' noted Zoe.

'Hi, girls!' Nelson jumped down beside Tina, goosing her in passing.

'Sheesh, Nelson, you made me spill my popcorn!' she protested.

'I'll help you pick it up,' he offered, eyeing her lap.

'You won't.' She brushed the kernels off her legs quickly.

'You're spoiling my fun.'

'Now that makes me feel a lot better.'

Nelson sighed dramatically, then settled back to watch the match. Since our conversation in the music room, I'd felt a lot of sympathy for Nelson and hoped his long term play to gain Tina's affection would succeed. She wasn't giving him much encouragement.

'Zed's in the zone today,' he remarked as the first man struck out.

'Yeah.' Tina absentmindedly offered him a handful of popcorn, too absorbed in the game to remember she was cross with him.

'He keeps looking up at this section of the bleachers between pitches, doesn't he?' Nelson took a gulp from her can.

'I wonder why,' Zoe said innocently, before spoiling the effect with a giggle.

'He doesn't even know I'm here.' I blushed as I realized I had as good as claimed to be the reason for his interest.

Nelson crossed his legs alongside Tina's. 'He knows, sweet thing, he knows.'

'Hold it a moment.' Zoe took a picture of me with her phone. 'I wanna capture this for posterity. The girl who caught the attention of the mighty Zed. All us locals have struck out with him.' She showed me the image for my approval; she'd used an app to add a crown but I still looked just a little better than on my school ID. 'He only dates girls from out of town. I think that's one of the exes down there, Hannah something, cheer captain of the Aspen team.'

I felt a totally irrational curl of jealousy. The girl had glorious legs from here to her armpits and a river of sleek auburn hair—the absolute opposite to me. Cheerleading, which I thought utterly ridiculous, was in her interpretation very sexy. I just hoped Zed hadn't noticed.

Of course he had. He was male, wasn't he? And he was welcome to her.

Tina, Nelson, and Zoe were still debating my love life while I was lost in my green-eyed haze.

'Being English means she's probably exotic enough for Zed's taste. Not from boring old Wrickenridge,' speculated Tina.

That was the first time anyone had implied that being English was an advantage. I'd been trying to blend but maybe difference was a good thing?

'I think it'd be better if he left Sky alone,' said Nelson, revealing his protective streak. Now I'd come to know him better I was considering recasting him as Doctor Defence.

Tina nodded. 'Yeah, we'd better gang up against him, keep her out of his way.'

Zoe poked her with her programme. 'What? And spoil the fun? Just think—Zed dating a girl from Wrickenridge—it'd be the most exciting thing to happen here since the Gold Rush.'

'And you're not prone to exaggeration,' said Tina, deadpan.

'Never!'

'Excuse me, guys, I am here, you know. It's nice of you to plan my love life or lack of it for me, but maybe I have an opinion,' I said, half amused, half exasperated by them.

Tina offered me her popcorn. 'And that is?'

'Actually, I haven't a clue—but I'm working my way to an answer. As I said to you before, Zed and me—that's not going to happen. I don't even like him.'

Zoe rolled her eyes at me. 'Sky, you don't need to like a guy like that. You just need to date him—once or twice would do it. It'd set your reputation up for the rest of your life.'

'What? Use him?'

'Oh yeah.'

'Zoe, that's sick.'

'I know. I'm great, aren't I?'

Excitement in the crowd built as a second player struck out.

Zoe leapt to her feet and did a little victory jig. 'If nothing else, that boy is hot, hot, hot! Coach is going to kill himself if he can't get him to try for a scholarship.'

Nelson whistled. 'He must: he's too good to waste his talent.'

But then something changed. I could see it in the shift of expression on Zed's face. His distant look faded, leaving him somehow more present, more like everyone else. His pitching went from remarkable to just very good. The next batter managed to hit him almost out of the diamond. The Wrickenridge students groaned.

'He always does this,' complained Zoe, 'gets so far then backs away. He had Aspen beat and now . . . !'

And now they were fighting back. Zed shrugged and relinquished the pitching spot to a team mate, leaving him the honour of finishing off Aspen.

He could have done it. I knew that in my bones. Zed could have fried them but he chose to back off. Like Zoe said, it was maddening.

'Why does he do that?' I wondered out loud.

'Do what?' Tina crumpled up the programme and chucked it in the bin. 'Draw back from the kill you mean?'

I nodded.

'He loses interest. Maybe his heart's just not in it. The

teachers are always telling him he's too arrogant to work on his inconsistency.'

'Maybe.'

But I wasn't so sure. He still played well, but I'm sure there was an extra edge he wasn't showing anyone. He was purposely keeping his play slightly blunted. I wanted to know why.

Wrickenridge beat Aspen but the man of the match went to a player in the visiting side. Zed melted away into the crowd around the captains, not seeking any attention. He accepted an enthusiastic hug from Hannah of the long legs but swiftly detached and moved on to shake hands with the opposing team. I knew about playing just to be a part of something—that was what an orchestra was about, not the individuals—but yet his unwillingness to stand out struck me as odd. He could have been the soloist, but he settled for second fiddle.

'Drive you home?' offered Tina. 'I'm giving Zoe and Nelson a lift.'

The others lived at the other end of town from me and she was always picking me up and dropping me off. And with only two seats, it was more than a squeeze—it was illegal. Besides, it might not do her any harm as she would drop Zoe first and then be alone with Nelson . . .

'It's OK. I'd like to walk. I'm going to pick up some groceries for Sally.'

'OK. See you tomorrow.'

The cars were queuing to get out of the car park. I stood back as the Aspen bus drew out, taking a wide swing to clear the corner. I then set off, leaving the crowds behind. The further I walked, the quieter it became. Mrs Hoffman scurried past, heading down the hill—Judge Merciless on a mission, shining slightly with a self-righteous blue. I rubbed my eyes and thankfully she went back to normal. She waved but fortunately was on the other side of the street so I did not have to stop and chat. Kingsley the mechanic drove by in his truck and tooted his horn.

In the store, Leanne, the sturdily built assistant who I had got to know over the past few weeks since the dill sauce episode, grilled me for a replay of the match as she packed my shopping. It continually surprised me how much local people cared about the fortunes of the school team. They treated it like Man U, not a bunch of teenage amateurs.

'How you finding school?' Leanne packed the eggs away carefully on top of the bag.

'It's good.' I grabbed a new graphic novel from the rack and tossed it into the basket. My parents made a point of despising them, which was probably why I liked them so much.

'I've been hearing nice things about you, Sky. You've a reputation for being very sweet. Mrs Hoffman has taken quite a shine to you.'

Yeah, a blue shine according to my batty brain. 'Oh, well, she's . . . she's . . . '

'Unstoppable. Like a heat-seeking missile. But it's better to be on her good side than her bad,' Leanne said sagely then ushered me out. 'You should head back before it gets dark, you hear?'

Shadows stretched across the road like big ink stains seeping into the ground. I felt cold in my light jacket and increased my pace. Wrickenridge was always vulnerable to the sudden changes of weather, the reality of life in the mountains. It was like living next door to our old neighbour in Richmond who had been a particularly cantankerous old man. I'd never known when his mood would change—one moment bathing me in grandfatherly sunny smiles, the next spitting out a hail of insults. Just now a light fall of sleet began to fall, splatting the pavement with coin-sized patches of slush, making it slippery underfoot.

As I turned down a quiet street, I heard someone approaching at a run behind me. It was probably just a jogger but still I couldn't help the nervous leap in my pulse. In London, I would have been really worried; but Wrickenridge just didn't feel the kind of place for a mugger to hang out. I clutched the handles of the shopping bag, planning to use it as a weapon just in case.

'Sky!' A hand landed on my shoulder. I swung the bag with a yelp—only to find Zed behind me. He caught the bag before it hit him.

'You almost gave me a heart attack!' I pressed my hand to my chest.

'Sorry. I thought I told you that you should take care walking home alone after dark.'

'You mean some boy might jump out and give me the scare of my life?'

He gave a flicker of a smile, reminding me of his alter ego, Wolfman. 'You never know. All kinds of odd people in the mountains.'

'Well, you've certainly proved your point.'

The smile became a grin. 'Here, let me take that.' He eased the bag from my fingers. 'I'll walk you home.'

What was this? Had he had a character transplant? 'No need.'

'I want to.'

'And you always get your way?'

'Nearly always.'

We walked on for a little while. I cast around for safe topics but everything I thought of sounded lame. I was uncomfortable in such close proximity to him after all my wild imaginings about him—I never knew if he was going to maul me or play nice.

He broke the silence first. 'So when were you going to tell me you're a savant?'

How's that for a conversation stopper? 'A what?'

He halted me under a street lamp. Flurries of sleet slid through the pool of light then winked out in the darkness. He turned up the collar of my jacket.

'You must realize how amazing it is.' His eyes fixed on mine—their colour intriguing, unusual to one of his Hispanic appearance. I'd tag them as borderline between blue and green. The colour of the Eyrie River on a sunny day.

Still, I couldn't understand the expression they held now. 'How amazing is what?'

He laughed; the sound rumbled deep in his chest. 'I see. You're punishing me for being a jackass. But you have to understand that I didn't know it was you. I thought I was warning some ditzy stranger to prevent her being knifed.'

I pushed his hands off my collar. 'What are you talking about?'

'I had this premonition a few nights before we met at the ghost town—you get them too?'

This conversation was beyond weird. I shook my head.

'You running down the street in the dark—a knife—screams—blood. I had to warn you—just in case it would do any good.'

O-K. I thought I had problems but *he* was seriously disturbed. I had to get away from him. 'Um . . . Zed, thanks for worrying about me but I'd better get back now.'

'Yeah, as if that's going to happen. Sky, you're my soulfinder, my partner—you can't just walk away from me.'

'I can't?'

'You must have felt it too. I knew as soon as you answered me—it was like, I don't know how to say this, like the fog lifting. I could really *see* you.' He ran a finger down my cheek. I shivered. 'Do you know what the odds of us finding each other are?'

'Whoa. Go back a little. Soulfinder?'

11

'Yeah.' He grinned and tugged me closer. 'No half life existence for us. It's taken me a few days to get over the shock and I've been waiting to speak to you so I can break the news to my folks.'

He had to be winding me up. I placed my hands on his chest and pushed him back. 'Zed, I've not a clue what you are talking about. But if you expect me to : . . to . . . I don't know what you expect, but it's not happening. You don't like me; I don't like you. Get over it.'

He was incredulous. '*Get over it?* Savants wait all their lives to find the one and you think I can get over it?'

'Why not? I don't even know what a savant is!'

He thumped his chest. 'I'm one.' He prodded me. 'You're one. Your gifts, Sky—they make you a savant. You must get that at least.'

I'd plotted stupid stuff in my head, but this was way beyond anything I could have thought up. I took a step back. 'Can I have the shopping bag, please?'

'What? That's it? We make the most astounding discovery of our lives and you're just going to go home?'

I took a quick look round, hoping to see someone. Mrs Hoffman would do. My parents even better. 'Um . . . yes. Looks like it.'

'You can't!'

'Just watch me.'

I tugged the bag from his fingers and hurried the last few yards to my house.

'Sky, you can't ignore this!' He stood under the street lamp, sleet settling in his hair, hands fisted at his side. 'You're mine—you have to be.'

'No. I. Don't.'

I slammed the front door.

Chapter 9

I couldn't sleep that night. Hardly surprising seeing what had happened out on the street with Zed. Arrogant jerk. Thinking he could just announce that I was his and I would fall into his arms. I might fancy him but that didn't mean I liked him. He was cold, abrupt, and rude. He'd crush me in five minutes if I was so foolish as to go out with him.

And as for all that soulfinder stuff—well, that was just bizarre.

And what the heck was a savant?

I got out of bed and pulled on a dressing gown, too restless to lie in bed turning the conversation over and over in my mind. There was so much I didn't understand but I was afraid to ask for an explanation. That premonition stuff had been plain creepy—he had me half believing him. But I didn't want to change my life just because a guy dreamt something might happen to me. What next? He could say I had to wear only orange or risk getting run over by a bus? Would I go to school looking like a tangerine on his say-so? No, it was all just a ploy to get me doing what he wanted.

Which was what?

The back of my neck prickled. The conviction grew that I wasn't alone. Nervous now, I moved to the window and gingerly drew back the curtain, *Psycho*-style music shrieking in my head.

'Sheesh!' Heart in my mouth, I found myself face to face with Zed. I literally had to bite my tongue to stop myself screaming. He'd climbed the apple tree and was sitting outside my room, straddling the branch. I threw open the window. 'What are you doing there?' I hissed. 'Get down, go away.'

'Invite me in.' He levered himself along the limb.

'Stop—get down!' Panicking, I wondered if I should call Simon.

'No, don't get your dad. I need to talk to you.'

I flapped my hands at him. 'Go away! I don't want you here.'

'I know.' He gave up on the idea of forcing his way into my room. 'Sky, why don't you know you're a savant?'

I contemplated slamming the window on this weird Romeo-and-Juliet scene. 'I can't answer that when I don't understand the question.'

'You heard me speaking to you—in your head. You didn't just follow my hint, you heard words.'

'I . . . I . . . '

You answered me.

I stared at him. He was doing it again—telepathy, wasn't it called? No, no, I was projecting—this wasn't happening.

'All savants can do it.'

'I'm not hearing anything. I don't understand what you're talking about.'

'I can see that and I have to know why.'

Confused, the only strategy I could come up with was denial. I had to get him out of my apple tree. 'I'm sure that's very fascinating but it's late and I want to sleep. So . . . um . . .

goodnight, Zed. Let's talk about this some other time.' Like never.

'You won't even give me a hearing?' He folded his arms.

'Why should I?'

'Because I'm your soulfinder.'

'Stop that. I don't understand you. You're nothing to me. You're rude, cold, you don't even like me and have taken every opportunity to criticize me.'

He shoved his hands into his pockets. 'So that's what you think of me?'

I nodded. 'Maybe this is, I dunno, your latest plot to humiliate me in some way—pretending you want me.'

'You really don't like me, do you?' He gave a hollow laugh. 'Great, my soulfinder doesn't understand the first thing about me.'

I folded my arms to hide the fact that I was trembling. 'What's there to understand? Jerks are pretty easy to read.'

Frustrated at my repeated rebuffs, he made a move towards me.

I took a step back. 'Get out of my tree.' My finger was shaking as I pointed to the gate.

To my surprise, he didn't refuse, just studied my face, then nodded. 'OK. But this isn't over, Sky. We've got to talk.'

'Get out.'

'I'm going.' With that, he dropped to the ground and disappeared into the night.

With a sob of relief, I slammed the window shut and collapsed on the bed. Tugging the duvet around me, I curled up, wondering what exactly was happening here.

And what I was going to do about it.

That night the dream came again, but this time with more details. I remembered the hunger—I'd barely had anything to eat for days except crisps and chocolate. They left me feeling sick. My knees were grubby and my hair matted on the side I preferred to lie on at night. My mouth felt sore, my lip swollen where it was cut on the inside. Sitting on the grass verge, I felt empty of anything but fear, a churning sense of panic in my stomach that I could only conquer by concentrating on the daisies. They were so white, even in the darkness they glowed against the grass, petals folded. I hugged my knees, gathering myself up like one of them.

I didn't like the smell here—dog, car fumes, and litter. And a bonfire. I hated fire. The roar of the motorway droned on; the traffic sounded angry and rushed, no time for a lost little girl.

I waited.

Then the dream changed. This time it wasn't a lady in a headscarf who came up to me—it was Zed. He stood over me and held out a hand.

'You're mine,' he said. 'I've come to claim you.'

I woke, heart pounding, just as dawn broke behind the mountains.

The next few days at school were a slow torture. Compared to the first weeks where I hardly ever saw him, I now ran across Zed at every turn. I could feel his brooding gaze as I walked through the dining hall or passed along the corridor. I begged Tina for lifts home and even dropped in on Mrs Hoffman when I got back so as not to be alone in the house. Zed was making me a prisoner. It was one thing to hanker after Wolfman from afar; it was entirely different to find him zeroing in on you.

Saturday morning and there was a knock on the door early. Simon and Sally were still in bed, so I went to answer it, mug of tea in hand, expecting it to be a delivery for the studio.

It was Zed, holding a massive bunch of flowers. He thrust it at me before I could shut the door on him.

'Let's start again.' He held out a hand. 'Hi, I'm Zed Benedict. And you are?'

I grappled with the flowers—they were my favourite colours—purple and blue.

'Go on—this is the easy part. "I am Sky Bright and I'm from England."' He put on such a ridiculous accent I felt some of my reluctance folding under the urge to laugh.

'I do not speak like that.'

'Sure you do. Go on.'

'Hi, I'm Sky Bright. I'm from Richmond, England.'

'Now you say, "Wow, what lovely flowers. How about coming in for a nice cup of tea?"'

That accent had to go. I threw a look over my shoulder, wondering if Sally or Simon would come down.

'They're asleep.' Zed nodded into the house. 'So?'

'Well, they are lovely flowers.' Perhaps we did have to talk. Here was better than school. I stepped out of the way. 'Coffee?' He didn't seem the sort for a cup of PG Tips.

'If you insist.' He smiled, a shade nervously for him, and entered.

'Come through to the kitchen.' I busied myself switching on the kettle and finding a vase for the flowers. 'Why are you here?'

'Isn't it obvious? I messed up. I want to say sorry.'

I tipped the plant food into the water. 'These are a good start.' Actually, it was the first time anyone had ever given me flowers. I felt less nervous in daytime, knowing my parents were just upstairs. I could cope with this conversation if he felt the urge to apologize. Tina would probably think it worthy of its own newsflash if she knew that the great Zed Benedict had stooped to humble himself to a girl.

Zed juggled with the cafetière. 'How does this thing work?'

I took it from him and showed him how much coffee to put in. 'You're not very at home in a kitchen?'

'Family of boys,' he said as if that explained it. 'We've a coffee maker—does great filter coffee.'

'And she's called your mum.'

He laughed. 'No way. She gets waited on hand and foot in our house.'

OK, I could do this. We were having a normal conversation about normal things.

He took his mug and sat at the breakfast bar. 'So tell me something about yourself. I play drums and guitar. How about you?'

'Piano, sax, and guitar.'

'See, we can talk without me freaking out on you.'

'Yeah.' I chanced a look at him; he was watching me like a bear crouched over a hole in the ice, ready to hook a salmon. 'You . . . you like all music, or just jazz?'

'All, but I like the freedom to improvise.' He patted a place next to him on the bench. I sat down, keeping a space between us. 'I like to cut free of what has to be. For me it's a kind of free fall with the notes as the parachute.'

'I like that too.'

'It's musicians' music. Not so straightforward as some but really repays when you get into it.' He gave me a look, asking me to understand there was another meaning below his surface words. 'I mean, you've got to be really confident to launch into an off-the-cuff solo and not make a fool of yourself. Everyone can make mistakes when they rush something, go in too early.'

'I suppose.'

'You really didn't know.'

Oh God, he was going to raise that savant stuff again.

He shook his head. 'And you've not the faintest idea why I

warned you that day. You think I've been trying to scare you.'

'Weren't you? All that stuff about knives and blood.'

'I didn't mean it like that.' He rubbed his thumb across my knuckles, clenched on the table between us. 'It's funny sitting with you. I get so much from you, like you're broadcasting on all frequencies.'

I frowned. 'What does that mean?'

He stretched his long legs out, gently bumping mine. 'It's difficult to explain. I'm sorry I've been rude to you.'

'Rude? I just thought that you had some weird allergic reaction to economy-sized English girls.'

He looked me over. 'Is that what you are?'

'Um . . . yeah.' I stared at my feet. 'Still waiting for that growth spurt Sally's been promising since I was fourteen.'

'Your height's perfect. I come from a family of giant redwoods; a bonsai makes a pleasant change.'

Bonsai! If I'd known him better I would have dug him in the ribs for that one. Too shy, I let it pass. 'So you're not going to explain what's been the problem with me?'

'Not today. I've messed it up once; I'm not going to risk spoiling it a second time by rushing. This is too important.' He picked up my hand and punched himself in the side with it. 'There—I deserved that.'

'You're crazy.'

'Yep, that's me.' But still he didn't explain how he knew I'd wanted to do that.

Zed released my hand. 'OK, I'll head out now. I don't want to push my luck. It was good meeting you, Sky. See you around.'

I didn't trust this reformed-bad-boy behaviour, but Zed clearly wasn't letting this go. On Monday at the end of school, he was waiting for me by Tina's car.

'Hi, Tina, how's it going?'

Tina stared at him, then looked at me, eyebrow quirked. 'Fine, Zed. You?'

'Great. Sky, ready to go home?' He held out a motorbike helmet.

'Tina's giving me a lift.'

'I'm sure she won't mind if I do that. I want to make sure Sky gets home, OK, Tina?'

Tina looked as if she did mind, not least because she didn't trust Zed any more than I. 'I said I'd take Sky.'

He held the helmet out to me. 'Please?'

Zed Benedict saying 'please'. Icicles were forming in Hell. And he was offering to fulfil one of my private fantasies: me riding out of school on the back of a hot bike. I knew it was a kind of cliché, but this rocked.

'Sky?' asked Tina, worried now.

I suppose such humility should be encouraged. 'It's OK. Thanks, Tina. I'll go with Zed.' I took the helmet.

'If you're sure.' She bunched her dreadlocks back, a gesture that I knew meant she was uncomfortable.

Not really. 'See you tomorrow.'

'Yeah.' Her last look left me in no doubt that I was going to get a grilling on what happened after she left.

Zed led me over to his bike. We were attracting quite a few astonished stares from the students milling about.

'I've never ridden one of these before,' I admitted as I climbed on behind him.

'The secret is to hold on tight.'

I couldn't see his face but I would've sworn he was grinning. I slid forward and looped my arms around his waist, my legs brushing his hips. Easing out of the car park, he turned the bike up the hill. As he pushed up the speed, I tightened my grip. I felt a brief caress of his hand on mine—a reassuring touch.

'Doing OK back there?'

'Fine.'

'Want to go a bit further? I can take you up into the mountains. There's about thirty minutes of light left.'

'Maybe just a little way.'

He went past the turning to my house and up the road. It became a switchback. There was little beyond here, only a few hunting cabins and a couple of isolated chalets. He pulled up on a promontory with a view back down the valley. The sun was setting ahead of us, bathing everything in a buttery gold light that gave an illusion of warmth despite the cold.

Parking the bike, he helped me dismount and let me admire the view in peace for a few minutes. The overnight frost still hung on in shady patches, the leaves, edged with white, crunchy underfoot. I could see for miles—the mountains which I had ignored all day thrusting themselves back into my conscious thoughts, reminding me of my insignificance in comparison to them.

'So, Sky, how was your day?'

Such a regular question from Zed was a surprise: Wolfman turning into puppy-carrying-slippers? I think not. It was kinda hard to trust him when he was acting so *normal*. 'Fine. I did a little composing at lunchtime.'

'I saw you at the piano.'

'You didn't come in?'

He laughed and held up his hands. 'I'm being careful. Very, very careful with you. You're a scary girl.'

'Me?'

'Think about it. You rip me up in the parking lot in front of my friends, save my best penalty kick, chuck me out of your apple tree—yeah, you're terrifying.'

I smiled. 'I like the sound of that.' SuperSky.

He grinned. He hadn't guessed my thoughts, had he?

'But what scares me the most is that there's so much riding on our relationship and you don't even know it.'

I huffed out a sigh. 'OK, Zed, try and explain it to me again. I'll listen this time.'

He nodded. 'I guess you don't know anything about savants?'

'I know more about soccer.'

He laughed at that. 'I'll just give you a little information now then, just to get us started. Let's sit here for a moment.' He boosted me up so I could perch on a fallen tree trunk, putting my eyes on a level with his as he leaned against it. It was the closest we'd been to each other since the raft and I was suddenly very aware of his eyes drifting over my features. It almost felt as if his fingers, not his gaze, were caressing my skin. 'Sure you want to hear? 'Cause if I tell you, I've got to ask you to keep it a secret for the sake of the rest of my family.'

'Who would I tell?' I sounded oddly breathless.

'I dunno. The *National Enquirer* maybe. Oprah. A congressional committee.' His expression was wry.

'Er, no, no and definitely not,' I laughed, counting them off on my fingers.

'OK then.' He smiled and brushed a tendril of hair off my brow. There was a quivering intensity to him, as though he was holding himself in check, afraid to let go of the reins. A little nervous, I groped for one of my usual distancing techniques, trying to recast this encounter as one of my comic strip imaginings, but found that I couldn't. He made me stay right here and now, completely in focus. The colours—his hair, eyes, clothes—weren't brash, but subtle, sparkling, multi-toned. High definition had switched on in my head.

'Savants: I'm one. All my family are, but I've got a heavy dose being the seventh son. My mom's a seventh child too.'

'And that makes it worse?'

I could count every single lash framing his spectacular eyes.

'Yeah, there's a multiplier effect. Savants have this gift; it's like an extra shift in a car, makes us go a little bit faster and further than normal people.'

'Right. OK.'

He rubbed his hand gently in circles on my knee, calming me. 'It means we can talk telepathically to each other. With people who don't have the savant *gene*, they would feel an impression, an impulse, not hear the voice. That's what I thought would happen when I spoke to you on the soccer pitch. I was pretty surprised when you understood me—blown away, in fact.'

'Because?'

'Because it meant that you are a telepath too. And when a soulfinder speaks telepathically to her partner, it's like all the lights coming on in a building. You lit me up like Vegas.'

'I see.' I didn't want to believe any of this but I remembered hearing his voice telling me to float when I'd fallen out of the raft. But it had to be a coincidence—I wouldn't allow it to be anything else.

He rested his head against mine. I made a subtle move to retreat but he curled his fingers around my nape, holding me gently to him. 'No, you don't. Not yet. There's more.'

The warmth of his hand seeped through to relax my tense neck muscles. 'I thought there might be.'

'When's your birthday?'

What possible relevance did that have? 'Um . . . first of March. Why?'

He shook his head. 'That's not right.'

'It's the day of my adoption.'

'Ah, I see. That's why.' He flicked his fingers lightly over the curve of my shoulder then let his hand drop to cover mine which I'd clasped on my lap. We stayed like that in silence for a while. I sensed a shadow—a presence in my mind.

'Yeah, that's me,' he said. 'I'm just checking.'

I shook my head. 'No, I'm imagining this.'

He gave a long-suffering sigh. 'I'm just checking my facts. I can't make a mistake about something like a soulfinder.' He moved away, the sense of him being with me receding, leaving me lonely. 'I understand now. You've come from a dark place, haven't you?'

What could I say to that?

'You don't know who your biological parents are?'

'No.' My nerves returned, coiling horribly inside me like maggots swarming out of a rotten apple. He was finding out too much. Letting people close hurt—this had to stop.

'So you never knew that you had a gift.'

'Well, that's because I don't. I'm ordinary. No extra shifts in here.' I tapped my head.

'Not that you've found. But they're there. You see, Sky, when a savant is born, his or her counterpart also arrives about the same time somewhere on the earth. It could be next door, or maybe thousands of miles away.' He linked his fingers with mine. 'You have half our gifts, I the other. Together we make a whole. Together we are much more powerful.'

I rolled my eyes. 'It sounds sweet, a nice fairy tale, but it can't possibly be true.'

'Not sweet. Think about it: the chances of meeting your other half are tiny. Most of us are doomed to knowing there's something better out there but we can't discover it. My parents were two of the lucky ones; they have each other thanks to a wise man of my dad's people with a gift for finding. None of my brothers have yet located their partner and each of them struggles with it. It's a killer, knowing things could be so much *more*. That's why I rushed. I was a starving man facing a banquet.'

'And if they never meet their soulfinder?'

'It can go many ways—despair, anger, acceptance. It gets worse as the years tick by. It hadn't really begun to worry me yet. I'm incredibly lucky to escape all that angst.'

I refused to believe this yarn he was spinning and took refuge in flippancy. 'Seems simple to me. Can't they run a savant match-making service on Facebook or something? Problem solved.'

He smiled wryly. 'Like we haven't thought of that. But it's not about your birthday exactly, but when you were conceived—that gives quite a lot of variation nine months on. Think how many people in the world were born on or around your birthday. Then factor in the premature babies, the ones overdue. You'd be trawling through thousands. Savants are rare—there's only one in every ten thousand or so. And not every savant lives in a country like ours with computers at home. Or even speaks the same language.'

'Yeah, I see that.' Sort of, if I was going to buy this whole thing, which I didn't.

He cupped my chin gently in his palm. 'But against the odds, I've discovered you. On a soccer pitch of all places. Sky Bright from Richmond, England.'

This was so strange. 'What does this all mean?'

'It means that's it for us. For life.'

'Joking?'

He shook his head.

'But I'm only here for, like, a year.'

'Just a year?'

'That's the plan.'

'And you do what then? Go back to England?'

I shrugged, assuming a calm I didn't feel. 'I don't know. It depends on Sally and Simon. It's going to be hard because I'll have done a year here and the course is completely different back in the UK. I don't want to start all over again.'

'Then we'll find a way for you to stay. Or I'll follow you to England.'

'You will?' I was hyper conscious that his fingers had once more entwined with mine. I'd never imagined what it would be like just to hold hands with a boy. It was nice but a bit scary at the same time.

'Hell, yeah. This is serious.' He squeezed my fingers, taking a better grip. 'So she doesn't run for the hills.'

'Meaning?'

He lifted one of my hands and tucked it into his jacket pocket. He kept his fingers still locked around mine as he leant beside me, looking out on the same view.

'I thought you might be a bit wary of me at first, until you got used to me. The nice me, not the jerk me.'

'Wary?'

'Wolfman, remember? You've got me down on the dark side; I saw that in your thoughts.'

He knew about Wolfman? Kill me now, why don't you?

'No way, it's cute.'

I gave a strangled groan of humiliation.

He chuckled. He was enjoying my embarrassment, the rat. 'I know I can be a bit hard to talk to sometimes—like when we met at the ghost town. I'm going through . . . ' he shook his head, 'it's tough right now. And sometimes, I just get, *overwhelmed*. Too much weighing on me.'

OK, I wasn't buying the soulfinder stuff, but I couldn't ignore that he had an uncanny ability to pluck thoughts from my head. 'You're not making this up? You do something, don't you?' I was thinking of the way he seemed to know what I was going to say before I said it.

'I do a lot of things.' The sun slid behind the horizon, the honeyed light fading to old gold. 'I'd like to do some things with you, Sky, if you want to. I was wrong to rush in claiming you as my soulfinder—you need to arrive at the same place with me. After all, we've the rest of our lives to get this right.'

I swallowed. Tina had warned me about this. What could be more alluring than a boy telling you that you were more or less made for him? That's what the evil guys always did to lure in those poor saps in the stories, wasn't it? But right now I couldn't think of that; all I could think about was Zed, standing there looking so . . . well . . . hopeful. 'What kind of things?'

He gently ran his free hand down my arm, linking fingers on my other side.

'Go for a ride.'

I smiled shyly. 'We've just been doing that.'

'Then we've ticked the first box already. Next we might go out to the movies in Aspen, or risk the diner in Wrickenridge and have everyone stare at us all evening.'

'The movies sound nice.'

'With me?'

I looked down. 'I might risk it. Once. But I still don't like you much.'

'Understood.' He nodded solemnly but his eyes were smiling.

'And this soulfinder stuff—I don't believe it. It leaves no room for choice, like some cosmic arranged marriage.'

He grimaced. 'We'll leave that aside for the moment then. One step. Go out with me?'

What should I say? I liked this Zed, the one that brought flowers and kicked easy penalties to stop a newcomer being humiliated, but I hadn't forgotten the angry, dangerous Wolf-man. 'OK, I'll give you a chance.'

He lifted my fingers to his mouth, gave them a playful nip, then let go. 'Then it's a date.'

chapter 10

I spent the next few days agonizing over my decision. Part of me was thrilled that I'd been asked on a date by Zed. I'd been manoeuvred into agreeing, that was true, but I wouldn't be human if I hadn't felt flattered. As Zoe had once told me, any female with a pulse would want to be asked out by a Benedict. Still, I didn't want to spill it even to my closest girlfriends, mainly because I daren't think it true. I had the crazy notion that saying it out loud might make it disappear like Cinderella's coach at midnight. I was also worried what Tina would say. Something on the lines of 'have you lost your mind?'. I feared if I talked to her, she'd persuade me that he was manipulating me, that he'd love me and leave me in the classic pattern of the bad boy. I wanted to believe in the new Zed: that I'd got him wrong, that he could be gentle, that we had common ground and could find more given time. But there was so much to take on board—the savant stuff (was that even real?), the soulfinder thing he was fixated on. My deepest fear was that he was just pretending to like me because he needed me in some way I couldn't yet fathom.

My mum noticed my distraction but she did not guess the cause.

'Sky, are you listening to me?'

'Um . . . yes?' I hazarded.

'You were not.'

'OK, I wasn't. What did you say?'

'I said we should buy you something special for the opening.' Sally eyed the limited contents of my wardrobe with her usual good taste. 'You've been worrying about it, haven't you? That's what's got into you.'

'Um . . .'

'I agree: you don't have anything here that will do. We'll have to get you a new outfit.'

The Arts Centre was marking the occasion of its formal opening with a black tie reception. Everyone in Wrickenridge was expected to turn out—after all, there wasn't much competition for entertainment until the ski season arrived. And if Sally thought I didn't have a suitable outfit I was in trouble: Zed was bound to be there.

'I'd like that but where can we go to shop? I can't face going all the way into Denver.'

'Mrs Hoffman—'

I groaned.

'*Said* there was a very nice boutique in Aspen, just forty-five minutes away on the interstate.'

In the end, Simon came too, saying we'd not spent enough time together as a family since arriving. He treated us to lunch in an Italian place, then made himself scarce while Sally and I hit the boutique.

'I might just get myself something new as well,' said Sally, fingering the rows of dresses with longing.

'Oh, now the hidden agenda is revealed!' I teased her, pulling out a long red number. 'This isn't about me—it's all about you. Try this on.'

After thirty minutes of indecision, we settled on two

dresses with prices that Sally tried to ignore. Aspen catered to the exclusive skiers, the Hollywood A list, so had tags to match.

'They are investments,' she said, pulling out her credit card. 'Yours will do for the ball in the summer.'

'Prom,' I corrected her. 'And I think parents are supposed to cough up for a new dress for that too. It's tradition.'

'Then I'll just have to sell a few more paintings.' She closed her eyes and signed the bill.

We were giggling like mad conspirators as we got ready that evening.

'Don't tell Simon about the shoes,' Sally warned. 'He doesn't understand about the need for coordination.' She bit her lip. 'They were horribly expensive, weren't they?'

'Where are my girls?' Simon shouted from downstairs. 'We'll be late!'

Sally went first down the stairs, posing for effect in her red sheath dress.

Simon gaped.

'I look good?' she asked, a small frown forming.

'I've changed my mind. Let's stay home.' He grinned, running his hand down her satin-clad back. 'I hope Sky is wearing something a little less revealing. I'll be chasing off the boys if she looks anything like you.'

I presented myself for his inspection. I had chosen a forget-me-not blue strapless dress that stopped short just above my knee. I'd let my hair loose, leaving it curling down my back, held at the front by two jewelled combs.

Simon shook his head. 'I don't think I can cope. Back to your rooms, girls.'

We laughed and seized him by the arms, towing him out to the car.

'But look at you, all dashing in your James Bond outfit!' I told him, straightening his bow tie. He made it a point of honour to use a real one, then always had to get us to tie it for him. 'Sally and I will be fighting the girls off with canapés and cocktail sticks.'

'I look to you both to defend me,' he said, winking at me in the rear-view mirror.

The Rodenheim Arts Centre had a roof line that echoed the peaks behind, sliced in two by an irregular glass pyramid lit up with a wash of blue light. On a crisp, cold night like this, the shapes made a dramatic contrast to the star scattered sky. It could almost be the prow of a spaceship travelling through the Alpha Quadrant. Through the glass front I could see the party was already in full swing. Mr Keneally was spruced up for the evening, providing light music from a piano in the foyer. Waiting staff slipped through the crowd with trays loaded with nibbles, ranging from elaborate sushi to spicy Mexican dips.

Tina manned the guest welcome. She didn't even bother with our name badges.

'Wow—just wow!' she exclaimed, taking in our little trio. 'You sure do wash up fine.'

'Most people do with just the right application of a credit card,' smiled Sally.

'And your shoes!'

'Don't mention the shoes,' Sally hissed.

'What's that?' said Simon.

'Nothing, darling.'

'Do you need any help?' I asked hopefully, wondering if I could be spared the painful small talk and sit out here with Tina for the evening.

She flapped me away. 'Don't you dare, Sky! Anyway, my shift's almost over. I'll come find you.'

Simon had already moved on, in pursuit of a waiter with a

tray of drinks. He snagged me a sparkling water and took two glasses of white for Sally and himself.

I lost my parents two minutes later. Sally got cornered by the local arts reporter from Aspen and Simon forgot his dislike of such events in a detailed discussion of Hockney with an earnest young student from Denver. At a loose end, I drifted, exchanging a few words with friends but not settling anywhere.

'Now there's a sight worth seeing!' exclaimed Zoe, licking sauce off her fingers. She nudged me towards the door. 'The whole Benedict clan has turned up—not a common event.'

So here were the fabled Benedict boys. Now, smartened up for the evening, I saw why people thought they could be trouble: they looked like a team of superheroes, though the jury was still out on whether they were on the side of good or evil. My eyes zeroed in on Zed first, who was looking really great in a black shirt and matching trousers.

Pants. The correction came through in my mind with the impression of a smile.

I don't want to know about those.

Don't you?

How could he make me blush from across the room? In fact, how could he even be talking to me? *Get out of my head.*

I can't cut it out now I've started. Has anyone told you that you could stop traffic in that dress?

Is that good or bad? I was mad replying to a disembodied voice.

It's good. Very, very good.

Oblivious to our conversation, Zoe giggled. 'Oh my, Zed's looking at you as if he's going to eat you! Be still my beating heart!'

I angled my shoulder to him, trying to regain some semblance of calm. 'He's not.'

'It's not me he's looking at, more's the pity. Then again, that still leaves Trace, Uriel, Victor, Will, Xavier, and my Yves to enjoy. Aren't they just—' She twirled her hand, lost for words.

'Which is which?'

'Xavier's the tallest. Just graduated. He's really serious about skiing. Got a chance at the Olympic slalom team if he keeps at it. Trace's a cop in Denver, I think. He's the cool, capable one who looks like he could eat razor blades without flinching. Uriel's at college, doing post-grad in forensic science. Will's the big, broad-shouldered guy, also at college, not sure what course he's taking. He's a bit of a joker and has a longer fuse than the rest of them. Hmm, who's left?'

'Victor.'

Zoe patted her chest. 'Oh, Victor. Really mysterious. Recently left town but no one knows what he's up to. Rumour has it he lives with Trace in the city, but I'm not so sure. I think he's a spy or something.'

'How do you remember who's who?'

'Easy: Trace, tough; Uriel, ultra intelligent; Victor . . . um . . . *very* mysterious . . . '

'Cheat.'

Zoe grinned. 'Will, wacky; Xav, X-treme sports; Yves, yummy—and I'll leave you to figure out Zed.' She hummed the alphabet song. 'If they used the Benedicts to teach letters, us girls would pay way more attention.'

I laughed. 'I wonder why they're all back this weekend?'

'A family birthday? Mr and Mrs Benedict are really nice—a bit weird at times, but always kind if you drop by the house.' She took a sip of her drink.

'I met Mr Benedict at the river.'

'Great, isn't he? Only strange thing is why anyone as clever as Mr Benedict would want to spend his life running the ski lift. You should see their bookshelves, crammed full of the kind of things my sister's reading at college, philosophy and stuff.'

'Perhaps they're outdoors kind of people.'

'Maybe.' She nudged me. 'But here's someone who doesn't want to be outdoors right now.'

Zed had left his brothers and was heading straight for us. 'Hi, Zoe, Sky.' He grinned at us both.

'Zed.' Zoe waved at Yves who was watching her across the room. 'Everyone home?'

'We had a bit of family business. You both look great.'

Zoe was reading the body language and, being the star that she is, decided to make tracks. She swung her long hair over her shoulder, her bracelets jingling.

'Thanks, Zed. You don't look so bad yourself. I'm just gonna go and catch up with Yves. See you.'

She slipped away, leaving us alone in our corner of the crowd. Zed stood in front of me, obscuring my view of the rest of the room so it felt as if it was just him and me.

'Hi, there,' he said in a low voice.

'I thought we'd said hello already.' Wow, this boy was sending out heat.

'I said hi to both you and Zoe before. That one was just for you.'

'Oh.' I bit my lip to stop my laugh. 'Hi.'

'I wasn't joking when I said you look amazing.' He reached over and brushed a loose curl back behind my ear. 'Where did all this come from?'

'I keep it tied back at school. It can be a nuisance.'

'I like it like this.'

'Well, you don't have to brush the tangles out each night.'

'I'm more than happy to volunteer.'

'Oh.'

'Yeah, oh.' He laughed and slid his arm around my shoulders. 'Shall we go mingle?'

'Do we have to?'

'Yep. I want you to meet my mom and dad.'

'Have you told them?' I didn't believe all this soulfinder talk, but if he did, I wondered what he'd done about it.

'No, I want you to be happy with the idea when we let them know. They'll be unbearable when I break the news.'

Was that the real reason, or was he just playing me, spinning a yarn to hook me in? I didn't know if I could trust my instincts when it came to him.

'What about your brothers? Can I meet them?'

'You can meet Yves as you know him already and the damage is done, but I want you to keep well away from the others.'

'Why? Wouldn't they like me?'

'How can anyone not like you?' He stroked my arm, sending goosepimples along the bare skin. 'It's not that. It's just that they'll tell you all the most embarrassing stories about me and you'll never speak to me again.'

'I don't think that's very likely.'

He looked down at me, his smile tender. 'No, I don't think so either.'

We paused by Mr Keneally, joining in the applause as he finished his set on the piano. Mr Keneally acknowledged his audience then frowned when he saw Zed was my escort.

'Would you like to play, Sky?' he asked, obviously thinking it a good way to separate us.

'No thanks, sir. Not tonight.'

Zed increased his grip on my shoulder. 'Would you like me to get you a drink, sir?'

Mr Keneally did a double take. 'That's very kind of you.' He reassessed our pairing. 'Glad to see she's a good influence on you.'

'Early days yet,' I murmured.

'I'll have a soda—a Coke.'

'Be right back.' Zed dropped his hold on me and dipped

into the crowd to catch a waiter. It was almost funny the way he was trying to impress on me that he could be polite when he put his mind to it.

Mr Keneally was obviously trying to think of how to broach a difficult subject. He shuffled the music. 'Settling in OK, Sky?'

'Yes, thank you.'

'Everyone looking after you?'

'Yes, sir.'

'If you have any . . . er . . . problems with anyone, you know there's a school counsellor, don't you?' Music Master leaping to my defence—though I don't think he was quite ready to take on Wolfman directly.

'Yes, Mr Joe told me. But I'm fine. Really.'

Zed returned. 'One Coke, sir. Ready to move on, Sky?'

'Yes. Bye, sir.'

Mr Keneally gave me a worried smile. 'Thanks for the drink, Zed.' He sat down and began to play Mahler's funeral march.

'Message for me?' whispered Zed.

'Or me. People can't work out why we're together.'

'Can't work out why I've got the prettiest girl in the room with me? Then they've no imagination.' He laughed when he saw he'd made me blush again. He brushed a thumb over my cheek. 'You are the definition of sweet, you know that?'

'I hope that's a compliment.'

'Meant to be. I knew it even when I gave you that warning—you know, about going out after dark. You listened, didn't you?'

I nodded, not sure what else to do. He seemed so serious about it.

He smiled and tickled my neck with a strand of my own hair. 'I was full of resentment that I had to do it because of my dream—I'm still worried about that—but even then, it did filter through that you were kinda cute.'

'You never showed it.'

His lip curled with wry self-knowledge. 'I do have an image to maintain, you know. I think I might have fallen for you that day in the parking lot. Nothing sexier than an angry woman.'

I so wanted him to be telling the truth, but I had my doubts. 'Cute and sexy? I'm not like that.'

'Sure you are. If I'm a tuning fork, you're the perfect A, making me hum.'

I was getting flustered. 'Zed, ssh!'

'What, you don't like compliments?'

'Of course I do—I just don't know what to do with them.'

'You just say, "Why thank you, Zed—that's the nicest thing anyone has ever said to me."'

'Will you stop putting on that fake English accent—it so doesn't work!'

He threw back his head and laughed, drawing many eyes to us. He swooped on my hand and kissed my palm. 'You are just great. You know, I can't understand why I was slow to realize what was going on with you.'

I wasn't ready to talk about feelings yet; I had to keep this practical. 'These dreams of yours—do they always come true?'

He frowned. 'One way or another. Don't worry, I won't let anything happen to you. I'm gonna take very good care of you, Sky.'

I didn't know what else I could say about such a vague threat, but he had me spooked. I changed the subject. 'You know, Tina doesn't think you're my type.' I gestured across the room to Tina who was chatting with Sally. She looked striking in her long green dress; Nelson hovered close—he'd not missed the fact that she was attracting many admiring glances tonight.

'Oh?' Zed looked amused. 'And your type would be?'

'Tina's opinion or mine?'

'Yours.'

I smiled down at my new shoes before risking a glimpse

of his expression. I was totally nervous, but I said it anyway. 'Right now my type seems to be tall, arrogant, angry and secretly really kind.'

'Nope, nobody I know.' His eyes glinted.

'Sky, isn't it? How are you?' Mr Benedict interrupted us, taking my hand in his large palm and holding it for a moment. His grip was warm and capable, work-roughened. If he was surprised to see me with his son after our last conversation in his presence, he didn't show it. Then again, I had the impression his face rarely betrayed his thoughts. By contrast, his wife was a bundle of energy with large dark eyes, face positively radiating her emotions, body held poised like a flamenco dancer. She was the one who had gifted her sons with the Hispanic looks. By the way Mr Benedict's arm rested on her shoulders, you could tell they had a special energy together, a quiet fizz of delight in each other.

'Sky.' Karla broke into my musing; she was smiling as she patted my wrist.

'Nice to meet you, Mrs Benedict.'

'Our boy apologized to you yet for how he spoke to you at the river?'

I glanced up at him. 'In his own way.'

'I see you understand him. I'm so pleased. It's difficult for him.' Mrs Benedict touched my cheek lightly, before her eyes lost focus and she became sort of *misty*. 'But you—you've seen these things too—lived them, which is much worse. I'm so sorry.'

My heart missed a beat.

'Mom,' warned Zed. 'Stop it.'

She turned to him. 'I can't help but see.'

'Yes, you can,' he ground out.

'So much sadness so young.'

'Karla, Sky is here to enjoy herself.' Mr Benedict herded his wife away from me. 'Come visit us anytime, Sky. You'll always be welcome.'

I wanted to run. These people were making me *see* things again. I couldn't. I'd squeezed those feelings—the colours—stuffed them away in a locked box deep inside. What was I doing here with Zed Benedict of all people? Who was I fooling? I couldn't handle relationships—I shouldn't have even tried.

'Sorry about that.' Zed tugged his collar awkwardly. 'Shall we get some air?'

'She's like you.' I could feel the shaking beginning. 'She was reading me—getting too much like you do.'

'Hush now.' He stepped closer to shield me from the rest of the guests. 'Don't think about it.'

'What am I? An open book or something?'

'It's not like that. It's not just you.'

'I think I'd like to go home now.'

'I'll drive you back.'

'No, it's OK. I'll get Tina to take me.' Right now I didn't want to be near any of the Benedicts.

'It's not OK. If you want to go, I'm the one who's going to take you. You're my responsibility now. I've got to keep you safe.'

'Safe' was the opposite of what he made me feel. I backed away. 'Just leave me alone. Please.'

Tina must've been keeping an eye on me all evening because she was at my side in an instant. 'What's the matter, Sky?'

'I . . . I'm not feeling well.'

Zed stepped between us. 'I was just about to drive her home.'

'I can take her,' Tina said swiftly.

'No need. She's with me. I'll look after her.' He was angry that I wanted to run from him, I could tell.

'Sky?' asked Tina.

I hugged my arms around my waist. It was easier not to argue. I just wanted to get home as quickly as possible, even if it meant a few minutes in the car with Zed.

'Zed'll take me. I'll just go tell my parents.'

I was feeling really shaken and some sign of that must have convinced my parents I'd be better off at home. Simon sized Zed up coldly before agreeing.

'Your dad does that well,' Zed said, starting the ignition in his family's jeep.

'What?' I suddenly felt tired—drained. I let my head flop against the side window.

'Do the ball breaker thing. He was letting me know that if I put a finger on his little girl, I'm already dead.'

I gave a hiccuping laugh. 'Yeah, he does get a bit protective.' A lot like Zed.

We left that hanging as Zed drove up the hill. A dangling crystal swayed from the mirror, catching the lights as it jiggled hypnotically to and fro.

'Why do you call them by their first names?' he asked, trying to steer us away from the swampy ground we'd just covered.

'I've only been with them since I was ten. We all agreed we were more comfortable with first names. They felt they were too old to start as Mummy and Daddy.'

'You agreed or they suggested?' He was right. I'd wanted to call them Mum and Dad, desperate to be like the other kids, but it hadn't been their style.

'I was fine with it.'

He let it go. 'My mom—she does that to people. What can I say? Sorry?'

'Not your fault.'

'I took you over to them. I should've headed her off. Don't let what she said worry you.'

'It's just not . . . not nice thinking someone can sense stuff about you.'

'You don't have to tell me—I live in the same house as her.'

'She can see stuff about you too?' That made me feel a lot better.

'Oh yeah. Being a Benedict is no bed of roses.'

We stopped outside the house. Only the porch lamp was on. I wasn't too keen on going in alone but didn't want Zed to think I was making him a different kind of invitation.

'So we'll keep it in the car then. Just one small step,' he said softly, then leant over and put his lips to mine for a kiss. It was incredibly soft. I felt as if we were melding together, barriers sinking under his gentle persuasion. Far too soon, he pulled reluctantly away. 'Where's your dad? Am I dead yet?'

'That wasn't a finger. You said my dad only thought about a finger.' My voice sounded distant to me. Panic faded and I began to enjoy being just here in the present—with Zed. Like he'd said, my body was humming to his perfect A.

'True.' He put his hands on my shoulders and trailed them over the skin. 'Sorry, I just had to do that. The dress should be outlawed.'

'Hmm.' Zed Benedict was kissing me—how could this possibly be real?

'Yeah, I really, really like you, Sky. But if I don't stop now, your dad *will* kill me and that will be the end of a beautiful friendship.' He took a last kiss and pushed away, coming round to my side of the car to help me out. 'I'll just go turn some lights on then head back to the party.'

'Thanks. I don't like going into an empty house.'

'I know.' Zed took the key from me and opened the door. I waited in the hall as he made a quick tour of the rooms.

He hovered on the porch, jingling his keys. 'I don't like leaving you alone. Promise not to go out?'

'I promise.'

'Are you sure you'll be all right?'

'Yes. I'll be fine.'

'And sorry again about Mom. If it's any comfort, her sister, Aunt Loretta, is worse.'

'Really?'

'Yeah. Hard to imagine, isn't it? Keep clear of our house at Thanksgiving—they're an unstoppable combination.' He drew me to him and kissed the tip of my nose. 'Goodnight, Sky.'

'Goodnight.'

Hand lingering on my cheek, he stepped back. 'Make sure you lock the door behind me.'

I did as he said and went upstairs to change. Looking out of the window I saw that he hadn't yet driven away. He sat there in the jeep. On guard until my parents came home. He was taking the threat to me seriously—which was both alarming and oddly comforting. At least tonight, I didn't have to be scared.

Chapter 11

We had our first light fall of snow in mid October. The woods looked incredible: leaves turning so many colours like the wrappers in a box of Quality Streets. Sally and Simon spent most days, fingernails ingrained with oils, bubbling over with excitement about the challenge they were facing when they painted al fresco. When they get like this, even when they try and remember, they often forget normal stuff, like their daughter's parent-teacher consultation and when they last saw her at meal times. It can be a bit lonely—at least I now had a piano at home to keep me company. But in Richmond, their studio was in the attic; here, they were a mile away at the centre.

So it was that they missed out on the little drama of which I found myself the focus.

The Wrickenridge High gossip machine was working overtime on the Zed Benedict/Sky Bright saga. I was determined that it was just 'going out'; Zed had his protect-Sky-and-be-her-soulfinder agenda but I refused to discuss either with him—all of which made for a stormy time. But with a boy like Zed, what did you expect? A relationship with him was never going to be plain sailing.

Tina dropped me at the corner of my street. She'd been giving me grief about Zed, not believing me when I told her that he'd been unfailingly kind to me since he'd decided to turn over a new leaf and work at persuading me we were a good idea.

'He doesn't kiss you on the doorstep and leave—he's not that kind of boy-next-door,' she insisted.

'Well, he did.' I was getting a bit annoyed with her now. 'He's much nicer than he seems.' At least, I think he was.

'Yeah, because he wants you.'

I fisted my hand in my hair, giving a sharp tug—an alternative to screaming. Everyone from my fellow students to the teachers was predicting some disaster to come from my relationship with Zed. They were all determined to cast him as villain and me as the clueless damsel about to get herself in distress. Nelson was perpetually worried, muttering dire warnings about what he'd do to Zed if things went wrong. I'd had coded advice from various female members of staff about not allowing myself to be pushed further than I wanted to go. I already had enough pessimistic thoughts myself; hearing them echoed by others was sapping my confidence.

'On your own again, Sky?' called Mrs Hoffman as I arrived back from school.

'I expect so.'

'Want to come in for a while? I've baked brownies.'

'Thanks, but I've . . . er . . . got homework to do.'

'Then I'll bring some over.'

'That'd be great.'

I'd got the hang of managing Mrs Hoffman now. You never went into her house unless you had a good hour to spare as it was impossible to break out of a conversation with her no matter how you wriggled like Houdini with the chains too tight. On your own territory, it was a bit easier and she always respected the demands of scholarship when offered as an excuse.

She left when I got out my text books. Munching on one of her biscuits, I went up to my bedroom to finish my history assignment.

Sky, are you OK?

After weeks of resisting, I'd finally had to admit that I could hear him in my head. *Zed?* I looked out of the window, half expecting his car to be on the street. *Where are you?*

At home. Do you want to come over?

How did you . . . ? No wait: how are we talking like this, so far apart?

We just can. Do you want to come?

A choice between sitting at home on my own or braving Zed's family?

Mom's in Denver. Yves's at some Young Einstein of the Year convention. It's just me, Dad, and Xav.

OK, I'll come over. You're up by the cable car, right? I think I can find you. I started downstairs, tugging my jacket off the newel post.

No! I don't want you out alone—it's getting dark. I'll come get you.

I'm not afraid of the dark.

I am. Humour me.

He shut the conversation off. I sat on the bottom step of the stairs and massaged my temples. It seemed harder to talk this way to him over a greater distance, more tiring somehow. Another thing I had to ask him about.

I heard the jeep ten minutes later. Slinging my jacket on and grabbing my keys, I ran out of the house.

'You must have broken every traffic law to get here so fast!'

He gave me a smooth smile. 'I was already on the way when I called in.'

'You think that's calling in?' I climbed into the passenger

seat and we headed off back through town. 'You could use a cellphone like other people.'

'The reception's bad out here—too many mountains.'

'That's the only reason?'

His mouth quirked at the corners. 'No. It brings you, well, *closer*.'

I'd have to think about that one. 'Do you talk to anyone else this way?'

'My family. We've the lowest phone bills in the valley.'

I laughed. 'Can you talk to your brothers in Denver?'

He put his right arm on the back of my seat, brushing the nape of my neck in passing. 'Why all the questions?'

'Sorry to break it to you, Zed, but it's not exactly normal.'

'It is for us.' He turned up the track running along the side of the ski lodges leading to his house. 'I'm going to pull over.'

'Why? What's the matter?'

'Nothing's wrong. I doubt if we'll have a chance to be alone when we arrive at the house so I just wanted to kiss you.'

I moved back a little. 'Zed, is this real? You wanting to be with me?'

He unfastened my seat belt. 'It most definitely is. You are everything I want. Everything I need.'

'I still don't understand.'

He rested his head against mine, breath warm in my ear. 'I know you don't. I'm trying to give you the time you need, let you get to know me enough so you trust me, trust this.'

'And the kissing?'

He chuckled. 'I have to admit that's for me. I'm selfish that way.'

Zed's dad met us outside the house, wearing work overalls and carrying a tool box; something about the way he handled himself said he knew what to do with his hands, a natural engineer. The Benedict home was a rambling clapboard lodge painted the colour of vanilla ice cream, snuggled next to the start of the cable car at the top end of town.

'There you are, Zed.' Mr Benedict wiped his greasy hands on a rag. 'I saw you coming.'

For some reason, Zed looked annoyed. 'Dad!'

'You know we can't control these things unless we concentrate. You forgot to shield. Sky, nice to see you again. I don't think we were properly introduced: I'm Saul Benedict.'

Xavier came jogging round the house. 'Hi!'

'Not you too,' groaned Zed.

'Why?'

'Dad *saw* Sky and me.'

Xavier held up both hands. 'Innocent. I wasn't anywhere near your mind, though I can guess what went on.'

'Don't go there,' warned Zed.

'What does he mean, about being "near your mind"?' I asked suspiciously.

All three men looked awkward. I could have sworn Saul's neck flushed.

'Were you *talking* to him when we were driving?'

'Not exactly.'

'She knows about that?' Saul said in a low voice. 'How come?'

Zed shrugged. 'It just happened. You heard what Mom said about her—she's a bridge. It's hard not to step over.'

A bridge? What was that?

Saul waved me to go ahead of him into the house. 'My son talk to you in your mind, Sky?'

'Um . . . maybe.'

'You've not told anyone else?'

'Well, no. It sounds a bit screwy.'

He looked relieved. 'We prefer people not to know about it ˙ so I'd really appreciate if you kept it to yourself.'

'Fine by me.'

'You don't have a problem with it?'

'Yes, but I'm more worried when Zed seems to know what I'm thinking before I do.' Not to mention the soulfinder thing.

Tiny lines deepened around Saul's eyes—silent laughter. 'Yes, we all feel that way about Zed. He never did buy the Santa-down-the-chimney story when he was small. But you learn to live with it.'

The house was very welcoming: an eclectic mixture of objects from all over the world scattered throughout the living rooms, strong on Latin America. I got the sense of a family rubbing along well together. I peeked round a corner and saw a huge amount of ski gear cluttering up the utility room.

'Wow.'

'Yes, we are serious about our skiing, though Zed here prefers to board,' said Saul with a fond smile.

'Public enemy number one,' commented Xavier pretending to shoot his brother.

'Boarders and skiers don't get on?'

'Not all the time,' said Saul. 'You ski?'

Zed must have read the answer in my mind. 'You don't?'

'England isn't exactly known for its powder snow.'

'Dad, we have an emergency. Intensive lessons starting from the first fall.'

'You bet.' Saul gave me a businesslike nod.

'I don't think I'll be very good at it.'

The three Benedicts shared a look.

Xavier gave a snort of laughter. 'Yeah, right.'

It was weird—there were definitely things happening here that I couldn't follow.

'What is it you're doing?

'Just looking ahead, Sky,' said Saul. 'Come into the kitchen. Karla's left pizza for us.'

There were more odd moments over dinner preparation. It started normally but then headed into la-la land. Saul took command of the sink and proved to be a competent salad chef. Xavier claimed that even Zed couldn't ruin pizza so let him take charge of the oven.

'His problem is that he sees the food already burnt and can't be bothered to change things.' Xavier put his feet up on an empty chair and rubbed his calf muscles. 'How's this one going to be?' he called to his brother.

What did that mean?

'This is going to be the best ever,' Zed replied confidently, shoving the baking sheet into the stove.

'So, Sky, how you finding school? Other students a pain in the butt, I bet?' Xavier threw a pretzel at his younger brother.

'It's OK. Bit different from what I'm used to.'

'Yeah, but Wrickenridge is way better than lots of high schools. Most kids go on to do what they want after.'

I took a handful of the snacks on the table between us. 'What about you? I was told you're good at slalom. Olympic standard good.'

He rolled his shoulders in a shrug. 'Could be—but I don't think I'll take it that far.'

'Is it because you can see yourself failing and can't be bothered to change it?'

'Ouch!' He laughed. 'Hey, Zed, your girl here has a mean streak. Getting back at me for ribbing you about your cooking.'

'Good for her.' Zed gave me an approving nod. 'Don't listen to any of his bull, Sky. I can cook.'

'Yeah, like Sky can ski.'

A lemon zipped from the fruit bowl and hit Xavier squarely on the nose. I jumped in my seat. 'What the—!'

'Zed!' said Saul in warning. 'We've a guest.'

I was still questioning what I had just seen. 'You've got, like, a poltergeist or something?'

'Yeah, or something.' Xavier rubbed his nose.

'Is anyone going to explain that?'

'Not me. What were we talking about before I was so rudely interrupted by a flying citrus?' He chucked the lemon towards Zed but it dropped suddenly halfway back into the bowl. 'Butthead,' grumbled Xavier.

'Um . . . we were talking about your skiing.' I looked at Zed but he was whistling innocently as he wiped down the work surface. Too innocently.

'Oh yeah. Well, I don't think I'll go the professional skier route. Got too much else I want to do with my life.'

'I can imagine.' But I wasn't sure he meant it. It felt like an excuse to me.

'I'm stopping as Colorado junior champion and retiring undefeated.'

'And never lets us forget it,' added Zed.

Something weird happened to the lemon at that point: it exploded.

'Boys!' Saul rapped on the counter.

'Sorry,' they intoned dutifully. Xavier got up to clean away the mess.

'No explanation, right?' I asked. They confused me, these Benedicts, but just at the moment I wanted to laugh.

'Nope, not from me. He's going to tell you.' Xavier chucked the rag at Zed. 'Later.' He made a sudden dash for the stove. 'Sheesh, Zed, you've let it burn! I thought you said this was going to be the best yet.' He grabbed oven gloves and dumped a slightly blackened pizza on the side.

Zed took a sniff. 'It is. Only singed. I'm improving.'

Xavier hit him round the head. 'What's the use of being a know-it-all when you can't even cook pizza?'

'I ask myself that every day,' Zed replied good-humouredly, getting out the pizza slicer.

After dinner, Zed suggested we went for a walk in the woods at the side of the ski run to burn off all that melted cheese.

'Xav's got clear-up duty as I cooked so we're free,' he explained, holding my jacket out for me.

'Cooked? Is that what you did?'

'OK. Charred.'

Taking my hand, he led me out of the back door. The house had hardly any garden, just a fence before the end of a ski run and the bottom of the lift. You couldn't see the peak of the mountain from here, only the steep slope of the forest climbing above the cable car station, firs closely packed to form a carpet. I took a breath, the air cold and dry on the back of my throat, making my skin feel tight across my face. My head felt slightly muzzy, which I put down to the altitude.

'Up or down?' Zed asked, gesturing to the slope.

Best to get the worst over with. 'Up first.'

'Good choice. I've a favourite place I want to show you.'

We passed under the trees. Most of the snow from a light fall earlier in the day had slid off the branches, melting away to reveal the dark green of needles and lighter shade of larch. The air was clear, brilliant like the dazzle of a crystal bringing the stars into sharp relief against the sky, pinpricks of light. We took it slowly, winding our way through the trees. A little higher and we hit snowdrifts, edging down the mountain as winter made its claim.

'Snow doesn't stay lower down till around Thanksgiving,' Zed explained.

We walked on hand in hand for a few more minutes. He gently brushed my knuckles through my glove. I found it strangely sweet that this boy, reputed to be the toughest nut in Wrickenridge, seemed content to walk like this. He was intriguing in his contradictions.

Unless, of course, Tina was right and he was just being what he thought I wanted. Way to go, Sky: how to spoil a lovely moment.

The snow was now ankle-deep and my valley shoes were not doing a very good job at keeping my feet dry.

'I should've thought,' I grumbled, kicking a clump of ice off my canvas toe cap before it could melt through.

'My sight isn't much help for practical stuff like that—sorry. Shoulda told you to bring boots.'

He was one strange boy sometimes. 'So, what powers do you think you have, aside from the telepathy thing?'

'Various, but mainly I can see the future.' He paused at a particularly beautiful spot, a clearing in the forest where the snow lay deep and pristine. 'Wanna make an angel?'

He dropped it so casually into the conversation, I was still reeling. 'You go ahead. Don't let me stop you.'

He grinned as he tumbled back into the deep snow, waving his arms and legs to make an angel shape.

'Come on—I know you're going to.'

'Because you can see?'

'Nope, because I'm gonna do this.'

He sat up quickly and tugged me down beside him before I had a chance to brace.

Well, now I was here, I had to make an angel, of course. Lying on my back, looking up at the patch of stars, I tried not to let my worries about being a savant and the possible danger coming for me sour the breathtaking beauty of the forest at night. I could feel Zed beside me, waiting for me to make another step towards him.

'So what can you see?' I asked him.

'Not everything and not all the time. I can't "see" my family's future, or only rarely. We're too close—there's too much interference, too many variables.'

'Do they do the same thing?'

'Only Mom, thankfully.' He sat up, brushing the snow from his elbows. 'The rest have other gifts.'

'You've seen my future? In that premonition?'

He rubbed a hand over his face. 'Maybe. But if I tell you exactly what I saw, I might either change things or be the reason it happens—I can't know that for sure. My sight gets more precise the closer I am to an event. I only know with any certainty something is going to happen a second or two before it does. Yet it can go really wrong. That's what happened in the raft—by interfering I helped cause what I was trying to stop.'

'So you won't tell me if I'm going to be a good skier?'

He shook his head and tapped my forehead. 'No, not even that.'

'Good, I think I'd prefer not to know.'

The breeze rustled the branches. The shadows were deepening under the trees.

'What's it like? How can you bear knowing so much?' I asked softly. He was my opposite in many ways: I knew so little about myself, about the past; he knew too much about the future.

Zed got up and pulled me to my feet. 'Most days, it's a curse. I know what people are going to say—how the film will end—what the score's going to be. My brothers don't really understand, or don't want to think, what it's like. We've all got our own gifts to handle.'

No wonder he was having problems getting along at school. If he was always ahead of the rest, always knowing, then he would be weighed down by a terrible sense of futility, not being able to change outcomes, like the pizza burning. It made my head hurt just thinking about it. 'This is all too weird.'

He put his arm round me, tucking me under his shoulder. 'Yeah, I get that. But I need you to understand. You see, Sky, it's like, I dunno, I suppose a bit like being in a lift with muzak. It's playing away in the background but you don't notice until you pay attention. But from time to time, I get a sudden trumpet burst of things. Scenes play out. I don't always know the people or understand what they mean. Not until later anyway. I may try and stop things but they usually just happen in a way I didn't anticipate. I try to block it out—I can for a time—but once I forget it comes back.'

I decided it sounded more like a curse than a gift. He'd be a little ahead of everyone when he tuned in.

Then I realized.

'You bloody cheater!' I elbowed him in the ribs. 'No wonder you are unbeatable when you pitch or kick goals!'

'Yeah, it does have that fringe benefit.' He turned to me and smirked. 'Helped you out, didn't it?'

I remembered the fluke save. 'Oh.'

'Yeah, *oh*. I sacrificed my perfect goal scoring record for you.'

'Hardly—you scored, like, twenty or something.'

'No, really. What are people gonna remember about that match? That I scored loads or that you saved that one? I'm never gonna live it down.'

'Idiot.' I swatted him.

He had the gall to laugh at me. 'That's done it. I'll have to distract you again before you hit me a second time.'

As he leant forward to take a kiss, he abruptly lunged, knocking me backwards. A tree trunk splintered five feet behind us. Simultaneously, I heard a report like a car backfiring.

Zed dragged me behind a fallen tree trunk and pushed me under, sheltering me with his body. He swore.

'This isn't supposed to be happening!'

'Get off me! What was that?' I tried to get up.

'Stay down.' He swore again, even more colourfully. 'Someone took a shot at us. I'm getting Dad and Xav.'

I lay quiet under him, my heart pounding.

Crack! A second shot struck the trunk not far above our heads.

Zed slid off me. 'We've got to move! Roll out the other side of the trunk and run for the big pine over there.'

'Why don't we just shout to tell them that they're shooting at humans?'

'He's not hunting animals, Sky: he's after us. Go!'

I squeezed under the trunk, scrambled up and ran. I could hear Zed just behind me—a third shot—then Zed tackled me from behind, his elbow connecting with my eye as we went down. A fourth shot hit the tree in front just level with where my head had been.

'Damn. Sorry,' Zed said as stars whirled. 'Saw that one almost too late again.'

Better stunned than dead.

Yeah. But still I'm sorry. Just stay still. Dad and Xav are hunting our hunter now.

I think there's more than one.

'What?' He lifted his head a fraction to look at my face. 'How do you know?'

'I don't know. I just feel them there.'

Zed didn't question my instinct and relayed the news to his father.

'I've told him to be careful.' Zed stayed over me, refusing to let me risk being in the line of fire. 'It could be a trap to lure him out. We've got to get back to the house. There's a stream just over that ridge. If we get there, we can stay hidden and circle back. OK?'

'OK. How do we get to it?'

Zed smiled grimly. 'You're amazing, Sky. Most people would have lost it by now. We crawl—make like lizards. I'll go first.'

He slithered on his belly over the ground then dropped over the ridge out of sight. I followed, trying not to think about what it would feel like to get a bullet in the back. It was too dark to see what was down there so I just had to trust him. I slipped head first down the bank, rolled and landed with my butt in icy water.

This way, said Zed.

Chapter 12

Keeping low, Zed led me down the course of a shallow stream that fed into the Eyrie. He was wearing walking boots, but my canvas sneakers had no purchase on the stones and I kept stumbling.

Hold on to my jacket, he told me. *Almost there.*

As the stream got deeper, the bank lowered allowing us to clamber out of the gully. We emerged on the grassy slope in front of the house.

'Sense anything?' Zed asked.

'No. You?'

'I can't see anything. Let's make a run for the house.' He gave my arm a squeeze. 'On three. One—two—three!'

Feet squelching in my shoes, I sprinted across the open ground and through the front door. I heard the lock click behind me without Zed touching it.

'Your dad and Xav OK?' I panted.

He looked distant for a second, checking in with the rest of the family.

'They're fine, but they lost the hunters. You were right: there were two of them. They took off out of town in an unmarked SUV. Black, dark windows. Hundreds of cars like it in the mountains. Dad says to stay here till he gets back. Let's look at that eye.'

Zed steered me into the downstairs bathroom and sat me on the edge of the bath. As he fumbled with the first aid box, I realized that he was shaking.

I put my hand on his arm. 'It's OK.'

'It's not OK.' He ripped open a pack of cotton wool, shooting the balls all over the vanity unit. 'We're supposed to be safe here.' Fury rather than shock was making him tremble.

'Why wouldn't you be safe? What's going on, Zed? You seem not really surprised that someone wanted to shoot you.'

He gave a hollow laugh. 'It does make a kind of horrible sense, Sky.' He rinsed out a flannel and placed it against my eye, the cold dulling the edge off the pain. 'Hold that there.' He then cleaned my cuts and scratches with the cotton wool. 'I realize you want to know why that might be, but it's better for you and for us if you don't.'

'And I'm supposed to be OK with that? I go for a walk with you, and get shot at, and I'm not supposed to wonder why? I can live with exploding lemons and the rest of it, but this is different. You almost died.'

He pushed the cloth back against my cheek where I had let it drop away. 'I know you're mad at me.'

'I'm not mad at you! I'm mad at the people who just tried to kill us! Have you told the police?'

'Yeah, Dad's handling it. They'll be along. They'll probably want to talk to you.' He took the cloth away and whistled. 'How's this for a first date: I've given you a black eye.'

That gave me a jolt.

'This was a date? You asked me here on, like, a date and I missed it?'

'Yeah, well, not many boys take their girls out on a duck

124

shoot with them as the target for a first date. You have to give me points for style.'

I hadn't got past first base yet. 'This was a date?' I repeated.

He pulled me up into his arms, my head against his chest. 'It was a date—I was trying to get you used to me, kinda in my natural habitat. But I can do better, I promise.'

'What? Gladiatorial combat next?'

'Now there's an idea.' He nuzzled my hair. 'Thanks for keeping a cool head out there.'

'Thanks for bringing us through it.'

'Zed? Sky? Are you all right?' Saul was shouting from the hallway.

'In here, Dad. I'm fine. Sky's a bit roughed up, but she's OK.'

Saul hovered in the door, his expression anguished. 'What happened? Didn't you see the danger, Zed?'

'Yeah, obviously I saw. I thought, "Let's take my girlfriend out for a walk and try and get her killed". Of course, I didn't see—no more than you sensed it.'

'Sorry, stupid question. Vick's on his way. I've called your mom and Yves back. Trace will be here as soon as possible.'

'Who was it?'

'I don't know. The two Kellys were sent down on Tuesday. It could be payback. But they shouldn't know where to find us.'

I turned in Zed's arms to look at Saul. 'Who are the Kellys?'

Saul saw my face properly for the first time. 'Sky, you're hurt! Xav, get in here.'

The bathroom was beginning to feel very crowded with so many Benedicts hovering over me.

'I'm fine. I just want some answers.'

Xav came running. 'She's not fine. Her face feels like it's on fire.'

I opened my mouth to protest.

'Don't bother, Sky, I can feel what you're feeling. An echo

of it.' Xav reached out and put his fingertip on the bruise. I experienced a tingling like pins and needles on the right side of my face.

'What are you doing?'

'Trying to stop you looking like a panda tomorrow.' He lifted his finger away. 'It's my gift.'

I touched my face cautiously. Though the bruise throbbed, the intensity of the pain had dimmed.

'You'll still have a bit of a bruise. I haven't had time to get rid of all of it. Pain's quick, bruises take more time to clear up—at least another fifteen minutes or so.'

'We'd better get Sky home. The further from this mess she is, the better.' Saul ushered us out of the bathroom.

'Won't the police want to take her statement?' Zed handed me a dry pair of socks from the clean laundry basket.

'Vick's sorting it out. He doesn't think we should involve the local cops; he'll get his people on to it. If he wants to talk to her, he can go to her to do so.'

Another thread for me to tug. 'And his people are?' I kicked off my shoes to rub my icy feet.

'The FBI.'

'That's like the CIA—spies and stuff?'

'No, not really. The Federal Bureau of Investigation deals with crimes that cross state boundaries. The big felonies. They're plain clothes. Agents rather than cops.'

I slipped the tie from my unravelling plait and clumped my hair together in a ponytail. 'Zoe always says Victor's a man of mystery.'

Saul flicked his eyes to Zed, clearly uncomfortable with how much I was learning about them.

'But the less that's known about his other life, the better, understood?'

'Another Benedict family secret?'

126

'They do seem to be piling up, don't they?' Saul chucked Zed a set of keys. 'Take Sky home on the bike—but don't go direct. We don't want you leading anyone to her.'

'You could take me to my parents' studio and they can run me back.'

'Good thinking. Zed, give my apologies to Mr and Mrs Bright for not taking proper care of their daughter.'

'What do I tell them about it all?' Zed asked, guiding me out of the house.

Saul rubbed the back of his neck. 'I'll get Victor to explain. He'll know what and how much to say. For now, tell them it was some idiot running wild in the woods. Ask them to keep a lid on it until the authorities have had a chance to deal with it. Is that OK with you, Sky?'

I nodded.

'Good. You did great.' Saul kissed the top of my head and hugged his son. 'Thank God we've only got one black eye to show for it. And thank you, Sky, for being so patient with us.'

I mounted the motorbike behind Zed, gripping on to his jacket like a lifebelt.

'I'm going to take us by some back roads that skirt round Wrickenridge to your side of town,' he warned me. 'Just in case.'

The so-called back roads proved to be little more than dirt tracks. To help myself cope, I fell back into my habit of seeing the drive in my head as a storyboard: headlamp cutting through the dark—startled deer bounding out of the way— bike weaving round a fallen tree—girl clutching on to boy. Music would be menacing, urgent—heavy metal maybe . . . But it didn't work—the danger was too real; I couldn't distance it with a story, not when I was one of the main characters.

I felt filthy and shaken up by the time we reached the Arts Centre. My head was pounding again.

'Can you do that thing Xavier does?' I asked, pinching the bridge of my nose after I took the helmet off.

'No, but I can buy you something for it at the drug store.'

'It's OK.'

Zed blew out a bracing breath. 'Come on; let's face the music from your dad.'

'Can you see how bad it's going to be?'

'Trying not to.'

The black eye was a bad enough introduction, but the news that we had been shot at by a madman in the woods was the last straw.

'Sky!' wailed Sally, her voice echoing around the clean white walls of the studio in the roof of the Arts Centre. 'What have we brought you to? This would never've happened in Richmond!'

'You might not believe me, ma'am,' Zed said politely, 'but it doesn't normally happen here either.'

'You're not to go out until this crazy man is caught!' Sally said, brushing my cheek and tutting over my bruise.

'And why didn't you tell us you were going out this evening, Sky?' Simon looked at Zed with open hostility, which was not surprising as Zed did look particularly menacing in black bike leathers. But I thought the question was rich coming from Simon seeing that they were hardly ever at home. The role of Strict Dad-Meister was at odds with the relaxed Bohemian Artist thing he had going, but for me he always managed to make an exception. In his mind, I was always to be ten, not sixteen.

'It was a last minute decision. I just went for supper. I thought I'd be back before you came home.'

Your dad is measuring me up for my coffin right now, Zed told me.

He's not.

128

I'm catching images here—all of them painful and detrimental to my future prospects of being a father.

'You're grounded, Sky, for going out without permission,' Simon growled. He was clearly channelling Dad-Meister at the moment.

'What! That's not fair!'

He's over-reacting because he's afraid for you.

Still not fair.

'I'm sorry, sir, it's my fault Sky went out tonight. I asked her over.' Zed tried to erect a force field between me and Simon's anger.

Dad-Meister zapped it down. 'That may well be, but my daughter has to learn to take responsibility for her own decisions. Grounded. For two weeks.'

'Simon!' I protested, embarrassed that Zed was witnessing this.

'Don't make me extend it to four, young lady! Goodnight, Zed.'

Zed squeezed my hand. *Sorry. He's not going to listen to me. I'd better get back.*

He left and then I heard the bike roar into life outside. Wolfman zipping off out of harm's way. Thanks a lot.

I folded my arms, my foot tapping in the way a cat's tail twitches when riled. If Simon was playing Dad-Meister, I was SuperAngry Sky. 'You expect me to sit at home while you and Sally play here but don't want me to enjoy myself with my friends!' I exploded. 'That is so unfair!'

'Don't you talk back to me, Sky.' Simon threw his brushes in the sink and ran the water too hard, the spray wetting his jumper.

'You're just saying that because you know you're in the wrong! I didn't complain when you stood up Mr Ozawa at school on Monday—that was *so* humiliating. I didn't know what to say to him. I didn't ground you for being crap parents.'

Simon shot Sally an embarrassed look. 'I phoned Mr Ozawa to apologize.'

'I know you only adopted me late in the day, but sometimes I think you forget you've got me.' I regretted the words as soon as I spoke them.

'Don't say that!' Sally put her hands to her mouth, eyes shining with tears, making me feel about an inch tall.

'So it's a bit much,' I continued. My hole was pretty deep now and I had to keep digging. 'A bit much for you to tell me off for not keeping you in the loop with what I'm up to. Half the time I've not got the foggiest where you are and I'm sure you don't realize it!'

'It's not the same,' snapped Simon, angry now I'd hurt Sally. He was probably hurting too. I know I was. 'Four weeks.'

I don't know what came over me. Normally it takes a lot to get me furious but I'd been shot at, had a load of secrets dumped on me by the Benedicts, ended up with a black eye, and Simon had turned it into something for which the juvenile punishment of grounding was thought an appropriate response.

'That's just a load of bull!'

'Don't you use that kind of language to me!'

'Urgh! Too American for you? Well, you brought me to this bloody country! I didn't ask to get shot at! I'm sick of it all—sick of you!' I stormed out and slammed the door behind me. Angry at him—angry at myself. I stomped up the road, kicking an empty can ahead of me, swearing with every rattle. No music inside to accompany this exit, unless you count the desire to clash bin lids together music.

I could hear someone running after me.

'Darling!' It was Sally. She grabbed me and folded me into a hug. 'You have to understand your father's afraid for you.

You're still his little girl. He's not used to seeing you with such a grown-up boy. And he certainly doesn't want you to get hurt by some trigger-happy redneck in the woods.'

Miserable under the weight of everything that had happened in the last few hours, I started to cry. 'I'm sorry, Sally. I didn't mean what I said—about the crap parent thing.'

'I know, darling. But we are crap parents. I bet you've not had a square meal this week—I know I haven't.'

'You're not. I'm a rubbish daughter. You took me in and put up with me and I . . .'

She gave me a little shake. 'And you have given us a hundred times more than we ever gave you. And we've never forgotten for one moment that we have you even when we are at our most unbearable. Give Simon a chance to cool down and I expect he'll even say sorry to you.'

'I was scared, Sally. They were shooting at us.'

'I know, darling.'

'Zed was really great. Knew what to do and everything.'

'He's a nice boy.'

'I like him.'

'I think you more than like him.'

I sniffed, fumbling for a handkerchief. I had no idea what I felt about him—confused about the savant connection, doubtful that anyone could want me as much as he claimed, just learning to trust him a little.

'Be careful, Sky. You are such a sensitive soul. A boy like that can crush you if you get too hung up on him.'

'A boy like what?' Why did everyone think they could put a label on Zed?

She sighed and steered me back to the car. 'He's good-looking, a little wild from what I hear. Few people stay long with their high school sweethearts—it's part of the training for life.'

'We've only had one date.'

'Exactly. So don't let your imagination go running off with you. Play it cool and you'll keep him interested.'

Him being interested wasn't the problem—I was the one keeping it light. But this was so like my mum—to worry about the heart when bullets had been flying. 'And this is, what, relationship advice according to Dr Sally Bright?'

'Do we need to have *that* conversation again? I thought we discussed it when you were twelve,' she teased.

'No, no, thanks, I've got the facts.'

'Then I trust you to apply them in practice.'

'You trust me, but Simon doesn't.'

She sighed. 'No, he's always felt really protective about you, maybe even more so because you were so hurt when we took you on. If he could lock you in a tower, dig ditches, plant a minefield and ring it all with razor wire, he'd do it.'

'I suppose I'm lucky I'm only grounded.'

'Yes, you are. I can probably beat him down to two weeks for you, but I think we can safely say you're grounded.'

chapter 13

The third eldest Benedict brother, Victor, came calling after
we'd gone to bed. I could hear Simon swearing as he fumbled
for his dressing gown to throw over his T-shirt and shorts. Sally
came to fetch me.

'Not asleep yet?'

'No. Wha'sup?'

'The FBI are in the kitchen. They want a word with us.'

Victor was with a female colleague. He had straight, long
dark hair tied back in a ponytail and wore a sharp black suit
with a silver tie. Like his father, he had a calm aura, as if he
could be surprised by few things. The colleague struck me as
more nervous. She was tapping her stylus on her electronic
memo, her hawkish face shadowed, her short brown hair
sleeked back behind her ears.

'Sky.' Victor held out a hand to me and led me to the seat
opposite him. It was strange how he acted as if he was in control in our kitchen. Sally and Simon had given way to him
without a murmur, hovering on the margins while he ran the
show. 'Do you mind if we record this?' He gestured to the
BlackBerry lying on the table.

I glanced at Simon. He shook his head.

'That's OK. I don't mind.'

He pressed a button. 'Record on. Incident seven, seven, eight, slash ten. Interview four. Present in the room are agents Victor Benedict and Anya Kowalski and witness, Sky Bright, a minor. Also in attendance are the witness's parents, Simon and Sally Bright.'

Cripes, this sounded like a trial.

'Have I done something wrong?' I asked, rubbing at the tea stain on the table top.

Victor's expression softened and he shook his head. 'Other than go out with my idiot brother, I'd say not. Sky, you're sixteen, is that right? What's your date of birth?'

'Um . . .'

Sally jumped in. 'No one is sure of her exact date as she lost her birth parents when she was six. We chose the day we adopted her—first of March—as her birthday.'

The hawkish agent made a note.

'OK,' said Victor, giving me a speculative look. 'Now, Sky, I want you to tell us in your own words, remembering as much detail as possible, what happened this evening out in the woods.'

Pushing a few stray grains of sugar to and fro on the table, I relived the experience for the record, running it in my head like one of my plots frame by frame, leaving out only the fact that for some of the time Zed and I had been using telepathy. Oh, and the kiss. I didn't think they needed to know about that.

'Zed said you were the one to realize that there was more than one shooter. How did you know?' Ms Kowalski butted in when I had reached that part in the story.

I wondered if I should make up something about hearing a noise or seeing another person, but decided I'd better stick to the truth.

'It was a gut feeling—you know, like an instinct.'

'Sky's always had good instincts,' added Sally, embarrassingly over-eager to assist the authorities with their enquiries. 'Remember how she never liked that tutor we employed for her that time, Simon? Turned out he'd been involved in a hit and run incident.'

I'd forgotten that—it had happened years ago. Mr Bagshot had made me feel panicky—guilty—when I was with him as if his emotions were spilling out and swamping me.

'Interesting.' Victor laced his fingers together. 'So you saw nothing, just felt it?'

'Yes.' I rubbed my temples, the headache back.

Victor dug in his pocket and pulled out a packet of aspirin. 'Zed sent these. He said you'd forget to take one.'

He'd seen this and not that we'd get shot at if we went for a walk? Second sight was annoyingly patchy. I took a tablet with a gulp of water and finished the story.

'Have you caught the men who did this?' Simon asked. Both he and Sally were pale: they hadn't heard the details of what happened, nor how close the bullets had come.

'No, sir.'

'Any idea who they were?'

'Not at this time.'

'Is Sky in danger?'

'We have no reason to think so.' Victor paused. 'I want to tell you something in confidence; you need to understand so you can make sure Sky is safe, but I have to ask you to keep it to yourselves.'

I wondered for a horrid moment if he was about to tell my parents about the savant stuff. They'd never believe him.

'You can trust us,' Simon confirmed.

'My family are here as part of a witness protection programme run by the FBI. We're afraid that news of their location must have leaked to associates of the people they helped send to jail. The attack was aimed at them, not your daughter, so we think she is under no further threat as long as she keeps her distance from us.'

'Oh.' Sally sat down, sagging like a collapsing inflatable. 'You poor things—to be living under that pressure.'

Simon had guessed the next step. 'Will you be moving now your location is no longer a secret?'

'We hope not. We all try and keep a low profile—'

'I'm stopping as Colorado junior champion and retiring undefeated', Xavier had said. He didn't want to become too well known across state boundaries. Zed had avoided making more than a good impression on the baseball diamond, ducking attention.

'But it's a bit early to say—and hard to uproot the whole family. Our preference is to deal with this threat, contain it, and see where we stand then.'

I drew a circle with my fingertip. 'And if you've a leak in the FBI, you have to plug it before moving or the problem would just follow you all.'

Victor's gaze sharpened. 'You're a bright girl, aren't you? No pun intended.'

'But I'm right, aren't I?'

'Yeah. We can protect ourselves better in a place we know until we can be sure it's safe.'

'I see.'

He got up and pocketed the recorder. 'Yeah, you do, don't you. You're sweet, just like Dad said you were. Thanks for your time, Sky, Mr and Mrs Bright.'

'No problem, Agent Benedict,' Simon said, showing them to the door.

Sally sat down next to me at the table. Simon sat on my other side and reached for my hand.

'Well,' he said.

'Yeah.' I leant my head on his shoulder, our earlier argument forgiven.

'I'm sorry, Sky, but we can't let you see that boy out of school, or any of his family for that matter, until this is all sorted out.'

'It's not fair.'

'No, it's not, darling. I'm sorry.'

Unable to see Zed in my free time, I couldn't wait to catch up with him at school to find out what was going to happen to his family. I felt very confused when he didn't turn up for the next few days. He'd left me worried sick and facing everyone with an unexplained black eye. It was totally embarrassing— the kind that makes you want to curl up quietly in a corner.

'Whoa, Sky, you take up boxing?' Nelson exclaimed in a loud voice on seeing me in the school hallway.

I tried to pull a hank of hair over my injury. 'No.'

Other students were now looking at me as if I were an exhibit. *Funny Girl with Black Eye*, roll up, roll up!

'How'd you do it then?'

I put on a spurt of speed, hoping to reach my form room before he got it out of me.

'Hey, Sky, you can tell me.' Nelson caught my arm, no longer teasing but serious now. 'Did someone hurt you?'

I shoved my hair off my face and looked at him straight. 'I ran into an elbow yesterday.'

'Whose?'

'Zed's. No big deal.'

'No big freaking deal! You're joking! Where is he?' Nelson looked fit to burst. 'I knew no good would come of it. He should take better care of you.'

'It's OK.'

'No, it is not OK, Sky. Zed's not right for a girl like you.'

'It was an accident.'

'So how it happen then?' He put his arm across the door, denying me entry. 'How you run into his elbow?'

What could I say? We were targeted by an assassin? That would be like setting off a box of fireworks in whole school assembly.

'We were mucking about in the woods and I kind of fell against him. Nelson, will you let me go in? It's bad enough looking stupid; I don't also want to be late.'

Nelson dropped his arm. 'But I got your back, remember? It may have been an accident but I don't see him here checking you're all right. I'm gonna have a word with Zed.'

'Don't.'

'Nothing you can do to stop me, Sky baby.'

So now I had something else to dread: Nelson ripping up Zed in the mistaken belief he was somehow defending me.

Zed turned up two days later. Victor drove both him and Yves to school in a sleek Prius with blacked out windows, dropping them near the door. I only saw them hurry in because I happened to be running behind too, having to function on 'Simon time' due to his insistence on taking me to class. Simon never started out until the moment he was supposed to be somewhere—OK for artists perhaps but not for students.

Seeing them run from the car to the front door, I thought the Benedicts looked harassed but otherwise fine.

Zed.

He heard me call out mind to mind, looked round, but Yves grabbed one arm and Victor the other, hurrying him under cover.

I'll find you later, he replied.

But I wanted him now. I had to swallow my disappointment

and go to explain to Mr Joe why I had missed registration for the second day in a row.

I hid in the library at recess. Outside the snow was falling and all of us were inside, scattered over the school, seeking shelter. I'd chosen the reference section of the library, hoping to attract fewer stares there. My eye was still a multicoloured humiliation. Since my brief glimpse of Zed that morning, I had the horrible feeling that maybe my feelings for him were leaping way ahead of his for me. I was all cut up about the tiny matter of a threat to his life and he hadn't even thought to call to tell me he was OK. Any thought messages I'd sent him had been left unanswered. Talk about blowing hot then cold. Perhaps that soulfinder rubbish had been just that—utter nonsense to win a few kisses.

But Zed found me in my bolt hole. Probably saw me there before I even arrived. He sat down opposite and just looked at me.

Sky, I'm sorry.

Hey, another benefit of this mind-talking stuff—not only do you have low phone bills but you don't get chucked out of the library. I pulled the P to Q section of the encyclopaedia towards me, pretending sudden interest in an article on penguins.

You mad at me?

No.

So why the cold shoulder?

I glanced up. He hadn't taken his eyes off me. Oh my, he looked good—I wanted to bury my face in his shoulder and just hold on tight.

Your eye hurt?

No, your brother fixed that; he just left me looking like a dork.

I couldn't come in until the area had been searched.

I guessed something like that was going on.

I couldn't text you because there's no network reception at home. I'm sorry.

No, don't apologize. I understand.

Do you really? Do you really understand how difficult it's been for me? I wanted to be with you—stay with you that day. You argued with your dad, didn't you?

Yeah, but we're OK now.

You're upset that I wasn't there to take the heat about your eye. People have been giving you a hard time.

Not hard, just awkward. Nelson's after you.

I deserve it.

You were saving my life.

You should never have been in danger in the first place. I should never have put you at risk. Look, can we go somewhere so we can talk properly?

I don't know if that's a good idea.

He pulled the book from my fingers. *Penguins, such fascinating creatures, but I didn't know you were studying them. What class is that you're taking?*

The 'we stupid looking creatures should stick together' class.

He tucked the book back on the shelf. 'Come with me.'

'Where?'

'Music practice rooms. I booked one out, just in case.'

Zed put his arm around my shoulder and led me out of the library, staring down Sheena and her gang who smirked at us. One look from him and they quickly found somewhere else to direct their gaze. When we got to the room, he first checked it was empty, then pulled me inside and shut the door.

'That's better.' He backed me against it and leant against me. 'Just let me hold you a moment. I've not had a chance just to touch you since those killers went for us.'

I let him hold me, feeling completely overwhelmed by his tenderness. There was a desperate edge to his embrace, perhaps we both knew that we were lucky to be breathing, let alone hugging each other.

'Sky, I couldn't bear it if something happened to you,' he whispered, his hands playing in the hair that I had let hang loose about my face to hide the bruise.

'Why? Is something going to happen? Have you seen something?'

'I told you, I can't tell people too much about the future. I might change it to be what none of us want if I do that.'

'So I take it mine doesn't look good?'

'Sky, please, I don't know. Don't you think I'd act if I knew what would help? All I know is I want you to be safe.'

It was so frustrating. These hints and half-spoken warnings were driving me crazy. Being a savant must really stink.

'Yeah, it does.'

'You're doing it again: reading my mind! Stop it. It's mine—private.' I folded my arms across my chest and moved away from him.

'I seem to be always apologizing to you, but I really am sorry. I can read you more clearly than I can other people—it kind of leaks out of you into my head.'

'And that's supposed to make me feel better?' My voice had a hysterical note.

'No, it's an explanation. You could learn to build shields, you know.'

'What?'

'Basic savant training. Living in a family of them, you soon learn to start shielding.'

'But I'm not a savant.'

'You are. And I think deep down you know it too.'

I fisted my hands in my hair. 'Stop it. I don't want to hear this.' *You're bad. Bad. Always making everyone unhappy.* 'No I'm not!' I wasn't talking to him any longer, but the whispers in my head.

'Sky.' Zed tugged at my fists, pulling them away from my

temples and drawing me towards him. His hands took up their slow caress again, running through the length of my hair, letting it fall back on my shoulders. 'You're beautiful. The furthest thing from bad that I've ever met.'

'What do you see—what do you know about where I came from?' I asked in a small voice. 'You've given hints. You know stuff about me that I don't.'

I could hear a sigh rumble in his chest. 'Nothing clear. Telling the past is more Uriel's gift than mine.'

I gave a shuddering laugh. 'Don't take this the wrong way but I hope I don't meet him.'

He swayed with me in his arms for the moment. It was like dancing without music, falling into the same rhythm.

'You want to know why I didn't call you?'

I nodded.

'I couldn't. We were on lockdown. I've got some more bad news.'

'What? Worse than some maniac being out to murder your family? I needed to know that you were all right. I needed to know *you* were all right.'

'Victor put us on code red. It means we can't communicate outside the immediate family.'

I couldn't help wondering where that put me in his order of priorities. He'd claimed I was his soulfinder after all.

'We don't know who might be listening in to our calls. I should've found a way to get a message to you but I was afraid to use telepathy.'

'Why?'

'That's the bad news. We think they've got a savant on the assassin team. They shouldn't have been able to get so close to us. Dad's gift is to sense danger. He should have known they were out there unless they were shielded by a powerful savant. You can listen in on telepathy just as you can with speech if you have the gift. I didn't want anything I did to tip them off about you.'

'So it's not just your family who can do telepathy?'

'No, there are a number of us we know about—and I guess many that we don't. You can turn a gift to evil as easily as choose to use it for good. The temptation is there, particularly for those who don't have the balance of a soulfinder.' He rubbed his chin against my hair. 'You're my balance, Sky. I was already slipping before I met you. I can't tell you what it means to me that you saved me from that grey existence.'

'You were slipping?'

'Yeah, big time. I'm not a nice person without you. It was becoming pretty tempting to use my gift to get my way, no matter how unfair or what the cost to other people was.' He grimaced, uncomfortable with what he was revealing about himself. 'You've given me enough hope now to hold on until you're ready to unlock your gift. Once that's done, there's no chance I'll ever return to what I was.'

'But you're not safe yet?' I hadn't realized I was holding him back. If something went wrong and he lost his balance, it would be my fault, wouldn't it, for not being brave enough to examine what was inside me? 'What should I do?'

He shook his head. 'Nothing. You need time. I'm more worried about getting this right for you than I am about me.'

'But I worry about you.'

'Thanks, but let's give you the space you need and deal with what we have to so we can keep you safe.'

Savant assassins—could this really be happening? The bullets had been genuine enough—I didn't doubt them. 'You think this savant has turned bad?'

'Yeah, he was working with the shooter. He might still be listening in—we just don't know. Telepathy over a distance is harder to channel to just the right person. We haven't come up against this before. We should have anticipated this.'

I sensed he was being hard on himself, frustrated that he didn't have all the answers for me. 'Why should you have done? You've only just got dragged in to this through the witness thing. When the trial's over, won't the threat pass?'

'Not exactly.' He looked a bit guilty for a moment, alerting me to the fact he hadn't been completely straight with me.

'Not exactly!'

'We aren't just witnesses—we're investigators. It's not just the latest trial—my family have combined their gifts to put away hundreds over the years. It's what we do.'

'So that means you have more enemies?'

'If they knew that we were behind their conviction—but they are not supposed to find out. Our information is used to steer the authorities to find evidence that will hold up in court. Our place isn't on the witness stand but behind the scenes.'

The full impact of what he was telling me took a while to set in. They were like a secret weapon for the law enforcers, up against evil day after day. 'How do you do it?'

He shut his eyes briefly. 'We work together—we see what happened.'

'You see it? See all that awful stuff—the killings—the crimes?'

'If we ignored what happened, that'd be worse. We'd share part of the guilt if we didn't act to stop crimes when we can.'

'But you suffer for it, don't you?'

He shrugged. 'What's that compared to the good we can do?'

I realized then that the Benedicts were brave and dedicated, putting aside their own ambitions to use their savant skills. They could be off seeking their soulfinders, but instead they risked everything to help victims of crime. But it also meant they would never be normal, never free to emerge from the shadows, stuck reliving the ugly scenes caused by the most vicious criminals. They had chosen the more difficult path; I didn't have it in me to be so noble. My life had been lived too much in shadows. I couldn't go back there—not even for Zed.

'I'm scared, Zed.'

'I don't think there's any threat to you as long as we aren't seen together out of school. I haven't even told my family about you. The only way I can think to protect you is by keeping my distance. If the rogue savant knew you were my soulfinder, it would put you in the centre of the target.'

'That's not what I meant. I'm scared you're going to get hurt.'

'We've got it under control now.'

'But you're going to have to keep hiding, aren't you?'

'I don't want to think about that.'

'Can I help? Is there some way I can make this easier for you?'

He shook his head. 'It would mean you releasing your gift and, as I said, I don't think that would be a good idea yet.'

'Releasing my gift? What does that mean? You savants speak in riddles.'

He laughed. 'Us savants, you mean. And if your gift were free, then you'd light up like I do when you're with me.'

I nestled closer to him, running my fingers over his chest, feeling as if I was leaving lines of fire behind. His heart picked up its beat. 'I already feel pretty sparkly.'

He kissed my hair, a gesture so tender it brought tears to my eyes. 'That's good—but you'd better stop doing that or we'll both be in trouble.' He caught my fingers in his hand, pressing them to his shirt.

'Zed, is this all real?'

'Yeah, it is. Your gift's just waiting for you to reach for it.'

'I'm afraid to do that.'

He rested his chin on the top of my head. 'I know. And I can wait—as long as you need. Come, sit on my lap for a moment.'

He led me over to the drum kit and sat on the stool.

'You want me to sit on your lap there? I'll fall off.'

'Not if you sit facing me.'

I laughed but it sounded kinda sad. 'This is crazy.'

'Maybe. But I'm going to enjoy it.'

I sat on his lap so I could rest my head on his chest, arms wrapped around him.

'You hold on now, you hear?'

'Uh-huh.'

He took the drumsticks and began to play the percussion part for the song we had first performed together as the jazz band. I hummed along.

'We could really do with the piano but I don't want you to move,' he said softly in my ear.

'We can imagine it.'

The beat was slow and hypnotic. Calming. I closed my eyes, listening as he began crooning the words to 'Hallelujah'. He had a nice voice—a tenor, pitch perfect.

'You just gonna sit there or sing with me?' he asked.

'I'm just gonna sit.'

'What's wrong with your voice?'

'I don't sing. Never have—not for a long time.'

'There's only me here. I won't laugh.'

All my life, singing had been a no-go area. I didn't want to bring that into this lovely moment. 'I'll just listen.'

'OK. But I'll get you singing yet.'

Chapter 14

The weeks that followed were frustrating for both of us. Only able to sneak a few moments alone at school, we could never just be together. We had to be careful not to be labelled a couple by other students in case word got out to whoever was after Zed's family. This led to guilt as I had to lie to my closest friends about what was going on. And there was still Zed's premonition to worry about—he was angry because he couldn't stick to my side to keep me safe and I was getting jumpy any time I was out after dark. The whole situation added up to major stress for us both. Two threats too many.

'Something happen between you and Zed, Sky?' asked Tina one afternoon as we helped decorate the form room for Hallowe'en.

I hung a row of pumpkin lights over the whiteboard. 'No.'

'You seemed on the point of something until he gave you that black eye. Was there more to that than you said?'

Yeah, just a bit. 'Like what?'

She shrugged, looking uncomfortable. 'He didn't hit you or anything?'

'No!'

'Just that the Benedicts are a little strange. No one really gets to know them. We talk about them, of course, but no one from school's dated them that I've heard about. Who knows what secrets they're hiding up there?'

I decided to fight fire with fire. 'You mean like their mad granny locked in the cellar? Or the voodoo dolls hanging by their necks over the corpses of their victims?'

She looked shamefaced now. 'I wasn't thinking that.'

'Zed does not beat up his girlfriends.'

She pounced. 'So you are his girlfriend?'

Oops. 'Not really. Just a friend.'

'Must admit I'm relieved to hear that.' Tina stretched out some cobweb material over the notice board. 'Did you know that Nelson went a round with him about what he did to you?'

'He didn't!'

'Yeah, in the guys' changing room after basketball practice.'

'I told him it was my fault, not Zed's!'

'Nelson has this protective streak a mile wide. You must have noticed. I think it's his version of his grandmother's desire to keep tabs on us all.'

'Did anyone get hurt?'

'No. Coach broke it up. Put them both in detention. Zed's on the watch list again for suspension.'

'I didn't want this.'

'What? Boys fighting over you? You should be flattered.'

'They're idiots.'

'Yeah, they're boys. Goes with the territory.'

I crossed my fingers. 'Look, Zed and me, we like each other, but it's not going to go any further.' At least, not until we'd sorted out the death threat.

'OK, I hear you. You're safe.' But I could tell she wasn't convinced. 'So, you want to come Trick-or-Treating with us?'

'Isn't that for little kids?'

'Doesn't stop us big ones having a party. We get dressed up, enjoy the show on the streets then go hang out back at someone's house. My mom said we can go to mine this year.'

'What kind of dressed up?'

'Any kind of fancy dress. Witch, ghoul, voodoo-doll-hanging-over-the-corpse-of-a-dead-granny-from-the-cellar—that kind of stuff.'

'Sounds fun.'

To my embarrassment, Simon was really into the idea of making a Hallowe'en costume. He often used materials in his art and got a bit carried away when I made the mistake of telling him about Trick-or-Treating. He constructed a skeleton suit for me out of material that glowed spectre-like in white light and a really convincing skull head mask. He made a costume for himself and Sally too.

'You're not thinking of coming with me?' I asked in horror as he displayed the masks in the kitchen on Hallowe'en morning.

'Of course.' His tone was deadpan but I caught the laughter in his eyes. 'Just what a teenager wants: her parents tagging along to a friend's party on her first evening out after grounding.'

'Tell me he's lying!' I appealed to Sally.

'Of course, he is. We were just reading up on the American customs at Hallowe'en and understand that it is our duty as fine upstanding citizens of Wrickenridge to man the door in as scary a fashion as possible and spread tooth decay among the younger part of the population.'

'You're going to hand out candy dressed like that?'

'Yep.' Simon tapped his skull mask affectionately.

'I'm glad I won't be home.'

My friends met up outside the grocery store at seven, forming a gaggle of witches, ghosts, and zombies. The atmosphere was perfect: dark, moonless, and there was even a mist to add to the ghoulish theme. Zoe had dressed in a fantastic vampire outfit with red-lined cape and white fangs. Tina chose the warlock look, pointy hat and long cape, face painted with silver stars. Nelson came as a zombie—a no-brainer (ha ha) for him. I felt a bit self-conscious in my figure-hugging skeleton suit.

Nelson rapped on the top of my plaster skull. 'Knock, knock, who's there?'

'It's me—Sky.'

'It's me, Sky who?'

'Shut up, Nelson.'

He laughed. 'You look great. Where did you get the suit? Did you hire it?'

I took off the mask. 'No, Simon made it.'

'Awesome.'

'He and Sally are sitting at home in similar outfits.'

He playfully began dragging me in the direction of my house. 'No way? We'll have to go up there.'

I jabbed him in the ribs. 'If you suggest that to the others, I will personally pull your dead brain out of your ears and feed it to your fellow zombies.'

'Ouch! Good visual threat—I like it.'

I was feeling a bit cold in my costume. 'Can we get moving, Tina?'

'Yeah, let's.'

Tina handed round pumpkin-shaped lanterns on the end of poles and we processed through the streets enjoying the show. Little children paraded past with their parents, dressed in a bizarre selection of costumes. The spooky theme seemed to have got diluted somewhere along the way because it was perfectly acceptable to wear your favourite princess costume if you were a kindergarten girl, or come dressed as Spider-Man if you were a boy. The emphasis was definitely on 'treat' rather than 'trick'. I saw a couple of older kids fighting each other with water pistols, but most were too busy racking up a sugar high to cause any damage to houses where they got no answer.

As we neared Tina's house, a werewolf emerged from the mist to join our group, complete with full face mask sprouting hair from ears, and a pair of shaggy paws. On any other night, this would be a cause for alarm; on Hallowe'en no one batted an eyelid.

The werewolf slipped through the crowd and sidled up to me. Bending down, he growled in my ear.

'Zed?' I yelped.

'Ssh. I don't want people to know I'm here. And don't, you know, *think* to me, in case someone's listening.'

I started to giggle, absurdly glad that he had sneaked out to see me. 'Ah, Wolfman, you are a master of disguise, fooling the bad guys with your cunning.'

'I blend, don't I? I knew you'd be out after dark, so here I am.'

I really didn't need a reminder of the real horror haunting us on this night of pretend terrors, but I did feel happier now he was beside me.

A shaggy paw insinuated itself around my waist. 'I'm not sure I approve of this costume of yours. Couldn't you put a cloak on or something?'

'I feel really cold. Simon didn't think of this when he made it for me.'

He shrugged out of his coat and slipped it over my shoulders. 'Your *dad* made this? Are we talking about the same guy who wants to lock you away until you're thirty? Has he had a personality change since I last saw him?'

'It's artistic. He wasn't thinking about how his daughter looks—just getting the right shape. He and Sally are at home in identical outfits.'

He chuckled softly.

'So, did you tell your parents you were going out?' I asked.

'No, they still think we need to circle the wagons back home. I'm tinkering with the bike in the garage. Xav's covering for me.'

'How are they going to react?'

He frowned. 'I can't see—it's hard with family. There are so many possibilities in a house of savants that I think the future gets fuzzy, like interference on a cellphone. And it's weird: I've noticed that the closer I get to you, the less I see about you.'

'Does that mean I could beat you at cards now?'

'Probably. But I might not be able to help you out with your goal-keeping either, so there's a drawback.'

'That's fine by me. It's not nice knowing you see so much all the time. Makes me feel, I dunno, *caged* by the future.'

'Yeah, I prefer it this way. It feels more normal.'

We reached Tina's house. She'd really gone to town: carved pumpkins grinned in every window and the porch was festooned with spiders, bats, and snakes. Her mum opened the door dressed as a witch, with massive false eyelashes and crimson nails. I could see Tina's older brothers out the back, forking garden trimmings on to a bonfire.

'Let's go in and stay for a while, then slip away,' suggested Zed. 'I really want to be alone with you for an hour or so. It's killing me having to steal all these moments at school, always worrying someone's going to walk in on us.'

'OK, but I can't bail out too early.'

'I'll keep away from you in there. If anyone recognizes me beneath the costume, they won't think anything of it. Tina did invite me.'

The party gathered in the kitchen. Tina's mum had a huge cauldron full of popcorn for us to eat and green jelly which we had to feed each other blindfold. Not possible when wearing a skull mask so I took this off and joined in. Zed hung back, keeping his werewolf gear on.

I drew Nelson as my jelly feeder with Tina shouting instructions. Inevitably he got more on me than in my mouth.

'Yuck. I'm going to need a shower now!' I squawked as the spoon hit my neck and jelly fell on my chest.

'Apple bobbing!' suggested Tina. 'That should help.'

I proved useless at getting my apple. Zoe was the best.

'It's her big mouth,' explained Tina, ducking as Zoe flicked water at her.

I had to be home at midnight, so if I wanted to spend some time with Zed, I needed to make my excuses at ten thirty.

'You OK getting back?' Tina asked, shuffling the songs on the iPod to start the dancing.

'Yes, I've got a lift arranged.'

'OK. See you tomorrow.'

'Thanks for the party. It was brilliant.'

She laughed. 'I love it when you speak Brit, Sky. *It was brilliant,*' she mimicked. Cackling with laughter, she swooped on Nelson and hauled him into the middle of the kitchen to dance.

I emerged on to the porch to find Zed waiting for me.

'Ready?' he asked.

'Uh-huh. Where are we going?'

'Let's head up to your place. There's a coffee bar on Main Street that should be open.'

'Is that safe?'

'Should be. We'll go to one of the booths at the back. As much as I appreciate the value of blending, I don't want to sit with this mask on all night.'

I held out the skull. 'Should I put this back on? I feel really stupid wearing it.'

'You might want to think that people can see who's wearing the skeleton suit if you don't.'

'Good point.' I put it back on then couldn't help laughing at us. 'This is our second date, right?'

'See, I told you I'd come up with something better.' He laced his fingers in mine: hairy claws to skele-bones.

The coffee bar was busy with parents taking a warming break after traipsing round after their hyper kids all evening. We had to wait for the back booth to come free.

'What'll you have?' Zed asked.

'Hot chocolate with all the trimmings.'

He carried over a tall glass brimming with cream and marshmallows, a chocolate stirring stick on the side. He'd chosen black coffee for himself.

'You don't know what you're missing.' I sighed with ecstasy as I took a hit of gooey marshmallow mixed with chocolate syrup.

'I think I'm probably getting as much pleasure watching you.' He sipped his coffee. 'I know it's a cheap date—sorry about that.'

'Yeah, you know me: I'm sitting here calculating how much you spent. Next time I'm expecting caviar at a five star restaurant.'

'I can stretch to a burger at the diner if you're hungry.'

I tugged a paw off. 'Don't be daft. My treat next time. Let's keep this equal.'

He stroked the back of my hand, sending a host of tingles dancing down my spine. 'I don't mind splitting the bill, but I kinda prefer buying for my date. I don't think I'd like it if you paid for me.'

I laughed. 'You grew up with cavemen, right?'

'You've met my dad and my brothers. I rest my case.'

We walked back through the now much quieter streets. The snow-capped mountains gleamed in the moonlight, the stars flecks of white in the black sky, so distant but acutely bright.

'Makes me feel very small,' I said, imagining all the miles between us and the nearest of them.

'I hate to break it to you, Sky, but you are small.'

I batted him in the stomach and he obligingly let out an 'oof' of air, though I doubted I'd done any injury to him. 'Look, I was having a moment here—one of those "isn't the universe mind-blowing?" things. Have some respect.'

He grinned. 'It's a challenge when you're wearing a bone suit. Do you realize you're shining in the moonlight? I've never had a date do that before.'

'And just who have you dated, Mr Benedict? Tina says your family don't go out with girls from Wrickenridge.'

'That's true. You're the exception. I dated a few—from Aspen mostly.' He squeezed my waist. 'How about you?'

I blushed, wishing I hadn't started this conversation. 'My friends back home did set me up with a boy once. It was a disaster. He was so in love with himself, it wasn't true.'

'So he wanted you for arm candy?'

'What?'

'For image.'

'I suppose. Only went out twice before I got fed up. So you see my experience is pretty limited.'

'Can't say I'm sorry to hear that. Did you enjoy the party?'

'The games were silly but fun.'

'I hoped you'd mention them. I was particularly intrigued by what happened to that jelly.' He started nuzzling my neck. 'Hmm. Yep, you definitely didn't get it all off.'

'Zed!' My protest was only half-hearted—I was enjoying his attentions far too much.

'Ssh! I'm busy here.'

When 'clean up' as he called it was over, we turned into my road. As we did so, two boys dressed as axe murderers ran out of the mist, yelling at the tops of their voices. Their hands were bloody and they had fake knives through their heads. One carried a blade in his hands.

'Here's some more to massacre! Kill the wolf! Kill the skeleton!' he screamed. 'Charge!' He ran straight for me; his bag of candy burst, scattering sweets all over the sidewalk. He didn't slow, his blood lust very convincing. The knife came plunging towards me even as I tried to duck out of the way. I screamed, half afraid of him.

Zed went crazy. He grabbed the boy's wrist and twisted so the knife clattered to the ground. He then jumped on top of him, pinning him down, wrenching his arms behind his back.

'Stop it, Zed!' I shouted, tugging my mask off. 'He didn't mean any harm—it's a fake.'

The other boy leapt on Zed and fists began to fly, the three of them rolling around in a mix of pretend blood and squashed sweets. I couldn't get anywhere near to pull the boys off Zed. My screams and the swearing from the fighters brought the neighbours running.

Mrs Hoffman bustled out of her door. 'Police! I'll call the police!' She disappeared back inside.

'No, don't! Stop it, Zed—stop it!'

Worse, my parents came out, recognizing my voice above the rest.

'Sky, what the hell's happening?' Simon shouted, sprinting towards me.

'Stop them, Simon, stop them!'

Simon weighed in and caught the smallest of the three by the back of his jeans. The little guy came up swinging just as a cop car turned into our lane. There was a short burst of siren, then revolving lights illuminated the scene. Two other neighbours reached the scuffle before the policeman could get out of his vehicle; they separated Zed from the remaining axeman.

The cop took one look at the mayhem and sighed. 'Who's gonna tell me what this is all about?' He took out his notebook. 'I know you, Zed Benedict, and these are the Gordano twins, yes? And this little . . . er . . . lady skeleton?'

'Her name's Sky, Sky Bright, my daughter,' Simon said stiff-ly. 'She wasn't fighting.'

'You're the English family, right?'

'Yes, sir.'

'I know these boys—they're good boys,' he said, looking at the twins. 'Never had no trouble from them. Who started this?'

The policeman's gaze turned to Zed and me. He thought he knew who was to blame.

'He attacked Sky.' Zed wiped blood from a split lip.

'Well, duh! I was just playing, man: it's Hal-oh-een, remem-ber? Zed went ballistic, Officer Hussein.' The axeman hugged his ribs.

'Let's take this down to the station, boys. I'll get the duty doctor to take a look at you and phone your parents.'

'Aw, officer!' groaned the twins.

'In the car.'

Zed shot me a desperate look. Our secret date was about to get exposed big time.

'And you, young lady, I think we'll need your side of this too. Perhaps your parents can bring you down. I seem to have my hands full of psycho killers and werewolves.'

'I'll bring her,' said Simon in clipped tones.

Great. Date number two ends in the police station.

Chapter 15

Officer Hussein wouldn't let us talk to each other until he'd had a chance to get our own version of events. I didn't dare risk telepathy, though the temptation was huge. But there was so much angry emotion rippling off Simon that I doubted any message would be able to penetrate the storm cloud.

'I'm not going to ask what you were doing with him until we get back home,' Simon fumed, as he gripped the steering wheel, driving me down to the station.

Now there was something to look forward to.

'But you are in trouble, Sky. You broke our trust. We asked you to keep away from him for your own safety.'

He was right. Of course, he was right. But it wasn't as if I'd planned it all. I'd just got carried away by the moment. We thought we'd taken enough precautions to make a simple date in a café a reasonable thing to do.

'And I did not expect to have to spend my evening ferrying you to the town lockup!'

I hugged my knees, my head buzzing.

'We're trying to make a good name for ourselves in Wrick-enridge, Sky. Your antics aren't helping. Mr Rodenheim might send us packing if we reflect badly on his centre.'

I dropped my forehead to my knees. I'd been bad.

Simon looked across at me, alerted by my silence that all was not well.

'Oh, bloody hell, darling, don't do that.' He pulled the car over and caressed the top of my head. 'I'm just scared for you.'

'Sorry.'

'You make me feel like a monster. I'm cross, but it's more at those idiotic boys than at you. I know you didn't have anything to do with that. Please.'

I looked up at him. He must have seen the tears in my eyes. 'I just wanted to be with him.'

'I know, love.'

'Is that wrong?'

'Not in the normal course of things, no.'

'We just went to the café. We kept our masks on almost all the time when we were on the streets.'

Simon heaved a sigh. 'Oh, to be sixteen again. Just a coffee and it's become a police matter.'

'Zed's on edge because of what happened in the woods. The axe boy was really convincing—and I screamed—I couldn't help myself. Zed thought I was in danger.'

'So, he over-reacted. I can understand that seeing how it's my fatal flaw. Let's go and find out what we can do for him then.'

Zed was sitting in the waiting area but the officer on duty ushered me through without letting us talk. I was taken into Officer Hussein's office as the Gordano twins were leaving in the custody of their mother. I wished I'd had time to change out of my skeleton suit.

'Not her fault,' mumbled the bigger twin.

'Looks like trash to me,' said Mrs Gordano, her nose in the air.

'Sky, take a seat.' Officer Hussein pushed a bottle of water towards me. 'I think I've got the full picture now, but why don't you tell me your story.'

I briefly ran through the events from leaving the café.

'What I can't understand,' said the officer, scratching his chest wearily—it had been a long night and it was only midnight, 'is why Zed couldn't see that it was a joke? He's a big guy, taking on a boy a head shorter than him. It just don't click for me.'

'Zed Benedict was looking out for his girl, officer,' said Simon, surprising me when he came to Zed's defence. 'He may be a head taller than that young man, but Sky is smaller than either of them. He would have seen a boy going for her with a knife. Sometimes you can't think straight when you are scared for someone.'

'Was anyone hurt?' I asked.

Officer Hussein tapped his pad. 'Not seriously. Ben Gordano has a couple of loose teeth but the dentist should be able to sort those out. It'll cost though.'

'Perhaps Zed could split the bill? It seems a suitable punishment,' Simon suggested.

Officer Hussein rose to his feet.

'Yeah, I guess that's right. No one need go away with a record for this.'

He led the way back to the waiting room. Zed's family had pitched up in the meantime—parents, Xav, Yves, and Victor all were there—and he was having to sit through a lecture on sneaking out and brawling in the streets. He looked frustrated rather than repentant, back to the sullen Wolfman of the first days of our acquaintance.

Officer Hussein clapped his hands to gain their attention.

'All right, all right, people, let's move this along. I want a word with Zed, then you can all go.' He took Zed into the back room, leaving me with the Benedicts.

Victor came forward. 'Mom, Dad, this is Mr Bright, Sky's father.'

Our parents exchanged stiff nods. I don't think Saul thought I was sweet any more. It looked more as if I left a sour taste in their mouths. Only Xav and Yves gave me a friendly smile.

'Like the suit,' whispered Xav. 'You and your dad thinking of starting a new fashion?'

Yves scratched his chin. 'Fascinating. Do you know, every bone is anatomically correct? Whoever made this has the mind of a medic.'

It only then struck me that Simon hadn't changed either. He'd thrown on a coat but there was unmistakable evidence peeking out that he too was wearing luminescent bones.

I groaned. 'Kill me now and bury me.'

'I thought the idea of the skeleton was that someone had already done that,' teased Xav.

'Word's going to get around, you know.' Yves's eyes twinkled behind his glasses.

'Well, isn't that a comforting thought.'

Xav rubbed his hands. 'Yeah, everyone's going to be talking about how Zed got cuffed and stuffed.'

'He wasn't cuffed.'

'But he was stuffed in the back of the police car. Besides the handcuffs make for a better story. You're both going to be quite infamous. I think Zed'll like the new edge to his rep.' He tweaked the unravelling end of my French plait. 'Don't worry, Sky, I'll still talk to you.'

'Thanks. You're a hero.'

Our parting from the Benedicts reminded me of an exchange of hostile prisoners in one of those old war films.

Zed and I were kept apart then frogmarched to our separate vehicles. He was looking ashen.

I feel like I've been suckerpunched. He risked the thought even though we might be heard. *I can't leave without saying sorry. Again.*

What happened?

I lost it, flipped out—all thanks to my freaking gift. I'd seen what was going to happen, you see, months back. Saw you being attacked with a knife. I hadn't realized it was a fake.

But that's good isn't it? The threat wasn't real.

Yeah, but you've just swapped my imagined threat for the real one of assassins. Congratulations and welcome to the wonderful world of the Benedict family. I'd better stop talking. Dad's giving me these weird looks.

Zed?

Yeah?

Take care.

You too. Love you.

He cut off.

'Sky, are you all right?' Simon asked, turning the key in the ignition. 'You're looking a bit pale.'

Zed had said he loved me. Was it just a throw-away comment or did he mean it?

'I'm fine. Just need to get some sleep.'

Simon yawned. 'We'll have to report to the boss first.'

Zed loved me—maybe. I wasn't sure if I wanted to believe him. The last thing I wanted was to fall in love because, deep down, I remembered that love hurt.

Our grand plan to pretend we weren't a couple had been blown apart by our visit to the police station. The gossip was too hot for me to put the fire out with indifference or denial.

162

Zed must've realized for he came to find me after my first class, not even bothering to hide the fact that he was towing me into an empty room.

'Are you OK?' He gave me a hug.

'Fine.'

'I've been hearing about this drop-dead gorgeous skeleton from everyone. Seems she had to report to a police station with some idiot who took on a couple of sophomores.'

'What did your parents say?'

He gave a hollow laugh. 'You really want to know? I'm going to have to work off my debt for Ben's teeth with extra chores and go round to apologize. I've had to swear not to sneak out with you again. They make me feel about nine years old. You?'

'It was OK. Simon blames you.'

'Great.'

I wanted to ask Zed if he meant what he said about loving me but was too scared to ask.

He hugged me. 'Yeah, I did.'

'Stop nicking stuff out of my head.'

He ignored my protest. 'I think I knew it from the moment you stood up to me in the parking lot, but, last night, when I saw you in the station dressed as a skeleton, defending me to the police, I knew for sure.' He gazed down at me, framing my face in his hands. 'I understand you still have issues with what I've been telling you, but it's more than just a random pairing, Sky: I really feel so much for you, it's scaring me to death. You are just . . . just everything—your smile, the way you think, the way you get embarrassed when I tease you, your stubborn streak.'

I sort of wanted to hear this—but also didn't: how mixed up is that? 'You've noticed I'm stubborn?'

'Can't miss it. To me, you're the theme that harmonizes

perfectly with mine.' He trapped my gaze with his. 'I'm in love with you.'

'You are?'

His eyes deepened to a darker shade. 'Sky, I've not felt like this before and it's terrifying.'

'Well, wow. Um . . . perhaps you should try to get over it. I'm not good at this relationship stuff.'

'Sure you are. You just need time to adjust.' He put his arms around me so I could rest my head against him and listen to his heart beating strong and steady.

I was so confused. Savants—soulfinders—all that did not hide that this was really about being committed to him. I'd spent many years defending myself by not exposing too much of my heart to other people; could I trust him enough to risk loving him back? What if I fell in love with him and got hurt? What if something happened to him?

'What's going on now? Has Victor had any luck finding the people after you or who betrayed you?' I asked.

Zed leant against a desk, positioning me so my back rested on his chest, his hands looped round me, chin on the top of my head.

'He thinks it's most likely it goes back to Daniel Kelly.'

I turned to look up at his face. 'Hey, I've heard of him. Doesn't he build skyscrapers?'

'That's only a tiny part of what he does. He's currently building a city-within-a-city in Las Vegas. It's a massive complex of hotels, casinos, and apartments. But he does it with dirty money—not that anyone dare say as they'd be crushed by a ton of lawsuits. He's got various relations heading different parts of his empire. Some are complete crooks—no better than the mafia. We caught a couple of them in Denver after a hit—we think on his orders, not that we could prove it; they went down for murder one a month ago—it was big news at the time.'

'I remember them talking at school about it.'

'Vick is trying to find out if they've got a savant on their payroll but it's tough. They're hardly going to talk to a Benedict and his sources are coming up dry. Kelly's got it in for us now. Will and Uriel are at college in Denver so they're watching each other's back. The rest of us are confined to barracks.'

I linked my fingers with his.

'What's Will's gift?'

'He's most like Dad, can sense trouble. He's great at telekinesis too.'

'What's that?'

'Moving stuff.'

'Like lemons.'

'Yeah.' He smirked. 'I'm way better than Xav at it.'

The bell rang in the hallway. 'I'm missing maths.'

'That's too bad. I've missed being with you.'

'I'll get detention.'

'Then I'll get it too. Great idea.'

'Won't you risk getting thrown out—Tina said you were in trouble again.'

'No, they won't dare. I'll send you along to the principal's office in your skele-suit. Man, I love that outfit.'

When no class came in, we realized we had another hour to ourselves.

'So are you going to tell me the rest of it, about your family?'

He sat on the windowsill and helped me up beside him. 'Yeah, I suppose it's past time. We all can do different stuff like telepathy, but we each have a main gift. You know about Dad sensing danger. Mom sees the future and can read thoughts off people: she's the most like me, I guess. Together they can maintain a guard around the house—it's part of their combined power as soulfinders. Trace can read objects. If he touches something, he can see the person or the event that brought it there.'

'Very handy for a cop.'

'We think so. It's either that or be an archaeologist. Uriel, I think I mentioned, sees the past. Victor can manipulate people's thinking . . . '

'What!'

'Yeah, he channels emotion and thoughts. Not so good when you find yourself agreeing to do the dishes when it's his turn. Xav's a healer. And Yves can handle energy, make things explode, catch fire and so on.'

'Bloody hell! Yves looks so . . . well, so friendly and studious.'

'It was scary when he was a toddler, Mom says, but he's got it under control.'

'How can your family do these things?'

'We just can. It's like why do you have blue eyes?'

The question fell like an ice cube down my neck. 'I guess I must have inherited them from my birth parents, but I wouldn't know, would I? They dumped me.'

'Sorry, that was stupid of me. I saw something about that in your memories.'

'Sally and Simon couldn't have children so took me on when everyone else thought I was too disturbed for adoption. I didn't really speak for four years until they rescued me. They had the patience to coax me out of my shell.'

'They're special people.'

'Yes, they are.'

'In the most important respect, they're your real parents now—I can see things from them in you.'

'Like what?'

'You're as nice as your mom about people and that stubbornness, that's from your dad.'

'Good.' I liked the idea of inheriting Simon's grit. 'He's a Yorkshireman. He'll be pleased to hear it's catching.'

'You shouldn't be scared of what you inherited from your

biological parents. I can't see anything to be ashamed of when I look at you.'

'Just don't look too hard.' I crossed my arms.

'I guess one of them at least must have been a savant.' He snagged a curl and twirled it playfully. 'My family comes from savants on both sides. Dad's people are part Ute—that's a Native American tribe. Mom says she has gypsies and all sorts in her bloodline. Dash of Irish somewhere along the way and a big dose of Mexico. I'd say we were doomed from birth.'

'That's how it works?'

'Yeah. My parents are both key players in the Savant Network—it's a kind of world-wide web for those of us with a gift. Mom's gift helps check those who join, making sure they are in it for the right reasons.'

'So bad guys need not apply?'

He shook his head. 'Not that they'd want to. The Net is about using our gift for the benefit of others. We keep ourselves secret so we can live as near to normal lives as possible, but that doesn't stop us helping where we can.'

'And you really think I'm a savant too?'

'Yeah I do.'

'But I can't move things.'

'Have you tried?'

'Well, no. I wouldn't know what to do. I thought I saw stuff once—aura, I suppose you'd call them—but I don't any more.' Not that I'd admit, anyway.

We sat for a while, hand in hand, gazing out of the window. The skies were thick with iron-grey clouds. Snow began to fall, thick and fast, gusts of wind driving it horizontal before letting it drop back to a gentle downward progress.

'I think this is it,' said Zed. 'The first proper snow. I'd love to be able to teach you to ski but it's not safe for you to be with me out there.'

'I suppose it wouldn't be a good idea.'

'You should get Tina to take you out: she's pretty good.'

'I might do that. But she'll laugh at me.'

'Yeah, she will.' He was doing it again—reading the future.

'Then again nothing can be as humiliating as the skeleton suit.'

'Don't knock the suit. I'm preserving that and gonna beg you to wear it on special occasions.'

I kicked myself. I really mustn't fall in love with this guy, but I wanted to curl up and tuck myself inside him, never to leave him. 'Will you teach me to shield? I don't want your family reading every thought that crosses my mind.'

He put an arm round me. 'No, we wouldn't want that. I catch some of them sometimes, you know. I like the one where you . . . ' He whispered the rest in my ear, causing me to die of embarrassment.

'Shields—I need shields,' I said when my cheeks stopped burning.

He laughed. 'OK. The technique is simple but it just takes practice. It's best to use visualization. Imagine building walls, putting yourself inside them, keeping the emotions, ideas, thoughts safe behind the barriers.'

'What kind of wall?'

'It's your wall; you decide.'

I closed my eyes and recalled the wallpaper of my bedroom. Turquoise.

'That's good.'

'You can see what I'm seeing?'

'An echo. When someone's shielded I see a shadow, a blank. Yours is a pale blue colour.'

'My bedroom walls.'

'Yeah, that's good. Safe, familiar. When you throw that up between you and anyone listening, they should find it hard to get behind it. But it takes work—and we all forget from time to time.'

'The savant working for the shooter—has he let his shield drop?'

Zed shook his head. 'That's why we know he's good—powerful. Either that or he's long gone, but we doubt it.'

'They'll try again?'

'We think so. We hope so, because now we are expecting them, we have a chance of catching them, and they might roll over on the mole in the FBI. But knowing what's in the wind, you be extra careful, promise?' He ran his finger lightly over the back of my hand, sending a shiver down my spine.

'I promise.'

'I'm keeping you a secret, even from my family. You're too precious to risk anywhere near this mess.'

Tina couldn't understand why I wasn't getting Zed to teach me to ski. 'You've got one of the best skiers in the district as a boyfriend—and I'm still angry with you for not telling me the truth about that, by the way—and you ask me to teach you?'

'That's right.' I picked up a scraper and helped her clear the snow off her car windscreen in the school parking lot.

'Why?'

'Because according to Zed you totally rock on the slopes yourself. You're my Obi Wan and I am your faithful apprentice.'

She preened with pleasure at the praise. 'Thanks. I didn't think he noticed girls like me.'

'He's not what you think. He's not as unapproachable as he seems. He's just got this . . . this problem with relaxing around people.' And he's stressed out half the time witnessing major crimes for the FBI, but she didn't need to know that part. 'And our parents aren't too keen we spend time together—not since we ended up at the police station.'

'Oh my God, it's like *West Side Story*!'

I didn't think that very accurate. If my memory of the musical was any good, I don't think either of them was pursued by assassins with extra-sensory perception.

'Fine, I'll teach you,' continued Tina. 'Besides, there's only so many times a girl wants to fall on her butt in front of the boy she's out to impress.'

Actually, she had a point. Perhaps it would be better to learn from her.

'Wisdom you speak, Obi Tina.'

She laughed. 'None of that—I'm the one who gets to speak backwards—no, we're both wrong—that's the little green guy, Yoda.'

I slapped my forehead. 'You're right. So I just get to pout and act badly when you try and teach me anything.'

'Try channelling Luke rather than Annakin—the outcome is better. I'll take you Sunday morning if you like, after church. We finish about eleven so I'll pick you up at quarter past.'

'Great.'

'Got any gear?'

'No. What do I need?'

'Don't worry. I'll bring you my old suit—I grew out of it years ago. You can hire skis at the sports store.'

'I can't wait.'

'Think you're going to be a natural?'

'Um.'

'Sure you are. Feel the force, Sky.'

I wasn't a natural skier—not by a long way. But I was a natural at falling over. My balance needed a lot of work. I'd been compared to Bambi before but today I felt like him when he first gets up on his hooves, legs slipping in all directions.

'Don't you sometimes have those daydreams,' I panted, spitting out snow after my most recent face plant, 'where you try something new and find yourself to be an undiscovered talent?'

Tina patted my back consolingly. 'All the time.'

'It's just not happening here.'

We were still at the foot of the nursery slopes. I could see the cable car doing good business taking the more experienced skiers up to the peak, Xav manning the ticket booth. It was a perfect day for skiing—sky pale blue, snow glistening with seductive promise, the heights beckoning. The mountains were at their most benign, Old Man Weather in his chair, rocking gently, no nasty changes of mood in mind.

Tina caught the direction of my gaze. 'Zed's probably up top. Mr Benedict pays the boys to work the weekend shift.'

At least he wasn't here to see my failure. I was providing Xav with enough entertainment as it was.

'OK, let's go again. Remember, Sky, it's just your first lesson.'

I watched with a sensation of despair as a little four year old whizzed by on mini skis. She wasn't even using sticks.

'You can't compare yourself to them. They don't have so far to fall and are indestructible at that age. Once more. Yeah, that's it. Keep the skis parallel. No, no, don't let them spread!'

'Ouch.' My thighs were screaming protests as I nearly did the splits.

'That was good—better.'

'Better than what?'

'Better than the time before. Had enough for today?'

'Oh yes.'

'Would you mind if I went up to do a run down?'

'Of course not.'

'You could come too.'

'You are joking?'

'You could take the cable car back again. You might like the view from the top.'

I grinned, pleased that Tina was coming round to Zed going out with me. She had dropped her dire warnings, decreasing the threat level to 'yellow alert' rather than 'crisis'. 'I might just do that.'

chapter 16

Skis on our shoulders, we trudged to the queue for the lift. Xav's eyes widened when he saw me at the kiosk. He shot a panicked look at Tina.

'Sky, sweetheart, don't you think it's a bit early to take a run from the top?' he asked.

'No, I feel just in the mood.' I suppressed my grin.

'Tina, you need to talk her out of this. She could kill herself.'

'Don't sweat it, Xav. She thinks she has undiscovered talent.'

He covered the ticket with his hand. 'Not selling you one, Sky.'

I rolled my eyes. 'For heaven's sake, Xav, I'm not completely stupid. I'm just going up for the ride. Tina's the one who's going to ski down.'

He laughed with relief. 'Great. No charge then. But just to be sure, I'll look after your skis.'

Tina flashed her season ticket and we climbed into the car. The view was spectacular. We hung over the roof of the Benedict house for a second then set off up the cable, brushing the tops of the firs until they too plunged away and we were swinging across a gorge. Below us antlike skiers zipped to and fro, making the whole business look so easy. Ten minutes later we got out at the station at the top. Zed was busy loading the car to go down—there were only a few sightseers like me so it wouldn't take long.

'Grab a coffee.' Tina nudged me towards the concession stand. 'I'll meet you back by the bottom of the cable car in half an hour.'

'OK. Have fun.'

Settling her feet in her skis, she propelled herself off the start of the black run.

'A coffee with milk and a doughnut please,' I asked the shiny faced man at the stall.

'Not skiing, hon?' he asked, handing over my pastry in a white bag.

'First time on skis. I'm rubbish.'

He laughed. 'So am I. That's why I stick to serving coffee.'

'How much?'

'On the house—to celebrate your first experience of skiing.'

'Thanks.'

Zed jogged up behind and scooped me round the waist, lifting me in the air, forcing a squeak from me. 'How's it going?'

'I'm crap at skiing.'

'Yeah, I thought you might be.' He spun me round. 'I've only a minute until the next car arrives, just enough to steal a bite of whatever you've got in there.'

'This your girl, Zed?' asked the stallholder.

'Yeah, José.'

'Why is it all the best ones are always taken? Ah well.' He passed over a Styrofoam cup and winked at me.

Zed took me back to his cabin at the head of the cable car. We could hear the creak and groan of the wheels running the lift. I studied Zed's face as he checked something on the control panel—the width of his shoulders as he reached to make an adjustment to the display, the muscles in his arms flexing. I hadn't got before why my friends spent so much time admiring boys in my old school; now I completely joined that party. Was this gorgeous guy really mine? It was hard to believe I had been so lucky.

'How do you know where the car is?' I asked as Zed absent-mindedly took a bite out of the doughnut. 'Hey!'

He laughed, holding the bag out of my reach, and pointed to a display. There was a series of lights counting down as the cars went over points. 'That shows me I've four minutes.'

Jumping, I grabbed the doughnut back and licked at the jam.

'Sweet tooth?'

'You've noticed?'

'The hot chocolate with everything was a bit of a clue.'

I took a bite then handed it back. 'You can finish it.'

He wolfed it down then took a slurp of coffee. 'Ugh! Milk. I should've guessed. I need something to take the taste away.' He tapped his chin, one eye on the monitor. 'I know!' He bent down and nibbled at my lips. I felt my body shift, a strange heaviness that urged me to hang on tightly to him or collapse in a heap at his feet. He gave a hum of pleasure and deepened the kiss.

We were interrupted by the arrival of the next batch of skiers. Unfortunately they consisted mainly of kids from high school who banged on the door and whistled when they saw what was going on in the cabin.

'Here, Zed, stop making out and let us out!' yelled a girl from my science class.

'Down, boy!' barked a guy from senior year.

'OK, OK,' replied Zed, dropping me back on my feet. He

looked pleased rather than embarrassed while my face was exploring all the possibilities in the red spectrum.

Once the skiers were off to their chosen runs, I stayed with Zed for another ten minutes then caught the car down the hill.

'Thanks for coming up,' Zed said, closing the door behind me. 'You've still got a bit of sugar on your lip.' He brushed a tender kiss over my mouth, then tugged my jacket straight.

'Hmm, I think I'll have to visit you again. It appears that the cable car is going to be more my thing than skiing.'

'Take care.'

'I'll try. You take care too.'

Tina persisted with my lessons to the point that, on the weekend before Thanksgiving, I could trundle down the nursery run without falling over until I reached the bottom.

'Woo-hoo!' She did a little dance on the spot as I made it. 'Jedi knights watch out!'

I struggled off the skis. 'I don't think I'm much of a threat to the Empire just yet.'

'It's a start—don't knock it.' She picked up her own skis. This Sunday was much cloudier than the first time out on the slopes, the top of the lift obscured from view, the weather in a sullen mood. We queued up for the lift to find Saul on the desk.

'Hi, Tina, Sky.' He let Tina through the turnstile but it didn't click for me. Saul was holding me back. 'No point you going up today, Sky. Xav's on duty. I gave Zed the day off to go boarding.'

'Oh, OK.'

The cable car was about to leave. Tina gave me a wave. 'Wait here. I won't take long skiing down. Weather's too horrid to hang about.'

I moved out of the way. The last of the queue filed inside.

'We can't keep you and Zed apart, can we?' Saul said, coming to sit beside me on a bench in the waiting area as the car began its journey up the hill.

'Seems that way.' I scuffed at the snow. I had an odd feeling that Saul was suspicious of me.

'We don't want anything to happen to either of you.' He stretched out his long legs, the gesture reminding me of his son.

'I know. It's been quiet, hasn't it?'

'Yes, it has. We don't know what to think. I'd like to believe that the threat has gone away but my mind tells me different.'

'They're lying low?'

'That's my guess. I'm sorry you got caught up in this. These people know that if they get one member of my family, they weaken all of us.' His profile looked noble staring out at the mountains, expression resolute. I sensed Saul belonged to the landscape around us in a way few residents did; he was in tune with it, part of the melody. MountainMan—standing as a barrier between his family and danger. 'Victor doesn't think they mind who they hurt,' he continued, 'just as long as the rest of us are so crippled emotionally that we can't function as a team. I've got everyone on lockdown, not just Zed. But we can't keep on like this. Our job's tough and our boys need to be free to let off steam, to forget. They can't if they're not allowed to act natural.'

'I know about the lockdown, Zed told me. But isn't he a bit exposed out here snowboarding? And Xav's up the mountain on his own.'

Saul brushed at the leg seam of his jeans, flicking away a speck of dirt. 'Don't worry about the boys. We've got security in place. Now we know the savant's using shielding, we know what we're looking for. That time in the woods, well, I suppose you could say we were caught with our pants down. Not again. And you, you're being careful?'

'I am. I don't go out on my own. Sally and Simon know to be wary of people we don't recognize.'

'Good. Don't let your guard down.' We sat in silence for a few moments, unspoken words hanging between us.

'Zed's told you, hasn't he?'

He reached out and squeezed my hand. 'Karla and I know. And we couldn't be more pleased. We couldn't help but notice that something momentous had happened to our son. For your sake, for Zed, for the others, we think he's right to keep it a secret until this is resolved.'

'The others?'

'Sky, I don't think you understand just what you're getting yourself into here. You are now Zed's number one priority, just as Karla is mine. Seeing him find that will be tough on the others. It will seem unfair, him being the youngest, that his soulfinder just fell into his lap while the others still have to look for theirs. They'll be delighted for him, but they wouldn't be human if they weren't jealous.'

'I don't want to create problems for your family.'

He patted the back of my hand. 'I know. Just give us time to get through this and they will look forward to welcoming you as one of us.'

'But I don't know about that yet. I'm only just getting used to Zed; I've not thought of anything beyond the next few weeks.'

Saul gave a knowing smile. 'You mustn't worry, Sky, all will fall into place in its own time. You haven't factored in that it's God and nature working this; you'll feel what you need to feel when you're ready.'

I hoped he was right. My feelings for Zed were deepening, but they weren't yet enough to think in terms of a for ever commitment, which is what they were expecting. I knew myself well enough to realize I'd back off big time if anyone forced the issue. So far, Zed seemed to understand that, but how long would his patience last?

I was really disappointed that I didn't see Zed that afternoon, despite hanging out at the end of the runs. Tina came down first, feeling pretty steamed over a boarder who had almost collided with her on the slopes.

'Not Zed?' I asked anxiously.

'No, just an idiot with an inflated ego and no brains, otherwise known as Nelson. He was trying to impress me.' She threw her gear in the back of her car. 'Ready to go home?'

'Yeah, thanks. So he's not persuaded you yet?'

She paused at the driver's side door. 'Of what? That we are perfect for each other? Pur-lease!'

OK: that didn't sound hopeful but I recognized a snit when I saw one and knew better than to try to advance his case when she was in this mood. I slipped into the passenger seat. She turned the ignition and the car took several tries to catch.

'Jeez. Sounds bad. It was working fine this morning.' She thrust into reverse. 'Heap of junk.'

'So I take it favourite brother is demoted?'

'You bet.'

We puttered back into town with the unnerving sensation that the car was about to stall on us every time she slowed for a junction.

'Ready to get out and push?' she joked darkly.

We got as far as Main Street when the electrics gave up on us.

'Tina, I think you'd best take this to the garage.'

'Yeah, I'm getting that message too.' She swung onto the forecourt of the Wrickenridge gas station. Only the pumps were open; the workshops closed for the weekend. Kingsley the mechanic was on duty at the till and came out when hearing an engine in distress.

'Pop the lid, honey,' he told Tina. He peered inside and scratched his head. 'Sounds like the alternator's gone.'

That made it much clearer—not.

He must have noticed our blank expressions. 'It charges the battery. Without it, the power drains and you get this.' He gestured to the car.

'A dead car.' Tina kicked the tyre.

'Temporarily dead car—it's not fatal. I'll fix it for you tomorrow.'

'Thanks, Kingsley.'

'I'll push it into the workshop. It'll be safe enough to leave your gear in the trunk.'

Passing over the car into Kingsley's capable hands, we were left without a ride.

'Well, that blows,' huffed Tina.

I knew the cure for that. 'Buy you a triple chocolate chip muffin?'

She perked up immediately. 'Just what I need. You're a good friend, Sky.'

We had a quick bite in the café. I managed to talk her out of her indignation against Nelson, pointing out that he was only over-eager, not malicious, in his attempts to gain her attention.

'I suppose, but sometimes he acts like a big baby,' she grumbled. 'Why can't he just grow up?'

'Maybe he's just on a steep learning curve.'

She smirked. 'Hey, who's Yoda now?'

I assumed my best wrinkled old man expression. 'Nelson, kind he is; chance you must give him.'

She burst into laughter. 'Get out of here. Yoda so does not have an English accent!'

I raised an eyebrow. 'Other than that you're saying I'm a dead ringer?'

'If the shoe fits.'

'Sheesh, I hate tall girls.'

Outside the café we had to go our separate ways. It was getting dark. Streetlights on Main stuttered on, making it seem even darker in the shadows.

'Thanks for the lesson and sorry about your car.' I zipped up my jacket.

'These things happen. I'll have to see if I can put some extra hours in at the store to pay for the repairs. See you later.'

I dug in my pocket for my mobile to tell Sally and Simon I was heading home.

'Hi, Sally? Tina's had car trouble. I'm walking from Main Street.'

I could hear the sound of tinny music in the background as Sally's voice came through. 'Not on your own?'

'Yes, I know. Not ideal. Can you come and meet me half-way? I don't want to walk home alone.'

'I'm leaving now. I'll see you by the shop. Stay where there are other people around.'

'Fine. I'll wait inside.'

I slipped the phone in my back pocket. There was about five hundred yards between the café and the shop, and I had to cross an intersection with traffic lights. I felt happy walking it as it was well lit and there were always lots of people milling about. Setting off up the hill, I wondered how Zed was getting on. He must have stopped boarding now it was dark. Would his dad tell him I'd been over hoping to see him?

I'd almost reached the intersection when a man jogged up behind me. I took a quick glance. Big. Heavy stubble. He had almost completely shaved his head, apart from a long tail of curly hair at the back. I moved to one side to let him pass.

'Hey, I think you dropped this.' He held out a brown leather purse.

'No, no, it's not mine.' I clutched my bag closer to me, knowing full well that my red wallet was tucked deep inside it.

He gave me an 'aw shucks' grin. 'That's kinda strange— because it has your photo in it.'

'That's not possible.' Perplexed I took the purse from him and flipped open the front section. My face stared back at me. A recent candid shot of me with Zed in the school yard. The note pocket was crammed with dollar bills, far more money than I ever had. 'I don't understand.' I glanced up at pony-tail guy. There was something off about him. I backed away, thrusting it in his hands. 'It's not mine.'

'Sure it is, Sky.'

How did he know my name? 'No, it's really not.' I broke into a run.

'Hey, don't you want the money?' he called, chasing after me.

I reached the corner but the traffic was going so fast I couldn't risk crossing without causing an accident. My moment's hesitation allowed him to catch up. He moved in and I felt something dig into my ribs.

'Then let me explain things more clearly, cupcake. You're going to get in the car with me now without drawing attention to yourself.'

I took a breath to scream, pulling away from his hand.

'Do that and I'll shoot.' He jabbed what I now realized was a gun in my side.

A black SUV with darkened windows screeched to a halt alongside.

'Get in.'

It happened so quickly, so smoothly, I didn't have a chance to formulate a plan of escape. He pushed me into the back seat, forcing my head down as he closed the door. The car accelerated away.

Zed! I screamed in my mind.

'She's using telepathy,' said the man in the front seat, sitting next to the driver. In his late twenties, he had short red hair and a mass of freckles.

Sky? What's wrong? Zed replied instantly.

'That's good. Let him know we've got you, darlin'. Tell him to come get you.' The passenger in the front had a strong Irish accent.

Immediately I shut off my link to Zed. They were using me to draw the Benedicts out.

'She's blocked him out,' said the red-haired man.

The thug in the back seat pulled me up by the scruff of the neck. I got a brief glimpse of my mum waiting outside the store, pulling out her mobile. The one in my back pocket rang.

'Is that him now?' the thug asked. 'Go on, answer it.'

He might not let me speak if I said it was my mother. I slid it from my ski suit but he grabbed it off me and pressed connect.

'We've got her. You know what we want. Eye for an eye, tooth for a tooth, two Benedicts for the two of ours.' He cut the call then chucked the phone out of the window. 'Who needs telepathy? That should do it.'

'It wasn't them—it . . . it was my mum.' I was beginning to shake. The few dull moments of shock were passing into bone-deep fear.

'Same difference.' He shrugged. 'Let her tell the Benedicts.'

I could hear the buzz of voices trying to reach me—not just Zed but the rest of the family too.

I couldn't stop myself answering. *Help me! Please!*

But then the noise deadened and faded out to nothing.

'I let her get one heart wrenching plea through.' The red-haired man rubbed his forehead. 'But those Benedicts are battering away at the shield. Let's get well away from here.'

So he was the savant.

'That's harsh, O'Halloran. You let them hear the little girl's final words and then stopped?' The thug was laughing.

'Yeah, I think it was a nice touch myself. Brings tears to the old eyes, don't it?' He turned round to wink at me. 'Don't fret, my darlin', they'll come for you. The Benedicts won't let one of their own down.'

I curled up into a ball, hugging my knees, putting as much distance as I could between me and the men. Closing my eyes, I concentrated on finding a way through the shield.

'Stop it!' snapped O'Halloran.

My eyes flew open. He was glaring at me in the mirror. I'd managed to affect him with my attempts but I was too clueless about savant stuff to know how to exploit it.

'I'll tell Gator to knock you out if you try that again,' O'Halloran warned.

'What she do?' ponytailed Gator asked.

O'Halloran rubbed his temples again. My assault and that of the Benedicts on his shield was getting to him.

'We have here a baby savant. I've no idea why she don't know what to do with her powers but she has some locked up inside her. She's a telepath.'

The thug looked unsettled now. 'What else she do?'

O'Halloran dismissed me with a shrug. 'Nothing, as far as I know. Don't worry, she won't harm you.'

Gator was scared of savants? That made two of us. But it was worth knowing—not that I could do anything with it at the moment. O'Halloran was right: I was a baby in savant terms. If I was going to help myself out of this mess, I had to grow up very quickly.

* * *

We had been driving for over an hour. I'd passed through abject terror and now felt a sense of deadening hopelessness. We were much too far from Wrickenridge for anyone to catch up with us.

'Where are you taking me?' I asked.

Gator seemed surprised to hear me speak. I had the impression that I was just a means to an end—getting the Benedicts—and no one in the car really considered me as a person.

'Shall I tell her?' he asked O'Halloran.

The savant nodded. He'd been silent, his battle on an invisible front as the Benedicts desperately tried to break his shield.

'Well, cupcake, we're taking you to see the boss.' Gator took a pack of chewing gum out of his breast pocket and offered me a strip. I shook my head.

'Who's your boss?'

'You'll find out soon enough.'

'Where is he?'

'At the other end of that plane ride.' He gestured towards an aircraft waiting on the tarmac of a little provincial airfield.

'We're flying?'

'We sure ain't walking to Vegas.'

We drew up alongside the jet. Gator pulled me out of the car and bundled me up the short flight of steps. As soon as the SUV was clear, the plane took off immediately, heading south.

Chapter 17

My room was on the top floor of a half-finished skyscraper hotel on the street in Las Vegas known as the Strip. I knew my location because no one made any attempt to stop me looking out of the ceiling to floor window. Lights from the casinos bled into the sky—neon palm trees, pyramids, rollercoaster rides, all glittering with zany promise. Beyond this thin layer of madness, past the twinkle of the suburbs, was the desert, dark and somehow sane. I leant my forehead against the cold glass, trying to calm the whirl of emotions beating away inside me. My head was on spin cycle.

After a long flight, we had put down at an airfield and I'd been bundled into another black car, this one a limo. My hopes of getting away from Gator and O'Halloran at the other end were dashed when we entered an underground car park and I was transferred into the hotel in a private lift. Whisked up to the penthouse, I'd then been left in my room and told to go to bed. My part was over for the moment, O'Halloran had explained, and he advised me to get some rest.

Rest? I kicked the white leather armchair stationed by the window. Five star accommodation didn't make this any less of a prison. They could take their flat screen TV, Jacuzzi bath, and four-poster bed and stick it . . . well, I had some creative suggestions as to where.

As no bodily harm had been done to me, I was less worried for the moment about my own fate. Most tormenting was the knowledge that Zed and my parents would be going through hell. I had to get a message through to them that I was all right. I'd already tried the phone—no surprise that it had no dial tone. The door was locked and I couldn't attract attention at this height from any living creature but the birds. That left telepathy. Zed had never answered my question as to whether he could talk to his brothers in Denver but he had managed to contact me over the couple of miles between his home and mine. Was it possible to communicate with him over the hundreds between Colorado and Nevada? I wasn't even sure exactly how far apart we were.

I rubbed my head, remembering the ache I'd got just sustaining that 'local' telepathic call. And there was O'Halloran to consider. Would he bother keeping the shield up now we were out of range? He knew I had few powers as a savant so probably didn't expect me to try anything so ambitious, but if he was playing safe and detected my clumsy attempts, he'd be furious and might punish me.

Fireworks went off in the distance, part of some nightly entertainment at one of the other casino hotels. Mine was called The Fortune Teller: I could see the crystal ball revolving on the roof in reflection in the windows of the building across the street. Only part of it was complete. 'T' shaped cranes stood sentinel over the rest—the offices, apartments, and malls that were waiting for the end of the recession so that their skeletons could be clad in something more attractive than iron girders. The rubble-strewn site to my right had weeds growing on the heaps, showing just how long the building project had been put on ice—ironically, given the name, not something the hotel owner had foreseen. He could've done with a savant to tip him off.

I hugged myself, missing Zed with a ferocity that surprised me. Unlike my boyfriend, I didn't know what the future held. I'd have to risk annoying O'Halloran but I could lessen the chances by choosing a time when he should be asleep. I checked my watch: it was midnight. I'd leave it to the small hours before making my move.

Turning away from the window, I contemplated my room, looking for anything that could help me. I'd already had to peel off the ski suit, being far too hot. I'd put on the hotel robe but I really wanted a change of clothes, feeling at a disadvantage in nothing but long thermals. There was a nightshirt neatly folded on one of the pillows. I shook it out: it bore the hotel logo and looked like the kind of thing you could buy in the gift shop. Wondering if someone had thought to provide more of the same, I opened the wardrobe and found a neat pile of T-shirts and shorts. Did that mean they expected me to be here for a while?

This was all too much for me to take in. I felt out of place, unable to focus. The wonderful high definition perception I had with Zed had collapsed, throwing me back into my old Manga-izing habits, flat colours, disjointed images. I hadn't realized until separated by hundreds of miles how I'd come to take his presence near me almost for granted. Even if we couldn't spend a lot of time together, I'd had the reassurance that he was there. He'd grounded me, making all that I was learning about the savant world less frightening. Now I was open to all fears and wild guesses as to what was going to happen. He'd been my shield, not the ones I'd practised in my head.

I hadn't seen it, but he had been acting as my soulfinder all along, even though I hadn't acknowledged him. Now it was too late to tell him.

Or maybe it wasn't. Maybe I could reach him.

Exhaustion crept up on me. I found my eyes blurring and I had to grab the wardrobe door as I swayed. If I wanted to have the energy for my plan, I needed to get some sleep. Even a few hours would make a difference. Changing quickly into the nightshirt, I set the alarm on the bedside clock and rolled under the satin sheet.

The neon lights were still pulsing outside when the alarm jolted me awake three hours later. A police helicopter circled overhead briefly then went north. On the street below, cars and hotel shuttles continued to cruise the Strip, gamblers unwilling or unable to stop even in the middle of the night. I dashed cold water in my eyes to clear my head.

OK. Time to take a chance on O'Halloran having gone to bed. I had to hope that abduction made for a tiring day for him.

Zed?

Nothing. I probed the darkness in my head, feeling the absence of the muffling blanket that had been in place in the car. That gave me hope that O'Halloran had dropped the shield.

Zed? Can you hear me?

No reply. I pressed my fingers to my temples. Concentrate. Perhaps Zed was asleep too?

No, he wouldn't be. He wouldn't be sleeping knowing I'd been taken. He'd be straining to hear the least word from me. Perhaps what I was trying was impossible?

I paced the room for a moment, my toes sinking into the deep pile of the rug.

Or maybe I just didn't know what I was doing? I thought back through the things Zed had told me about telepathy, how he had made contact with me despite himself. He'd said I was a bridge.

Perhaps it would work like shielding, but in reverse? Opening up and building a link rather than closing down and constructing barriers?

I tried again, imagining I was building a thin arching bridge between my mind and Zed's. I saw it like an image stretching out of a comic book frame, breaking the conventions to close the distance to the next picture.

After an hour of migraine-inducing thought, I felt a change, a subtle flow of energy in the other direction.

Zed?

Sky? His thoughts sounded faint, moving in and out of reach like a thread of a cobweb dancing in the wind.

I'm in Vegas.

His shock was clear enough. *You can't . . . How can you . . . me . . . Vegas?*

You tell me. You're the savant, remember?

. . . miracle . . .

I'm OK. They've got me on the top floor of the Fortune Teller.

Can't . . . you. Breaking . . .

Fortune Teller. Top floor.

My head was screaming with the pain of maintaining the bridge but I was determined to get my message through.

I . . . you.

He wasn't hearing me. I repeated my location.

. . . love you. . . . come for you.

No!

Easier . . . closer.

No, no. It's a trap. The bridge was collapsing. I could feel it going, feel my stomach churning, head pounding. Just a moment longer. *I love you too, but don't come. It's what they want.*

190

Sky! He'd felt the link fracture, scrambling my last words.

'Zed.' I was on the floor, perspiration running down my back, nausea gripping my stomach. I crawled on hands and knees to the bathroom and was sick. Though shaky, I felt a little better for it. Hauling myself to the bed, I fell on the covers face down and passed out.

Chapter 18

I did not wake properly until mid morning. The sky was a pale blue through the tinted windows, tiny puffs of cloud smudging the perfect surface. Feeling numb, I cleaned my teeth with the hotel-supplied brush and paste and got dressed. It seemed odd to be wearing shorts in the middle of winter but the climate controlled environment of the hotel meant it was always summer inside. My stomach growled. I investigated the contents of the mini bar and helped myself to a chocolate biscuit and bottle of Coke, then sat down to wait. I was in the middle of a crisis but things were strangely calm. The eye of the storm.

I didn't dare risk trying to contact Zed again. O'Halloran would probably be up and about and I didn't know enough about shield-busting to give it a go. I just hoped Zed got my message not to come rushing in. We needed a plan to get me out, not a second hostage.

There was a knock at the door. Not behaviour I expected of my kidnappers. It opened to reveal Gator carrying a tray.

'Rise and shine, cupcake. You slept well?'

'Not really.'

Ignoring this, Gator dumped the tray on a table by the

window. 'Breakfast. Eat quickly. The boss wants to see you.'

I wasn't sure I could manage anything. Deciding not to rile him by refusing co-operation over so small a thing, I lifted the lid. Nope, I couldn't stomach those eggs. I sipped at the orange juice and nibbled a slice of toast instead. Gator didn't leave. He stood at the window pretending to shoot at the birds flying over the buildings, giving me a good view of his ponytail which he'd secured back with a leather tie. He seemed in a cheerful mood, not at all on edge for someone who was part of a kidnapping. It struck me then that whoever was behind this must control this entire hotel or Gator would be less relaxed about holding me here.

'I've had enough, thanks.' I stood up. The fact that I was meeting the boss face to face did not bode well for what they had planned for me. I tried to think up a scenario where they didn't kill me to protect their identities at the end of this and couldn't imagine one.

'OK, let's go.' He took a firm grip of my upper arm and marched me out into the hallway. We turned left, walked past the elevator and on into a waiting area. Through the frosted windows, I could see people sitting around a boardroom table. Gator knocked once, waited for the green light, then entered with me in tow.

Fear made the images sharp. I tried to absorb as much information as I could just in case by some miracle I did get free. Three people sat at the table. My eyes were drawn to the oldest: a man with dyed black hair and dodgy tan, punching away at his BlackBerry. His suit screamed designer, though his choice in ties did not: today's a tangerine shade that clashed with his skin. He had the seat at the head. On either side sat a younger man and a woman. The family resemblance was strong enough for me to hazard a guess that these were his children or close relatives.

'Here she is, Mr Kelly. I'll wait outside.' Gator gave me a little push towards the table and walked out.

Mr Kelly sat looking at me without speaking for a while, his fingers touching in an arch. The others were clearly waiting for him to make the first move, which left me stranded. I knew only that the Benedicts had helped in the conviction of two of the Kelly family. From the way he sat so confidently in the head chair, I guessed I was looking at the famous Daniel Kelly himself, head of the Kelly business empire, the man whose face appeared more regularly in the business pages than Donald Trump and Richard Branson combined.

'Come here.' Kelly beckoned me closer.

Reluctantly, I walked round the table.

'O'Halloran said you are a savant?'

'I don't know.' I tucked my hands in my pockets to disguise the fact that they were trembling.

'You are. I can tell. It's a shame really that you've been caught up in this.' He flashed me an unapologetic grin, displaying improbably even teeth.

The man on his right stirred. 'Dad, are you sure the Benedicts will trade themselves for her?'

'Yes, they will try. They won't be able to stop themselves trying to protect an innocent like her.'

The younger Kelly poured a cup of coffee. 'And the police? They must be involved by now.'

'They will never be able to trace it back to us. And she will tell them exactly what I tell her to say.' Mr Kelly leaned back in his chair. 'Fascinating. There are such dark spaces in her mind.'

I stepped back in alarm. He was reading my mind somehow. Zed had said I always gave too much away to another savant. I threw up walls as fast as I could.

He drummed his fingers lazily on the table. 'Turquoise. Such a girlish colour, don't you think?'

'Not very strong though,' commented the younger woman; she had the sleek looks of a wild cat, groomed but deadly. 'I could break them for you, Daddy.'

'Oh no, I don't want her broken just yet.'

The bottom fell out of my world. The Benedicts had thought there was only one savant involved; what they had failed to anticipate was that the Kellys had powers like theirs. This had suddenly got a whole lot more complicated.

'You're wondering what we're going to do with you, aren't you, Sky?' Kelly held out a hand to me, his face lined with dissatisfaction. He looked as if he was suffering from deep disappointment and wanted others to suffer with him.

I'd prefer to touch a snake so I kept my hands in my pockets.

'We're not going to kill you, if that is what you are thinking. You are not our enemy.' He let his hand drop. 'I'm a businessman, not a murderer.'

'So what are you going to do with me?'

He stood up, tugging his jacket straight. Approaching me, he walked round, assessing me like an art critic at a showing of a new work. His presence grated on my nerves like a piece of discordant music.

'You are going to become my very good friend, Sky. You are going to tell the policemen that neither I nor my family had anything to do with your kidnapping, that it was two of the Benedict boys who took you for their own disgusting and evil purposes.' He smiled with evil relish. 'You know how savants can so easily go wrong—too much power, too little to hold them sane. The fact that they died trying to stop you escaping is no tragedy but saves the American taxpayer the money for housing them for the rest of their natural life in jail.'

'I like that,' commented the young man. 'I think disgracing them is better than just killing them.'

'I thought you would, Sean. I told you that you could trust

me to think up a suitable payback for your uncles.'

I gaped at them. 'You're mad! There's nothing you can do or say to make me tell the police such a lie, even if you threaten me! And I won't let you kill Zed or . . . or his brothers! I won't!'

Kelly found my anger funny. 'Such an amusing little foreigner, isn't she? All hissing and spitting like a furious kitten and about as threatening.' He laughed. 'Of course you will say what I tell you, Sky. You see, it is my gift. You will remember what I want you to remember. People do, you know, like the prison guards who will very soon be letting my brothers out of prison, thinking they received word from the governor to release them. There's no point resisting. Bending people to my will is what I am good at. I've built my fortune on it and you'll be no different.'

Oh my God, he was like Victor. But could he really make me say and do something so out of character? I could see that making a couple of guards misinterpret their duty might be possible, but to fabricate a whole complicated lie that flew in the face of the evidence, surely I wouldn't go along with that? Could I forget myself so far as to betray Zed? Betray my soulfinder?

I slammed that thought deep behind all my barriers. Kelly must not learn what Zed was to me—he'd exploit that weakness without mercy, knowing what savants would do for their other half.

Absolutely brilliant, Sky. I kicked myself. *What a time to accept Zed is your soulfinder.*

I'd been scared before; now I was terrified.

'I see you are beginning to believe that I can do it.' Kelly tucked his BlackBerry away in his breast pocket. 'Don't worry: you won't suffer. You'll think you're telling the truth. I'll have to keep you close by, of course, to make sure you carry on singing the same tune for a year or so until everyone forgets, but we can see to that can't we, Maria?'

The younger woman nodded. 'Yes, Daddy. I think we can make a place for her in housekeeping in one of the hotels when she drops out of high school to live in Vegas. Tragically, the memories of Wrickenridge will be too painful for her to return.'

'But my parents . . . ' This was worse than a nightmare.

Kelly gave an insincere sigh. 'They'll feel they failed to protect you and I'll persuade them that they want to give you the space our doctors say you need after your trauma. We know all about them and your adoption—how fragile your mental condition is. I'm sure they'll be too busy with their careers to worry too much as long as you tell them you're happy—and you will tell them so.'

How did he know so much? 'You're taking my life away from me.'

'Better than killing you, and that's the only other option.'

Sean came to join his father. He was a good head taller, but much fatter, his belly rolling over the top of his thin leather belt that kept up his sagging trousers. He had a Zorro-style moustache arching over his lip which looked ridiculous on someone who had only a few years on me, like someone had drawn it on him for a joke while he slept and he hadn't yet noticed. 'You say she has darkness inside her?'

Kelly frowned. 'Can't you sense it?'

Sean seized my hand and pulled it up to his nose, sniffing the palm, eyes closed as if reaching for a faint perfume. I tried to tug free but his grip pinched. 'Yes, I can feel it now. Wonderful seams of pain and abandonment.'

As he touched me I could feel my panic heighten; the calm I'd struggled to maintain was being shredded away like paper ripped off a present.

'Why not give her to me? I would enjoy draining her of her emotions—I can sense she would provide hours of entertainment.'

Daniel Kelly smiled indulgently at his son. 'Is her emotional energy that strong?'

He nodded. 'I've not felt anything like it.'

'Then you can have her after she's served her purpose with the Benedicts. Just keep her well enough to convince her family she's here of her own free will.'

'I'll take care of it.' Sean Kelly kissed the palm of my hand and let it go. I wiped it on my shorts with a shudder. 'Hmm.' He licked his lips. 'You and I are going to get to know each other very well, my sweet.'

'What are you?' I hugged my arms to my sides and retreated to the window. I wanted to scream in his face but it would only show them how scared I was.

Maria Kelly rolled her eyes impatiently. 'My brother's an emotion miner—gets his kicks from drawing the stuff out of other people's brains. I could've done with a new maid, Daddy: it's not fair. Not even good business. She won't be any use if Sean gets his hands on her—you know that. The last one only lasted a month before we had to get rid of her.' Her voice rose in a whine.

'I'll make it up to you, darling.' Daniel Kelly stamped his authority on the situation with a slice of his hand. 'Now enough of this: I must get to work on our guest. The police search for her is well under way and our source has reported that the Benedicts have made their move from their base. It's time the authorities were pointed in their direction. Come, Sky, I have something I want you to remember.' Daniel Kelly looked round for me but I was already running. No way was I meekly going to succumb to his mind-manipulation.

'Sean!' he barked.

I was faster than that doughnut. I burst out of the doors and bolted for the elevators, hoping to find one waiting or at least a stairwell. But I'd forgotten who was outside. I got as far as the hallway before Gator tackled me. He took me down, forcing all the air from my lungs. My head cracked on the tiles but I continued to kick and bite as he hauled me up. He held me at arm's length and shook me.

'Stop it, cupcake. If you do what the boss says, you won't get hurt.'

Blood dripped from a cut on the side of my head. My vision was greying at the edges.

'Bring her back here,' Kelly ordered.

Gator dragged me into the boardroom. 'Don't be too mad at her, Mr Kelly,' he pleaded. 'The girl's just scared.'

'On the contrary, I'm not angry; she's playing into our hands.' Kelly checked his flashy Cartier watch. 'When we release her to the authorities covered in blood, they'll believe her more readily. Now sit her down. I'll start on her now.' He was so cold, acting as if I were just another boring item on the meeting agenda to be got through.

I tried to scratch my way free. 'No, leave me alone!'

Gator dumped me in a chair and tied me to it with some flexi-cuffs. I couldn't even wipe the blood off my cheek and had to let it trickle down and drip on to my chest. I was shaking.

'She's in shock,' Maria said in disgust. 'You'll not get much into her brain when she's blank like this.'

Sean slithered up behind me and put his hands on my shoulders, inhaling deeply. 'She's not blank. Lovely—fear, out-rage, and horrible anticipation—a wonderful combination.'

Maria knocked his hands away. 'Don't. You're magnifying her emotions. We don't want her going catatonic on us.'

'Oh no, there's too much fight in her to take that route so soon.'

Gator shifted awkwardly. 'Are you going to do that mind stuff on her, Mr Kelly?'

The businessman glanced up. 'Yes. Why?'

'Just don't seem right,' Gator muttered.

Maria pushed him away. 'Oh, you're pathetic! We know you hate our powers but remember who pays your wage, Gator.'

'You should've let me just shoot a couple of them Benedicts,' grumbled Gator.

'But you missed,' Maria said tartly. 'Oh, I've had enough of this. Daddy, can we get on? I've the linen inventory to oversee.'

Daniel Kelly seized my head and held it tightly. I could feel his presence pushing at me, trying to take control. Merger and acquisition. I threw up my walls, imagining piling the dressing table, bed and anything I could get my hands on to stop him getting past my shield. I couldn't help but catch glimpses of what he was trying to plant in my brain. He was seeding pictures of Zed and Xav luring me off the street and imprisoning me in the boot of a battered old car. They'd kept me there while pretending to join the search for me, then driven off with me under the nose of the local police force. They'd held me in an abandoned warehouse, laughed at me for believing Zed loved me, tormented me . . .

No! I slammed the door on his suggestions. The Benedicts did not do that—would never do that to anyone. Remember the truth. Gator and O'Halloran. The plane. The hotel. Think where you are.

The Benedicts hate you. Zed's too everything for you—too cool, too good looking—of course it had to be a set up. You suspected that. He's been using you. He and Xav do this to girls all the time. They had to be stopped, officer. I had to shoot them. It was their gun I used.

No, no, no. I could feel my brain buckling under his assault. I've never shot anyone.

The image of the gun in my own hand was so strong, right down to the bitten nails.

That's not me. Zed and Xav are still alive. I haven't shot them. My eyes flew open. 'You're going to shoot Zed and his brother?'

Daniel Kelly couldn't hide his flare of shock that I had slipped out of his control. His clunky signet ring dug into my cheek, making my eyes water. 'You may not pull the trigger but you will think that you did.'

The images flooded back into my brain, bright reds, ink blacks, primary colours whirling. *The heavy weight of a handgun in my palm. Zed dead by my hand. Xav too. I was a murderer, even though it had been in self-defence.*

No.

Yes. That was how it happened. I was wrong about them. The Benedicts were a sick family. They just want to torment those who fall into their hands. All of them sick, sick, sick.

This was wrong. Wrong.

I blacked out.

Over the next few hours, whenever I regained consciousness, I felt as if I had glass splinters burrowing into my brain. I couldn't think straight. I had the impression of several sessions with Daniel Kelly's dark eyes burning into my mind, my head held rigid in his grip. Sometimes Sean was there too, drinking in the backwash of my distress, making everything much worse. Kelly seemed angry that I was still resisting but eventually I was so confused my mind was crying out for me to take the easy way out and agree with what he was insisting was the truth.

'Tell me again what happened, Sky,' he ordered me for what seemed like the hundredth time.

'You . . . you saved me.' Images of him sweeping into hospital to offer comfort after the bloodbath in the warehouse flickered before my eyes. He'd come to my parents' rescue, found us a private room, paid for their accommodation. Been so generous to the poor English family he'd heard about on the news.

'That's right. And who took you from the street?'

'The Benedicts. They're sick and evil.' No—yes. I didn't know. 'I want to go home.'

'No, you don't. You want to stay here in Vegas where you feel safe.' An image forced its way into my head: a room with strong doors and barred windows where no one could reach me.

'I feel safe.'

'With the people who helped you. Sean has been so kind.'

'Kind. Gator's been kind. He brought me breakfast. Asked that I not be hurt.'

'Not Gator. My son, Sean. He's going to help you heal.'

'He is?'

'Yes, take all that nasty emotion away from you.'

I nodded. That sounded good. I didn't want to feel.

Maria came into the room with O'Halloran and Gator behind her. 'Is she ready? It's taking too long. The Benedicts are already in town and that slimeball Victor Benedict has applied for a warrant to search our properties.'

Daniel Kelly pinched my chin. 'Yes, I think she is. A little confusion will make it more convincing. Get her in position then send the message to the Benedicts that they can find her in the warehouse on the old airfield. The two boys have to come alone or the deal's off.'

'They won't come alone—the rest won't let them.'

'They will try to make it look like they are alone and that will be enough. The others will be too far away to stop what's going to happen. We'll alert the police ourselves. A dash of interagency confusion into the mix always helps.'

I held my head. This didn't make sense. It had already taken place, hadn't it? I'd been in the warehouse—knew who got shot. There was blood on my hands.

Maria smiled. 'Our little savant is having a hard time getting her facts straight.'

'She'll be all right. All she need do is sit there with the gun in her hand while the FBI and the police argue why it all went down so badly. O'Halloran, you've got a damper on telepathy?'

He nodded. 'It'll hold until she gets close to one of them.'

'Make sure you take them out swiftly. Dump the gun in her hands and get away before the FBI and police arrive. I want them wondering what the hell happened.'

'Sure, boss.'

Kelly cracked his knuckles. 'After today, the Savant Net will know that no one who interferes with my people gets away unscathed. They'll leave us alone in future. Now, Sky, this is goodbye until we meet again for the first time in hospital. *When I say the word, you forget everything that happened since yesterday and remember only what I told you.*'

Gator was apologetic as he tied my legs and left me sitting in the middle of the empty warehouse.

'Just do as I tell you and then this will be over,' he told me, tucking my hair behind my ear.

I was shivering, despite being dressed in my ski suit. My body was acting like it had a fever it was trying to throw off. Nothing felt right. Gator took up position a few feet further back, sheltering behind a barrier of crates. I could hear him checking the magazine in the gun.

Was he here to defend me? I couldn't remember. I wasn't even sure who he was. What was wrong with me? My brain felt like cotton wool.

After what seemed like an age, there was a scuffling sound at the far end. The sliding door edged back a few inches.

'It's us. We've come alone like you demanded.' It was Xav

Benedict. My enemy.

'What have you done with Sky? Is she all right?' His brother, Zed. I knew him, didn't I? Of course, I knew him. He was my boyfriend. He said he loved me.

He doesn't love you—he's just playing with you. The words floated in my brain but I couldn't remember why I thought that.

I kept quiet, drawing my knees up to my chest.

Sky? Please answer! I'm going crazy here. Tell me you're OK.

Zed was in my head too. There was nowhere to hide. I couldn't help myself—I let out a whimper.

'Xav, that's her! She's hurt.'

Xav held him back. 'It's a trap, Zed. We do this as we agreed.'

They hadn't yet come in sight.

'Tell us what you want in exchange for Sky and it's yours.' Zed's voice was unsteady.

None of this made sense. I'd shot them. Why were they here? Why did I have to relive the nightmare?

'Just step out where I can see you and I'll tell you,' said Gator.

'The thing is, we're not stupid. You can tell us while we stay where we are.'

'If you don't come out with your hands up, I'll put a bullet in your little girlfriend.'

This wasn't how it was meant to be. I'd got the gun in the struggle with Zed and shot both the Benedicts. I'd seen it happen—it was there in my brain.

'Zed?' My voice was thin, quavering in the emptiness of the warehouse.

'Sky? Hold on, baby, we're going to get you out of this.'

Wrong—all wrong. My memory felt like a comic strip with the key frames ripped out. The Benedicts had hurt me—yes they had. Locked me in the boot of their car for hours.

'Go a . . . way!' I choked. I saw movement down the far end, the tips of someone's fingers as they rose up from behind the container that they had been hiding behind. It was Zed.

My brain seemed to explode with conflicting emotions and images—hatred, love, laughter, torment. Colours in the warehouse went from flat to multi-toned and complex.

His eyes zeroed in on mine. 'Don't look at me like that, baby. I'm here now. Just let me talk to the man who's got you and we'll get you free.'

He took a step closer.

How many of them are there? Has he got a gun on me? Zed's voice echoed in my head again.

I don't shoot people. The images of my hands holding the gun flicked on and off like the neon signs.

What's wrong with you, Sky? I can see what you're seeing. Your mind feels different towards me.

'He has a gun,' I said aloud. 'Gator, don't shoot anyone. We mustn't. I've killed them already but they don't die—they just come back.'

'Quiet, Sky,' said Gator from behind me. 'And you, come where I can see you. I'm sure you'd prefer me to have you in my sights than your girlfriend.'

Zed stepped into plain view. I couldn't help but devour him with my gaze; it felt as if he was alternating between two masks, one where he was kind and tender, the other vicious and cruel. His face wavered in and out of focus.

'Now your brother. I want both of you where I can see you. Come a bit closer to Sky. Don't you want to see what we've done to her?' Gator taunted.

I had to choose. Which did I believe? Kind Zed; cruel Zed.

Zed took two steps forward, hands rock steady in the air. 'You don't want her. The Kellys' quarrel is with the Benedicts—not her. She's nothing to do with this.'

What should I do? Who should I believe? *Sky has got good*

instincts. My mum had said that, hadn't she? Instincts. More than instincts. I could read people, know their guilt, tell good from bad. I'd buried it but it was there inside me under all the gibberish in my head ever since I was six. Locked it away. But now I had to reach out with my gift.

I closed my eyes, feeling inside for the door that would release my powers. I opened my mind.

My power of perception went through the roof. The sensations flowing in the room were formidable. I saw them as streams of colour. The red of excitement and a bit of black fear from behind me; the gold glitter of love and green tinge of guilt from Zed.

Soulfinder.

The knowledge was there, as deeply rooted in me as DNA. How had I not seen it? My body retuned to Zed's note; perfect match, perfectly in harmony.

So why did he feel guilt? I probed the green: Zed felt terrible because he had let me be taken and that I had suffered instead of him. He'd wanted it to be him sitting there with blood on his face and clothes.

I didn't know why my brain was so scrambled but I now knew where I stood.

'Zed!' I screamed. 'Get down.'

The gun went off. Zed was already moving, alerted by his foreknowledge. A second crack. There was another shooter—O'Halloran—up in the rafter, trying to pick off Xav by the door. Instead of diving for cover, Zed ran for me. I screamed—my mind playing a version of this where he had attacked me and I had shot him. But my hands were empty. No gun.

Victor. Code Red! Code Red! Xav punched the message through O'Halloran's shield with all the strength he could muster, broadcasting on a wide channel for any telepath to hear.

Zed threw himself over me as I sat curled up, clutching my knees. 'Keep down, Sky.'

'Don't shoot!' I pleaded. 'Please, no!'

I sensed Gator's aggression and determination to kill swell in a flood of red colour. Zed's back presented a clear target, his only hesitation that the bullet might pass through and get me too.

'No!' With a burst of strength brought on by desperation, I used my legs to boost Zed clear. The bullet meant for his back hit the ground between us, ricocheting wildly off the concrete. Then everything went to hell. Gunshots rang out; agents burst through the door, screaming that they were FBI. Something hit my right arm. Pain lanced through me. Sirens and more shouting. Police. I curled up into a ball, sobbing.

In the confusion, someone crawled to my side and crouched over me. Zed. He was swearing, tears running down his face. He clamped his hand over the wound on my arm.

After several staccato explosions, the guns fell silent. I sensed that two presences had gone from the room—O'Halloran and Gator. Had they fled?

'Get me a medic over here!' yelled Zed. 'Sky's been hit.'

I lay quietly, biting down on the urge to cry out. No, they'd not fled. They'd been killed in the exchange of fire, their energy snuffed out.

A police paramedic rushed over.

'I've got her,' she told Zed.

He released his grip on my arm, my blood on his hands. The medic ripped my sleeve open.

'From the looks of it, just a graze. Possibly she caught a ricochet.'

'They're dead,' I murmured.

Zed caressed my hair. 'Yeah.'

'What happened to me?'

The medic looked up from her treatment of my arm. 'You hit your head too?' She saw the blood in my hair. 'When did this happen.'

'I don't know.' My eyes turned to Zed. 'You locked me in the boot of your car. Why did you do that to me?'

Zed looked shocked.

'No, I didn't, Sky. Is that what they did to you? Oh God, baby, I'm sorry.'

'We'd best get her checked for concussion,' said the medic. 'Keep talking to her.' She signalled for a stretcher to be brought over. Zed untied my legs.

'I shot you,' I told him.

'No, you didn't, Sky. The men were shooting at us, remember?'

I gave up. 'I don't know what to think.'

'Just think that you are safe now.'

I had an image of an orange-skinned man in a suit swooping into the hospital to save me. Who was that?

The two medics lifted me onto the stretcher. Zed kept hold of my uninjured hand as I was wheeled out to the ambulance.

'I'm sorry I shot you,' I told him. 'But you were attacking me.'

Why would my soulfinder attack me?

I could see other Benedicts gathering around my stretcher. They were evil, weren't they?

Zed wiped the blood from my cheek. 'I wasn't attacking you and you haven't shot me.'

The last I saw of the rest of the Benedict family was a grim-looking Saul as I was loaded into the ambulance. Zed tried to get in but I shook my head.

'I shot him,' I told the medic seriously. 'He can't come with me; he hates me.'

'I'm sorry,' the woman told Zed. 'Your presence is upsetting her. Where are her parents?'

'They're booked into a hotel off the Strip,' said Saul. 'I'll let them know. Which hospital are you taking her to?'

'The Cedars.'

'OK, I'll stay away, let her calm down if you think that best,' said Zed reluctantly releasing my hand. 'Sally and Simon will be there. You hear that, Sky?'

I didn't reply. As far as I could remember one or other of us should be dead. Perhaps it was me. I closed my eyes, my mind so overloaded I had to check out for a moment. Then I was gone.

Chapter 19

It was the sounds that first alerted me to the fact that I was in hospital. I didn't open my eyes but I could hear the hushed noise in the room—a machine humming, people murmuring. And the smells—antiseptic, unfamiliar sheets, flowers. Surfacing a little more, I could feel the pain, dulled by drugs but still lurking. My arm was bandaged and I could feel the pull of a dressing in my hair and the itch of stitches. Slowly, I let my eyes flutter open. The light was too bright.

'Sky?' Sally was at my side in an instant. 'Are you thirsty? The doctors said you must drink.' She held a beaker out, her hand shaking.

'Give her a moment, love,' Simon said, coming to stand behind her. 'Are you all right?'

I nodded. I didn't want to speak. My head was still messed up, full of conflicting images. I couldn't work out what was real and what was imagined.

Supporting the back of my head, Sally held the water to my lips and I took a sip.

'Better now? Can you use your voice?' she asked.

There were too many voices—mine, Zed's, a man saying

he was my friend. I closed my eyes and turned my face to the pillow.

'Simon!' Sally sounded distressed.

I didn't want to upset her. Perhaps if I pretended I wasn't there, she would be happy again. That sometimes worked.

'She's in shock, Sally,' Simon said soothingly. 'Give her a chance.'

'But she's not been like this since we first had her. I can see it in her eyes.'

'Shh, Sally. Don't jump to conclusions. Sky, you take all the time you need, you hear? No one's going to rush you.'

Sally sat down on the bed and took my hand. 'We love you, Sky. Hold on to that.'

But I didn't want love. It hurt.

Simon switched on the radio and tuned in to a station playing soft classical music. It flowed over me like a caress. I'd listened to music all the time during the years in a succession of foster and care homes. I'd only spoken by singing strange little half-mad songs I'd made up myself, which had led the carers to assume I was crazy. I suppose I had been. But then Sally and Simon had met me and seen that they could do something for me. They'd been so patient, waiting for me to emerge, and gradually I had. I'd not sung a note since. I couldn't put them through that again.

'I'm all right,' I rasped. I wasn't. My brain was a junkyard of bits and pieces.

'Thank you, darling.' Sally squeezed my hand. 'I needed to hear it.'

Simon fiddled with an arrangement of flowers, clearing his throat several times. 'We're not the only ones who want to know you're OK. Zed Benedict and his family have been camping out in the visitors' lounge.'

Zed. My confusion increased. Panic zapped through me like

an electric shock. I'd realized something important about him, but I'd slammed the door closed again.

'I can't.'

'It's all right. I'll just go and tell them you've woken up and explain you aren't up to visitors right now. But I'm afraid the police are waiting to talk to you. We have to let them in.'

'I don't know what to say.'

'Just tell them the truth.'

Simon went out to give the Benedicts the news. I gestured to Sally that I wanted to sit up. I now noticed that her face looked strained and tired.

'How long have I been here?'

'You've been out for twelve hours, Sky. The doctors couldn't explain why. We were very worried.'

Something made me glance up. The Benedicts were leaving the hospital. Zed slowed by the window in the corridor that looked into my room and our eyes met. I had a horrible sensation in the pit of my stomach. Fear. He stopped, placing his hand on the glass as if to reach for me. I clenched my fists on the cover. Deep inside I could hear a ringing note, discordant, violent. The water jug on the bedside table began to judder; the overhead light stuttered; the buzzer to summon the nurse jumped off the rail and crashed to the floor. Zed's expression became darker, the sound harsher. Then Saul came up alongside and said something softly in his ear. Zed nodded, gave me a last look and walked on. The note stopped, snapped off; the vibrations ceased.

Sally rubbed her arms. 'Strange. Must have been a tremor.' She returned the buzzer to its original position. 'I didn't know Vegas was in an earthquake zone.'

I couldn't tell if it had been me or Zed. Was he so angry at me he wanted to shake me? Or had that been my fear trying to push him away?

Feeling numb, I let Sally brush and plait my hair for me.

'I won't ask you what happened, darling,' she said, taking care not to pull the hair around my cut, 'as you'll have to go through it for the police and FBI, but I just want you to know that whatever happened wasn't your fault. No one will blame you.'

'Two men died, didn't they?' My voice sounded distant. I felt I was watching myself go through the motions of talking to Sally while really I was hidden deep inside, hiding behind so many doors and locks that no one could reach me. It was the only place I felt safe.

'Yes. The police and FBI arrived at the same time acting on separate tip-offs—it was a massive mix-up in communications, the left hand not knowing what the right was doing. The two men were killed in the exchange of fire.'

'One of them was called Gator. He had a curly ponytail. He was nice to me.' I couldn't remember why I thought that.

'Then I'm sorry he is dead.'

There was a cough at the door. Victor Benedict stood in the entrance with an unfamiliar man in a dark suit.

'May we come in?' Victor was looking at me with particular intent. The tremor had not gone unnoticed and he looked, well, *wary* of me, as if I was an unexploded bomb or something.

'Please.' Sally got up from the bed and made space for them.

'Sky, this is Lieutenant Farstein of the Las Vegas police department. He's got a few questions for you. Is that OK?'

I nodded. Farstein, a sun-bronzed, middle-aged man with thinning hair, pulled up a seat.

'Miss Bright, how are you?' he asked.

I took a sip of water. I liked him—my instinct was that he was genuinely concerned. 'A bit confused.'

'Yeah, I know the feeling.' He pulled out a notebook to check his facts. 'You've got the police departments of two states and the FBI in a spin, but we're glad we found you safe and well.' He tapped the page thoughtfully. 'Maybe you'd best start from the top—tell us how you were snatched.'

I strained to remember. 'It was getting dark. I'd been skiing—well, falling over on skis really.'

Victor smiled, his face reminding me so much of Zed when it took on a softer expression. 'Yeah, I'd heard you were taking lessons.'

'Tina's car had a problem.'

Farstein checked his notes. 'The mechanic discovered that someone messed with the leads to the battery.'

'Oh.' I rubbed my forehead. The next steps were shaky. 'Then Zed and Xav persuaded me to get in a car. They locked me in the boot. No, no, they didn't.' I pinched the bridge of my nose. 'I can see them doing it but it doesn't feel right.'

'Sky.' Victor's tone was low and insistent. 'What is it you're seeing?'

Farstein cut across him. 'Are you saying, Sky, that two of the Benedict brothers were responsible for your abduction?'

Something clicked in my head. The pictures flowing easily, smoothly, without pain.

'They pretended to be my friend, wanted to hurt me.'

'You know that's not true, Sky.' Victor was furious, his lips compressed.

Farstein shot him a quelling look. 'Agent Benedict, you should not interrupt the witness. And bearing in mind your relationship to those she's accusing, I suggest you step outside and send in a colleague who can listen impartially.'

Victor stalked to the door, his back to the room, but didn't leave. 'What she's saying is impossible. I was with my brothers, lieutenant; they had nothing to do with her kidnapping.' *Sky, why are you saying this?*

I looked frantically to Sally. 'He's talking to me in my

224

head—tell him to stop.' I pressed my fists to my temples. 'It hurts.'

Sally took my hand, standing between me and Victor. 'Mr Benedict, I think you'd best go: you're upsetting Sky.'

I turned tear-filled eyes to Farstein. 'I shot them, didn't I?'

'No, Sky, you weren't responsible for the deaths of those men.'

'Zed and Xav are dead?'

Farstein threw Sally an anxious look. 'No,' he said carefully, 'the two men who staked out the warehouse are dead.'

'Gator and O'Halloran,' I repeated, remembering them. 'The savant.'

'The what?' asked Farstein.

Which one, Sky? asked Victor urgently.

'Go away from me!' I pulled the covers over my head. 'Get out of my head.'

Farstein sighed and closed his notebook. 'I can see we are doing more harm than good here, Mrs Bright. We'll leave Sky to get some rest. Agent Benedict, I want a word with you.'

Victor nodded. 'Down the hall. Take it easy, Sky. It'll come back.'

The two men left. I lowered the covers to find Sally watching me with fear in her eyes.

'I'm going mad, aren't I?' I asked her. 'I can't remember—and what I remember feels wrong.'

She brushed her thumb over my knuckles. 'You're not mad. You're recovering from trauma. It takes time. We think the people who did this to you are probably dead, killed in the shootout. The police are just trying to tie up the loose ends.'

I wish someone would tie up the loose ends in my brain. My thoughts were like ragged bunting from some abandoned party whipping about in the wind—no purpose, no anchor.

'If Zed and Xav didn't kidnap me, then why do I think they did?'

Thanksgiving came and went, the only sign the turkey dinner in hospital. My mind was no clearer. I felt like a beach after the passing of a tidal wave—odds and ends thrown up on the shore, all out of place, smashed to pieces. I was aware of the passage of great emotion through me but I couldn't sort it out, what had been real, what had been false. I'd let something loose inside and not controlled it—the result had been devastating.

Zed and his brother were cleared of all suspicion by the Las Vegas police department. So why had I accused them? I was racked with guilt that I had involved them in this, too embarrassed to see any of the Benedicts. I made my parents promise that they wouldn't let them in—I couldn't face them. I wasn't able to keep Victor out though; he came several times with Farstein to see if I remembered any more. I apologized to him, and the policeman, for getting it wrong, but I wouldn't be surprised if Victor hated me now.

'Nightmares, Miss Bright—that's what they are,' Farstein said in a practical tone of voice. 'You've gone through a terrifying experience and your mind got muddled.'

He was being kind but I could tell he dismissed me as next to useless in his enquiries. Everyone agreed that I'd been kidnapped, but no one could prove that anyone beyond the two men in the warehouse had been involved. I was the key but I wasn't opening any doors for them.

Farstein brought me a pack of cards and a bunch of flowers on his last visit. 'Here you are, Miss Bright, I hope these help you feel better.' He split open the packet and shuffled. 'I imagine you must be bored stuck in here. My city is a good place to

visit for most folks; I'm sorry you had such a bad time with us.'
He cut the cards and dealt me a hand.

Victor was hanging back, watching us from the doorway.
'You're not corrupting the girl, are you, Farstein?'

'Can't leave Vegas without taking one gamble.'

'I don't know many games,' I admitted.

'Let's keep it to Snap then.'

'If I win?'

'You get the flowers.'

'If I lose?'

'You still get the flowers, but you have to give me one for my buttonhole.'

Farstein left with a carnation pinned to his lapel.

Victor stayed behind. He stood looking out of the window for a moment, his disquiet clear.

'Sky, why don't you want to see Zed?'

I closed my eyes.

'He's really cut up. I've never seen him like this. I know he blames himself for what happened to you, but it's knocked him off his stride in a major way.'

I said nothing.

'I'm worried about him.'

Victor was not one to confide in someone outside the family. He really must be concerned. But what could I do? I could barely find the courage to get up in the morning.

'He got in a fight last night.'

A fight? 'Is he all right?'

'From the brawl? Yeah, it was more words than fists.'

'Who did he fight?'

'A couple of guys from Aspen. He went looking for it, Sky. And in answer to your other question, he isn't all right. He's hurting. It's like he's bleeding inside, somewhere he thinks no one can see.'

'I'm sorry.'

'But you're not going to do anything about it?'

Tears pricked the back of my eyes. 'What do you want me to do?'

He held out a hand to me. 'Stop shutting him out. Help him.'

I swallowed. There was a streak of ruthlessness to Victor that wouldn't let me duck behind the excuse of my confusion—it was both scary and challenging. 'I'll . . . I'll try.'

His hand curled into a fist before he let it drop. 'I hope you do, because if something bad happens to my brother, I'm not going to be pleased.'

'Is that a . . . a threat?'

'No, just the truth.' He shook his head, his irritation clear. 'You can get through this, Sky. Start looking outside yourself— that'll help you heal.'

At the end of November, I was released from hospital but my parents had decided on the advice of the doctors not to take me straight home.

'Too many distressing associations in Wrickenridge,' Dr Peters, my consultant psychiatrist, told them. 'Sky needs absolute rest and no stress.' She gave them a recommendation for a convalescent home in Aspen and I was duly registered and assigned my own room, something we could only afford thanks to the generosity of an anonymous benefactor from Vegas who had heard about my case on the news.

'This is a loony bin, isn't it?' I asked Simon bluntly as Sally unpacked my few belongings into the chest of drawers. My room had a view of the snowy gardens. I could see a girl walking round and round the pond, lost in her own world, until a nurse came out to fetch her in.

'It's a nursing home,' Simon corrected me. 'You're not fit to go back to school yet and we couldn't afford to stay in Vegas any longer, so this is the best we could come up with.'

Sally stood up and shoved the drawer closed. 'We could go back to the UK, Simon. Sky might feel better among her old friends.'

Old friends? I'd kept up with some of them on Facebook but somehow the old closeness had evaporated the longer I was away. It wouldn't be like going back to how it had been.

Simon gave me a one-armed hug. 'If that's what it takes, we'll do it, but one step at a time, eh?'

'We've got classes we have to teach at the Arts Centre,' Sally explained. 'But one of us will be over every day. Do you want to see your friends from Wrickenridge?'

I played with the curtain cord. 'What have you told them?'

'That you've had a bad reaction to the trauma of your kid-napping. Nothing too serious but you need time to recover.'

'They'll think I'm crazy.'

'They think you're suffering—and you are—we can see it.'

'I'd like to see Tina and Zoe. Nelson too if he wants to come.'

'What about Zed?'

I leant my head against the cool glass. The gesture gave me a sudden flashback—a tall tower, neon signs. I shuddered.

'What, love?'

'I'm seeing other stuff now—stuff that makes no sense.'

'To do with Zed?'

'No.' And it wasn't, I realized. Zed hadn't been there. And I'd been stalling. I'd promised Victor I would try. Maybe if I saw Zed, it would help get things straight. 'I'd like to see Zed too—just for a little while.'

Simon smiled. 'Good. The boy's been worried sick about you, phoning us every hour of the day and most of the night.'

'You've changed your tune about him,' I murmured, sud-denly remembering clearly the argument we'd had about him a month ago. Hadn't Zed said he loved me? So why did I feel as if he was my enemy?

'Well, you can't help but like someone who walked into a trap to get his girl out.'

'He did?'

'Don't you remember? He was there when you were injured.'

'Yes, he was, wasn't he?'

Simon squeezed my shoulder. 'See, it's coming back.'

The next day passed quietly. I read my way through a pile of novels, not leaving my room. My carer was a motherly woman from California who had a lot to say on the subject of the Colorado winters. She came in and out all day, but left me largely to my own devices. At around five, just before she went off shift, she knocked on the door.

'You've visitors, honey. Shall I send them up?'

I closed my book, my heart rate accelerating. 'Who is it?'

She checked her list. 'Tina Monterey, Zoe Stuart, and Nelson Hoffman.'

'Oh.' I felt a mixture of relief and disappointment. 'Sure, send them up.'

Tina put her head round the door first. 'Hi.'

It felt an age since I'd seen her. I hadn't realized how much I'd missed her explosion of ginger brown dreadlocks and her outrageous nails.

'Come in. There's not much room but you can sit on the bed.' I stayed in my chair by the window, knees drawn up to my chest. My smile felt fragile so I didn't push it too far.

Zoe and Nelson followed her, all looking a bit awkward.

Tina put a pot of pink cyclamen on the bedside table. 'For you,' she said.

'Thanks.'

'So . . .'

'So how are you, guys?' I asked hurriedly. The very last thing I wanted was to explain my totally messed up brain. 'How's school?'

'Fine. Everyone was worried about you—really shocked. Nothing like this has ever happened in Wrickenridge before.'

My gaze drifted to the window. 'I don't suppose it has.'

'I remember joking with you about that when you first came—I feel awful that you had to find out I was wrong. Are you, you know, OK?'

I gave a hollow laugh. 'Look around you, Tina: I'm here, aren't I?'

Nelson got up abruptly. 'Sky, if I could get the guys who did this to you, I'd kill them!'

'I think they might be dead already. At least, that's what the police think.'

Tina hauled Nelson back down on the bed. 'Don't, Nelson. Remember, we promised not to upset her.'

'Sorry, Sky.' Nelson put his arm round Tina and kissed the top of her head. 'Thanks.'

What was this? I couldn't help but grin—my first genuine smile in a very long while. 'Hey, are you two . . . ?'

Zoe rolled her eyes and offered me a stick of bubblegum. 'Yeah, they so are. Driving me crazy, the pair of them. You've got to get straightened out, Sky, and keep me sane at school.' Thank God for Zoe making fun of the madness—it made me feel a lot more normal.

'When, how?' I mimicked one of Tina's favourite gestures— a pale imitation of her long-nailed beckon but it was something. 'Give me the details, sister.'

Tina looked down, a little embarrassed. 'When you were, you know, *taken*, Nelson was really great. Stopped me losing it big time. I thought it was my fault—what with the car and everything.'

Nelson rubbed her forearm. 'Yeah, Tina saw my good side for once.'

'I'm so pleased—for you both. You deserve each other,' I said.

Tina laughed. 'Is that, like, a Chinese curse?'

'No, you dweeb,' I threw my cushion at her, 'it's a compliment.'

They stayed for about an hour. As long as we kept off the subject of my abduction, I felt fine. I had no problem remembering things about school, no pain, no confusion. I began to feel like my old self.

Tina checked her watch and gave the others a nod. 'We'd best go. Your next visitor is due at six.'

I gave them each a hug. 'Thanks for coming to see the poor crazy girl.'

'Nothing wrong with you that a little time won't put right, Sky. We'll be back the day after tomorrow. Sally said she thought you'd be here at least until the end of the week.'

I shrugged. Time didn't seem to mean so much to me. I'd stepped out of my normal routines. 'I expect so. See you then.'

They left, exchanging greetings with someone in the hall. I went to the window to watch them go but I couldn't spot the car park from my room.

There was a soft knock at the door.

I turned, expecting to see Sally. 'Come in.'

The door opened and Zed stepped over the threshold. He paused, unsure of his welcome.

'Hi.'

My throat seized. 'H . . . hi.'

He pulled a massive gold box tied with a red satin ribbon from behind his back. 'I come bearing chocolate.'

222

'In that case, you'd better sit down.' I sounded calm but inside my emotions were tossing like palm trees in advance of a hurricane. That tidal surge of feeling was coming back.

He didn't sit. He put the box on the bed then came to stand beside me at the window.

'Nice view.'

I clenched my teeth, keeping the door in my head firmly shut against the surge. 'Yeah. We crazy people get to go out earlier in the day. I'm told there's a snowman down in the orchard that looks like the head nurse.' My fingers were shaking as I rested my hands on the sill.

A warm hand moved to cover mine, stilling the trembling. 'You're not crazy.'

I tried to laugh but it came out wrong. I quickly wiped away a tear. 'That's what everyone keeps telling me but my brain feels like cold scrambled egg.'

'You're still in shock.'

I shook my head. 'No, Zed, it's more than that. I see things that I don't think happened. I've got all these terrible images in my head—stuff about you and Xav. But you're not like that— part of me knows this. And I think I shot you both. I wake up in a cold sweat dreaming there's a gun in my hand. I haven't even touched a gun in my life so how do I know what it feels like to shoot one?'

'Come here.' He tugged me towards him, but I held back.

'No, Zed, you don't want to touch me. I'm . . . I'm broken.'

I don't want her broken, not yet. Oh God, who had said that?

He refused to listen to me and pulled me firmly into his arms.

'You're not broken, Sky. Even if you were, I'd still want you, but you're not. I don't know why you see those things, but if you do, there's a reason for it. Perhaps that dead savant messed with your mind somehow? Whatever it takes, we'll find out and we'll help you.' He sighed. 'But Xav and I, we weren't anywhere near you until we found you in the warehouse. Do you believe that?'

I nodded against his chest. 'I think I do.'

He ran his hands up and down my back, kneading out the knots from my muscles. 'I thought I'd lost you. I can't tell you what it means to me to hold you like this.'

'You came for me even though you knew they might shoot you.' I remembered that much, thanks to Simon.

'I was wearing a bulletproof vest.'

'You still could've been killed. They could've taken a head shot.'

He cradled my face in his hand, rubbing his thumb over the dip in my chin. 'Price worth paying. Without you, I'd become the coldest, most cynical tough nut on the planet, worse even than the guys who took you.'

'I don't believe that.'

'It's true. You are my anchor, keeping me on the right side of wrong. I've been drifting since you shut me out.'

Guilt swamped me. 'Victor told me.'

Zed frowned. 'I told him to leave you alone.'

'He's worried about you.'

'But you come first.'

'I'm sorry I wouldn't let you visit. I was so ashamed of myself.'

'You've nothing to be ashamed of.'

'I left you to suffer.'

'I'm a big boy—I can take it.'

'You got in a fight.'

'I'm also stupid.'

I smiled, rubbing my nose against the cotton of his shirt. 'You're not stupid; you were hurting.'

'It's still stupid to take that out on a couple of Frat boys for looking at me the wrong way.' Zed sighed at his own behaviour, then gave up the subject. 'I know you're confused about a lot right now, Sky, but I want you to know one thing for sure: I love you and would give my life for yours if it meant I could save you.'

Tears, always near the surface at the moment, brimmed in my eyes. 'I know. I felt it. I could read your emotions. That's what told me my mind was lying to me.'

He kissed my forehead.

'And I think,' I continued, 'that under all this, when I find myself again, I will also find that I love you too.'

'That's good to know.'

And so we stood, watching the stars come out, both praying that the explanation for why I was so messed up would not be long delayed.

chapter 20

Sally and Simon took me home a few days into December. Some early celebrators had already strung up their Christmas lights. Mrs Hoffman's house was a blaze of colour, enough to be worth a detour off the highway. Our home was dark, not a candle or a bauble in sight.

Simon opened the door. 'Now you're back, Sky, we can get decorating.'

'So, do we go for tasteful Olde England or brash new world?' asked Sally too cheerfully.

I played along, knowing they wanted to think I was better than I was. 'If we do, can I have an inflatable Santa hanging out of my window.'

'Absolutely, as long as I can have flashing reindeer on the roof.'

Flashing lights—a palm tree, rollercoaster rides.

'What is it, love?' Simon put his arm round me.

This was happening all the time now: I'd see glimpses of things—a chair, a jet plane, a bed—none of which I understood.

'Nothing. Just having one of my moments.'

I dumped my case on my bed and sat down, staring at the walls. Turquoise. I'd quite forgotten to practise shielding. I must be leaking thoughts and feelings to Zed all the time but he'd been too kind to tell me. Somehow I didn't have the energy to pick up where I left off. He'd told me I'd contacted him while I was being held by my mystery kidnappers. I'd claimed to be in Las Vegas, which he'd found hard to believe until I turned up in the warehouse. He thought I'd tried to tell him exactly where I was but he had missed most of my message. The Benedicts had acted on what I'd managed to say and travelled to Vegas because the city was Daniel Kelly's powerbase—the coincidence was too much to be ignored. They still believed there was a link: Gator, the man who had died in the warehouse, had been employed by Kelly's corporation, but the police had been unable to connect the kidnapping back to the head man.

Victor was feeling pretty steamed about the whole thing. To add insult to injury, the two Kellys the Benedicts helped put away had slipped out of jail a few weeks ago; no one quite knew how they did it.

'Sky, supper's on the table!' Sally called.

I went down and pretended to have a greater appetite than I did. Sally had cooked my favourite pasta and bought in a tub of special ice cream. We were all making an effort to make the evening a success.

I toyed with the spaghetti. 'Do you think I should go back to school?'

Simon topped up Sally's wine then poured himself a glass. 'Not just yet, love. Actually, I've . . . er . . . been wondering.'

'Hmm?' Sally looked up, hearing the cautious note in his voice.

'I heard from this lady from Las Vegas today—Mrs Toscana. She runs one of those casino hotels. Turns out she was behind the secret donation that paid for the convalescent home.'

'Oh, how kind of her.'

'That's what I told her. Anyway, she heard about the kidnapping and has seen our portfolio on the web; she wondered if we might consider a new contract advising on the art acquisitions made by the hotel chain. They've got hotels all over—Rome, Milan, Madrid, Tokyo, London, as well as throughout the States. It would last longer than a year and allow Sky to finish her schooling in one place. She mentioned there were some excellent high schools in Vegas. She even recommended a few.'

Sally swirled her wine in the glass. 'I don't know, Simon. If we move anywhere, I'd prefer to go back to England. I don't think our American adventure has been a great success. And Vegas—well, the memories aren't pleasant.'

Simon twisted the spaghetti expertly around his fork. 'I didn't commit us. She suggested that we talked more about it, explored the possibilities before rejecting the idea. She invited us down for a weekend—Sky too.' He took a bite. 'I must say the salary she mentioned far exceeded my expectations.'

'Sky? What do you think?' Sally asked.

'Huh? Oh, I wasn't really listening.'

'Do you need a change from Wrickenridge?'

'I don't think I want to move again just now.'

'Can you face school here knowing that everyone is aware what happened to you? We wouldn't blame you if you wanted a fresh start somewhere else.'

'Can you let me think about this?'

Simon nodded. 'Of course. We can go take a look without making any commitments. It'll help you decide. After all, you didn't really get to see Vegas, just the hospital and that . . . that warehouse. You might enjoy the city.'

'Maybe.' I shelved that for the moment, my mind too

caught up with getting used to being home again to think about moving.

Karla and Saul Benedict came to call on Saturday morning. I'd never felt at ease with Zed's mother since our first meeting, but she was on her best behaviour today, giving no sign that she was reading me. Ironically, I wouldn't have minded someone telling me what was going on in my head as I hadn't a clue. I remembered the conversation I'd had with Saul about my relationship with their son; would they still be so keen on having me in their family now they knew I'd cracked up in Vegas?

Sally and Simon sat with me as we entertained the Benedicts in the kitchen. There was none of the zany fun I'd had in the Benedict home when I'd gone there. They exchanged a few stilted pleasantries, talking about the concerts planned for Christmas and the busy season on the slopes. I felt sad that I wasn't taking part in the music as I had planned to do. Rehearsals would be going on at school without me. Finally, Saul turned to me, coming to the point of the visit.

'Sky, it's good to see you back in Wrickenridge.'

'Thanks, Mr Benedict.'

'Zed's told us what you said to him about having false memories.'

I looked down at my hands.

'We think we can help you.'

Simon cleared his throat. 'Now, Mr Benedict, I appreciate you coming here, but we've got Sky an excellent doctor. She's seeing to her treatment. I don't think we should mess around with it.'

'That would be all very well in the normal course of things,' said Karla, her tone betraying an edge of impatience, 'but we believe Sky's problem might lie out of the realms of normal medicine.'

The look Sally and Simon exchanged was clear. They were hostile to any suggestions out of their control; the Benedicts were not the only family who knew how to circle the wagons.

'That may be so, but she's our daughter and we will decide with her what's best.' Simon stood, signalling that as far as he was concerned this friendly visit was at an end.

Saul kept his eyes on me. 'We would like you to spend some time with our family, Sky. When we get together, there are things we can do to help someone in your situation.'

The prospect terrified me—but I also knew I wasn't getting anywhere under the doctor's methods for all Sally's and Simon's optimism.

'It is time spent with your family that got Sky into the fix she's in now!' Simon no longer bothered to hide his anger. 'Look, Mr Benedict—'

'Please, call me Saul. We've been through too much together to still be so formal.'

Simon sighed, wind taken out of his sails. 'Saul, we like Zed—he's a fine boy—but Sky's not likely to be around much longer to spend this time you're talking about. Please, just leave us alone now. Sky's had enough to put up with in her short life; don't add to the stress she's already under by making claims on her.'

Sally knitted her fingers together, clenching them tightly. 'We've always known, since she was a little girl, that Sky's mental condition is delicate. It's not your fault, but it's turned out that the association with your family with its exceptional problems has upset that balance. Please, leave her alone now.'

The argument was carrying on over my head. It was almost as if I wasn't there.

'Sally, please.'

'It's all right, Sky. It's nothing to be ashamed of.'

'Your daughter needs us,' said Mrs Benedict.

'I'm sorry, but I don't agree.' Sally joined Simon by the door, body language crystal clear. 'We know what's best for Sky. She's been ours six years now and I think we know her rather better than you do.'

'Stop it, all of you, please.' I felt like a bone being quarrelled over by a pack of dogs. Everyone was so busy telling me they knew best, I couldn't decide what that might be for myself.

Saul rose from the table. 'Karla, we're distressing Sky. We'd better go.' He darted a glance at me. 'The offer stands, Sky. Just think about it. For Zed's sake, as well as yours.'

The Benedicts left with a slamming of car doors and strained goodbyes at the front gate. I remained behind in the living room, running my fingers over the piano keyboard. Was it my imagination, or did it sound out of tune too?

'Well, really,' said Sally, coming back into the house in a huff. 'Is there nobody in Wrickenridge who doesn't think they know better than us?'

'Sorry you had to sit through that, love.' Simon ruffled my hair. 'I think they mean well.'

'Right now Las Vegas is looking very tempting,' added Sally.

Simon's eyes glinted, like a driver seeing a gap in the rush hour traffic, knowing he could make a break for it. 'Then I'll give Mrs Toscana a ring, see what we can fix up.'

I didn't want this attitude of full steam ahead to a new life; I wanted time to adjust to the one I'd been making for myself here. I wanted time to find out what there was between Zed and me. And for all this I needed my head back in the right place.

I closed the piano lid. 'Can we not just think for a minute about what Mr and Mrs Benedict said? Maybe they can help.'

'Sorry, Sky, but once bitten, twice shy.' Simon flipped

through the business cards until he found the one for the hotel in Vegas. 'Getting tangled up in that family's business has been a disaster. We don't mind you seeing Zed here, but you're not to go over to his house. You're making progress, we don't want any setbacks. I'll just make this call.'

I had little energy for a fight at the moment so I made no promises, just got up, saying I was off to bed. I could hear Simon talking animatedly to his new contact, mentioning what weekends we had free and how much we were looking forward to visiting. I had no desire to go back to Vegas; why would I? Everything I wanted was here.

I sat at the end of my bed looking out of the window long after my parents had retired for the night. The sky was clear, moon shadows turning the snow a bruised blue. Winter had set in, the snow packed down, prepared to stay till spring. The thermometer was well below freezing, the icicles dripping from the eaves, lengthening daily. I scratched at my arms. I couldn't bear this. I wanted to scream, pummel my head until it was back in shape. I was trying hard to pretend I was getting better but in fact I felt I was getting worse. I clung on to sanity, stepping lightly on the thin ice protecting my mind, but I feared that this was an illusion: I had already plunged through the cracks.

I stood up abruptly and walked to the window, fists clenched. I had to do something. There was only one place I could think of to go to prevent the damage spreading. Grabbing my dressing gown, I shoved open the casement. I knew what I was contemplating was mad, but then again I thought I was crazy, so what the hell. Regretting that my snow boots were downstairs—I didn't want to risk alerting my parents to my plan—I climbed on to the porch roof, slid down to the edge and dropped to the ground. My soft shoes were immediately soaked but I now felt too driven by the belief that this was my one last hope to care.

I started to run down the road, feet crunching in the powder snow. I travelled from shivering cold to not feeling. Passing our car parked in the garage, I spared a wish that I had taken the opportunity of Coloradan laws letting sixteen year olds behind the wheel—Zed had once said he'd give me lessons but we'd never got to it. Never mind, it was only a couple of miles across town. I could make it.

I was walking by the time I turned into the steep road behind the ski lodges that led up to the cable car. The snow here was stamped down, freezing in icy ridges. When I looked at my toes, I realized the soles of my shoes were in shreds and my feet bleeding. Oddly, I couldn't bring myself to care too much. I approached the Benedict house cautiously, wondering what security they had installed. They'd been expecting an attack and wouldn't have let down their guard yet. A hundred yards out, I did feel a barrier—not a physical one but a sensation of unwillingness and fear compelling me to turn back. Slamming up my shield, I pushed on through, my determination to reach Zed far stronger than this counter-instinct. When I broke free, I sensed that I'd tripped some kind of alarm. Lights went on in the house ahead, first upstairs in the bedrooms, then down on the porch.

What was I thinking? I was planning to go knocking on their door in the middle of the night? This was gun-toting America, not England: I'd probably get shot before they realized who it was. My certainty that this was a good idea evaporated. I stood irresolutely on the path, considering if I had the energy to turn round and go home.

'Stop right there. Put your hands up where we can see them.' A man's voice—one I didn't recognize.

I was frozen to the spot—too cold to move, to think.

There came the unmistakable sound of a rifle bolt being slid—something I'd only ever heard in the movies. Images spun:

Bugsy Malone—'come out with your hands up'. I swallowed a hysterical gulp of laughter.

'Step into the light so we can see you.'

I forced myself to move.

'And I said "hands up"!'

I raised my hands shakily.

'Trace, it's Sky!' Zed burst from the house only to be pulled back by his arm. His oldest brother, Trace, the policeman from Denver, wasn't letting him go.

'It might be a trap,' Trace warned.

Victor stepped out of the darkness behind me. He'd circled round to cut me off, gun trained on my back.

'Let go of me!' Zed struggled, but Saul joined the blockade.

'Why aren't you using telepathy, Sky?' Saul spoke calmly, for all the world as if it were natural to have a girl turn up in her dressing gown at three in the morning.

I swallowed. There were too many voices in my head already. 'Can I come in? You said I could come.'

'Is she alone?' Trace asked Victor.

'Seems so.'

'You ask her, just to make sure.' Trace lowered the gun. 'We can't risk a mistake.'

'Don't you touch her, Vick! Leave her alone!' Zed burst from his brother's grasp and jumped the steps.

'Zed!' shouted Saul.

But too late. Zed reached me and folded me in his arms. 'Oh baby, you're freezing!'

'I . . . I'm sorry to come like this,' I murmured.

'Stop being so damn British about it—you don't need to apologize. Ssh, it's fine.'

Saul reached us but didn't have the heart to separate me from his son. 'It's not fine, not until we know why she's here. She walked right through our security perimeter. She can't have done that without help. Her powers aren't that strong.'

Victor eased me away from Zed's chest and held my eyes with his steely gaze. *'Tell us why you're here. Did someone send you?'* He was using his gift, layering his words with a compulsion to answer. I could hear it like a harmony running under the melody. It hurt. *'Sky, you must tell me.'*

'Stop it, stop it!' I sobbed, pulling away from them, stumbling backwards. 'Get out of my brain, all of you!' I tripped over, ending up sitting in the snow, head squeezed between my hands.

Zed shoved Victor out of the way and scooped me up in his arms. He was furious. 'I'm taking her inside and I don't care what you say. She's mine—my soulfinder—and you'd better not try and stop me.'

This announcement was met with shock from his brothers, resignation from Saul.

'Look at her—she's blue with cold.' Zed shouldered his way past his family and took me into the kitchen. Xav was there, along with Will, one of the brothers I was yet to meet properly; they were checking a monitor that had been set up on the kitchen counter.

'She walked in,' Will said. He was running some CCTV coverage of the gate to the cable car compound. 'No sign of anyone else.'

'Sky, what are you playing at?' Xav moved towards me, then spotted my feet. 'Sheesh, Zed, didn't you notice she's bleeding? Put her on the counter.'

Zed held me to him as Xav eased off what was left of my shoes. He closed his eyes and placed his palms on the soles of my feet. I immediately felt a tingling sensation like pins-and-needles and then pain as sensation flowed back into my toes.

Victor dropped his gun on the counter and took out

the magazine. 'Will, Xav, there's something little brother's forgotten to mention.'

Trace shook his head. 'Yeah, meet his soulfinder.'

Xav's touch pinched for a second, a jolt in the flow of energy, then he went back to healing.

Will whistled. 'No kidding?'

'That's what he says.' Trace glanced at his father, seeking confirmation. Saul nodded.

'Well, wha'd'ya know.' Will grinned at me, his happiness genuine. 'Got any older sisters, Sky?'

Zed smiled at him gratefully. 'Not that she knows—but we'll try and find out for you.'

'Don't forget the rest of us,' said Trace, his smile a little forced. 'Some of us are running out of time.'

Saul clasped his son's shoulder briefly. 'Patience, son. You'll find her.'

'You walked here all on your own?' Zed asked gently while the healing was progressing. 'Why?'

'I need help,' I whispered, wishing I could burrow into his chest and disappear. He was so warm and I was so cold. 'I needed you.'

Trace and Victor were still suspicious about my strange arrival. I could feel the waves of emotion flowing off them. Oh God, my gift had switched on again. I'd read the emotions in the warehouse but deadened myself to them ever since; here, in this house of savants, the ability to see people from their feelings came rushing back.

'I want your brothers to know I'm telling the truth.' I didn't need to open my eyes to be aware where everyone was. The two older Benedicts hovered protectively by the door into the rest of the house. Their father's emotions were mixed—fear, concern for me, and puzzlement. Will leaned on the counter, glowing with a cheerful spring green. Xav was concentrating on healing my feet, his presence a cool blue of concentration. And Zed, he was glowing with golden love and a purple edge of desperation to do something to help me.

'You don't think I'm here because someone sent me to hurt you, do you?' I murmured, rubbing my cheek against his sweat-shirt.

'No, baby,' he replied, nuzzling my hair.

'Your dad said I could come.'

'I know.'

Saul picked up the phone lying on the table. 'What's her number?' he asked.

I'd forgotten all about my parents. 'They don't know I'm gone.'

'Better to wake them up to tell them you're safe than to let them discover your empty bed and worry.'

Zed reeled off the number and Saul had a quick conversation with Simon. I knew they would want to jump in the car and fetch me, but I didn't want that after having come all this way.

'I want to stay,' I whispered. Then I found a stronger voice. 'I want to stay.'

Saul glanced at me and nodded. 'Yes, Simon, she's OK, a little cold but we're looking after her. She's sure she wants to stay. Why not come and collect her after breakfast? No point turning out in the middle of the night when there's no need. Yep, will do.' He put the phone down. 'He'll drive over in the morning. He says that you were to get some rest and not worry.'

'Am I grounded again?'

Zed ruffled the hair at the back of my neck.

'He didn't mention that.' Saul smiled.

'I bet I am.'

'Until you're fifty,' said Zed.

'I thought as much.'

Xav let go of my feet. 'I've done what I can for your soul-finder.' He used the term with relish. 'She needs to keep warm and sleep it off now. The cuts are pretty much healed.'

'Thanks.' Zed lifted me up. 'I'll put her in my bed for tonight. Mom's going to lend her some dry nightclothes.'

Snug and warm under Zed's duvet, I didn't feel sleepy. He was sitting on the window seat, guitar in hand, running through some soothing tunes. Karla had clucked a little about me being in Zed's room but when it was clear he was not going to let me out of his sight, gave in, saying she trusted us to behave.

Zed leant his forehead against his mother's, a gesture I found oddly touching seeing how much taller he was than her. 'Tell me what you see, Mom. I've dropped my shields.'

Karla sighed. 'I see you standing guard over her and behaving like a perfect gentleman.'

'That's right.' He winked at me. 'Sometimes having a mom who sees the future is a blessing.'

Now gazing at him framed by the night sky, I thought I'd never seen anything more perfect.

'I love you, Zed,' I said softly. 'I don't need to wait to sort out my memories; I know I do.'

He stopped playing. 'Well, now.' He cleared his throat. 'That's the first time you've said it to me face to face like this.'

'I've told you before; I'm sure I have.'

'No, you've hinted but you've never just come out with it.'

'I do, you know—love you, I mean. I'm a little shy so I don't say it easily.'

'A little shy? Sky, you're possibly the shyest person I've ever met.'

'I'm sorry.'

He came and sat on the edge of the bed. 'Don't be. It's part of what I love about you. You never think anyone's going to like you and have this vaguely surprised expression when we all fall for you. It's cute.' He tapped the end of my nose.

'I don't want to be cute.'

'I know, you want to be taken seriously.' His expression was solemn but his eyes were laughing. 'And I do—I swear it.'

'You don't—not about this.'

'You don't believe me?'

I shook my head. 'I can read emotion you know.'

He brushed the hair off my forehead. 'I may not have a poker face but I can't believe I'm that transparent.'

'You don't understand. It's my gift—I really can read what you're feeling. My gift—it unlocked.'

He sat back, his colours shifting into the mauve of bewilderment. I could see him processing what I said, the emotions moving to the warm colours of his love for me as he came to terms with it. 'That's OK then, so you know that when I say I love you, I really mean it. You know you're my soulfinder.'

'Yes. But I can tell if you lie to me too about other things. People have a shifty yellow cloud to them when they tell a fib.'

'Oh, well now, that isn't fair.'

'You can see the future.'

''Not all the time—and not so much with you now.'

I smiled sleepily. 'Then you'd better watch your step with me.'

He trailed the back of his hand over my cheek. 'You're enjoying having the advantage for once.'

'Yeah, I'm ahead of the curve, or whatever you say here.'

'God help us all.' He nudged me over and stretched out beside me. 'When did you discover this?'

'In the warehouse. It was how I knew that you hadn't hurt me even though my brain was telling me you had.' I paused, the images were still so vivid. 'Are you sure I never shot you—not even in make-believe like that fake knife?'

He groaned. 'Don't remind me of that. And yeah, I'm sure. It's not something I'm likely to forget now, is it?'

'I'm crazy, Zed.' There, I'd admitted it.

'Uh-huh. And I'm crazy too—about you.'

Chapter 21

I came down to the kitchen wearing clothes much too big for me, jeans and shirt sleeves rolled up, a pair of Zed's woolly socks on my feet instead of slippers. I was getting used to seeing my parents regard me with that shocked, disappointed expression, the one where I knew I'd let them down but they were too scared to tell me off in case I collapsed on them.

'Hi, love, ready to come home?' asked Simon, a touch impatiently, jingling the car keys in his palm.

Zed came up behind, giving me the silent encouragement of his presence.

'I'd like to stay a while, please. I think they can help me.' I reached for Zed's hand at my back.

Sally touched the base of her throat. 'For how long?'

I shrugged. I hated hurting them. 'Until I know if this is going to work.'

Karla closed her eyes for a moment, feeling out to the future. She smiled when she looked at me. 'I honestly think we can help Sky, Sally. Please trust us. We're just a short drive away. You'll be able to reach her in a few minutes if you're worried about her.'

'Love, are you sure?' asked Simon.

'I'm sure.'

Sally hadn't reconciled herself yet to this separation. 'But, darling, what can they do for you that we can't?'

'I don't know. It just feels right.'

She hugged me tight. 'OK, we'll try it. You've got your boy to take care of you then?'

'Yes, I have.'

Sally nodded. 'I can see that. If it doesn't work, don't worry. We'll just try something else and keep on going until we solve this.'

'Thanks.'

My parents reluctantly headed back home leaving me with all nine Benedicts in their kitchen.

'I like your parents,' Zed said in a low voice, putting an arm around me. 'They keep on fighting your corner, don't they?'

'Yes. I'm lucky to have them.' I was very aware of our audience. I was still to meet Uriel—he was the slim dark one standing next to Will, both were eyeing me as if I was an exotic creature. Zed's soulfinder. The least physically imposing of the Benedicts, Uriel was the one I most feared—the one who could read the past.

Karla clapped her hands. 'Right, my little ones—'

Little ones? She was the smallest of the family by a long chalk.

'Breakfast! Trace and Uriel—plates. Xav—knives and forks. Yves and Victor—you make the pancakes. Will—get the maple syrup.'

'What about Zed?' grumbled Yves, getting out a mixing bowl.

Karla smiled at us. 'He's got his hands full, comforting his girl, and is just where he should be. Sit down, you two.'

Zed pulled me into his lap in the breakfast nook and I sat back to enjoy the show. The most dangerous boys in

Wrickenridge were completely different at home. Though Trace and Victor were grown men, they did not dare sass their mother and buckled down to the tasks with everyone else. Not having to hide their powers in front of me, I soon got used to seeing the Benedicts summon things they needed, floating it to hand. It was fascinating. I realized I could see them doing it. The power showed up to me as a white light, very faint, like a thread. I had to concentrate or I missed it. I wondered if I could do the same thing. I watched as Trace levitated an egg from the box and then, giving in to impulse, I imagined lassoing it with my own power. To my utter shock, the egg veered from his control and zoomed towards us. Zed made me duck just in time. The egg hit the wall behind us and slid to the floor.

'Who did that?' shrieked Karla in outrage. 'Xav? I will not have you throwing eggs at our guest!'

Xav looked most offended. 'It wasn't me. Why do you always think it's my fault?'

'Because it usually is,' said Will drily, as he nudged Xav from behind, making him drop the cutlery on the table.

'Who did it?' Karla repeated, determined to get an answer.

'Whoever it is will have the rest of the eggs shoved down their neck,' growled Zed, putting an arm protectively around my waist.

'Who?' repeated Karla, revealing that height was not needed to look scary.

'Um . . . I think it was me,' I confessed.

Zed's jaw dropped. I discovered that astonishment was coloured glittering silver.

'I was seeing you do stuff—and wondered if I could do it too. I lassoed the egg.'

Will guffawed, making the cutlery dance into place with a wave of his hand. They bowed to me before arranging themselves neatly.

Saul took a seat at the table. 'You saw? What does that mean?'

I could feel my cheeks go pink. I wished I could find a button to switch off my propensity to blush. 'Um . . . well, moving things—that's like a white line. I suppose I'm sensing energy or something.'

'She sees emotions too, Dad,' Zed added. 'She can tell if you're lying.'

'Very useful.' Victor looked at me with a calculation I wasn't sure I liked. He was very low emotion compared to the others, or maybe he was just better at shielding.

I turned my eyes from him. 'Healing is blue. When Mrs Benedict dipped into the future, she sort of faded a little. I'm not sure about the rest, but I think each power has its own identity.'

What about telepathy? asked Saul.

I flinched, still not liking the feeling that someone else was in my head. 'I can't see that—at least, I don't know what to look for.'

'It takes the lowest energy of all the gifts when done close to the person you are communicating with. The signs might be too subtle to pick up.'

I rubbed my temples, remembering the pain of talking to Zed at a great distance. Where had I been when I'd done that? The warehouse?

Zed tugged me back against him. 'Don't think about it right now, Sky. I can tell it's hurting you.'

'Why can't I remember?'

'That's what we're going to find out,' Saul said firmly. 'But after breakfast.'

'What about school?' I knew Zed and Yves should have left already.

'Family powwow—we get to skip classes.' Yves grinned,

putting the first pancake in front of me. His boffin image slipped somewhat when I saw how happy he was to cut school.

'Like that day, back in September?' I turned to Zed. 'You missed a Friday.'

'Oh that. Yeah. We were helping Trace hunt down the people who shot that family in the drugs deal.'

I remembered now how drained he'd been that Saturday when I'd met him at the ghost town on the hillside.

'And these family powwows—you get to see what happened?'

'Yeah, but we get results,' said Trace, sitting down with his own plate. 'We got the bas—' he glanced at his mother's frown, 'son of a gun. He's up for trial early next year.'

'You mustn't worry about us, Sky,' Zed added, knowing my thoughts even though he didn't have my gift for reading emotions. 'It's what we do.'

'The family business,' agreed Xav, tipping the maple syrup on to his pancake. 'The Savant Net working as it should.'

'And we're proud of it,' concluded Victor, tapping the empty space in front of him. 'Where's mine?'

A plate containing a freshly cooked pancake hovered in the air towards him. Zed clapped his hands over my eyes. 'No lassoes.'

I laughed. 'I promise—no more experiments with food.'

The mood turned sober after breakfast. Saul went out briefly to check his assistants had everything under control on the ski lift, then returned, shaking the snow off his boots.

'We're all set,' he announced. 'Let's do this in the family room.'

Zed led me into a space at the far end of the house which doubled as a games room. Trace and Victor moved the table tennis table back while Uriel and Yves gathered floor cushions in a ring.

'We just want you to sit with Zed,' Saul said, taking his place opposite me.

'What are you going to do?' I was already feeling nervous. What had I let myself in for?

'We're treating this like an investigation.' Trace sat down at my right hand. 'Which is appropriate because we believe something's happened to you as a result of a crime.'

'I do feel like I've been brain-mugged,' I admitted.

'Each of us is going to use our gift to read you—nothing invasive, just a touch to sense which is the strongest lead.' Trace flicked his eyes to Zed. 'I'm gonna need to hold your hand if Zed will let go—I have to be in contact with my subject to allow my gift to work. I should be able to tell where you've been recently—before the warehouse. You don't have to remember; if you were physically there I should be able to track you. Wonder boy here, as the seventh son, he gets to channel it all as he's the most powerful of us.'

I swivelled to look up at Zed. 'Is that true?'

'Yeah, I'm like the screen to display the information. Compare the results. I can see what everyone else is seeing.'

'And he doesn't even need batteries,' quipped Will, slumping down on my other side.

They were making fun of it but I could now understand some of the darkness I'd seen in Zed, the strain of the evil he had been forced to witness. It wasn't just his own insight but everyone's that channelled through him, meaning he saw it in all ways and in greater depth than the rest. Little wonder he had felt he was slipping in that ugliness until he found an anchor.

The second son, Uriel, the post-grad student, nudged Will aside.

246

'Hi, Sky, we've not met properly yet. I'm the only sensible one in the family.'

'I can see that.'

'My gift is to read memories, anything to do with the past. I know you're afraid I might blurt out your secrets, but you mustn't worry: I can't force you to show me the past, I can only open doors which you unlock.'

'I understand.' I drew strength from feeling the warmth of Zed's chest against my back as I sat between his legs. 'And if I want to keep the door closed?'

'Then you do. But we think that you need to start building up a complete picture of everything that's happened to you to understand what's real and what you've imagined.'

I frowned. I didn't like the sound of that.

'It's like music, Sky,' Zed said. 'Orchestrating the score one instrument at a time. You've been running on the melody for a while now and we think you've been leaving out the bass, or the foundation notes.'

'You mean, about what happened when I was little?'

'Yeah. It's there.'

Dark spaces. *Wonderful seams of pain and abandonment.* Who had described me like that?

'We think that when you've seen what's behind all your doors, you'll find it easier to close them on others, stop people reading you so easily. In turn, it should give you control over the more recent memories, like discovering the key pieces in a puzzle.'

That was definitely something I wanted, no matter how scared I was of the process. 'OK, let's sort me out.'

Mrs Benedict drew the curtains while Yves lit candles around the room with a click of his fingers—this was the guy who could make things explode, I recalled. I was relieved to see the evidence that he had his gift well under control. The candles smelt of vanilla and cinnamon. The house was very quiet. We could hear the distant sounds of people enjoying the slopes, the rumble of the cable car going over the points, the sound of the trees rustling, but in this room, this haven, all was peace. I could feel the different gifts of each Benedict brush me—just a gentle caress, nothing to alarm. Zed kept his arms looped around me, relaxed, unworried.

Xav the healer was the first to speak. 'Sky, there's nothing medically wrong with you—I can see no sign of mental illness, though I could feel your distress.'

Zed rubbed the nape of my neck. 'Not crazy after all.'

'I can't read the future clearly,' admitted Karla. 'There are many possible paths leading out of this moment.'

'But I know where she's been recently,' Trace said. 'She's been in a room in a first class hotel—satin sheets, lots of glass, you touched something made from white leather and a deep pile carpet. It is safe to say you were held somewhere before you ended up in the warehouse. If we got hold of the clothes you were wearing, I could probably tell you more.'

'The threat's not gone,' said Saul, using his gift to sense the predators after us.

Will nodded. 'I sense more than one person looking for you, Sky.'

I turned to Zed. 'Did you get all that too?'

'Uh-huh. I also got that the two in the warehouse were the two who shot at us in the woods that day. O'Halloran was a savant, extraordinarily good at shielding. I wondered if that was why I could feel a layer in your mind—something alien. Did you see that, Uriel?'

Uriel touched my knee comfortingly. 'Yes, and I think I know what it is even if I don't know how it got there. Sky, your parents are artists, aren't they?'

I nodded.

'You know what sometimes happens to Old Masters? Someone takes them and paints over the surface and you have to strip off a layer to get back to the original? Well, someone has done something similar to your memories.'

That felt right. 'So what's the original and what's the forgery?'

'That's where we need to take it back to the base.'

'Will everyone see?' It was bad enough bringing out my past for my own eyes; I didn't want an audience for it.

'No, just Zed, me, and you,' Uriel said, his colours pulsing with the gentle pink of compassion. 'And we won't tell anyone unless you want us to.'

I really didn't want to do this but knew I had to.

'Don't be frightened,' whispered Zed. 'I'll be there with you.'

'OK. OK. So what do I do?'

Uriel smiled reassuringly. 'Just relax and let me in.'

It started out fine. I felt him examining my memories—the ones where I met my adoptive parents and how music helped heal me. I hadn't buried those. It was when he pushed on the door leading back that I felt fear.

Don't fight, Zed said. *He's not going to hurt you.*

But it wasn't Uriel I was scared of: it was what lay beyond the door.

Nothing we see there will make us feel any different about you, he assured me.

I could feel waves of calm emotion coming from the other members of the Benedict family; Xav was doing something to reduce my racing pulse.

I took a deep breath. *OK.*

Uriel pushed the block aside and images began to stream through like a crowd rushing the turnstiles.

A cold night. Seething anger in a car.

'I've had as much as I can take of this kid. She ruins everything!' A man beating the steering wheel while a

249

hollow-cheeked woman fixed her make-up in the mirror. She looked a bit like me but her skin was really bad, as if she'd not eaten properly for months. The layers of foundation didn't hide the blemishes.

'What can I do? I'm the only family she has.' The woman made kissy noises as she patched up her blood-red lipstick.

A door opened further back in time. Other lips, bubblegum pink, kissing my cheek. My mummy had been Red Lips's sister. She smelt of light perfume and had a silvery laugh. Her long fair hair brushed my tummy when she leant over to tickle me. I giggled.

The doorbell rang.

'Stay here, poppet.' She put up the side of the travel cot.

A rumbling voice in the corridor. Daddy. We didn't want him to find us, did we, Mummy? Why was he here? I clutched my lop-eared rabbit tight, listening to them in the hall.

'But you're not my soulfinder, Ian—we both know that. Miguel is. I'm going to him and you can't stop me!' Mummy's voice was ugly. She was really cross, but she was also scared. I felt scared.

'What about the child? What about me? You can't leave England with her!'

'You never wanted her before—you're just jealous!'

'That's not true. I'm not letting you do this.'

'I have to be with him. You of all people should understand.'

'Go then. But I'll take my daughter with me.'

They were getting nearer. I whimpered. The room was red with anger and the brash gold of love. A shadowy man plucked me from my bed and hugged me to his chest. The mouse nightlight exploded—bulb fragments flying.

'Mouse!' I screamed.

Mummy was shaking with anger. 'You lost Di too young—lost

your soulfinder—and I'm really, really sorry, Ian. But against all the odds, I found mine after I'd given up and I have to go to him. Now just put her down!'

Daddy squeezed me tighter. He was shaking. 'Why should I be the one left with nothing, Franny? I won't stand for it.' As she moved to take me back, he threw his hand towards her and my books leapt off the shelf, bombarding her.

The carpet began to smoke under his feet. I sobbed.

'Stop it, Franny. You'll set the whole bloody house on fire!'

'You're not taking her from me!' Mummy's temper flared and my bed went up in flames. 'I won't leave my baby behind.' She reached out, tugging at my sleep suit.

The burning bed spun in the air and slammed into her, throwing her into a wall.

'Mummy!' I screwed my eyes shut.

I never saw them again.

Another image. Auntie Red Lips had collected me from the hospital. I was the only one to have survived the fire—miraculously floated out of the house by unseen forces and found curled up on the dew-damp grass. Now we lived in a flat. I was still cold, my dress filthy. I was tiny—my head not even reaching the door handles. There was loud music in the main room; I'd been told to keep out of the way so was hiding in the hallway.

'Don't look at me like that!' It was the driver man again; he had a friend with him this time. He kicked out when I didn't move fast enough. I scurried back, pressing myself against the wall, trying to pretend I wasn't there. I watched as he passed the other man something and got money in exchange.

'He cheated you,' I whispered.

The second man stopped and knelt beside me. His breath was horrible, like fried onions. 'What you say, little chicky?' He seemed to find me funny.

'He lied. He's pleased he tricked you.' I rocked to and fro, knowing I was going to be punished but at least He would be too.

'Hey,' He said, smile insincere. 'You're listening to my girlfriend's little brat? What she know about anything?'

The onion man took the package out of his pocket and pressed it between thumb and finger, no longer smiling. 'This pure?'

'One hundred per cent. I give you my word.'

'He's lying,' I said. The Man's colours were sickly yellow.

Mr Onion held it out. 'Thanks, chicky. I want my money back. Your word isn't worth fifty quid.'

The man handed it back, swearing his innocence.

Next came pain.

Later, I heard Him telling the doctor how I'd fallen down the stairs and broken my arm. I was clumsy. A lie. He'd got angry with me.

Then we were back in the car. Another day. On the move again before anyone got too interested in us. Auntie Red Lips was feeling jittery. She'd been moaning, said He was about to ditch her because of me. She didn't like me either. I saw too much, she said. Like a witch. Like her stupid, dead half-sister.

'We could give her to the social services in Bristol, say we can't cope.' Auntie glared at me.

'First rule—never let the authorities even know we exist. We're not going back to Bristol—we've moved on.' He cut up another car undertaking on the motorway.

'Since when, Phil?'

'Since the police busted the Cricketer's Arms.'

I gazed out of the window at the blue sign—I saw it had a little symbol of a plane at the top. The road was going somewhere, taking off on a jumbo jet. I wished I could. I started to sing. *Leaving on a jet plane* . . .

'That's it!' The man indicated, taking us off the road and into a service station. 'We're dumping the freak here.'

'What!' The woman glanced across at him in bewilderment.

Slime green malice emanated from the man; her colours were dark purple, with a hint of green. It made me feel sick to look at them. I looked at my grubby shorts instead.

'You're joking, right?'

'Wrong. I'm leaving her here. You can either stay with her or come with me. Your choice.'

'Bloody hell, Phil, I can't just dump her!'

He pulled over into a space towards the rear of the car park, checking his mirrors nervously. 'Why not? I can't operate with her around. Some do-gooder will find her. She'll be their problem, Jo, not ours. She's just Franny's mistake. She should've got rid of her. She's nothing to do with you—with us.' He leant over and kissed her, his colours a horrid yellow which signalled a big fat lie.

The woman bit her lip. 'All right, all right, give me a moment. God, I need a drink. Won't we be traced?'

He shrugged. 'Car plates are false. If we don't get out, we won't be caught on camera. No one in England knows her. Parents died in Dublin—unless they think to check abroad, she's nobody. Who's gonna recognize her after all this time? She's not even got the accent.'

'So we leave her and someone else looks after her. She doesn't get hurt.' Auntie was trying to persuade herself she was doing the right thing.

'But she will if I have to come back for her. She's bad for us—ruining what we've got.'

Summoning up the courage, the woman nodded. 'Let's do it.'

'We just need a chance to get clear.' The man turned round and grabbed the front of my T-shirt. 'Listen, freak, you be quiet, no fuss, or we'll come back and get you. Understand?'

I nodded. I was so scared I thought I might wet myself. His lights were pulsing a violent red like just before he hit me.

He reached over and opened the door. 'Now get out and sit over there. Don't cause trouble.'

I unclicked my belt, used to looking after myself.

'Are you sure about this, Phil?' the woman whined.

He didn't answer, just pulled the door closed. The next thing I heard was the car accelerating away.

I sat down and counted daisies.

When I opened my eyes this time, I wasn't in a car park, but sitting in the circle of Zed arms, warm, cared for.

'You saw that?' I whispered, not daring to look at him.

'Yeah. Thank God they dumped you before he killed you.' Zed rubbed his chin lightly over the crown of my head, the hair catching in his stubble.

'I still don't know who I am. I don't think they ever said a name.'

Auntie Jo, Phil, and the freak—that's what we'd been when I was six. If my mother and father—Franny and Ian—had given me a name, I'd forgotten it. My parents had been savants; they'd killed each other because they hadn't controlled their gifts, leaving me with a junkie as my guardian. I felt so angry with them for that betrayal.

'A truth-teller don't go down too well in the house of a dealer.' Zed circled my wrists with his fingers, brushing my palms to gentle out my clenched fists. 'I've seen scum like that before working for Trace and Victor. You were lucky to get out.'

As a child, I'd not understood the transaction in the passageway, but I did now. 'I spoiled things for Phil big time—that man was his best customer. I did that more than once.'

'And he hurt you more than once.'

I cringed, hating having so much ugly stuff exposed like this before the Benedicts. 'I think so.'

Zed's anger was crimson, not directed at me, but out at the one who had dared hurt me. 'I'd like to get him, make him feel what he did to you.'

'He was an evil man, using my aunt. She was mostly OK—but couldn't be bothered with me. I don't suppose they're still together.'

'They're probably both dead. Drugs and dealing don't make for long happy lives,' said Uriel matter-of-factly.

I sagged back against Zed, exhausted and raw. I needed time to put what I'd seen in place, adjust my memories. We weren't talking about it, but I had to come to terms with what my mum's obsession about going to her soulfinder had done to us all. It crept like an ugly stain seeping across what I thought I had with Zed. I felt dirtied by it—threatened.

'You've seen enough,' said Zed. 'We don't expect you to remember everything right away.'

'But we've found the foundation,' said Uriel. 'We can build on that.'

Looking round at the others in the room, I could tell they weren't expecting any answers today. Victor and Trace were the most impatient for information but trying to hide it.

'You need a break. Take the girl snowboarding, Zed,' said Trace. 'We'll make sure you're safe.'

I pushed away the grim memories with an effort. 'By break, do you mean I should break a leg, because that's what's going to happen if I try to board.'

Trace laughed, the serious cop-face relaxing into a fond smile as he regarded his kid brother. 'No, Sky, I don't. He'll take good care of you.'

Chapter 22

It was a relief to get outside. The memories were hanging over my head like a poisonous cloud but the pristine white slopes blew them away—for the moment. Everything sparkled. If I concentrated, I could count every pine needle, every cone, every snowflake, my perception was so clear. The mountains didn't daunt me today but exhilarated.

I'd borrowed a snowsuit from Karla, which made me look like a dumpling, but Zed seemed to think it was cute.

'Nursery slopes?' I asked, my breath puffing like a dragon.

'No, too many people.' Shading his eyes, he studied the mountain, giving me the chance to appreciate how long and dangerous he looked in his close-fitting navy ski suit, a shark on the slopes. He flashed a grin when he caught me admiring him and waggled his eyebrows teasingly. 'Like what you see?'

I elbowed him. 'Shut up! You really need to work on that humility thing.'

He laughed. 'I will—if you'll promise to teach me.'

'I think you're a lost cause.'

That provided him with even more amusement. When he'd finally stopped laughing, he hugged me to his side. 'So, Sky, are you ready? Because we're going up. There's a peaceful place. I was going to take you there that day we got shot at in the woods, but I think it's even better in winter. We'll catch the lift up and walk down to it.'

The top of the mountain was much quieter than at the weekend. José wasn't manning his stall so I couldn't stop for a doughnut and a chat as I usually did. Zed led me away from the busy runs and into the woods.

'Is this a good idea? You know what happened last time we went into the forest.'

Arm looped over my shoulders, he rubbed my upper arm in reassurance. 'Dad and Mom are holding a barrier around the place. Trace, Vick, and Will are on lookout. We should be fine.'

'A mind barrier?'

'Yeah, it sends people away, makes them think they left the headlights on or got to meet someone in town. Which reminds me: how did you get through ours last night?'

I shrugged. 'I felt it, but I was too desperate to care.'

'You shouldn't have been able to do that. It was why Trace and Vick were so suspicious of you just turning up out of the blue.'

'Maybe this barrier isn't as strong as you'd like to think.'

'Maybe you're stronger than we realize. We'll have to find out.'

'Not just now, please.' I didn't want anything more to do with savants—their powers were too freaky.

'No, not now. This is playtime.'

We broke out into the open and the ground dropped away in an awesome sweep, smoothly curved like a J. The peaks across the valley towered on the horizon like an audience of giants come to watch the show.

'Wow.'

'Great, isn't it? Not many people come here because it heads nowhere, but I like it. You can do some extreme boarding here without pesky skiers like my brother getting in the road.'

'I'm not ready for extreme.'

'I know. We can do slow and gentle too.' He flipped the board down on to the snow. 'Been surfing?'

I laughed. 'You don't know much about London, do you? We're not exactly beach babes in Richmond.'

He grinned. 'So what did you do all day?'

'We have a deer park. You can go riding. There's the Thames if you like rowing.'

'Spill it.'

'I . . . er . . . shopped. I've got an Olympic gold in that. And I had my music, of course.'

'Time to broaden your horizons. Take a run then slide.'

'What?'

'Trust me, just do it.'

Feeling more than a bit foolish, I did as he asked.

'OK, so you lead with your right foot.'

'You can tell that how?'

'It's the foot you chose to slide with. Now, I'll get you in the right stance.' He adjusted the board and showed me where to put my feet. He put his arm around my waist and rocked me to and fro. 'It's about balance.'

'This is just an excuse for you to get your hands on me.'

'I know. Great, isn't it?'

To my surprise, I proved much better at boarding than ski-ing. I fell over lots, of course, but more like the average learner than the complete idiot I was on skis.

'Let me see you do your thing, Hot Stuff,' I teased Zed after I felt I'd sat enough times on my butt to call it a day.

'OK, Short Stuff. Make yourself comfortable over there and don't move. I'm gonna show you how it's done. I've just got to go up the hill some.'

I sat in the shelter of a little cliff, watching the slope for any sign of Zed but he seemed to be taking a very long while to get to the beginning of his run.

'Woo-ee!'

A board shot overhead and Zed landed six metres in front of me, weaving his way down the hill.

'Show off!' I had to laugh. I should've guessed he'd do that.

He took a while to trudge back up to me, board on his shoulder, but he was grinning every step of the way.

'What d'ya think?' he called.

'Hmm.' I examined my nails. 'Passable.'

'Passable! That was perfect.'

'You see, this other guy came by and did a somersault. I gave him a ten.'

He dumped the board and tackled me down on to the snow. 'I want a ten too.'

'Uh-uh. Not without a triple axel.'

'That's skating, you dork.'

'My guy, he did one of those on the way back. Got maximum points.'

Zed growled into my neck. 'I'm your guy. Admit it: there was no one else here.'

I giggled. 'Still can't give you a ten for that jump.'

'How about I try and bribe you?' He kissed his way up my neck to my lips, taking time to hit all the right spots. 'So? How did I do?'

Hoping his future sense was on hold for the moment, I quietly took a handful of snow. 'Hmm, let me think. It seems to me . . . you still need practice!' Before he could react, I stuffed the snow down his neck, producing a squawk I'd not heard from him before.

'Right, this is war.' He rolled me over but I scrambled free, gasping with laughter. I ran but he caught me in a few steps and lifted me off my feet. 'It's into the snowdrift for you.' Finding a deep patch, he dumped me down so I was half buried.

'All the more ammunition!' I made a quick snowball and chucked it at him.

It veered in the air and came back to hit my face.

'You cheater!'

Zed bent over with laughter at my outrage.

'That does it! Two can play at that game.' Remembering my egg lasso, I imagined pulling the branch over his head down then let go. It sprang up, showering him with snow. Pleased with the effect, I brushed my hands nonchalantly together. 'Take that!'

Zed shook the ice off his hat. 'We should never have told you about being a savant. You're dangerous.'

I leapt up, clapping my hands. 'I'm dangerous—dangerous! Woo-hoo, I'm dangerous!'

'But not yet skilled!' The snow shifted from under me and I was on my back in the snowdrift with Zed kneeling over me, a threatening snowball in hand. 'So what was that about my snowboarding?'

I smiled. 'Definitely a ten. No, an eleven.'

He chucked the ball aside. 'Good. I'm glad you've seen reason.'

I spent some time on my own later in the day, walking in the woods at the back of the house, sorting through the memories Uriel had unlocked. After my parents' murderous argument—I couldn't bear to dwell on that—my early childhood had been a chaotic nightmare of constant moves, haphazard care, and no love. It hadn't become completely terrible until my aunt had hooked up with the drug dealing boyfriend.

What had happened to the rest of my family? I wondered. Had my mother and father no parents or grandparents, or other brothers or sisters for me to go to? It was a puzzle, and I suspected the answers would not be happy ones. At six, I'd only had a vague grasp of my circumstances, knowing I counted on two unreliable adults to look after me. It had been a horrible existence; not knowing how to make them love me, I had retreated into myself and taken small steps against Phil the bully who had made a project of hurting me.

I rather admired my child-self for that, even though I could have avoided some pain by keeping silent.

I strained to remember more. My name. It seemed a simple thing, one I should remember.

'Sky, are you all right?' Zed thought I'd brooded for long enough and had come in search of me bearing a takeaway cup.

'I'm OK. Just thinking.'

He handed me the container. 'You've done enough of that. Here, I made you hot chocolate. Not as good as the café's, I know, but it should warm you up.'

'Thanks. I need a chocolate hit right now.'

He took my elbow, steering me back towards the house. 'Did you know that chocolate had special chemicals in it to make you feel happy?'

'I don't need an excuse for chocolate.' I sipped, glancing at him sideways. The front of his hair where it was not covered by his hat carried a few snowflakes. His eyes were cheerful today—the pale green-blue of the river shallows in the sunshine. 'And you, have you been sneaking some of the same chemicals?'

'Hmm?'

' 'Cause you look happy.'

He laughed. 'No, not chocolate, just you. That's what being a soulfinder is all about—you're my happiness shot.'

No, that wasn't right: my parents proved that having a soulfinder spelled destruction. I was pretending to Zed that everything was OK but I just couldn't do it—couldn't take the risk. That crushing realization made me feel as if I'd just skied off a cliff and was still in freefall. How was I going to tell Zed—and his family—that after seeing what had happened to my mum and dad, I couldn't be what they expected? When I landed with that news, everything was going to turn really ugly. Zed was going to hate me—and I already hated myself.

I was so scared.

With that hanging over me, the Benedicts chose that evening to begin preparing their house for Christmas. I felt like the Judas at the feast. Saul and Trace disappeared up into the attic and emerged with boxes upon boxes of decorations.

'You take this seriously, don't you?' I marvelled, fingering a beautiful glass bauble with a golden angel suspended inside. That was me—trapped in a bubble of panic, unable to break free.

'Of course, Sky,' said Karla. 'We collect as we travel. My family in the Savant Net, they send me special decorations to add to it each year. It would be an insult to the giver if we did not use them.'

Zed, standing behind his mother, rolled his eyes. 'Mom doesn't think one decoration enough when ten will do. You'll think you're standing in the Christmas department of Macy's by the time we finish.'

No inflatable Santas for the Benedicts. Every artefact was exquisitely handmade and unique. I found a carved nativity set from South America, a string of icicle lights from Canada, and Venetian glass baubles. Part of me craved to belong to this wider family of people with the same kind of gifts, but I didn't deserve to, not when I rejected their ways. I was going to have to say something and soon—it wasn't fair to let them all treat me like one of them when I'd already made my decision to cut myself off from that future. But as each moment ticked by, I couldn't find the courage to speak.

The 'boys', as Karla termed her menfolk, hauled back a fir tree cut from the family plot. It was twice my height and filled the family room to the ceiling. After the customary swearing over faulty bulbs and missing extension cords, Saul and Victor wrapped it in lights. The younger members of the family got to put on the decorations, Zed lifting me up on his back so I could put my choices on the higher branches. Karla recounted a tale for each one, either something about the person who gave it to her or about the place she had bought it. I got an impression of a huge extended family from here to Argentina with far flung branches in Asia and Europe. It made my own family of three seem very small.

'Now we have the carols!' declared Karla, returning with a tray of mulled wine, more hot chocolate for me, and sweet cinnamon biscuits.

Trace pretended to groan and complain. From the amused lights that shone around him, I guessed he was merely fulfilling his expected role as family musical failure. I settled back on a beanbag, keeping out of the way with my guilty conscience for company, and watched Saul tune up his fiddle, Zed get out his guitar, and Uriel assemble his flute. They played a selection of traditional carols beautifully, some of the tunes so haunting I felt I was transported back in time to when these were first sung. It was only then that I realized Uriel was glowing gently with a bronze light. He was not only playing tunes from the past, I could see that he was partly there.

'We need a vocalist,' Uriel announced. 'Trace?'

Everyone laughed.

'Sure, if you want to spoil the moment,' he said, half getting up before Will wrestled him back down.

'Sky?' suggested Yves.

I shook my head. 'I don't sing.'

'You're really musical—I've played with you, remember,' he coaxed.

A flutter of panic made me want to hide. 'I don't sing.'

Uriel closed his eyes for a moment. 'You did.'

'Not any more.'

'Why not, Sky?' asked Zed softly. 'That's behind you now. You've looked at the memories and can put them away. Today's a new start.'

Just not the start he was expecting. Oh God, help me.

Karla passed around the plate of biscuits, trying to break the tension. 'Leave the poor girl alone, you three. No one has to sing if they don't want to.'

But I did. Underneath the alarm, I knew that as a musician I would love to sing, use my voice as another instrument.

'Come on, I'll sing with you.' Zed held out his hand.

'We'll all sing,' suggested Uriel. ' "Joy to the World"?'

'I'll play my sax,' I prevaricated. My mum had dropped it by earlier, knowing I needed music as a comfort when I was distressed.

The Benedicts then proved they not only sang but they harmonized as well as any choir I'd heard. Even Trace ventured a few bass notes without disgracing himself.

At the end, Zed gave me a hug. 'You've a great touch on the sax. You know it's the closest instrument to a human voice.'

I nodded. My tenor sax had been a way of singing without it actually being me. It might be close but I sensed it wasn't quite enough for Zed. He wanted everything and knew I was holding back.

Zed gave up his bedroom to me that night to bunk with Xav. Despite my anxious state of mind, I was so mentally exhausted, I managed to sleep, the first really unbroken rest I'd had since my kidnapping. I woke the next morning to find

264

my mind had been working in the night to sort itself out like a computer going through a defragging process. Having stumbled past my early memories, I remembered everything about Las Vegas. Kelly had taken me apart bit by bit. He'd made me think such terrible things about Zed and Xav, sprayed his graffiti all over my mind—I hated him for that. But now I was back in charge; I could tell truth from falsehood and that was worth celebrating at least. Desperate to share the discovery, I rushed to find Zed.

'Hey!' I burst into Xav's room which was next door. Zed was still zipped up in a cocoon of a sleeping bag on the floor, Xav sprawled on the bed, mouth open, snoring. 'Zed!'

'W-what?' He scrambled out and grabbed me close, assuming we had to be under attack. 'What's happened?'

'I know who took me! I remember it all.'

Xav tumbled out of bed. 'Sky? Wha's'matter?'

I suddenly became conscious that I was standing there in nothing more than a long T-shirt and knickers. I should have stopped to put on more clothes.

'Um, can you get Trace and Victor, Zed?' I asked, edging back. 'I've got something to tell them.'

Zed had had time to surface from sleep. He grinned and patted my butt. 'Go put on my dressing gown. I'll get them out of bed and meet you in the kitchen. Mom and Dad will want to hear this too.'

I told them what I remembered over a cup of tea—my English drinking habits surfacing when I felt most uncomfortable. The memories were frightening: the hotel, Daniel Kelly forcing images into my head, the son circling me like a blubbery great white shark.

Victor recorded what I said, nodding as if I was confirming things he had suspected.

'Another family of savants outside the Net,' mused Saul

when I'd finished. 'Ones with no soulfinders to add balance. And they had O'Halloran on the payroll. Sounds to me that there's more out there than we thought.'

'I know how to manipulate people's minds,' said Victor, tucking the recorder in his pocket, 'but I would never think to do it to such an extent.'

'That's because Kelly's evil and you're not,' I suggested. 'I'm not joking when I said it was like brain mugging. He stole from me, trying to make me hate you.' I reached for Zed's hand under the table. 'The pictures are still there in my head even if I know they're false.'

'Have you heard of a gift like the son's before?' Zed asked Saul, squeezing my fingers in reassurance. 'I don't like the way he went after Sky, making everything worse.'

Saul rubbed his chin in thought. 'The Ute talk of people who thrive on the emotion of others. They are the parasites in the savant world.'

'And the daughter, what can she do?' asked Trace.

'Maybe she has a gift with shields—at least she talked about breaking through mine but it wasn't strong enough to stand up to Daniel Kelly. He's very powerful. I resisted for as long as I could.'

'Probably longer than she expected,' commented Victor. 'And it didn't take properly, did it? You questioned all the time.'

'Are you going to arrest him?'

'Ah.' He sipped his coffee. 'The thing is, Sky, this isn't evidence that I can use to apprehend Daniel Kelly. He's a powerful man; his money buys a lot of silence. No judge would accept your account, especially after the confused version you've already given to the Las Vegas police accusing others.'

'Zed and Xav.'

'Yeah. They dropped their investigation when I proved that

266

they couldn't have had anything to do with your abduction, but it discredits you as a witness.'

'I see. So there was no point me telling you all this?'

'Of course there's a point. We have the truth now and it ties up the things we didn't understand or couldn't know. It is invaluable that we are aware that there are other savants out there working on the dark side.' He curled his lip ironically at the Hollywood echo. 'Yeah, we have a dark side too in the savant world. We could've walked into all manner of traps if we'd remained in ignorance. And it raises the possibility that the mole in the FBI does not even know they're doing it. Daniel Kelly could have got to one of my colleagues and forced them to betray us. I'll have to review who's had contact with him.'

I felt better to know that I had been of use. Revived by this thought, I checked the clock: seven thirty.

'You know something? I want to go to school today.' I'd give anything to feel normal again—to be with friends who couldn't change my thoughts, read my mind, or make things explode. It would also delay having to have the big conversation with Zed that I knew was coming.

'What?' Zed rubbed his rough chin. 'You have the perfect excuse to miss class yet you want to go?'

'I don't like skiving. It makes me feel as if I'm sick, as if I'm letting Daniel Kelly win.'

'Well, if you put it like that, then we have to go. I'd better get ready. Man, I didn't bother to revise for my physics test thinking I'd be with you here today.'

Saul frowned. 'If you're using Sky as an excuse to duck work, Zed . . . '

Zed was up and away. 'Meet you down here in twenty minutes, Sky.'

'I'll just let my parents know what I'm planning.'

Sally and Simon were really happy that I felt well enough to face school.

'You were absolutely right, darling,' bubbled Sally over the phone, 'you needed a change of scene and the Benedicts were the best place for you to go.'

'But I'll come back home tonight.' Being here was too painful as I'd made up my mind to reject the savant world.

'Wonderful. We're planning a treat for you—a little trip.'

'Not Vegas?' I groaned, remembering Simon's new idea.

'If you're feeling better, then we should put the bad memories to bed—see what the city has to offer.'

'I don't want to move there.'

'Nor do I, darling. But you know Simon, he has to follow this to the end and then he'll decide our way in any case.'

I had no desire to go back to a city holding the Kellys. 'This woman who has got in touch: who is she again?'

'Mrs Toscana—a friend of Mr Rodenheim apparently.'

'What hotel does she manage?'

'I forget. Circus Circus was it? Something like that.'

It rang no bells but the coincidence was too suspicious; I decided I'd mention the approach to Victor just to be sure. 'OK, Sally. See you later.'

chapter 23

I walked into Wrickenridge High at eight thirty flanked by Yves and Zed. It felt strange: I'd only been away for a few weeks but it could have been months. As I anticipated, I attracted guiltily intrigued stares. I didn't need to read their minds to know what they were thinking: *There she is—the girl who was kidnapped. Cracked up, we hear. Gone crazy.*

'That's not true, Sky,' murmured Zed. 'No one thinks you're mad. They understand.'

We walked into the office to register my return. Mr Joe practically leapt the desk to give me a hug.

'Little Sky! You're back! We've all been so worried!' He wiped a tear from his eye and sniffed, part genuine, part enjoying the drama. 'Are you quite sure you are ready?'

'Yes, Mr Joe.'

He gave the Benedicts an assessing look. 'You're going to make sure she's all right?'

'Yes, sir,' promised Zed.

'You do that.' Mr Joe handed me a card to take to my form room. 'Now get along with you. You don't want to be late on your first day back.'

And that was what it proved to be like: everyone was bending over backwards to help me settle in again. Even Sheena and her Vampire Brides were nice to me as if, like a spun glass bauble, I might shatter if they said anything cruel. Weirdly it made me miss their stupid bunny comments. I had got behind on all subjects but rather than present this as a problem the teachers organized 'catch-up' packs for me and students offered me the use of their notes. Tina had already photocopied hers. It dawned on me that somewhere along the way I had been accepted as belonging to the school and they were looking out for me as one of their own.

At lunch, I went along with Zed to the music practice. I wasn't expecting to do any more than watch but Mr Keneally was having none of it. He put me back on piano.

'But the concert's next week!' I protested.

He produced a score from his bag with a flourish.

'You're right. Plenty of time to learn the piece I picked out for you.'

'You're expecting me to perform on my own?'

I looked round the room hoping to find some support from my fellow students but even Nelson was grinning at Mr Keneally's tactics.

'You were expecting not to? Why learn an instrument if you don't want to be heard?' asked the teacher.

I didn't think he'd understand the pleasure I took in playing for myself so I kept quiet about that. 'I'm not sure I'm feeling up to this.'

'Nonsense. Best response to a hard knock like you've had is to fight back.'

I suppose I shared that philosophy. 'OK. I'll have a look at the music.'

Mr Keneally moved on to the violins, saying over his shoulder. 'You'd better do more than look. Your name is already on the programme. I told Nelson to put it back on as soon as I heard you'd come to school this morning.'

Victor was lounging against his car at the end of school, waiting for us to emerge. He had some bad but not entirely unanticipated news for me.

'Maria Toscana—better known as Maria Toscana Kelly.' He displayed a photo of Daniel Kelly's daughter on his laptop as we sat in the back seat of his Prius. 'She married an Italian Count but she dumped him two years ago and joined Daddy's empire. Lucky escape for him, I'd say.'

So my instinct had been right. 'They're trying to get to me through my parents.'

'And through you to us. The Kellys' score with the Benedicts has grown longer since we took out two of their men at the warehouse. It might be the lead we're looking for.'

Zed's arm was draped around my shoulders. He now sat up straight, alerted to the dangerous situation that was brewing.

'You can't use Sky and her parents in this, Vick.'

Victor shut the lid of the laptop. 'We're beating our heads against a brick wall at the moment, not least on the whereabouts of the two escapees. The whole family should be behind bars, but we can't even keep those we put there under lock and key. It's frustrating to say the least.'

'What do you think I can do?' I asked.

'I had in mind that you could wear a wire when you meet Maria Toscana Kelly.'

'But she'll be walking into a trap!' protested Zed. 'Vick, she's not doing that.'

'Not if we know about it first—then we can reverse it, catch them instead. These people won't stop coming after us until we get them. I'm thinking of her as well as us—she's one of us too.'

271

I toyed with the straps of my schoolbag. I could help the Benedicts if I did this. If nothing was done, they'd never be able to breathe freely. It was the least I could do as I had been increasingly panicking about the savant thing and was coming to the conclusion that the best thing I could do—the safest—was to run. I'd have to tell Zed that I had no intention of being anything more than his temporary girlfriend. Very soon I'd go back to England and leave the savant world behind.

'Don't listen to him, Sky,' Zed said softly.

'But I can help.'

He looked resolute. 'I'd prefer to know you're safe and well even if it means that the danger doesn't go away for my family.'

'What's the use of that? We'll all be in a kind of prison—one run by Daniel Kelly.'

'Oh God, Sky, don't do this to me.' Zed put his forehead to mine, his distress reaching me in black waves shot through with lightning flashes of silver.

He was so quick to protect me; it was about time he allowed me to return the favour. I wasn't the frail damsel in distress he seemed to think; I had my own power, my own agenda. If I couldn't be the brave partner he needed, the least I wanted was to make sure he and his family would never be harmed by these people.

'No, I won't be doing it *to* you, I'll be doing it *for* all of us—and because it's the right thing. I don't want it on my conscience that I did nothing when I had a chance to make a difference. Who else will Daniel Kelly mind-mug if I don't help stop him?'

'Vick!' pleaded Zed. 'You can't let anything happen to her.'

Victor nodded solemnly. 'I promise. She's one of us, isn't she? I wouldn't let those creeps get us, so I won't let them touch Sky. And she won't be going in without protection.'

Zed was still unconvinced. In some ways he was like my

parents, seeing me as too delicate to face the threats out in the world. I wanted to prove him wrong. I could handle this.

'What kind of protection?' I asked Victor.

Zed wasn't having it. 'Sky, just shut up. You're not doing this. I've seen what these people can do—I'm not letting you get messed up in that.'

I thumped him in the ribs—hard. 'You have no right to tell me to shut up, Zed Benedict. You act like I have to be kept in cotton wool. I've seen bad stuff too—you know I have.'

'Not like this. I don't want it touching you.'

'So it's OK for you to fill your head with these horrors, but not me?'

'Well, yeah.'

'That's just stupid—and sexist.'

'Zed, we need her,' added his brother.

'Keep out of this, Victor,' I snapped.

'Yes, ma'am.'

I glared at them both. 'I've been wanting to say this to you for some time now. You need help, Zed, help coping with the stuff your family dump in your head. I know it makes you angry and frustrated and you take it out on other people, like the teachers, because you can't reach the people who did the bad stuff . . . '

Zed tried to cut me off. 'Just a moment, Sky . . . '

'No, you wait a moment, I'm not finished. I happen to know rather more than most about what bad experiences can do to your head and you need time to sort yourself out without Kelly's threat hanging over you. So to give you that, I'm going to Las Vegas to . . . to kick Daniel Kelly's butt.'

'Well said, Sky,' Victor applauded as Zed glowered at me.

'Now, back to business,' I said briskly. 'What protection did you have in mind?'

'We're not finished here,' growled Zed.

'Yes, we are. Victor, you were saying?'

Victor grinned at his brother. 'The lady's made up her mind, Zed. I'd drop it if I were you. Sky, I'll work with you on your shields. Last time, they were pretty weak. Bedroom walls, right?'

I nodded.

'This time it'll be Windsor Castle thick, rings of protection, OK?'

I smiled. 'OK.'

'And I have a few ideas of what you can do to that scum, Sean, if he goes sniffing around your emotions.'

'Even better.'

Victor patted my hand. 'I like you, Sky. You're a fighter.'

'I am, aren't I? Hear that, Zed? No more Bambi comparisons. I'm a Rottweiler—with a temper.'

'A very small Rottweiler,' said Zed, still not convinced.

The biggest issue as the weekend approached was how much my parents should know about the set up. As a mother herself, Karla was in favour of full disclosure; I was against, knowing they'd immediately ban me from going and pull the meeting, tipping off the Kellys that we were on to them. Victor agreed with me; in the end it was decided that he should have a talk with Sally and Simon about the possibility of those behind the kidnapping still being out there, without actually naming Maria Toscana Kelly.

On Friday evening, my last day before the trip, I lay curled up on the sofa at the Benedicts' house next to Zed while he watched baseball. He had an arm around me, the other digging into the large bowl of popcorn. Everyone else in the family had made themselves scarce, knowing that Zed wanted this time alone with me before sending me off to Vegas in the morning.

Less interested in the mysteries of baseball than studying him, I gazed at the curve of his neck, the line of his jaw, and the slope of his nose. How could anyone be so outrageously . . . well, the only word I could come up with was 'hot'? It didn't seem fair to the rest of us tepid mortals. I thought he was too hooked by the game to notice my study, but I was wrong. He started to laugh.

'Sky, you're being sappy again.'

'Is sappy the same as the English soppy?'

'I guess.'

'But I like looking at you.'

'I'm trying to watch baseball here—it's, like, a sacred pursuit.'

I snuggled closer. How much longer would I be able to do this? 'I'm not stopping you.'

'You are. I can feel your eyes on my face almost as if you were touching me.'

'You've got a very nice face.'

'Why, thank you, Miss Bright.'

'You're welcome, Mr Benedict.' I waited a moment, then whispered. 'Now you're supposed to say "And yours isn't bad either."'

He removed his attention from the screen to look down at my upturned face. 'There's a script for this? What, in "Romance 101"?'

'Uh-huh. One compliment demands one in return.'

He wrinkled his brow in thought. 'Well then, Miss Bright, you have a mighty fine . . . left ear.'

I pelted him with a handful of popcorn.

'I blew it?' he asked innocently.

'Yes, you did.'

He removed the ammunition from my reach, kicked his legs up on the sofa and pulled me on top of him so I lay with my head on his chest, toes touching. I traced little circles on his chest, enjoying his shiver of pleasure. He was so different from me—strong where I had always been slight.

'That's better. Then let me say, Miss Bright, you have the most beautiful left ear, right ear and everything in between that I have had the privilege of seeing. I'm particularly fond of your hair, even though it does get everywhere.' He brushed a strand off his mouth.

'Well, if you do insist on kissing it.'

'Yeah, I do insist. I'll have to get it written into the constitution as my personal inalienable right. I'll send a letter to the president tonight.'

'Hmm.' I turned my head to the screen. 'What's the score?'

'Who cares?'

Now there was the right answer.

A few minutes of just lying together passed. I felt at peace, despite what was waiting tomorrow. Complete. But then, idiot that I am, I had to chisel at the harmony and let the first crack develop between us. 'Zed?'

'Hmm?'

'Don't you think this attempt to get me back to Vegas is, well, a bit obvious?'

I felt him tense. 'What do you mean?'

'The Kellys—Daniel Kelly and Maria at least—they struck me as being clever. Surely they know you would still be keeping a lookout for me? They'd expect you to be suspicious of an invitation out of the blue like this.'

His fingers stroked along my spine, sending little electrical pulses zipping throughout my body. 'Yeah, you've got a point. So what does that mean?'

I shrugged, wishing I could concentrate on the lovely sensations he was provoking rather than fixate on my anxious thoughts. 'I can't work it out. Can you see what's going to happen?'

He was silent for a moment. 'No, I can't. I see you in

Vegas—a flash of a casino—but it doesn't go any further. Like I said, I don't control what I see and with you and my family, at this distance from the events, there are too many variables to get a clear picture.'

'What if they're using me to draw your family in again? They might guess Victor will be on hand to protect me. I might be leading my parents and your brother into real danger.'

'You forget to mention yourself. You know I'm against you doing this. If you've got doubts, it's not too late to back out.'

'But that would still leave us with your family under threat.'

'Yeah, it would.'

'It's not fair.'

'No, but I believe we do good work when we use our gifts together. It's worth it. No one else in the Savant Net can do quite what we do.'

I pushed up on my elbows. 'I couldn't live that way.' I slid off him, sitting on the edge of the sofa. He was already half killing himself with the strain of his work. He'd never said, but I would put money on him having nightmares about the things he had witnessed. What would he do when he realized I wasn't going to stick around—that I was running scared because I feared the soulfinder thing far more than I feared Daniel Kelly?

He must have overheard an echo of my fears because he caught me by the waist to stop me putting more distance between us. 'I want you to be happy. We'll work it out.'

No, we wouldn't. 'You say that now, but people do let you down, you know.' I was trying to warn him not to invest too much in me. 'Things change. I mean, I doubt many people stay with their high school sweethearts.'

His expression clouded. 'You're not being fair, Sky. I've sensed for a few days now that you're shaken up by the soulfinder thing, but soulfinders have nothing in common with high school sweethearts—it goes much deeper.'

We were still side by side but no longer moulded to each other; I only had myself to blame because I was the one who had taken a step back.

I tried to sound mature and reasonable. 'I think I am being fair. I think I'm being realistic.'

'Is that how you see me?' Zed's face hardened, reminding me he didn't have a reputation for trouble without cause. 'Haven't you felt what I feel? Are you still closing off your gift?'

Of course, I'd felt it—too much and it was scaring me. 'I don't know what's normal and what's not. I know I love you but I just can't do this.' I gestured between us.

'I see.' He sat up and moved down the far end of the sofa. 'Well, while you think that one out, I'll just watch the rest of the game.'

'Zed, please. I need to talk about this.'

He floated the popcorn bowl to his lap. 'We've been talking. So far we've established that I'm just a boy you're dating. You're running from the miracle that we've found each other.'

I wrung my hands. I hadn't wanted to upset him but how could I not when I was fighting for my emotional survival? He didn't understand what was at stake for me.

'Look, Zed, my parents killed each other over my mother's soulfinder. I don't want history to repeat itself. I don't have that kind of strength in here.' I tapped my head.

He gave a curt nod. 'I understand. Your mom and dad lost it, so we will too. It doesn't make a blind bit of sense but you probably know that. The way I see it, your parents got into problems because Fate pulled a mean trick on them and your mom ran out on your dad when she should've handled finding her soulfinder more fairly. They made a mistake and you paid for it.'

I didn't like his criticism of my mum for running. 'I'm trying to explain how I feel, Zed.'

'And what about how I feel, Sky?' He pulverized a handful of popcorn, struggling to keep his temper. 'I'd walk across burning coals for you. Hell, I walked in front of a gun for you. But is that enough to prove I love you? That you are it for me? I don't know what more I can do.'

'Please don't be angry.'

'I'm not angry. I'm disappointed.'

God, that was worse. 'I'm sorry.'

'Yeah, well.' He pretended to watch the game but I could see that his emotions were fluctuating wildly between anger and hurt.

I felt absolutely gutted by what I'd just done. He'd offered me love—it was something unique—like a Fabergé egg—which I'd proceeded to smash. To have your soulfinder reject you was like tearing yourself in two, but somehow I couldn't help myself. I was hurting him because I was plain terrified. Like that mountaineer who cut off his own hand to save himself, pain now was better than more suffering later, wasn't it? Oh God, was I right or just running?

Confused and scared, I switched off the television.

'Hey!' Zed reached for the controller.

'Just give me a moment then you can switch it back on.' I tucked the controller behind my back. 'I really am sorry. This is me—I'm not the most confident person. You said once I always act surprised when someone likes me—but it isn't an act. I don't expect people to like me—let alone love me. I just don't feel that lovable and now you can see why. I suppose it's kinda your bad luck to end up with me as a soulfinder.'

Zed ran a hand across his face and through his hair, trying to muster his thoughts. 'I don't blame you.'

'I know you don't. You've seen what's inside me, warts and all.' I gave a slightly hysterical laugh. My heart was pounding: I'd messed up big time but I couldn't leave him thinking I didn't have strong feelings for him. Maybe I couldn't be what he wanted, but I could prove I loved him. 'You said you walked in front of a gun to show that you loved me. Well, I suppose I can only do the same for you. I'm going to Vegas tomorrow—and I'll be doing it for you.'

He shot to his feet. 'No way!'

I chucked him the controller which he caught on reflex. 'I'm not as sorted as you are about this savant stuff and we both have to live with that. I just can't risk being that way with you—I don't think I'll survive the life.' I took a breath. 'But Victor's plan is the only way I can think of to give you proof that, despite my messed-up head, I do love you.'

There—I'd said my piece. I couldn't read Zed's response—his emotions were confused and he was ominously silent.

'So, you can . . . um . . . get back to the game. I'm going to turn in—get an early night.'

He held out a hand to me. 'Sky?'

'Yes?'

'I still love you—more than ever. I'll wait till you're ready.'

I felt a huge rush of guilt. I'd never be ready.

'I don't want you to put yourself on the line for me.'

I folded my arms. 'Yeah, I kinda guessed that bit.'

He tugged me closer, his large hand rose to cradle the back of my head, warmth seeping through to the skin. 'I'll talk to Victor about your worries. I'm gonna insist I come. My future sense works well just before an event even with interference. I can help anticipate problems.'

'From a safe distance?'

'From a reasonable distance. Close enough to be there to help, but not so close to hand the Kellys the advantage.'

'OK.' I rubbed my palm over his heart, silently apologizing for the heartache I was causing. 'I can cope with that.'

chapter 24

The female FBI agent I'd encountered months ago met me in the washrooms at McCarran airport, Las Vegas, to fit me with my wire.

'Hi, Sky. Anya Kowalski. Remember me?' she asked, getting out her kit.

'Yes, of course.'

She smiled at me in the mirror, her sleek brown hair glowing in the spotlights. 'We appreciate what you're doing for us.'

'Can you hurry, please? Sally might come looking for me any moment now.'

She grinned at my worried reflection. 'That's not likely. She's being interviewed by a local reporter on her views on airport standards. He's not letting her get away.'

'And he is?'

'One of our men.' She slipped a tiny microphone into the elastic of my bra. 'That should do it. Try not to cover up too much and remember not to bash it with anything—purse, whatever—as it gives our listening post a nasty headache.'

'OK. That's it? No battery or wire?'

'Nope. It's got its own little power pack and will run for

about twenty-four hours. No wires to give it away.'

'But it emits a signal, right?'

'Yes, it transmits sound. What you hear, we hear.'

'Can anyone tell?'

'Theoretically. But only if they have the inside track on FBI frequencies. We've not had a problem before.'

'But if Daniel Kelly has got this information from one of you already?'

She grimaced. 'Then the proverbial hits the fan. But we'll get you and your parents out, don't worry.'

Sally was preening when I returned to her side.

'That young man was really interested in my views,' she said. 'He said he totally agreed that the airport was bland and could do with some more challenging artworks—maybe a Damien Hirst cow or diamond skull—this is Vegas, after all.'

'Why not go the whole hog and have the Emin bed?' grumbled Simon, who didn't think highly of installation works. 'Most people bumming about airports look as though they could do with a good sleep.'

'I should have thought of that.' Sally winked at me.

'I think one of Dali's melting clock faces is more appropriate—time seems like fudge for international travellers,' I suggested.

My parents stopped and stared at me in amazement.

'What?' I asked, embarrassed.

'You understand art!' Sally gasped.

'Yeah, so?'

Simon laughed with delight. 'All these years and I thought it wasn't rubbing off on her!' He gave me a smacking kiss.

'I'm still not going to go splash paint on unsuspecting canvases,' I mumbled, pleased I'd given them something to celebrate. I felt bad enough about letting them walk into this blind.

'We wouldn't expect you to. In fact, I think I'd forbid you to try. Imagine having another scatty artist in the family!'

Simon linked his arms in mine and Sally's and waltzed us out of the airport to the waiting car.

Sliding into the back seat, the reality of what was happening rushed back. It wasn't the same vehicle I'd been carried in to the warehouse—just an innocuous hotel shuttle to the airport—but I still felt a chill run up my spine.

Zed?

It's OK, Sky. Victor and I are two cars behind. We'll drop back and pass the tail over to another agent in a moment, but we won't lose you.

Is it OK to talk like this?

Until you reach the hotel. We're guessing Maria Kelly is the surviving shield expert so we mustn't take risks.

Tell me again, how much do I have to get for the FBI to move in?

We need them to admit to involvement in the kidnapping or to do something illegal on this trip, like try to falsify your memories—that's the most likely. An added bonus would be any sight or sound of the two Kelly escapees.

How do I get them to do that? It seemed far more difficult now I had to execute the strategy I'd only thought about in the abstract.

They've set things up to bring you here so they must have a plan. Go along with things as far as you can. We're guessing they're going to try and separate you from Sally and Simon.

And I let them?

I could tell Zed was uncomfortable with the answer. *They'll be safer that way.*

Don't worry about me.

No can do.

We turned into the covered drop-off area for The Fortune Teller casino hotel.

'That's what it's called!' said Sally, clicking her fingers. 'I knew it was something to do with fairs.' She smoothed her Matisse silk scarf over the jacket of her light wool suit. 'Do I look OK, Sky?'

'Very professional.' I regretted that she was wasting her efforts on a criminal.

Simon always screamed 'artist' whatever he was wearing. Today he'd put on his favourite black denim jacket with his jeans—his version of a suit.

'What an amazing place!' he marvelled as we strode through the foyer with its ranks of slot machines and waitresses in skimpy gypsy costumes. It was a maze—many of the shops selling cheap rubbish right next to designer label stores. 'So absolutely tasteless, it is quite a work of art in itself.'

To our right, a klaxon sounded and coins began to pour from a machine into the lap of an ecstatic man in a shiny blue tracksuit. There was a momentary lull as the gamblers glanced over at the lucky winner, then business as usual.

'I'd like to paint the faces,' mused Sally, eyeing a woman with an acutely desperate expression perched on a stool by her chosen fruit machine. 'You can smell the hope and the hopelessness. The lack of natural light gives it an underworld feeling, doesn't it; land of lost souls?'

Underworld? I was thinking Hell myself with the Kellys as the ruling demons.

A bellboy led us to the bank of lifts. 'Mrs Toscana will see you in her office,' he explained. 'West Tower, third floor.'

The mirrored lift took us to the mezzanine level. A balcony overlooked the main floor of the casino, a variety of games under way from roulette to poker. As it was mid afternoon, most people were casually dressed and the atmosphere relaxed. I'd expected James Bond sophistication and got seaside amusements. The baize shone with the rich green of dubious promise, plastic chips which in truth represented millions of dollars thickening the illusion that this was all just a harmless bit of fun. Our guide showed us to a double set of doors with 'General Manager' inscribed on a brass name plate. Once we were through, we left behind the garish fortune teller flash of the hotel decor for quiet and refinement: an elegant white L-shaped sofa for visitors; fresh flowers on a low glass table; and a neatly dressed secretary who greeted us and showed us into the boss's inner sanctum.

The first thing I noticed was the bank of screens showing activity in all parts of the hotel. There were close-ups of the card tables as well as more general views of the public areas. Then I noticed Maria Kelly standing by the window looking out on to the hotel atrium, her hand outstretched. My hackles rose: she was poison and I didn't want her anywhere near my parents.

'Simon, Sally, delighted to meet you in person after our phone calls. And this must be Sky?'

Her smile was friendly, but her emotions told another story, flickering between cool blue calculation and a tinge of red violence. I hoped my face did not betray my revulsion at seeing her again. I had to pretend I still did not remember.

'Yes, it is,' said Simon. 'Thanks for inviting us.'

She waved us to three chairs across the desk from hers. 'I was hoping that this weekend would give you a chance to understand my hotels, what kind of clientele we cater for, and what artistic tastes they might have. I think you'll find our rooms range from the economy to the exclusive and our guests' preferences are on as wide a scale.'

This job was bogus—I could see it in the yellow lights now glowing around her. She was enjoying spinning the tale, like a cat playing with mice.

'I've got a full programme worked out for you and one of

my assistant managers will be dedicated to facilitating your visit. But that no doubt sounds very boring for your daughter.'

'Sky's happy to fit in with us,' Sally said. 'She'll be no bother.'

'No, no, that won't be necessary. I thought she might prefer to find out what Vegas has to offer young people.'

Simon shifted in his seat. 'Well, now, Mrs Toscana, that's really kind of you, but you know what Sky's been through recently; we don't want to leave her on her own in an unfamiliar place.'

'Naturally, I couldn't agree more. That's why I've asked my younger brother if he could spare the time to look after her. I'm sure he'll show her a good time. Maybe they could catch an afternoon show. The Cirque du Soleil is amazing—she can't miss that!'

Sean Kelly's idea of a good time was to drain me of all my emotions and mess around with my head. So this was the plan: to throw me to the Sean-lion while my parents were shepherded off to play in the hotel. I only hoped Victor and Zed were getting all this and would step in before things went too far.

'Would you like that, darling?' Sally asked.

'That's fine,' I replied, not quite able to bring myself to thank Maria.

'Lovely.' The lines around Sally's eyes crinkled into a relieved smile. 'Then we'll see you back here this evening for dinner, darling.'

'I've booked my private dining room for us, so you can meet other members of the senior staff.' Maria smiled, displaying an expensive set of teeth. 'But Sky might prefer to grab a burger with Sean. He's waiting for her just outside. I've got a few business matters I'd like to discuss with your parents, Sky. I hope you don't mind.'

'Fine.' She was a real cow—sending me off with the creep outside while pretending she was doing me a favour. 'I'll see you later then.'

'Let's play it by ear,' Simon said happily. 'Come back when you've had enough, love.'

Reluctantly, I got up. The only redeeming part of this plan was the fact that my parents were going to be far away from any danger. I checked my new phone was in my jeans' pocket. Victor had given it to me that morning, saying he'd programmed in his and other emergency numbers just in case. 'Keep your phone switched on, Simon—I'll call when I'm finished seeing the sights.'

'Don't rush if you're enjoying yourself.' Sally smiled conspiratorially at Maria.

That was highly unlikely—not unless it involved seeing our hosts led away in handcuffs.

I'd forgotten just how repulsive Sean was in the flesh. It wasn't the fact that he was overweight—that could have made him friendly and jolly—it was the dampness of his palm, the smarminess in his smile, the little moustache that looked like an earwig.

'Sky Bright? Delighted to meet you.' He held out a hand which I had to take but I slid free as soon as possible.

'Hi. You're Sean, right?'

'Yes. Maria's asked me to take care of you.'

I bet she has.

'What do you want to see first? The tables?' He led the way to the lifts.

'Am I allowed to gamble? I thought I was under-age.'

He gave me a wink. 'Let's say it's a special arrangement just for you. I'll get you some chips on the house and you can have a play without losing a dime of your own money. I'm generous—I'll let you keep any winnings.'

'That's really kind of you.' *Not.*

He took me to the cashier's window and drew out chips worth a thousand dollars. 'That should get you started.'

'I don't know the rules of any of the card games.'

'Then let's try roulette—that's child's play.'

This whole thing was like a spin of roulette. Black or red? Would we come out a winner or the Kellys?

'OK. That sounds fun,' I said with feigned enthusiasm.

I swiftly lost half the money through bad guesses, then won a quarter of it back with a lucky punt. I could see how the game could become addictive. There was the hope that the next spin would favour you. No skill was involved; only good fortune.

'Another go?' Sean raked in my winnings for me.

'OK.' I shoved nearly all of my money on an outside bet on the evens square.

I lost.

'Hey ho,' I sighed, trying not to be bothered by all this money going back to the hotel. It was only leprechaun gold, like in *Harry Potter*.

Put everything on the fifteen, Zed whispered.

I hid my smile behind my hand. I knew he'd be unbeatable at gambling. I placed my remaining chips on fifteen. Sean shook his head.

'Are you sure, Sky? A bet like that is called a straight up—a risky move.'

'Yeah, I like to live dangerously.' I gave him a brash smile.

The other participants chuckled indulgently at my rookie's enthusiasm.

'Well now,' drawled a Stetson-wearing good ol' boy from Texas, 'if the pretty lady says black fifteen is lucky, I'll put my money where she's put hers. Thirty-five to one—great odds—if you win.'

From the gentle orange glow around the man, I could tell he was only trying to make me feel better about my rashness in the spirit of 'misery loves company' when I inevitably lost it all.

'Trust me,' I told him seriously. 'I'm feeling good about this.'

With a laugh, he shoved a sizeable chunk of his money on the fifteen. Catching on to the fun of the moment, several other people risked a chip or two on the same square.

With a confident smile, the croupier spun the big wheel and dropped in the ball.

'First time, honey?' asked my Texan, tucking his thumbs into his belt.

'Yes.'

'You've got a nice accent there.'

'I'm English.'

'Pleased to meet you. Now, little lady, don't go getting upset when you lose your money—treat it as a lesson. Wish I had when I was your age. I'd've had myself a nice condo in Florida if I hadn't wasted it all in places like this.'

I smiled and nodded, turning my attention back to the slowing wheel. Little did he know but he was one step closer to that retirement place.

The ball jumped, clattered, then dropped into its slot. The croupier looked down and swallowed. 'Black fifteen!'

There was a gasp from all at the table, bar me. Then . . .

'Yee-ha!' The Texan threw his hat in the air. Next he picked me up and spun me round, giving me a kiss on both cheeks. 'Luck is a lady and here she is!'

Our joint winnings were impressive. I walked away with nearly five thousand dollars, the Texan with several hundred thousand, much to Sean's horror.

'Promise to spend it on a place in Florida?' I asked the Texan, who introduced himself as George Mitchell the Third.

I could just see him handing it all back to the Kellys with another rash bet.

'I promise, honey. And even more, I'll call it after you. What's your name?'

'Sky Bright.'

'Perfect. Bright Skies here I come.' With a wave of his hat, he headed for the cashier's office, hitching his trousers up by the belt.

Gamblers being a superstitious bunch, I found myself besieged by requests for tips for the next spin. Sean pulled on my arm.

'I think we'd best be heading out,' he said smoothly, his lights pulsing an angry red.

'OK. Whatever you want,' I replied sweetly.

'I'll make sure your winnings get to you. A cheque OK?'

'Um . . . to my parents, please. I haven't opened my own bank account in the US yet.'

'Fine.' His grip on my arm was just the far side of comfortable, showing that his control was slipping. He tried to make a joke of it. 'I should take you out of here before you break the bank. How about you go ruin some of our competitors?'

Did that mean he suspected I had used savant powers to beat the roulette wheel?

'I think I've had enough. Beginner's luck and all that. Don't want to push it.'

He mastered himself, getting back on track. 'OK, let's go eat then. We've got an excellent restaurant on the top floor, views across to Red Rock Canyon. I'll just drop your chips in the office.' He headed for the cashier's window. I could tell from the aura of satisfaction that surrounded him that he had no intention of me seeing a cent.

I couldn't resist checking Zed was still listening even with the risk. Maria Kelly had to be busy, didn't she? *You get that?*

Yeah. I'm still laughing about the roulette—well done, baby. I couldn't help giving you the tip—Victor's not amused.

Hearing his voice in my head grounded me, lessened the fear. *One of my finer moments, thanks to you.*

There was a pause. *I've got to be quick. Victor says Daniel Kelly is up top. We think this might be it.*

They're going to try and wipe my mind again?

Very likely—but we won't let that happen. Don't forget to keep your shields strong. We're moving in to position, got a team on the floor below posing as a cleaning crew.

Where are you?

Close. I'd better stop talking to you now in case Sean picks it up.

I don't think he can, but maybe Maria is about the place somewhere. She's the more powerful savant, I'd say.

Then we must break this off. Stay safe.

Yeah, you too.

Chapter 25

The trip up in the lift was one of the hardest things I have ever done. I had to hide the fact that I was feeling sick with nerves, remembering all too well what had happened last time I'd been alone with Daniel Kelly and son.

'So, what you fancy? They do a good club sandwich,' Sean said, rubbing his hands together. All he needed was a black cape and to cackle 'bwa-ha-ha' to complete the bad guy act. I found him pathetic.

'Um, yeah, that sounds lovely.'

'You like Las Vegas?'

'It's unique.'

He sniggered. 'It is that. A manmade playground.'

'You in college?'

'No. I went straight into the family business.'

'Hotels?'

'And other things.'

It was the other things he preferred—the racketeering and the violence. I could sense he thought of himself as following in Dad's footsteps. He was quite pitiable really, with none of the edge his father and sister had. He was only truly frightening when he threatened to suck the emotions out of me.

The lift doors opened on an all too familiar corridor. I couldn't help hesitating before I stepped out.

'Problem?'

'Er . . . no, just a moment of déjà-vu.'

He stroked his moustache to hide a grin. 'I know the feeling. Look, Sky, I just want to introduce you to my father; he's CEO of the family business. It won't take a moment. Is that OK with you?'

I shoved my hands in my pockets, glancing down quickly to check that my microphone was not visible in my cleavage. 'OK.'

I'm doing this for Zed, I told myself as I followed Sean into the boardroom.

As he had been that day weeks ago, Daniel Kelly was waiting at the head of the table. 'Ah, Sky, good to see you again.' He got up and waved the door closed with his telekinetic powers.

The lock clicked.

What? He wasn't even bothering to hide that he was a savant.

'I've met you before?' I asked, hoping I sounded genuinely puzzled.

'You can drop the pretence now. I'm fully aware that the FBI has sent you to us in the vain hope we'll incriminate ourselves. But that's not going to happen.'

Then why was he talking like this? I couldn't help but glance down again.

'You can forget about the wire. Maria's running interference. They'll just be getting static. Sean, where are your manners? Show our guest to a chair.'

Sean seized my shoulders and pushed me down on to a seat on its own by the window.

'What are you getting from her?' Daniel Kelly tapped his fingers on his crossed arms.

'The smug confidence has gone.' Sean inhaled deeply. 'Fear—wonderful fear.'

'Take as much as you like,' his father said. 'She's cost us enough with that stunt she pulled in the casino.'

I shuddered as Sean bent to my neck and rubbed his cheek against mine. I felt like a tyre developing a puncture, air rushing out. My training with Victor fled with it; I couldn't remember what I was supposed to do. Fear escalated; I was shivering uncontrollably. Worst of all, I couldn't feel Zed with me any more. All the most frightening times in my life crowded to the fore: my parents' argument, Phil's beatings, abandonment, being shot at in the forest, the warehouse.

'Wonderful,' murmured Sean. 'She's like a vintage wine— intoxicating, potent.'

Daniel Kelly decided he had indulged enough. 'Stop now, Sean. I want her conscious.'

Sean brushed a sweaty kiss on my jaw and stood up. I felt clammy and washed out, energy having drained away with the emotion. I hugged my arms around me.

Think, I ordered my fractured mind. *There's something you can do. Windsor Castle.*

But my shields were a house of cards, tumbling down at the first shock.

'If I am right, the FBI will be trying to gain access to this floor so we don't have long. Unfortunately, Sky, you are going to go on a teenage rampage, your doubtful sanity having given way. Seizing this gun,' he indicated a handgun lying on the table, 'you're going to run through the casino shooting at innocent guests. The FBI will have to take you out to stop you—sacrifice their pawn. Rather poetic isn't it?'

'I won't.'

'You will. Of course, they'll suspect the truth but there will be no evidence, what with you being dead and all.'

'No.'

'How tragic for the Benedicts.' He perched on the edge of the table, checking his watch. 'You see, Sky, I've decided that to make them instrumental in the death of innocents is the best revenge. They'll have to live with the knowledge. It'll cripple them permanently and the FBI wouldn't dare use them again.'

I had to get a grip on myself. Victor had told me what to do if I faced mind-mugging again. I had to get it right as not only my own life was at risk this time. I couldn't imagine anything more horrifying than causing the death of others. He was not going to do this to me. I refused to let him.

I clenched my hands on the arms of the chair and began to project waves of my power. The table shook; a glass carafe juddered to the edge and crashed to the floor; a crack developed in the window, snaking up to the ceiling.

'Stop it!' Kelly said sharply, slapping me round the face. 'Maria! Sean, drain her!'

Maria rushed in as Sean bent once more to my neck. I felt him this time before he could begin absorbing the emotion. I pulsed out one beat of anger, hitting his mind like a punch to the chin. He reared back.

'What the—!' Sean grabbed his head, blood dripping from his nose. 'You little witch!'

'Maria, do something!' ordered Daniel Kelly as the ceiling panels began to fall into the room.

Maria thrust both palms towards me. It was like hitting a wall after freewheeling down a hill. I was thrown back in the chair, ending up on the floor, my attack cut off.

'Our little savant has learned to use her powers, has she?' With a wave of his hand, Daniel Kelly righted my chair. 'But you don't seriously think you can match the three of us, do you? No, I can see from your eyes that you don't. You're still waiting for your cavalry to charge in and save you, but the bad news for you is that they won't. This floor is locked down and they have no warrant. By the time they get one, the drama will have relocated to the casino.' He grabbed my head between his hands and squeezed. 'Now sit back and relax. This won't take long.'

The next thing I remember is walking out of the lift into the hotel lounge. A pianist sat at his instrument crooning a song about people needing people. But I didn't need anyone. I wanted to shoot them, didn't I?

I strolled into the casino, gun tucked in the small of my back under my shirt.

'Hey, it's Lady Luck!' George Mitchell the Third swooped on me.

'What you still doing here, George?' I asked him. Was I supposed to kill him too? I felt a bead of sweat run down my face. I wiped it away.

'Just saying goodbye to the tables. I swore to you I wouldn't be back and I'm a man of my word.'

'That's good, George. You best get going.'

'Yeah, I'm saddling up and heading out.' He tipped his hat to me, then squinted at my face. 'You don't look so good, honey.'

'I feel a bit strange.'

'Go lie down. Take a load off. Can I get someone for you?'

I rubbed my forehead. I wanted someone. Zed. He was close.

'Your parents?'

Artists. Art. *Didn't know you understood art.* Old Masters. Layers. It was important but I couldn't remember why. Images were flicking through my brain like wind stirring the leaves of one of my graphic novels, opening on random pages.

'I'm OK. I'll go up to my room in a moment.'

'You do that, honey. It was nice meeting you.'

'And you, George.'

He turned his back, walking away with a wide-legged gait.

Shoot him.

No!

Take out the gun and shoot him.

My hand crept round to the gun in my waistband, fingers curling round the butt, drawing it clear. Then someone screamed—Maria Kelly rushed for the security guard and pointed at me.

'She's got a gun!' she shrieked.

I looked down at my hand. So I did. I was supposed to run and fire the thing at random.

Do it.

Old Masters. False memories. Scrape away.

The security guard hit the alarm. I stood irresolute in the middle of the casino as gamblers dived for cover. A slot machine paid out a win to an empty stool.

'Sheesh, honey, you don't want to fire that thing!' called George from the safety of the other side of a pinball table.

My brain was screaming at me to act. I couldn't stop myself— I raised the muzzle to the ceiling and squeezed the trigger. The recoil was incredible, jarring my wrist. A chandelier shattered. How could I have done that? I was trapped in a nightmare with my body and brain no longer under my control.

That's it—now target the people.

No, this was wrong. I hated guns. I stared down at the big black thing in my hand as if it was a cancerous growth, wanting to drop it but my mind shouted at me to start firing.

Then, scrambled from the upper floors of the hotel, the FBI made it into the casino, pushing hotel security aside. I must have looked odd, standing in the middle of an empty floor, surrounded by spilled cards and chips, a ticking roulette wheel, but making no effort to defend myself.

'Drop the gun, Sky!' called Victor. 'You don't want to do this. This isn't you.'

I tried to shake it loose but my fingers wouldn't uncurl, my brain over-riding the command.

Turn the gun on yourself. Say you'll kill yourself if they come any closer. Daniel Kelly's words brought the muzzle under my ear.

'Don't come any closer,' I said in a shaky voice.

There was a scream to my left. Security guards were restraining my parents as they tried to reach me.

'Sky, what are you doing?' Sally cried, her face drained of colour.

'Come on, love, put the gun down. You need help. No one's been harmed—we'll get you help,' Simon said desperately.

Somehow their words didn't penetrate. More powerful were the whisperings that I should end it all, punish the Benedicts for using me.

'Stay back—no one come any closer!' My finger tightened on the trigger. There seemed no other way.

Then Zed stepped out from behind Victor, shaking his brother off when he attempted to stop him.

'She won't shoot me,' he said calmly, though his lights were flickering red with anger.

Was he angry with me? I hadn't done anything, had I?

No, he's not angry with me. With someone else. The Kellys.

Zed came towards me. 'Second time I step in front of a gun for you, Sky. We've really got to stop meeting like this.'

He was making fun of me? I was threatening to kill myself and he cracked a joke? This wasn't the script. People were supposed to run in terror—I was supposed to die in a hail of bullets.

'You shouldn't be here, Zed.' Thirsting for something that

made sense in this madness, I drank in the sight of him—broad shoulders, the strong lines of his face, the deep blue-green eyes.

'Sky, you have to understand that now I've found you, I'm not going away. Deep down you don't want me to either. Soulfinders don't hurt each other. We can't because it would be like harming yourself.'

'Soulfinder?' What was I doing? The internal compulsion to pull the trigger melted like frost in the sun. This all felt wrong because it wasn't my script. My destiny stood in front of me, loving me enough to risk me shooting him. Soulfinder. The Kellys hadn't known that I had a power they could not defeat; I'd already been found—I'd managed to protect that secret when they'd destroyed all my other defences. Recognition of my soulfinder punched through the suffocating false layers with a strength not even a skilled savant could counter.

It all became clear. My fingers loosened on the gun butt and I let it drop to the floor.

I gave a shaky shrug.

'Um . . . what can I say? Sorry?'

Zed rushed the last few yards and grabbed me in a hug. 'Those Kellys got you again?'

I buried my head in his chest. 'Yeah, they did. I was supposed to punish you by either doing myself in or getting gunned down by the FBI.'

'Clever—but they can't beat my girl.'

'They almost did.'

'No!' Daniel Kelly stormed into the casino flanked by Maria and Sean, hungry for a consolation prize as the main one eluded him. 'I'm pressing charges against this girl. She threatened my guests with a gun—shot at my property—disrupted play. Arrest her.'

My parents reached my side seconds before the Kellys.

'What's going on, Sky?' Simon looked ready to punch Mr Kelly.

'Sally, Simon, meet Daniel Kelly and family.' I waved at them. 'They're responsible for my kidnapping last time and tried to brainwash me this afternoon into going on a shooting spree down here.'

'The girl is mad. She's already spent a month in a mental facility. She is totally unreliable.' Daniel Kelly got out his BlackBerry, speed-dialling his legal team. 'She needs to be locked up for the safety of the general public.'

Victor scooped up the gun with a handkerchief and tucked it in an evidence bag.

'Very interesting, Mr Kelly, but I beg to disagree. I believe Sky is right to say you've been manipulating her.'

Sally looked horrified. 'You mean drugged her—or . . . or what? Hypnotized her?'

'That's right, ma'am.'

'You've no evidence of that,' sneered Maria Toscana, shoulder to shoulder with her father. 'But we do have ample footage from the CCTV of this girl storming in here and shooting wildly. Which of us is a judge going to believe?'

'Sky.' Victor grinned wolfishly. 'You see, I worked out, Mr Kelly, that you'd got to Agent Kowalski when she had you under surveillance in October. As she was my partner, you couldn't resist, could you? Once I realized who was leaking information about our investigation, things such as who Sky was, intelligence only Kowalski and I knew, I expected her to inform you about the tap we put on Sky. Kowalski never had a clue you were using her, did she?'

'I'm saying nothing,' Daniel Kelly said through his teeth.

'That's fine, because I have plenty of talking to do. Agent Kowalski fitted Sky with a standard FBI wire—the one you were blocking—but she didn't know anything about the recording device in Sky's phone.' He pulled my mobile from my back pocket and tapped it. 'Every word you said to Sky is captured, preserved for the judge and jury to hear. I'm sure it'll make interesting listening.'

'I want a lawyer.'

Victor's grin widened. 'Excellent. My favourite four words. Daniel Kelly, Maria Toscana Kelly, Sean Kelly, I am arresting you for kidnapping and conspiracy to murder. You have the right to remain silent . . . '

Six uniformed officers stepped up to cuff the Kellys as Victor continued to recite their rights. Zed led me apart and hugged me tight, rocking me to and fro so only my toes brushed the carpet.

'Isn't that a lovely sound—to hear their rights read to them?' he murmured in my ear, kissing the very same place Sean had slobbered over, taking away the shivery feeling. I was safe. Home.

'I hope they lock them up and throw away the key.'

'From Vick's expression, I think he's pretty confident of that.'

'Did you know about the phone?'

'Yeah, but I couldn't tell you in case the Kellys picked it out of your mind.'

I rested my palm over his heart, listening to the steady beat as I came down from my adrenaline high. I couldn't stop trembling. 'Then you're forgiven.'

'I never dreamed they'd make you do something like this, baby.' He gestured to the mess I'd made of the casino.

'I didn't do anything, remember? Well, except for shooting that chandelier but, as it's an offence to good taste, I was in fact doing everyone a favour.'

'You really OK?'

'Yes, I am. Uriel helped me last time to sort out true from

false; this time, once I sensed the fake stuff, it all fell into place much more quickly thanks to my soulfinder. But I've got a headache though. And I made an even bigger mess of the penthouse—shook it up a bit.'

'Yeah, we felt that. I'm impressed. You pack a powerful punch into your five feet and one debatable inch.'

I looked up to see the Kellys being led away. 'Someone needs to make sure Daniel Kelly doesn't use his gift to get them out of jail.'

'Victor's on to that. He's got procedures set up to make sure Kelly can't get his claws into anyone.'

'What about the two Kellys that got away from jail?'

Zed ruffled my hair. 'Come on, Sky, three collars for one day isn't bad going. We'll get them sooner or later. What I want to know is when you're going to stop running from me.'

I rested my head on his chest. 'Running?'

'We're not like your biological parents. We can make this work. Just trust me. Please.'

Standing peacefully together in the chaos of the casino, I took a deep breath, relishing his scent of woodsy soap and something that was purely him. That was what he was to me: my resting place. I'd been stupid to think I could survive without him. My fears had blinded me to the prize I had been about to throw away. 'I think I might've stopped running when you stepped out in front of me. I hit my wall.'

He kissed the top of my head. 'And I'm not moving.'

'OK. You're my soulfinder. There, I've admitted it.'

He gave a shudder of relief. 'Painful?'

'Yes, very.'

'Scared?'

'Out of my wits.'

'Well, don't be. The only really scary thing would be not to stay together.'

Sally and Simon approached with my new friend Texan George.

'This gentleman here told us what happened,' Sally said, looking at me warily.

'I'm OK now, Sally. Victor will tell you all about it when he gets back.'

George nodded sagely. 'It was the damnedest thing, Mrs Bright. I knew there was something wrong with your gal the moment I saw her eyes—all glassy. Reminded me of a cabaret act I saw in the Paradise Lounge one time. Hypnotist made the man from the audience sing like Elvis until he clicked his fingers and broke the spell.' He winked at me. 'But those bad guys couldn't get you to go against your conscience, could they, Sky?'

'I suppose not, George.'

'See, hypnotism has its limits.' He patted my hand in a grandfatherly fashion. 'Go get yourself some rest, Sky.'

'And you go take your winnings away from the tables.' I pointed to the exit.

He tipped his hat. 'Sure will, ma'am. There's a condo in Florida with your name on it just waiting for me.'

When he'd left, I turned to my dad. 'So, do you still want to move to Vegas?'

Simon looked at Sally, then at Zed and me, standing together. 'I think that would be a "no"—a very big "no".'

Epilogue

To my horror, photos of me standing in the casino, shooting at the chandelier, made it into the papers. Daniel Kelly's fall was such big news any part of the transaction made headlines. The account of exactly what I was doing there was understandably garbled; most made me out to be an FBI plant working undercover to expose the criminal dealings of the Kelly family. It made a good storyline but that didn't wash at school where they knew me.

'Hey, Sky!' called Nelson, practically tackling me in the hallway. 'What the heck were you doing in Las Vegas last weekend?'

The Benedicts and I had discussed what story would best explain my uncharacteristic behaviour. Nelson was the first person on whom I was to try out the tale.

'Oh that?' I gave an airy laugh. 'Can you believe the papers? It was a stunt I was doing for a British TV programme—a reconstruction; they're doing this feature on American gun crime. Bad timing on the producer's part as we happened to be there at the same time as the hotel management got arrested. Some health and safety violation or something, my mum said.'

Nelson shook his head. 'No, Sky baby, the Kellys are very bad guys—wanted for conspiracy to murder.'

'Really?' I opened my eyes wide.

Don't overplay it. Zed came up behind. *Nelson's no fool. He'll expect you to know about Kelly.*

'Well, wow. That's very interesting,' I said, toning the innocence down a notch. 'I should've paid more attention.'

'So you're gonna be on TV?' Nelson was off on another track.

'Yeah. It's a programme for kids, called . . . um . . . *Blue Peter.*'

'Cool. Gun crime—sounds real cutting edge stuff.'

'Absolutely.' Use round-ended scissors and no one gets harmed.

'Awesome. Let us know when they show it—make sure you get a copy.'

'Will do.'

Nelson jogged away, stealing a kiss from Tina in passing. 'Sky's gonna be on British TV!' he shouted. 'She's a stunt girl.'

Well, that was one way of spreading the story. Stunt girl? I rather liked that. Much better than nutty fruitcake who shot up a casino.

'Come on, Sky, what are you daydreaming about?' Zed asked, tugging me back into walking.

'Oh, just stuff.'

'You'd better snap out of it because we've got some serious rehearsing to do. Concert's the day after tomorrow.'

'Bummer. I forgot.'

'It's nothing. If you can operate as part of an FBI investigation, you should think nothing of a little concert to friends and family.'

Little concert? Huh, Mr Benedict, I'll be having words with you later.

Zed's little concert turned out to be a massive gig with everyone from the vicinity crammed into the school auditorium. The mood was festive. Sheena's cheerleaders came sporting Father Christmas hats; the baseball team had opted for reindeer horns. Every instrument was bedecked with tinsel. The geeks had done themselves proud with an impressive video presentation of the year so far that played on the white screen over the stage. I was particularly embarrassed to see my goal-keeping debut got its own segment. It was a good save though. Parents mingled with each other, exchanging gossip and jokes. The Benedicts were out in force. I was thrilled to see Yves chatting to Zoe; she looked starry-eyed to be singled out for his attention. He was certainly making her day, proving that studious-looking guys also had some pretty cool moves. Sally and Simon were in deep conversation with Tina's mother. When I approached, I heard them talking not about me—sigh of relief—but about Tina's artistic talent.

My friend beckoned me over, flashing her newly painted silver nails for me to approve. Voluntarily excluding herself from singing for the sake of our eardrums, Tina was doing a fine job selling programmes.

'Sally just offered to give you extra lessons free; she thinks very highly of you,' I announced.

'She does?' Tina's smile was a dazzling hundred watts. 'Then you get this one free too then.' She passed me a programme. 'I see you're playing a solo.'

'If I don't manage to make a run for it before Mr Keneally shoves me on stage.'

'Don't you dare! I'm counting on you. I've been promising everyone our stunt girl will be the star of the show.'

I wasn't going to live that one down quickly. 'I'll give it my best shot.'

'Ha-ha.'

I frowned. 'What did I say?'

'Best shot—stunt girl?'

'Oh. I didn't mean the pun.' Just then the screen flashed up an image of me shooting the chandelier. 'Where on earth did they get that?'

'The internet's a bitch,' said Tina philosophically, before turning to bellow, 'Dig deep, folks. All proceeds go to the Aspen convalescent home.'

I glanced down at the programme to find my name at the top of the bill. Surrounded by Vegas style lights of all things.

That was it—I was so out of here. Nelson and Tina had turned me into the main attraction. I bolted for the exit, only to run slap into Zed's chest.

'Going somewhere, Sky?' he said with a knowing smile.

'Home.'

'Uh-huh. And that would be because . . . ?'

I lowered my voice. 'Everyone's going to be looking at me!'

'That's kinda the idea when you perform.' He steered me back behind stage.

'Nothing you can say will make me go out there,' I hissed as the audience took their seats.

'Nothing?' His mouth quirked into a smile.

'Nothing.' I dug in my heels.

He bent down to my face and whispered: 'Chicken.'

I folded my arms. 'Too right I am. Cluck-cluck.'

He laughed. 'OK. How about I give you another of my special boarding lessons if you do this?'

The knot of panic loosened at the happy memory of our time on the slopes together. Zed always knew what I wanted—where I needed to go to feel safe. 'Really?'

'Yeah. I'll even promise to do a double axel and a somersault.'

'Triple.'

'Triple?'

'Triple axel. And there has to be hot chocolate.'

He feigned a frown. 'Good grief, girl, you drive a hard bargain.'

'With marshmallows. And kisses.'

'Now you're talking.' He held out his palm. 'Done.'

I couldn't wait. Laughing, I took his hand and, before I could protest, he escorted me to the piano to the sound of applause from our friends.

'Don't worry,' he whispered. 'I won't leave you—not ever.'

I sat down and opened up the first piece of music. My future looked very promising—and he was standing right beside me.

About the author

Joss Stirling lives in Oxford and has always been fascinated by the idea that life is more than what we see on the surface. Researching *Finding Sky* saw her travelling in the characters' footsteps, from the awe-inspiring landscape of the Rockies, down a white-water river on a raft, and to the artificial skyline of Las Vegas. You can visit her website on www.jossstirling.com